The Gilded Lily

A Novel

DEBORAH SWIFT

St. Martin's Griffin
New York

This is a work of fiction. All of the characters, organizations, and events portrayed in this novel are either products of the author's imagination or are used fictitiously.

ISBN 978-1-62090-923-2

The two children were so fond of one another that they always held each other by the hand when they went out together, and when Snow-White said, we will not leave each other, Rose-Red answered, never so long as we live – and their mother would add, what one has she must share with the other.

Traditional fairy tale

Westmorland 1660

Chapter 1

Netherbarrow

Anyone else would probably scream – woken in the night like that, with a hand clamped over the mouth in the pitch black. But not Sadie, she knew it was Ella, even though she heard not a single word, for the smell of her sister's skin was as familiar to her as her own.

A blast of cold air buffeted her through her thin shift as the covers were wrenched back over her feet. Sadie scrambled out of bed. Silently she felt the floorboards for her clothes, shivering as she slipped her arms awkwardly into her bodice and tied on her skirt, with fingers fumbling in half-sleep. She tripped as she put on her clogs and one of them clattered down.

'Sshh,' said Ella. They listened in breathless silence for a sound from below. Sadie could hear nothing, except her own heart beating.

A cuff round the ear. 'Carry them, mutton-head.'

Sadie felt a strong grip steering her shoulder and Ella's voice hissed in her ear. 'If you waken him, I'll do for you.'

Ella pushed her down the stairs and out of the front door into the wet, before she had time to catch her breath. In the white chalk of the lane Ella was silhouetted in the darkness; Sadie could just make out her dark eyes in the pale oval of her face and the outline of her hair, which had escaped from her cap and sprung into curls from the damp.

'Is it time?' whispered Sadie. 'Have you come for me already? What shall I fetch over?'

'Nothing,' said Ella shortly, almost dragging her along the road. 'Hurry, can't you.'

Sadie hopped along, trying to fit her clogs on her feet as she went. This was not what she had imagined at all. When Ella had left home to be the Ibbetsons' lady's maid she had promised Sadie she would come back for her, as soon as she could find her a position in the household. But surely they wouldn't be asking for her in the middle of the night.

'Why are we in such a fret? What's the matter?'

'Muzzle it. Or I'll leave you behind.' She set off at a run, with Sadie hanging onto her sleeve, haring down the road through the sleeping village, under the shadowy dripping trees. Though at fifteen she was three years younger than Ella, Sadie was almost as tall, but she was not used to running and soon had to let go of her arm.

Ella did not slow – her skirts were hoisted up over her knees, her feet kicked up gobs of dirt as she ran. Sadie dropped behind, clutching a stitch in her side, but when she saw the flash of her sister's white calves getting smaller she forced herself to sprint on behind her, pounding through the puddles, her eyes screwed up against the sting of the rain.

The big house loomed up ahead of them. The windows were blacked-out holes, no smoke came from the chimneys. They stopped on the front step, both of them doubled over and panting. Ella produced a key to open up and thrust Sadie into the hall.

Sadie tried to calm her breathing, expecting to see a housekeeper, a footman or other staff. From long-standing habit she pulled her hair forward over the left side of her face to hide the wine stain on her cheek. Strangers often feared this birthmark as a sign of bad luck. But she need not have worried – there was nobody there. She rubbed her eyes and wiped the drizzle from her face with her sleeve, letting her dark hair fall back. It was the first time she had been inside the Ibbetsons' house. She peered around eagerly.

Ella took out a tinderbox from the drawer and lit a candle on the side table. Sadie gasped as it illuminated a sudden sheen of polished wood panelling. Ella turned around to face her, holding the candle. She was breathless, her face grim. In the flickering light her eyes were like swimming fish, darting from side to side. A dread settled on Sadie's shoulders like a cloak. Something was wrong.

'The dawn's coming, and we must be away before 'tis light. Listen to me. There's no time to explain. Get ahold of that basket and fill it with aught you can find that's worth having. Silver plate, linen – naught too big, but we've got to be quick.'

Sadie whispered, 'You mean, just take it?' She did not move, holding tight to the fabric of her skirt with both hands.

'Oh, for God's sake.' Ella grabbed hold of her arm and pulled her towards the stairs. 'Come here. I'll do it. Take the basket, will you? We'll start up there.'

The house was eerily quiet. Not a sign of anyone else, and the fires were cold in the grates. Where was everyone? Why was Ella allowed to roam the house alone at night? The stairs creaked. Sadie's wooden clogs scraped on the edges of the steps, despite the fact she did her best to tread quietly. She clasped the basket in both hands, staring round her in astonishment. Ella seemed to know exactly what she was doing. They cleared a room of a lady's things – a silver mirror, glass scent bottles still reeking of lavender, lace gloves, thimbles, a mother-of-pearl fan. Ella shovelled armfuls of lace into the basket, leaving all the drawers gaping.

Sadie pushed the door of the second room; it swung open silently at her touch. In the gloom she glimpsed a mound of blankets and the top of a stubbled head.

She scuttled backwards onto the landing. 'There's someone asleep in there.' She could barely speak and caught hold of Ella's arm to stay her. Ella shook her off and pushed past her, the candle in one hand, the basket with its trailing lace balanced on her hip.

'Get that trunk –' Ella pointed under the bed – 'we'll need that too.'

Sadie tiptoed over and inched out the trunk in case she should wake him, but the man on the bed slept on. Even when Ella cleared his side table of its ivory combs, brass candlesticks and magnifying lens on a stand, he did not stir. Ella jammed all the things hastily into the basket, packing them tightly round with nightcaps, gloves and hose dragged from the linen press at the end of the bed.

Sadie stood up; the man remained hunched under the bed-covers. She leaned over and peered down at him. His eyes were like two whelks staring up at her.

She stepped back and almost lost her balance as her heel banged into the trunk. A part of her would have fled, but she could not take her eyes away. His mouth was slightly open as if he was about to speak. In an instant she knew. No more words would come.

Sadie felt a lurch in her chest and a pounding in her ears as if the silence had suddenly become too loud. She stood stock-still. The room whirled to a stop.

'Don't just stand there. Get his watch,' hissed Ella.

Sadie glanced at the window. The first stirrings of the dawn had crept in unnoticed through the shutters, making a stripe of gold on the floor. Ella rifled through a leather pouch, and Sadie watched her wrinkle her nose in disgust when it contained only a few tokens and a silver toothpick.

'Go on,' Ella said.

Sadie swallowed hard and raised her eyebrows in question.

'In his pocket.'

Sadie shook her head and stepped further away from the bed.

Ella strode over and stood over the man. Her hands hovered in mid-air a moment before she jerked back the blanket. Sadie saw the quick movement of a mouse flash across the pillow and the room filled with the stench of death. She brought her hand up to her mouth. Ella started; her lower lip trembled and she bit down on it. They did not look at each other. Sadie saw her steel herself, squeeze her eyes shut, take a deep breath and thrust her hand into the pocket of his waistcoat. She withdrew the watch with its ruby seal hanging from its chain. Without looking at her, she pushed it into Sadie's open hand – its cool slinking weight dropped into her palm. The touch of it repulsed her. She let it slither straight into the basket and scrubbed her hand on the rough linen of her skirt.

'Come on,' said Ella, in her angry voice, 'downstairs.'

After that, Sadie followed Ella in a daze. By the time the birds were in full song, Ella had picked the house bone-clean.

They took the mule and cart, driving it hard down the dripping country lanes, the rain stinging their faces, the baskets and trunks sliding from side to side behind them. By milking time they were almost at Lancaster. Sadie was in the driver's seat, as the reins were greasy and Ella acknowledged she had always been the better driver. On the road they saw only two other conveyances – one a canvas-covered miller's cart and the other a carriage drawn by a pair of high-stepping chestnut thoroughbreds.

When Ella saw the dark blur of that carriage in the distance she yelled, 'Pull off the road!'

Sadie skewed the cart into an open gateway, spraying grit and mud, and hauled it to a standstill behind a hedge. A few moments later the carriage bowled past. Through its open window Sadie caught a glimpse of a dour-faced man and a woman in a fine hat.

'It's them,' muttered Ella. 'It must be them.'

'Who?' asked Sadie.

For the first time that night Ella answered one of her questions. 'His brother and his wife. Neighbours sent for them. When word got out he was ill. We'd best get a pace on, we've not got much of a start. And keep your face covered.'

'Where are we going?'

'London. Where no folks know us and no one can ask questions. The centre of the world.' Ella paused, added, 'Where the sun always shines, the streets are paved with gold, and everyone is always smiling.' They both fell quiet, mulling over this obvious untruth.

Sadie could not imagine it. London. It was too far away, she had never been to a city before. She knew it only from the childish rhymes they sang as they played skip-rope or bull-stones. *Oranges and lemons, saith the bells of St Clements, I do not know, saith the great bells of Bow.* Eventually she said, 'When will we be able to come home?' She asked it, even though in her heart she already knew the answer. Ella did not speak, just twitched the reins out of her hands and clicked her tongue, setting the mule going again with a start.

Sadie turned around, craned her neck, looked back over the jolting road and saw the hills of Westmorland, grey behind the morning mist, already fade into memory.

Chapter 2

Sadie glanced up at the sky. The moon was up and floated like a ghost in and out of the clouds. Under a tree on the other side of the track Ella sat on the pigskin trunk, with the other baskets and boxes piled up beside her. They had sold the mule and cart on the second day and hitched a lift this far with a boxwagon. The weather had worsened and now they had taken shelter by the side of the track. The rain dripped insistently off the branches but Ella huddled under the shelter anyway, her cloak dark on the shoulders with the wet. On the other side of the track the Thames slid by, black as molasses.

'By, I could sleep stood up, I'm that tired,' Ella said, 'but the light's not far off and we'd best keep our eyes skinned. Soon as we can hie a lift, we will.'

Sadie's eyes followed the snaking line of the river into the distance to where the moonlight caught the edge of a carbuncled silhouette – the city of London. Her stomach was hollow with hunger, and with apprehension. She turned away from the city and leaned against the comforting solidity of the tree, looking back up the track whence they had come. She drew her old shawl tight, pulling at the frayed fringe with her fingers.

'Don't fash yourself,' Ella said. 'No footpad or bezzler in their right mind would be out at this time of night in this weather.'

'I'm not scared,' she said. Then after a moment, 'It's just that I can imagine the folk that must have travelled this road. All on their way to London. I feel like I can hear footsteps, horses even, passing right through where we're standing. Kings and ordinary folk. It makes me giddy. And there'll be others after us too, maybe hundreds. Don't it make you feel small?'

Ella sniffed. 'I tell you, 'tis good London's so big – more chance to lose ourselves in it. And we've got a grand start with what's in here.' She thumped the side of the pigskin trunk. 'It's just us now. No wife to tell us what to do or what to buy. No father ready to batter us if we don't hand over our earnings. No master wanting us to fill his bed before he fills our bellies. We'll be able to afford a house with glass at the windows and proper furnishings. Drapes and all.'

'And will there be a plot for biddy chickens to scratch in, and a place to grow beans?'

'Bet your life there will. And we'll get new shoes made of soft leather, and starched white chemises, and we'll sleep on clean linen too.'

Sadie came to join Ella and edged up next to her. 'Do you think they'll send someone after us?'

'They might. But they'll not find us in London, needles in a haystack we'll be. We'll lie low a while. They'll soon give up.'

'What about Da?'

'Forget him.' Ella's arm came round her waist. They sat a moment in silence before Ella said, 'Sarah in the village says her cousin works on Bread Street. And that there's a Milk Street and a Honey Street and even a Pudding Street. We'll get our puddings on Pudding Street, hey, Sadie?'

Sadie contemplated this a moment, the pictures forming into a biblical promised land of milk and honey.

'Tell us more about how it will be, Ell,' Sadie said, elbowing closer.

Ella slapped her arm a stinging blow, suddenly impatient. 'How should I know? We haven't got there yet.' She stood up and went to look up the track. 'It's all the waiting. We seem to have been on the road for ever. I just want to get there now. What time is it?'

'I heard a church strike the four a while back.'

'A trap should be along soon then. I'm fit to drop. If I nap, will you keep an eye out and wake me if something comes?'

'Course. You rest up, it's foolish the both of us watching out.'

'Just a little while, then it'll be your turn.'

Ella swirled her woollen cloak around her, and sat back down. She swaddled it tight across her chest, leaned back against the tree and closed her eyes. Sadie watched her upturned face grow passive and still. Asleep, Ella looked a different person – her arched eyebrows relaxed, her mouth settled into an expression of innocence. All boldness and bluster gone, she looked like a child. Sadie snuggled closer, put her hand out to touch the bumpy shape of her elbow under the rough texture of the cloak. Her sister did not move but her breath came heavy and even. The rain had turned to sleet, which fell onto her forehead through the tree canopy, and Sadie brushed its icy granules away with the tips of her fingers. Even then, Ella did not stir.

Sadie's chest constricted with tenderness, she thought she had never seen a more beautiful sight. Just the two of us, Ella had said, starting a new life together. She had the urge to hold on to the moment, to press it in a book the way ladies pressed wild-flowers, to preserve their beauty before they faded.

She stood to stretch her legs and looked towards the city for a long time. To watch quietly had always been her way. She had never drawn attention to herself and consequently had always been on the fringes of things. In the village the other children had called her 'patch-eye' and 'dog-face', told her she was ugly, squealed and run away from her, shouting out that she'd the Devil's pawprint and would hex them all. When she was little, she had not known what they meant, but when she was about four summers old she looked in the glass window of the bakehouse, and she saw that there was a blood-red mark staining the side of her face. It went from her cheek, round her eye and up onto her forehead, as if someone had thrown a pail of paint. She had spat on her palm and rubbed and rubbed, but it did not shift, and she had felt suddenly sad, and old beyond her years, for she knew that like a skewbald's blaze it was something that could never be cured, was with her for life.

She looked back to the tree where Ella was snoring gently. A swing of light in the distance alerted her and she hurried over to the bank, where a makeshift jetty stuck out into the water. A few moments later she heard the slap of oars. A small craft came round the bend in the river, its sail furled to the mast, a single lantern illuminating the two occupants who were rowing steadily, their shoulders swaying back and forth.

'Ell, a boat. Wake up.' Ella shifted slightly but did not open her eyes. Sadie shook her by the shoulder. 'Someone's coming, Ell.'

Ella stumbled to her feet. 'Where?'

'On the river – look.'

'Leave it. I'd rather go by wagon.'

'But it could be hours yet. Let's try.' Sadie knew Ella hated the water. She could not swim and could never be persuaded to paddle in the tarn with the other girls of the village. 'I know you're scared of the water, but—'

'Am not. Who said that? It's just—'

'Go on, Ell. You shout – they'll listen to you.'

Ella stood a little back from the edge. Her bravado had returned as soon as Sadie challenged her. 'Oy!' she yelled, 'you going downriver?'

One of the men started and let go of his oar. 'What the—?'

'We need a ride,' she called. 'You got any room?'

'Damned fool woman, made me lose my oar,' said the man, ignoring her and floundering over the edge of the boat to retrieve it. 'Charlie, paddle over a bit, I can't reach it.'

The oar floated towards them and Ella began dragging the trunk towards the jetty. She signalled silently to Sadie, who scrambled past, her head down, to drag all the other bags and baskets to the edge.

'We can pay you,' Ella said, throwing her winning smile at Charlie, who stared from under his slouch cap first at her, and then more dubiously at Sadie and the jumble of bags on the jetty.

Ella leaned forwards and unwrapped her shawl to show her white throat, smiling at him as she withdrew a small bag from her stays. Sadie just waited and watched. She saw Charlie smile back – no man seemed able to resist Ella's dimples once she had a mind to use them.

'Where are you going?' Charlie said. She knew then that their lift was secure.

'Come on, let's not waste our time,' scowled the other man, slotting the oar back into the rowlock. 'Pull on those oars.'

'Wait a while, the ladies have said they'll pay.' He smiled up at Ella, who beamed back. Sadie hung behind her like her shadow.

Ten minutes later their luggage was on board and Ella had been helped into the prow. Sadie saw her hands clinging to the wooden seat although her face was haughty and serene. She would never admit she was afraid of anything. Sadie, meanwhile, was squashed up with the trunk digging into her thigh and a pile of baskets and boxes wobbling on her knee. She pressed one hand on top of her load but peered sideways at the passing trees, looking for the houses and taverns that would signal their arrival.

'Where you going?' she heard Charlie say.

'London,' Ella said.

'Very droll,' Charlie's friend said. 'He means where shall we let you off?'

'Where are you going?' Ella asked.

'St Olave's Wharf.'

'Well, that's mighty strange, that's where we're bound too,' Ella said.

Sadie hid her smile behind a wicker basket. The dawn was coming up and the sky had lightened. Now there was a pale yellow smudge on the horizon so that she could make out distant spires and rooftops, and there were more taverns by the side of the river and jetties with punts tied alongside. The river was sluggish, but soon it became more of a highway with small craft appearing from nowhere, some under brown sail and some under manpower. Near the edge horses trudged the bank, pulling long barges of goods wrapped in oiled canvas, and punts skimmed by, stacked with barrels of ale. In the pall of mist on the surface of the river it looked as if the men were gliding upright, standing on the water.

The sides of the river became more crowded until she saw at last the city walls and a jumble of blackened half-timbered houses. She realized she was holding her breath trying to take in all the new sights and sounds, and had to let it out in a long sigh. But then she would catch her breath again as some new wonder came into view. By now the river was thick with craft of every shape and size and the air was a Babel of men and women, all shouting to each other in an accent Sadie could barely fathom. She wrinkled her nose; there was a smell, like something rotting.

'Oh my word,' said Ella, pointing ahead to a huge mountain of a bridge so log-jammed with boats trying to get through that the river itself was all but invisible underneath them. Some boatmen had clearly given up and made their way to the jetties, but on the other side of the bridge the banks were thick with boats waiting to carry them on.

'We'll never pass through there,' she said, but Charlie and his mate rowed steadfastly, making for one of the larger barges loaded with crates of squawking chickens, just ahead. It was pulled by a grey Percheron horse with hooves the size of trenchers. The barge thrust everything else out of its way as the horse trundled up to the bridge. There it was unharnessed and the barge continued to move by its own momentum under the bridge. Once on the other side the horse was hastily put back in traces. Their boat simply followed close behind in the barge's wake. Sadie saw Charlie wink at Ella. Ella was white-faced. A small tic moved in her cheek but she forced a tight-lipped smile. Sadie peered over the side at the water but withdrew as she saw a scum of jetsam and a bloated dead rat, partly submerged in the water.

A few minutes later they drew up at a wharf, the boat lurched and Charlie threw the rope out to the ground. Several ragged children with grey faces and enormous eyes fought with each other to take the rope and tie it round the post, screaming insults, kicking and punching each other in their hurry. Their arms were thin as kindling, they looked half starved. One of the lads armed with a broken spar of wood swung it out until the others cowered back, making himself room until, triumphant, he grabbed the rope and in a deft movement wound it round a mooring. Charlie alighted and threw him a coin. He snatched it from the air and scurried away. The rest of the filthy gaggle of children left them be and ran further up the bank to where another boat was just landing.

Ella sat stock-still, clinging to the wooden seat. 'Here, let me help you,' Charlie said, offering his arm.

Sadie jumped out and began to heave their luggage onto the wharf.

'Careful, it's heavy,' said Ella.

After a few moments, Charlie's companion reluctantly lent a hand. Sadie vaguely heard Ella ask about finding lodgings but paid no attention to the conversation, she was too busy looking round, amazed at all the comings and goings, clutching her shawl to her stomach.

As she was staring, a huge woman, long-stemmed pipe still a-smoke in her mouth, loaded up a basket with carrots from a barge stacked with crates of vegetables. She swung the basket onto her back as if it weighed nothing and swayed off along the quay. Sadie stared at her departing rump.

'Hey,' Ella shouted. A wiry child with sticking-out ears had picked up one of their baskets and was dodging his way through the crowd.

Ella lunged towards him and grabbed him by the shoulder. 'Oh no you don't, you little mongrel,' she said, seizing the basket back.

Charlie took hold of him by the waist and delivered a punch to the side of his head so the boy reeled and stumbled. 'Sorry, mister,' he said, but Charlie kicked out at him another vicious blow to the shins. 'That'll learn you,' he said, hitting him again with a sideways look at Ella. The boy crouched, shielding his head with his skinny arms.

'Oh please stop,' Sadie said. Charlie and Ella turned to look at her and the boy made a grateful escape. Charlie continued to stare at her face, likely he had not noticed it in the dark.

'Why wasn't you watching our bags, you lummock?' Ella said, back to her usual self now she was safely on dry land. 'We could have lost that basket then. 'Tain't no use staring into the air like a halfwit. Wake up, can't you.' Sadie flushed and looked down.

'Maid like you needs a buck to look out for you,' Charlie said to Ella.

'Have a care.' Charlie's friend was suddenly at his side. 'What about Joan?' he whispered.

'What about her?' Charlie was sullen.

'Come on, now. The ladies don't need our company.'

Ella smiled at him. 'Oh but we do. Charlie promised he'd help us fetch our bags to the Bear's Head. We've no lodgings yet, see. And my sister, well, she's only thirteen and we're fair worn out with travelling . . .'

Thirteen? Sadie took a sharp intake of breath and looked down at her feet, embarrassed. Ella knew full well she was way past her fifteenth birthday.

'We'd be that grateful if you'd help us with our trunks.' Ella looked up at the two men through her eyelashes.

'Well, I . . .' Charlie's friend said, but Ella picked up a box and thrust it out towards him. Sadie saw the reluctance still on his face, but nevertheless his arms reached out to take the box. Within a few minutes the two men were carrying the trunk between them, piled with all the boxes, leaving Ella and Sadie to follow behind with the handbaskets.

The Bear's Head had a sign hanging half off, with a picture that must have once been a bear but now was so worn that only a vague silhouette and pig-like eyes were visible beneath a layer of grime. They went through the squat wooden door into a tavern full of low-lying smoke, as airless and sunless as the bottom of a barrel.

'Is this it?' Ella said. She sniffed, turned to Sadie and shrugged her shoulders. A brass bell stood on the bar. Ella shook it till the clapper brought the alewoman.

'Bring them in,' Ella said, beckoning impatiently to the two men. They struggled through the door with the luggage. Ella supervised them, until they had dumped it, then brushed them aside to haggle heatedly with the alewoman, leaving the men standing uncertainly under the lantern in the passage. 'You can go now,' Ella said, handing them a single token.

'Now just wait a minute—' Charlie said.

'Well, if you don't want it—' Ella said.

'Thank you for bringing our things,' Sadie spoke quickly, to try to stave off an argument. Charlie's friend stared at her as though he had only just seen her. His eyes rested on her cheek a fraction too long. He pulled them away to look at Ella, but they slid back to Sadie. Sadie ignored him, acted busy by repacking one of the baskets.

'Come on, Charlie, let's go.' He tugged at Charlie's sleeve.

Charlie was hovering, still trying to attract Ella's attention, but Ella was oblivious, persuading the alewoman to let them have a room at the front overlooking the street. Finally his friend took him by the elbow and propelled him out of the door. Ella did not turn to bid them the time of day as they went.

They took a room for one night and Sadie watched Ella count out the coins from Thomas Ibbetson's black leather purse. She remembered seeing it in his chamber, and how she watched Ella slide it into her palm, then tie it into the string of her skirt and tuck it down inside. Now Ella was counting out an enormous sum for just one night in this filthy tavern.

Their room was furnished with a stiff horsehair bed, propped up with an old chopping-board where the leg had been broken off, a side table with a dusty washbowl and jug, and a window looking out onto the street. Together they brought up their things, carrying them between them and bumping the trunk up the stairs. Ella began to unpack straight away, laying out a few of the lady's things on the washstand as if they were her own.

Sadie went straight over to the window, rubbed away the layer of greasy dust with a fingertip until the window squeaked. Below, folk on horseback rode by and tradesmen carried goods on their heads. From here she saw right inside their baskets – nosegays of dried flowers, orange-coloured salted fish, bundles of lace and ribands, dried wafers of apple threaded on strings. The apples made her wonder where they had come from, whether they had come from the country, maybe from a farm near their home in Westmorland.

'Ella, where do you think apples come from in London? Are there apple trees in the city?'

'I don't know. I don't think so.' Ella brought out some crocheted gloves and arranged them on the table, patting them gently into place. She had found a silver-backed brush to tease her soft brown hair into waves over her shoulders. Then her face darkened and she put the brush down and shook her head as if to shake some unruly thought away.

She turned to Sadie with a false gaiety. 'Isn't this fine?' Ella said. 'No more slaving in Netherbarrow, we've left all that behind. A whole city waiting for us. Nobody knows us here. We can be anything we like, start over.'

Sadie looked at Ella's hopeful face and wanted to believe it, but for her Netherbarrow seemed as much a part of her as the stain on her face. She shivered, unable to quash the feeling that the past clung on and would let neither of them go so easily.

Ella walked to the window beside her and stared out as a cobbler's boy set up his mending last in the street. 'There must be thousands of young men in the city,' she said. 'How'd you fancy it, Sadie? A London lad!'

Sadie laughed, but it was a brittle sound. Her heart sank. How could she have been so stupid? So it was not to be just the two of them after all. She watched Ella stroke her hair over her shoulder. Ella was set on finding a young man, already planning on making it a threesome though she had been in London less than half a day. And then Sadie would be on her own. Her throat tightened; there were so many people in London it made her feel as if she were drowning. She came away from the window, she had no taste any more for the sights of the city.

'Tomorrow,' Ella went on, 'we'll find work and proper lodgings. A room, just for the two of us. Now we've sold the mule, we've enough here so's we won't have to share.' She tapped the purse where it lay against her skirts. 'Shall I go out and find us some snap? A pork pie, or a suet muffin?'

Hunger took over her judgement. Ella meant nothing by it, just talk – that was what it was. Sadie beamed. 'Gradely, Ella.'

Ella pulled on the crocheted gloves. 'You can stay here and mind us things.'

Ella hurried out onto the street, looking about to get her bearings. There was a pall of mist over everything, and the stench of coal. Opposite was a narrow alleyway where there were stalls set up. The street was thronging. Ella blew out through her mouth, a long sigh. Free. She was free. She looked around. Netherbarrow seemed a dark and distant dream already. London was altogether another world. Not a speck of green in sight – no hills, no trees and no gossiping neighbours. Nobody to whisper about her behind her back. The Ibbetsons would never find her here.

She pulled her shoulders back and ran across the road with a little skip. She smiled at everyone she passed – the cobbler lad, a boy selling lampreys in a wriggling mass in a big bowl and a woman hawking oranges from a basket balanced jauntily on her head. She even gave a smile to the pieman, who was a youth of about her own age, his skin marked with the pox, his hair tied up in a greasy pigtail. She paid tuppence for the pies, ignoring his leers as she took the purse from her bodice.

'You wanna watch out,' he said, 'put that purse somewhere less tempting.'

Ella smiled pleasantly, but turned away, thrusting her wrapped parcel into her basket. Lads like him were beneath her. She'd enough money to afford a chamber and a new gown – she was going up in the world. She'd have to help Sadie though, make sure she got some proper employment. Like a babe she was – a proper greenhorn. At home, if a piglet or a kitten was born weak or with some sort of deformity, her da would have dispatched it, with the blade of his shovel. But you couldn't do that with people, could you? And the stronger ones had to look out for the runts in the litter, that was always the way of it. Still, London might toughen Sadie up.

She worried about Sadie's face, though. In the village some had taken against her – thought it was ill-luck to be seen abroad with her. It made her angry when they did that – it hurt, as if somehow the taint stuck to her as well. And Sadie was a sweet-natured soul, always ready to believe the best of folk. Likely the poor thing would be hard-pressed to find a sweetheart, so she'd need some useful craft to keep her occupied without a man to take care of her. Sooner the better, Ella thought. She didn't want her hanging round her apron, putting off all the young bucks.

Ella saw a man climb out of a shiny black sedan and dismiss the bearers with a wave of his hand. They jostled the contraption away up the street. The people stepped aside to let them stagger by. The occupant was elegantly dressed in claret brocade with a broad-brimmed hat over a full wig. A footman walked a few steps behind him, his hand on his sword. She watched covertly as he walked over to the market and a wave of anger washed over her. She hated the way he ignored his servant and those stepping out of his path. Immediately the anger was replaced by longing.

Someone like him, she thought, that's the sort for me.

Chapter 3

The Rectory,
Netherbarrow by Kendal,
County of Westmorland
27th day of October 1660

To Mr T. Ibbetson Esq.

Sir,

It is with regret I inform you your brother is gravely
ill. I have no doubt that his sudden collapse has been
brought about by the unfortunate fate of his wife. I fear
your brother is no longer capable of managing his affairs,
so I appeal to you to come without delay. It grieves me
to see your brother thus brought down. Needless to say,
he is daily in our prayers.

Yours faithfully,
Charles Goathley
Rector of the Parish of St Mary's

Titus Ibbetson clutched the piece of paper in one hand, steadying it on his knee. The sky was sullen with rain, and damp had blurred the ink, but he almost knew the words by heart, he had read it so often. The journey through a never-ending wasteland of mud and trees had taken its toll on his patience, and he snapped at his wife Isobel when she kept complaining about the state of the track. He could not think of anything else except the fact that his twin brother Thomas was seriously ill.

The village was scarcely more than a clutch of rough pigsties, and at first he was unsure if this really was Netherbarrow, so he stopped a sleepy farm labourer with his hoe over his shoulder to ask for the Ibbetsons' house. He pointed them 'up yonder, second house past the green'. Titus scanned the horizon; there were indeed several more imposing dwellings clustered together around the church.

He had never understood why his brother chose to live in this hellhole of a village and not in the more prosperous town. When Titus had asked him, he had replied that he could not abide the smoke of Kendal, and the country air was good for his shortness of breath. Though Titus had to confess, from this distance his brother's house looked substantial enough, a square stone box half covered in ivy, with large glazed windows.

Isobel pushed her head out of the carriage window. 'Oh hurry,' she called to the driver. The horses sprang forward.

'Don't shout like that,' Titus said.

'But will you look there,' Isobel said, 'that dolt of a housekeeper's left the front door flapping open, in this weather.'

He peered out, and immediately pulled his head back in. He got out a kerchief and rubbed a spatter of mud from his face as they pulled to a halt. 'Wonder he puts up with her, letting the heat out like that. Mind, there's no smoke from the chimneys, so I guess there's no fire lit.'

They looked at each other. That was not right – no fire, and Thomas ill abed. Titus rubbed his palms together, surprised to find them sticky with sweat.

'Stay in the carriage, whilst I go in,' he said, but Isobel had already alighted and pushed past him towards the gate.

The door was open but the hallway was gloomy and still. Once inside the front door he called out, but there was no reply. Their footfalls rang loud on the flagstones, and the rest of the house was ominously shuttered and dark.

'Wait there, I'll get these open,' he said. He tugged at the shutters in the drawing room so that the grey light flooded in, revealing gaping cabinets and all the drawers wrenched out of the side table and cast aside. Concerned now, he strode past Isobel in the dim hallway and took the stairs.

One look through the door was enough.

He pulled out the muddy kerchief and held it to his nose, panting for breath.

'Isobel,' he shouted, 'have the carriage take you to the rectory, and call for the curate.'

'What is it? Is it Thomas?' He heard the rustling of her skirts on the stairs.

'No, don't come in.'

'Is he –? Let me see.'

'I said don't –' He tried to usher her out of the room.

She pushed past him, but stopped dead. Her throat made a small choking sound. She opened and closed her mouth, lost for words. But then she raised a quavering finger. 'God preserve us. Look,' she said, 'look at that.'

'What?' he said, having no desire to look further.

She pointed again. The feather pillow was not where it should have been, under Thomas's head, but on the coverlet next to his face, as if someone had just put it down. She moved closer.

25

'Look at his face,' she said. 'Someone's killed him. Suffocated him with his own pillow and left him for dead.'

'No, surely not. Not Thomas. No one would want to kill Thomas.'

'But –' She touched a forefinger towards the pillow, her eyes wide.

'Calm yourself. You are being fanciful.'

'Your own brother lying there like that, you cannot tell me it's not suspicious. I tell you, Titus, 'tis not right. I have a feeling, just here.' Her hand pressed the space between her eyebrows.

'You and your feelings. Not now, I say. Come away and leave him in peace.'

Isobel's narrow eyes ranged around the chamber, taking in the open kist, the strangely bare surfaces. 'Odd things have gone on here – Devil's work. His wife accused of witchery, and now this.' She pointed to the kist. 'Look at that, not a speck left, not even a button.' At this she began to weep and he had to drag her away, prop her on his arm to help her down the stairs.

Titus could not quieten her. It was as if he was viewing her through thick glass, standing outside a window looking in. He bundled her in the carriage and sent a farm boy for the local constable. The news of Thomas's death soon seeped out, with villagers arriving in dribs and drabs to stand silently watching them whilst they waited for the wretched constable to arrive. Titus slammed the door on the locals and shut himself in the cold parlour. He was shivering, his teeth chattered together, the noise of them penetrating the silent room. Here too all the drawers were out and there were half-empty cutlery boxes on the floor as if someone had left in a hurry. He began to put them back, to tidy it, to restore order.

A sound in the garden made him jump and he spun round. He ran to the door and hurled a lump of coal from the scuttle to shoo some barefoot lads away – surely they had something better to occupy their time? Soon more gawping strangers clustered at the windows of the carriage where Isobel had shut herself in and was weeping, her veil pulled over her face. Titus rubbed his coal-stained palms on his buff breeches, where they left a black smear. He stared at it thinking, no matter, he would be in mourning tomorrow and all his clothes would be black.

Surely Thomas had not been suffocated. Isobel was mistaken, he was sure; her weaker constitution made her prone to the vapours and these odd notions. Nobody had any reason to dislike Thomas, he had always been the good one: mild-tempered, easy-going – some might say idle – nodding at everyone and everything like he was still a small boy. His mother had told everyone that he, Titus, was the roguish one who would get himself into trouble, and not the beaming angelic-faced Thomas. Thomas had never had any self-discipline or sense of duty at all, thought Titus. A lump came to his throat. He swallowed and drew himself upright. He would not cry. He had always had to help Thomas, ever since he was a small boy, whereas he himself had never in his life asked anyone for help. Silly fool. He couldn't help him now.

When the country constable finally arrived, in his too-small coat, he insisted on interviewing Titus as if he was at fault. Isobel remained in the carriage, pretending the whole affair was beneath her. It became clear from the constable that the housekeeper, Ella Appleby, and her sister had planned the whole robbery together. The mule and cart were missing from the stable, and nobody had seen either girl since the night before. The constable rocked on his heels and asked questions in his barely intelligible Westmorland drawl. Titus gritted his teeth. It was frustrating, to be confined in Netherbarrow when the Appleby sisters could be halfway to Lancaster by now.

Finally, he could bear the constable's questions no longer.

'Should you not take horse after them?' he asked.

'Better give me full particulars first. Let us make a stock list of the items missing from the gentleman's cabinets.'

'Good sir, I do not know all my brother's possessions. And besides, it is of no earthly use to inventory items of cutlery when my brother is dead, his house has been ransacked and the miscreants are galloping further away by the minute. If you will not go after them, then I will do it myself. Excuse me.'

'You'll not be catching them now. Not before nightfall anyhows.'

Titus scowled and climbed into his carriage. 'We'll see,' he shouted. 'Lancaster,' he said to the driver, despite Isobel's teary protestations. As the carriage lurched forth, he caught sight of the Rector and Mrs Goathley hastening towards them up the hill, so he leaned out of the window and requested that they arrange for someone to sit with his brother until he returned. Mrs Goathley said she would sit there herself, though no harm would come to him, no more than he had already suffered.

As the carriage lumbered down the track, Titus turned and looked back at the diminishing village. He suppressed the overpowering urge to go back, to tell Thomas to stop jesting, to stop being so idle and to get up and get dressed. He felt a lurch in his stomach, like a child's seesaw when someone suddenly jumps off. Their lives were bound together. That Thomas could be dead was impossible. Thomas had always been a part of his life, since he was a few minutes old and had slipped out of the womb after Titus, his cord still wrapped round Titus's ankle.

A lump rose to his throat; he gripped Isobel's hand as the carriage bumped on the uneven track. He wished he had visited his brother more often, but he was always so busy. And Thomas was always needing something. His business ventures often ran into trouble and then he would come bleating to Titus for help. Lately his requests for assistance had become tiresome. Titus owned he should perhaps make more effort to stay in touch. He would make the time. But then he realized there was no more time.

'You're hurting,' Isobel said, pulling her hand away. 'Thank goodness we are leaving this festering climate. I cannot wait to be home. Some strange malady is at work here, best not to tarry.'

'We are not going home. Not until we find them.'

'What?'

'You heard. You were witness to the exceeding speed of the Netherbarrow law,' he said. 'If you want something doing properly, best to do it yourself. I have no confidence in that constable. I am going to find those girls and make them return every last farthing.'

'But I have a dressmaker's appointment the day after tomorrow . . .'

'For God's sake, Isobel, have you no sense of propriety? My brother is dead and you see fit to chatter about your dressmaker? One word more, and I'll put you off and you will walk home from Netherbarrow.'

Isobel turned her back to him with a heavy sigh and they continued the journey in silence. After a while, Isobel said, 'What about Alice?'

Titus did not answer. Of course he knew they should inform the wife, but Titus had never been able to bear her. She was no use at all to Thomas as far as he could see. Titus never saw the point of her wasting her time with her insipid paintings, her hair all hanging wild and in disarray, her sleeves dribbled in paint. And besides, the constable had informed him she was in the gaol at Lancaster. Accused of meddling in the black arts. It was outlandish – bizarre – that any member of his family should be so accused. He would not want his hands tainted with that. Did not he have enough to deal with? His friends in the guild would laugh at him. No, he told himself, find the thieving sisters first and restore order to Thomas's estate. The wife would have to wait.

Lancaster. Preston. Warrington. Newcastle-under-the-Lyme. Eccleshall. At each town they had reports that the girls had just left. Desperate and sleepless, for this was now Titus's fourth uncomfortable day in a tooth-rattling carriage, he made several wild goose chases, until he got word of a mule and cart sold just outside Lichfield. They galloped there, to discover no trace of the girls or the goods.

Isobel refused to get back in the carriage. 'No more,' she said.

'We will try Coventry, now get in.'

'No. I refuse to go a single furlong more. What if we never find them?'

Titus looked at her blankly. 'Get in, or I shall go without you else. You are wasting time.'

Isobel sat down on the carriage step and began to weep. 'I want to go back.'

'I will not return to Netherbarrow until I find them.'

'Not Netherbarrow,' she blubbed, 'home. I want to go home.'

'We are going to Coventry. Now stop greeting, it does nobody any good,' he snapped. Her crying annoyed him. Men were not allowed such displays of feeling. She didn't understand, he could no more think of Thomas not existing than he could think of waking up without an arm.

Isobel wiped her eyes again and climbed back into the carriage. She twisted her kidskin gloves in her hands and stared out of the window.

'We will take respite at an inn on the way,' he said, but Isobel did not reply.

That evening Titus was forced to leave the coach and four at Coventry, for he could not make the beasts go any further no matter how much he told the driver to apply his whip. The ostler at the inn had nearly set on him and had insisted he change horses. But there were no matching pairs to be had, so he had been forced to take a single mount. It wasn't much of a horse for the money, a ridge-backed roan with splinty legs. He thwacked it a cutting blow to keep it to speed. A great anger had seized him, he scarcely knew what he did.

Isobel had not hidden her relief that the lack of a coach meant she had to stay behind in Coventry. He had shouted at her like a common man then, but worse, he had also had to leave behind his driver and negotiate the wild countryside to Banbury unaided, and be forever unsure if he was on the right road.

But they couldn't be that far ahead, and he was convinced he was on their tails. The bitter wind drained the blood from his hands and blew his sparse hair into his eyes. He was cold and hungry, and unused to the saddle. Rage at the fact that he was forced to take horse like this made him kick the horse's ribs until it galloped wildly into the wind. The cold stung his eyes, but then he could tell himself it was the wind, not grief, that made his eyes water so.

Chapter 4

Madame Lefevre's, Perruquier, Friday Street, London
January 1661

Sadie heard the slap of the leather measuring tape a fraction before she felt its sting on the back of her neck. Nobody spoke. It was silent except for her sharp intake of breath. She shot upright in an instant, the back of her neck hot and tingling, but she knew better than to turn round, for Madame Lefevre would still be there, raking the room with her eyes, ready to pounce on any shirker with the stab of a pin in the back. Or worse, the whip-like crack of the measuring tape, perfected through years of vengeful practice. This was her usual habit, to punish the nearest girl if any one of them stopped for breath.

Sadie watched Ella hurriedly grasp the bone handle of the hook and bend again to the wig block, her face flushing scarlet, for she was the one who had been staring into space.

Still smarting from the lash of the tape, Sadie doubled her speed, her thin white hands flashing over the pins, working each single hair through the tulle netting, twisting and knotting it before laying it flat against the base. Half the block in front of her was already covered with a long dark fall of hair. She looked down. Her fingers were thick with grease, the skin rough with tiny cuts. You would not think that horsehair could be sharp, but it was – edges like razors making countless small cuts. The hairs snagged in the cuts making her work slow and painful.

In, out, twist, pull. In, out, twist, pull. Over and over, twelve hours a day.

Across the room, Ella's work remained a small patch, sprouting like black moss. Madame Lefevre clacked across the room on her heels and poked Ella in the back.

'Get on with it, or she'll get another.' She came round the front of the bench, swept up the wig block and inspected it. 'Barely covered a farthing's worth. No dexterity. Your fingers are too fat and clumsy. Like potatoes.'

Madame Lefevre held the wig block up above her head to show it to everyone. Her eyes were like cinders even through her thick glass lunettes.

'Look at it. Just about fit for a farm labourer. And how many of those do we get in here?' She gave a mirthless laugh.

Some of the other girls sniggered, until silenced by a look. Madame Lefevre was the only one allowed a sense of humour in the wigmaker's. She banged the block back down so the pins on the bench sprang up.

Ella stared back at her, her blue eyes unblinking. Sadie was uneasy. She knew Madame Lefevre detested this the most – not Ella's lack of skill, but her refusal to be broken. Madame Lefevre expected to be able to pull everyone's strings, to dandle everyone to do her bidding. Ella's mutinous demeanour was guaranteed to rile her, but so far she had kept her on because Sadie had an uncanny knack with the knotting.

The bell on the door sounded. Madame Lefevre reluctantly let Ella fall from her gaze, like a cat dropping a mouse to which it would return, and hurried upstairs into the front of the house, hitching up her stiff black skirts. Sadie watched her slightly stooped, angular figure go.

'Sow,' Ella muttered under her breath.

Madame Lefevre disappeared into the upper room, where she received the gentlemen for their fittings, talking now in a sing-song, in what Sadie had nicknamed her 'parlour voice'. Sadie heard a man's voice greeting her with her proper name, Widow Lefevre, which he pronounced in the English way as 'le fever' and not in the French way. The girls themselves called her Old Feverface when she was out of hearing. Widowed when her French wigmaker husband had been trampled by a horse, she had continued his business with the grim air of someone determined to prove she could run the business better than he ever could. And now that the fashion was for ever more opulent wigs, she was making a good living. She never dressed in anything but black, her flapping skirts and shoulder cape reminiscent of a nun, keeping order over about ten young girls, heads bowed over their wig blocks as if in prayer in the dingy back room of her workshop.

Whilst Madame Lefevre was occupied with the customer, the girls took their chance to chatter amongst themselves in low whispers. Corey Johnson was always the first to start a conversation. She was a short fair girl, broad-boned with a pugnacious face and stubby capable fingers, and amongst the girls she was the one who had worked there the longest.

'Buckingham's up to his old tricks,' Corey said, pushing her cap back behind her ears. 'My mam heard it down the flea-market.'

'What?' Ella asked.

'The Duke of Buckingham. His new club. It's called the Wits – all the well-to-do gents are in it, but they've caused no end of a ruckus in the Pelican Coffee House. They got well leathered and kidnapped one of the serving maids. One of the dandies stole her clothes and made her wear his. They found her later wandering the streets, wearing only a man's breeches. Raving, she was.'

Sadie shook her head, it sounded a far-fetched tale to her. 'What will happen to them?'

'What do you mean?'

'Well, won't someone go after them, these Wits, or whatever they're called?'

The other girls laughed. 'Them? No, you goose. Nothing'll happen to them.' Betsy giggled. 'They're friends of the king. And a right merry king he's turned out to be. No, there's different rules for them and us, same as always. We had one of them in here once, just afore Yuletide I think it was. He's one of the Wits now, Lord Buckhurst. You never saw such fancy clothes in all your life.'

'What sort of fancy clothes?' Ella asked.

'Pale tabby satin suit with real gold embroidery. It even had little red poppies fashioned on the pockets, with scarlet buttons,' Betsy said. 'And his cuffs were made of acres of Brussels lace, and shoes with diamond buckles. I'm not jesting, each of the diamonds must have been the size of a knuckle.'

'And I was putting away the pattern book when he came in, and Old Feverface's jaw nearly hit the ground when she saw him,' Alyson said.

'You're making it up. Who's up there with her now?' Ella said.

'Don't know. Didn't recognize his voice. Can you see?' Corey leaned over her bench to look.

Sadie watched Ella peer up the stairs to where Madame Lefevre seated the gentlemen in a big chair. Usually the girls could not see anything, because there was always a heavy mustard-coloured curtain dragged across the doorway – whether to shield the customers' privacy, or just because the front room was Madame

Lefevre's exclusive territory, she did not know. Or perhaps it was because of the steam and stink in the wig room below – the smell of unwashed horsehair, sheep's wool and the greasy locks of the nuns. The best wigs were made of imported hair shorn from the heads of Italian nuns. It made Sadie shiver to touch the hair shorn from those poor Italian girls.

But today the curtain was left open by mistake.

As a child Ella had always loved to peer through keyholes, over fences and in through back doors. She could never resist looking where she was not supposed to look. Unlike Sadie, Ella had noticed the curtain straight away, and leaning backwards on her stool she had a clear view of a shaven-headed man sitting in the wing chair.

He had probably just come from the barber's next door, Ella thought, for his head was smooth as an ivory ball, and his cheeks, pink and shining, showed not even a sign or shadow of a beard. He had a long aquiline nose and expressive dark eyebrows. She looked him over, to see if he was dressed like the man Betsy had just been telling them about. It was an incongruous sight, a young man in fine navy silk breeches and flowing shirt, all flounced lace and ribbons below, but topped by an impossibly small head. Ella could not resist a smile as she watched Madame Lefevre stretch the measuring tape around his naked temples and chalk the numbers onto a slate. Madame Lefevre treated everything as if it was her personal enemy – her lips pursed in concentration, she splintered the chalk as she stabbed down the figures.

Whilst she was writing, the man caught Ella staring at him, and without moving his head or changing his expression, he slowly raised his eyebrows. She fixed her eyes back on her wig stand, annoyed to have been caught looking. She threaded a hair into the hook and dug it under the mesh again, pulling a few more strands of the dark hair through before she dared to look up again. He was still staring at her, like a hawk fixes its prey. She felt herself blush as their eyes met. He kept glancing at her, keeping his head still as Madame Lefevre fussed around him, measuring across the top of his head. She pretended to be working, all the time conscious of his eyes watching her. Eventually she dared a small smile. Madame Lefevre, sensing there was something going on she had not sanctioned, glared at Ella, grabbed hold of the curtain and yanked it shut.

Now she was out of Madame Lefevre's view, Ella stretched her back and circled her shoulders, which were stiff from hunching over the wig stand. She glanced at Sadie, who was still industriously knotting. The room grew darker, the day's sunlight had passed the two small windows and they were shadowed by the building opposite. None of the girls would have the welcome squares of light from the windows over their workspace now. Madame Lefevre was stingy with the rushlights, waiting until nightfall before handing them out one at a time. Each day as evening came, they had to bend closer to the work, straining to see the minute filaments of tulle and hair.

Ella saw Sadie gingerly feeling the back of her neck, and mouthed at her, 'Does it hurt?'

Sadie shook her head.

'Let's look.' She stood up and went over. Sadie's brown hair hung over one side of her face as usual.

The other girls crept over too, full of ghoulish curiosity.

'Move your hair, so's we can see,' Corey said.

'No,' Sadie said, but she tilted her head forward to expose her neck.

'That looks nearly as sore as what she gave Kitty Hazlitt,' Corey said, 'but not as bad as the time she caught—'

Suddenly the mustard curtain was hauled aside again and the

DEBORAH SWIFT

girls scurried back to their places and bent over their work. The man ducked under the lintel and came down the few steps into the room, immediately followed by Madame Lefevre pecking at his heel. From a sidelong glance Ella saw that he was sporting a simple dark tied wig, and that his head now appeared to be of normal proportions. He was fingering the brim of his hat and looking at her again.

Madame Lefevre was obviously uncomfortable with the visitor's venture into the back room.

'There's not a deal to see, Mr Whitgift,' she said, 'the girls are only just beginning this week's orders. If you would care to return to the parlour I will show you some of the finished periwigs.'

He picked up a hook from the bench, juggling it in his fingers.

'But I like to see how they are made. I enjoy good craftsmanship.' He flashed Madame Lefevre a smile that showed surprisingly white teeth. 'Does each girl take on the whole article, from start to finish?'

'Usually yes, though for ladies' styles there are two Frenchmen who come in to curl the wigs on a Friday. Gentlemen's styles are not so difficult and can be styled by my good self. But the girls do all the knotting. Never fear though, sir, I have hand-picked them for their skill.'

'Well, in that case, I would like this girl to make mine.' He waved his hand at Ella. She was mortified and felt her face grow hot and red.

Madame Lefevre's mouth fell open, before she clamped it shut again.

'Sir, I am sure we are most flattered, but this girl is new, her training is not yet complete – O'Malley over there is a more experienced knotter, she does a very neat job.' Pegeen lowered her head as if she wanted to disappear into the pile of black horsehair on the bench.

'No, I have made up my mind. I want this girl to make it.' He gave Ella a dazzling smile. Ella saw Madame Lefevre's eyes on her and kept her expression stony.

'Anyway,' he said, 'she will weave it beautifully, I can see it.'

Ella bobbed deferentially. Mr Whitgift seemed amused by this coyness and tried to smother a smile.

Madame Lefevre pursed her lips. 'Very well, sir. Her sister can help her. Are you listening?' Sadie tilted her head from under her hair. 'Now then, please follow me through to the parlour and we will look at a few styles in the book. Buckingham sports side curls now and all the gentlemen want them.' Madame Lefevre guided him back to the curtain like a bad-tempered collie rounding up a stray sheep. She herded him back upstairs, threw Ella a malevolent glance over her shoulder and whipped the curtain shut.

'Who is he?' whispered Ella to Corey, who was known to be a storehouse of names and faces, having lived in London all her life. Most of the other girls were incomers – Irish or Dutch.

'Josiah Whitgift, son of Walt Whitgift, the pawnbroker down by Broken Wharf. People call him Jay, you know, like the bird.'

Ella strained her ears to hear what might be going on upstairs, but the voices were muffled and indistinct. She swallowed, unease settled on her shoulders like a cloak. Her knotting was clumsy and she knew it. She caught Sadie's eye and Sadie shook her head. And this Mr Whitgift – he was well-to-do. You only had to look at his clothes to see that. She had been too rash, she should not have been so brazen as to exchange glances with him. Madame Lefevre would be on her back all the time now with her eagle eye. And clearly the gentleman would expect something in return. She did not want to be beholden to anyone. She knew well enough men like that only single you out for one thing.

Ella turned back to Corey and hissed, 'Are you sure he's a pawnbroker's son? He doesn't look or sound like one. Too flash.'

'His pa's shop is the grandest in London. It's nearly as wide as the Thames.' Sadie and the rest of the girls leaned in to hear Corey's conspiratorial whisper. 'It's not supposed to be a pop shop, just a second-hand shop, but we all know it as the pop shop. They say if a lord gets burgled or set upon by a highway thief, there's only one place he should look for his missing watch – Walt Whitgift's.'

'Is he a rogue then?' Sadie said, with a worried frown.

'I'm not saying that. Walt Whitgift's got a reputation for being straight as an arrow, see. But there's always rumours about *him*.' She wagged her head in the direction of the curtain.

Corey opened her mouth to continue, but buttoned up again as Madame Lefevre appeared like a bitter gust of wind through the curtain.

'You.' Madame Lefevre clawed Ella's arm with her gloved fingers and hoisted her to a standing position. 'What did you say to him?'

Ella remained silent, her face unmoving, eyes staring ahead like a wax doll. Madame Lefevre started to shake her.

'She didn't say a thing, Madame Lefevre,' said Sadie. 'Nobody did.'

Madame Lefevre pursed her lips into a round, hard hole and thrust Ella back down onto her stool.

'Get those fat fingers moving. He wants the wig Wednesday week.'

She did not respond, and Madame Lefevre moved around to the front of the bench and brought her face up close. She addressed the top of her head as if she would spit on it.

'Did you hear me?'

Ella closed her nose against the sickly sweet odour of Madame Lefevre's breath and gave a barely perceptible nod. Her eyes stayed downcast, watching a flea appear and disappear between the sprouting hairs on the work in front of her.

'And you –' Madame Lefevre's eyes alighted on Sadie – 'I can't have dead wood cluttering my shop. I've got my reputation to think of. There's plenty more out of work and looking. It's got to be right, or she'll be out. Make sure she ties it neat and proper.'

'Oh, she will, madame – it'll be as fine as any wig in London, ain't that right, Ella?'

Sadie looked to her in appeal. Ella lowered her eyes guiltily. Half of her wanted to placate Sadie and avoid trouble by becoming a model worker overnight, to surprise them all by making a perfect wig, but the other half of her wanted to spite Madame Lefevre and the world in general by refusing to lift a single finger to the task. She heard Sadie give a small sigh, and knew that her sister had understood all of this without a word being exchanged between them. Her guilty feeling increased all the more.

'He'll be back Friday for a fitting and he wants you there.' Ella flinched as the words were accompanied by a sharp dig in the back. 'Lord knows why. Or in your case – the Devil knows why. This is your last chance.'

Ella slowly and deliberately picked up the hook and separated a hair very carefully from the foul-smelling heap by her elbow. She relished the slowness of her movements because she knew it was guaranteed to goad Madame Lefevre all the more. She enjoyed the feeling of everyone's eyes upon her, it gave her a sense of power to have all their attention. She drew the hair inchmeal through the mesh. It was almost with satisfaction that she felt the thwack of the measuring tape sting the back of her neck. She did not falter but continued the slow pulling of the hair. Shortly afterwards she heard the tap-tap of Madame Lefevre's wooden heels as she swept away into her private quarters, followed by the slam and rattle of her door.

When she raised her eyes it was to see Sadie looking at her

with a mixture of fear and reproach. She quickly returned to her work but her stomach squirmed, and when she tried to hook the next hair through, she fumbled and got it all tangled. 'Devil fetch it,' she cursed.

Chapter 5

Bread Street

'Come on, you've not eaten enough to keep a mite alive.'

'I'm not hungry,' Sadie said, pushing away her half of the cold potage. 'I'm afraid, Ella. What if Madame Lefevre gives us the elbow? How'll we pay our way then?'

'Are you saying my knotting's no good?'

'No, Ell. No. It's just she picks fault in everything. I'm afeared she'll find something ill with it and throw one of her rages.'

'She won't get rid of us. You're her little pet. Soon as you showed your needlework, she knew you'd take to the knotting. You're quick as a fox. She'd be a bedlam fool to let you go. Nah, she'll keep us both on.' Ella slicked the remaining potage from her bowl with a wipe of her bread, unconcerned.

'But what if she don't?'

'Tush, Sadie. We'll brook that when it's in front of us. No point thinking of that now. Anyway, we'd get taken on someplace else. I'm not after being stuck in that scum-hole for ever, not me. I've got my eyes peeled for something better.'

'Wig shop pays scarce a scab, I know, but work's hard to

come by. I reckon we're lucky. It's not bad work, not like the fishwives, or tanners. And we've got a house to live in, and food on the table, it's more than most.'

'Lucky? Huh. Some place. I sure as eggs don't want to live here for ever.' Ella screwed up her face at the thought of it. 'Eat up, don't waste it.'

Sadie spooned another mouthful of the grey oatmeal, forced herself to swallow. She had realized within hours of coming to London that the poor here were always hungry, for nothing grew here. Livestock was not fed corn, but existed on scraps hurled from the back doors, if they could get to it before the foraging packs of yellow dogs that hung on every street. She had seen an old man bloody another's nose when he thought his neighbour was trying to steal his mangy chicken – poor pathetic creature, surely all gristle anyway.

Ella had been used to better, Sadie thought, what with living in as a housemaid at the Ibbetsons'. But to Sadie it was no worse than the house she had come from, except of course it was crammed up in Cooper's Yard with a score of others. London was tight as a closed fist round them, so tight you could smell its sweat.

The dwelling was furnished with only two chairs, a table and the trunks they had come with. Dingy and smoke-stained, it was a single room of crumbling lath and plaster more often than not damp and cold. As yet there was not enough money from their earnings for a fire in the hearth every day, only on the coldest days or cooking days. Up a splintered ladder at the back of the room there was a sleeping platform, partitioned off. Inside, a sagging truckle bed leaned against the wall, and under it a pot. By the door stood a bucket and ewer for washing.

But it was their own. Ella had insisted on that when they fled Westmorland. London was full of shared rooms where two or three families were crammed together, and everyone hung on each other's shirt tails. No, Ella had said, no shared lodgings for them. She'd had her fill of being at someone else's beck and call.

They sold most of the goods straight away at Ella's insistence – anything that wasn't too valuable or ostentatious: the unremarkable watch, the lace and linen, all the silver plate. She knew how much Ella had wanted to keep it all by the way she handled the goods as she parcelled them up to be sold. But London was expensive, much more expensive than Ella had reckoned on, so the proceeds had only been just enough to rent this small chamber on Bread Street on a three-month lease. Bread Street was not as wholesome as its name, ramshackle and with a ditch running down the centre always full of pigshit. The yeasty residues and bakery waste attracted the pigs, but at least there were ovens going most of the day and that meant it was warmer than other places.

When Sadie had first seen it, she had mistakenly queried whether Ella had made a good bargain, and Ella had cuffed her and said she had not wanted to haggle and draw attention to herself – she did not want Thomas Ibbetson's family to trace them. Sadie had watched as she had a smith put a great iron lock on the door straight away.

Just looking at that lock still gave Sadie gooseflesh.

She put down her spoon, the bowl empty except for a ring of dried crust. She followed Ella's eyes as they ranged round the room. 'Do you think he's still looking for us?'

'I don't know. No. Shouldn't think so. Not after all these weeks.'

Sadie swept up both bowls to take them for scrubbing in the sand pail.

'It's a kennel,' Ella said, still looking about her with a disgruntled air, 'but at least it's our own, and I suppose we'll get by.'

'Then promise me you'll be right particular with Mr Whitgift's wig. Old Feverface will throw us out if it's not up to the mark.' She grabbed Ella's hand and squeezed it, searching her face, looking for an agreement.

Ella slid her eyes away, avoiding her, so Sadie dug her fingers further into Ella's hand. Eventually Ella sighed. 'If it means you'll stop looking so mardy. But I'm telling you, Sadie, when I see her claws picking over my work as if I'm somehow not good enough, it makes me so mad I could grind her bony fingers into dust under my boot.'

Sadie withdrew her hand, shocked by the venom of her sister's words.

'Don't look at me like that. You know as well as I, she never shows her real face in the shop, acting all meek-mannered with the customers under her fancy black lace. But we know the sting of that tape. I'd like to see her grovel. Her, and all the folk like her.'

Ella's face darkened and a shadow passed over it, the way clouds alter the colours of the hills as they drift by. 'It's always us or them, isn't it?'

'Aw, come on, Ell, don't start on that again.'

'Or at least, mostly.'

Astonished, Sadie saw that Ella's eyes had grown full of tears. 'He weren't like that though – not Master Thomas,' Ella said.

Sadie put down the crocks and went over to put her arm round Ella's shoulder, but Ella shrugged away, as if she wanted to gather herself together, folding her arms tight across her chest.

'I never would have thought it, but I miss him that sore. Before he fell sick, he were kind, and he treated me like a proper woman, not a servant. Oh aye, I had to roll over for him like any man, but come morning he'd help me dress, bend down and put my two clogs side by side for me to slip my feet into, just like I were any lady.' She stood up hurriedly and moved over to the grimy window. 'But I don't know that I deserved him.' Her mouth twisted into a wring of pain, her voice was choked as though in mid-swallow. 'He shouldn't have died. We were happy. Comfortable. He should have got better, the physician said so. But then he went and—'

She came back to the table, eyes streaming. She brushed the wet across her cheeks and into her hair. 'Do you think the dead can see us?'

'Well, I don't know . . .'

'His wife cursed me. If it weren't for her . . .' She took a deep shuddering breath. 'She hexed me – I saw her give me the cold eye when she was in the dock. She saw to it we'd have no peace. We would have been happy, snug and safe in our warm little house.' Ella took hold of Sadie's arm and pulled her close. 'You could have had your own little room under the eaves. He were soft, a good provider, and he loved me. He would have done anything for me. Even though I were just a maidservant. He called me his little chicken.' Ella's lower lip trembled, and she let go. 'Stupid bloody man. Why did he have to die?'

Sadie sat back down and pulled her hair forward, tugging it between her fingers. She was unsure what her sister meant – their flight from Netherbarrow had been hurried and confusing. She was confounded by this strange talk of hexes – all she had understood was that Ella's employer, Mr Ibbetson, had died and Ella had lost her position.

She knew of course that they had taken a large quantity of goods from the house – this alone made her quake, the value of the goods was far more than twelve penn'orth, and that on its own was a hanging offence – but now here was Ella talking of curses too. Sadie shivered and looked behind, as if something might be lurking in the dark recesses under the platform. She stared at Ella, standing now head tilted up towards the ceiling, her mouth twitching, as if she were chewing the inside of it.

Ella was serious. A chill ran through Sadie's spine. 'What do you mean, Ella? What sort of hex?'

Ella grabbed hold of the back of her chair, her hands white, the tears were gone. Her eyes turned hard and defiant. 'I know folks think it sinful, what I did. But it didn't feel wrong. Maid-servants are two a penny, and if one dies, then another mooncalf steps straight in to fill her boots, and most times the mistress don't even notice the difference. As long as their bloody fires are mended. Filled with her own importance she was, Mistress, like I didn't have no feelings nor nothing, lording it over us all with her jangling keys.'

She paced the floor, her hands crushed into fists. Her voice took on a flinty edge. 'It were time for Mistress to know what it feels like, to be left waiting.'

Sadie twined her hair round her index finger. She did not know how to respond, so she simply sat and waited for Ella to burn her-self out. Even when they were small, she had often watched as Ella's storms blew up and then abated, and like the weather they seldom lasted too long. Ella had the knack of setting things to one side, putting them away neatly in sealed boxes in her mind and pretend-ing that they never happened, whereas Sadie could never stop one thought from leaking into the next, so that her thoughts crashed into each other in a sea of worries. Now her disquiet began to mount as she tried to make sense of the fragments of Ella's story.

'What is it?' Sadie whispered, when Ella stopped pacing and her shoulders showed that her breathing had settled. 'What is it you're telling me?'

Ella turned half away as if ashamed.

'Go on,' Sadie said.

'He needed someone to love him, see. Great soft thing. But

now I'm thinking, mayhap I was wrong, and Alice Ibbetson might be a witch after all. She cursed me afore she went – not in words, but I caught it well enough. It were a look of hell and brimstone and I'll not forget that look as long as I live.'

Sadie stared. 'Is she dead?'

Ella did not look up.

'Did they hang her?'

Ella nodded, as if she could not trust herself to speak.

There was a moment's pause. Pigeons cooed in the rafters.

'Then she can't harm us,' said Sadie, 'whatever's passed between you. God rest her soul.' But the words seemed hollow and empty. She had not forgotten the sight of the body in the bedroom, and here was Ella talking about another death. She had a sense that she had only just scratched the surface of the story; that the events of the night they left Westmorland were like an underground river, deeply hidden, treacherous, so that the ground beneath them might suddenly collapse and drag them down and sweep them away in a black tide.

Ella's face took on a closed look. She took hold of Sadie's shoulder and her fingers pressed into her collarbone. 'Never go out without locking that door. And keep your head down when you're out and about. That's why I bought you that hooded cloak. That stain marks you out.'

Sadie felt her words like a slap. Ella hardly ever referred to her face, though plenty of other people used it as a stick to beat her with. But her sister had always ignored it, treating her with a rough tenderness, partly bullying, partly loving, and for this she had been grateful.

Sadie went red, and her hand sprang up to her forehead as if she was pressing it over a headache. It was a gesture she used often, her hand resting on her eyebrow, half cupped over her left eye, shadowing her cheek.

49

Ella looked uncomfortable. She picked up the potage bowls and took them purposefully out of the front door to empty the dregs into the gutter, before dropping them into the sand bucket next to the fireplace. Sadie watched her sister scour the bowls with sand, rubbing hard round the edges with a cloth, put the lid back on the cooking pot with a clatter and wipe her hands. She turned back to Sadie, a softer look on her face.

"'Tis only for a time. Till the fuss dies down,' she said, gruff now, almost apologetic. 'Come on, brace up. That potage were foul. I'll go out to the pie shop and get us a savoury to share.'

'Can we manage it?' Sadie said. 'There's not much left from selling that ring, and you said it had to last us a month.'

'I know what I said,' snapped Ella, suddenly belligerent again. 'Just stop moaning, will you. Lock the door after me, and don't open it till you hear my knock – two short raps. D'you hear?'

Sadie nodded and stood up as Ella unlocked the door with a key hung inside her petticoat on a long grubby string and took out the black leather purse of coins. When she got to the door she called back, 'Lock it after me, I said.' And Sadie slid the two bolts on the inside, though the door frame was that rickety and rotten she doubted it would hold up against someone who was really determined to get in.

She turned her back on the bolted door and saw anew the small square box they lived in. It was smaller than the stall they kept their cows in at home. The pang of homesickness took her by surprise. A longing that seemed to spring straight up from her heart. She pulled her shawl more closely round her shoulders and tied the ends. It was one she had knitted herself with Herdwick wool. She brought it up to her face and inhaled. It was shabby and worn, with a tatty fringe, but it smelt of Westmorland. She liked it better than the cloak Ella had bought her.

The smell took her straight home. She pictured her father's

back straining against his yoked shirt, bent over the fire to see what was cooking. She missed her da. Fifteen years she had spent hating him, dreading him coming home, fearing his drunken footsteps outside the door. At night she used to lie awake and dream about the day Ella would come back in her fine lace and satin and take her away from him. Ever since she was small she had been his scapegoat, someone he could hit when he was angry, someone who would cringe and beg, make him feel powerful, like a man, when in truth he wasn't a man at all – just bones held together by beer. Yet now she missed him and it shamed her. But at least he was predictable, not like Ella who blew hither and thither like chaff in the wind.

She went to the window and opened the shutters to look out on the street. She wondered what Da thought when she had disappeared. Since coming to London she played out imaginary scenes in her head, where he wept and told her he loved her, begged her to come home, said he'd never forgive himself. Maybe he was out searching for her right that minute. But deep down she knew he would not, that he had just drowned it as usual.

She turned away from the window and hoicked the bowls out of the sand where Ella had left them, then dried them on her apron. She rubbed the cloth around the inside, staring into space. Da. The memories flooded back. She realized she had not thought of him since Christmas Day. She knew it was Christmas Day because she and Ella hunkered up in front of a big fire with a meal of roasted pigeon and boiled taters, courtesy of selling another pair of candlesticks, and Ella had even bought a sprig of holly for the windowsill. At the first mouthful of pigeon she had felt a sudden grief, wondering how he was managing with nobody to fetch their share of the goose from their neighbours. That day Sadie saw Ella's faraway look and knew that, like her, she was remembering other feast days and holidays, the May Day carousings and the warm fires of the Candlemas supper. But there was no snow in London, no village fiddler coming door to door, no mummers play, and the grey damp was unabated.

She had reached across the table then and given Ella her last boiled tater, even though she'd been saving it till the end because it was the biggest.

Sadie looked down at the two bowls. What was she doing standing about like a lummock? She stacked the bowls on the shelf and pushed her memories away. The pain of them scalded her too much. She ached for the beauty of the hills – the open skies with their scudding clouds, the hawthorn's scarlet berries, the sweet tang of cow dung. She sat back on the hard wooden chair, winding her hair in her fingers, the stench of horse urine, bird droppings and soot in her nostrils, the incessant noise of iron-shod hooves drowning out the vermin scratching in the rafters.

She waited for Ella to return and wondered if she had ever really known her sister. There was something in Ella's tale that made her spine prickle, for she knew that Ella never told anyone the truth when a lie suited her better. With Ella there was always the feeling that the truth moved about, like tussocks on shifting sand, and that sometimes when you thought you were on solid ground, it would tilt and sink beneath you. And that fact alone made her shiver, and not just from cold.

Chapter 6

Jay Whitgift hurried down the narrow alleyway towards the Pelican Coffee House. The icy rain was like pitchforks so he was anxious to get away from the midden of the narrow unswept streets with their seeping piles of horse excrement and into the dry darkness of the Pelican, where he was to meet Allsop, a client. As he rounded the corner into Cooper's Yard, he almost tripped over a chapman whose tray of pamphlets was jutting out into the main thoroughfare. About to curse the man, he turned to face him but was arrested by a pair of familiar eyes.

'Josiah Whitgift.' The man moved out from under the upper storey and pushed his tray under Jay's nose. 'Well, I never.'

Jay did not reply and stepped away. He had no wish to linger and speak with him for he recalled him well.

'Don't go running away from old friends now. There is an almanac here would suit you very well.' He fished amongst the damp pile of thin booklets in his tray.

Jay shifted uncomfortably from foot to foot. 'Sorry, Tindall, I'm meeting someone, maybe another time, eh?'

Tindall fixed Jay with his eyes. 'Take my advice, you ignore the stars at your peril. A wise man takes them into account or he cannot move with the tides.'

Jay looked over his shoulder, seeking an excuse to leave.

'There is a message here could be made for you,' Tindall went on, 'and you would do well to heed it. There is a conjunction of Saturn and Mars coming, the reaper and the firebrand. It will mean great upheaval, not least for those born under the twins, such as yourself.'

Curse the man. He would walk past, but it was evident that Tindall was not going to let him by unless he made a purchase. It was embarrassing to see him standing out on the street in such a condition. The last time he had seen him was in his father's warm parlour, where in his fancy velvet coat it seemed as if he was doing them a favour by calling at all. Now astrologers had fallen from the king's favour, and like all the others Tindall must be finding it hard to earn a living.

'Very well, I'll take this.' Anxious to move on, Jay picked out the first chapbook that came to hand, giving it a cursory glance to see the price. He turned it over. It showed what appeared to be a depiction of Hell – burning skeletons flailing behind a wall of forked-tongued flames. In the background, a building that looked like St Paul's Church was toppling into the fiery sea.

He stuffed it into the top of his breeches and held out a penny.

'No. It is not that one you need,' said Tindall, his eyes dark and shifting behind his dribble of greasy hair, and he took out a thinner handwritten paper from under his coat.

Jay sighed and reached for another coin. Tindall took it. His cuffs were thick with dirt, the edges frayed.

'This is the one,' said Tindall, holding out the paper, which was peppered with diagrams and symbols and tiny writing. 'But you will not make much sense of it without my interpretation – you would do better with a full consultation.'

Jay snatched the paper impatiently. 'No, I don't think so.' He looked at Tindall almost apologetically. 'You must know, nobody bothers with astrology these days. My father doesn't need your help. We are men of reason now – I even have my own telescope. We don't need old-fashioned notions of predatory comets and portents of doom. We've moved forward with the king, into a new age.'

Tindall shook his head and said nothing, just stared at him intently, a look of pity in his eyes. Jay shifted his gaze, feeling uncomfortable, and having said his piece thrust his way past and continued up the road, screwing up the paper in his fist and throwing it down onto the road in disgust.

Tindall watched him go. He dodged a passing handcart to retrieve the paper, unfolded it and smoothed it out. Through narrowed eyes he glanced at the sign of the Pelican, carefully shielded the paper from the rain, refolded it and put it back inside his waistcoat.

'That's as may be,' Tindall said, drawing the oilskin cover over his wares. He shrugged and moved off. In a moment he was swallowed up by the crowd of itinerant hawkers, pedlars and barrow boys.

Meanwhile Jay swung in through the door of the coffee shop and looked for a place to sit in the fug of steam and tobacco smoke. The stalls were full, but the occupant of one of the round tables near the bow window sprang to his feet and beckoned him over.

'Over here, Whitgift.' Allsop removed a glove and held out his hand, and Jay took it, noticing that it was immaculately manicured as always, the nails white curves above smooth pink flesh. Jay's sharp eyes also saw that Allsop wore a mourning ring, presumably for his late mother. It was a particularly fine example, an ebony mount with engraved doves. He mentally assessed its worth as he gave Allsop's hand the briefest of shakes. He recoiled a little for the hand was slightly damp. Sweat also stood out like dew on Allsop's forehead.

They sat, Allsop having some difficulty in forcing his large frame into such a tight corner, for he was a giant of a man, barrel-chested, like a mastiff, but with the jowls of a bloodhound. He was impeccably attired, in a tight-fitting plum-coloured damask coat. He snapped his fingers at the molly behind the counter and ordered more coffee, before leaning in to speak.

'Look here, Whitgift, I'm going to need another loan. The burglary cleared me out. I'd hoped selling my late mother's collections would clear my debts, but until the stolen goods are recovered I find myself in a bit of a tight spot.'

'You realize the other loan is still outstanding?'

'It's a short-term difficulty. I am in poor health. I need to pay the apothecary and the physician, and they do not come cheap. It's nigh on ten shilling these days just to get bled. Twenty pounds should cover it.'

Jay whistled through his teeth. 'That's a fair amount on top of what's owed.'

'If the silver that was stolen is recovered – and I know you will let me know if it shows up at Whitgift's – then obviously I will pay off both loans together.'

'You know there's no guarantee—'

'Come on, Whitgift, I've always paid my dues on time, have I not?'

'I can let you have ten. It's all I have brought with me.' Jay had been prepared for this. He brought out his satchel from under the table and counted out the amount, before pushing the book across for Allsop to make his mark.

Allsop made a great fuss of uncorking the ink and wiping the quill afterwards with unsteady hands. He pushed the book back.

'I don't know, I seem to be bedevilled – what with the burglary, and now I am unwell. And there's more.'

Jay raised his eyebrows in question.

'We are in a bit of difficulty. The matter is somewhat awkward . . .' He paused to wipe his forehead with his sleeve. His eyes shifted sideways, not meeting Jay's gaze.

Jay did not like the sound of the 'we'. He put his elbows on the table and pushed his hat back on his head to get closer. 'What is it?' He sensed trouble coming.

'There has been an oversight . . .'

'Tell me straight. What's the flutter? Is it horses again?'

'No, not that. The list of my late mother's jewellery, the one I sent over to Whitgift's last week, from the burglary . . . well, there was something I missed, something I didn't know was gone . . .'

'Another jewel? It can easily be added to the inventory, you know, just give my father—'

'No, no, it's not that. This is a little delicate . . . if it was to fall into the wrong hands, it would ruin me. And bring you down with it.'

'Go on.' The hairs had risen on Jay's neck.

'I got the idea from my friend Pepys, it is a kind of notebook – a private diary.'

Jay's stomach sank. He grasped immediately the implications of that confession. 'What's in it?' Allsop shifted in his chair. The man was red in the face and sweating even more profusely under his full-bottomed wig. A drip ran down his forehead. 'Is my name in it?'

'I think not. But you see, I cannot exactly recall. But I'm afraid it—'

'You know what this means. We've got to get it back before it reaches someone who can read. What does it look like?'

'Well, it's a small leather-bound book—'

'I know that, how the deuce am I supposed to—?'

'– about a handspan tall and four digits wide. Buff calfskin, gold-tooled binding . . .'

'For God's sake.' It had just started to sink in. 'And you say it gives details of our transactions?'

'Not just yours. I write them all down, see, afterwards. The doxies. So I can read it over again another time for my own pleasure, and you know my tastes are not straightforward. But it's not just that – if anyone read it, I would be finished.' Allsop clutched Jay's arm and looked up at him through panicky eyes.

'Now look here, you'd best level with me, if my name's in it and my neck's at stake. What else?' Jay lowered his voice. 'Is it . . . gentlemen?'

'Of course not. What do you take me for?'

Jay looked at him coldly and stood up. 'I will need ten pounds to pay my men to track it down. And you do not need me to tell you how urgent that is.'

'Ten pounds? No. That is outrageous. You know I cannot pay that.'

''Tis cheap enough in this circumstance. Why did you not have the damn thing under lock and key?'

'How was I to know I would be turned over like that in the night?' He looked sulky. 'I sacked the porter; he must have been sleeping on the watch.'

'Well, do you want it back or no? Ten pounds and I guarantee you it will be back in your hands by the end of the week. But I need to know what's in it first.'

'No, it's private. I can't tell you that here. Just get it back to me, that's all.'

'When I locate it, I will read it anyway. So why this pretence at coyness? That is, unless you want it left abroad and your rutting habits bandied about the city.'

Jay watched him squirm. He usually enjoyed playing this game. He knew its rules well, like a game of chequers, he understood the unspoken patterns of advance and retreat. But this was something different entirely. He was uneasy, sensing his own neck at risk. Damn Allsop. He was becoming tedious. He leaned in and fixed Allsop with a stare. 'Tell me what's in it. It will be safe with me,' he lied. He knew half of London's underworld would have to hear of it for him to stand any chance of tracing it. Books were risky because they always crept their way upwards to the learned, and therefore the more influential. They were of no value to most folks except as fuel. 'Tell me,' Jay said.

'Stop pressing me! I said no.' Allsop thumped his fist on the table.

The molly arrived and set down a steaming pot of coffee and two porcelain bowls before them. The occupants of the stalls behind peered over the tops of the partitions to find out the cause of the sudden noise. Jay smiled thinly at them to reassure the curious faces there was nothing amiss, and poured a thick sooty stream into the bowls before turning his attention back to Allsop. Jay flicked his head to the side and the molly took his signal, swung her tray under her arm and sashayed away.

'It's a catastrophe. I will be ruined,' said Allsop. Jay waited as he twirled the spoon in his bowl. Allsop finally whispered, 'It has my accounts in it, my debts, all listed in the back. They can see I am not worth a penny pittance. I'll be a laughing stock. You will find it, will you not?'

'If it mentions my name, I'll find it all right. And burn it.'

For a moment Allsop looked as though he might crumble into his own boots, but then he stood up as if catapulted out of his seat, his face the colour of cochineal. 'You will not. It's my property. When you find it, you will return it to me. Or I will let loose my tongue.'

A childhood in the East End of London, where he had been bullied within an inch of his life, followed by an even more brutal spell at St Paul's School had left Jay impervious to threats or violent behaviour. He pulled his hat further down on his head, and opened the door as if preparing to leave.

'And who would believe you, eh?' he hissed. 'A bankrupt with a whore and gambling habit, against the son of Fair Square Walt Whitgift of Friargate.'

Allsop, who had followed him, grabbed him by the sleeve. 'I do not trust you, Whitgift. So help me God, if I'm going down, you'll be dragged down with me, so you'd better play straight and return my property to me.'

'No one is going down,' said Jay quietly, removing Allsop's hand from his arm. 'Threaten me all you like, but it will not bring you back your book. May I remind you of your obligations as agreed. You have thirty days. Should the required amount not be forthcoming, I will send a friend to help you reconsider. And when I find this scurrilous diary, which I assure you I will, then, after a little pruning, I know of a very good printer in Whitechapel. Good day.'

Jay held onto the brim of his hat and ducked under the doorway, leaving Allsop to pick up the bill in the Pelican. His mind was already working. If there was to be any sort of scandal, he must be in control of it, make sure it fell to his advantage. He would find that notebook and remove any reference to himself. He was always careful to cover his own tracks. Damn Allsop, the pudding-brained simkin. Men like him deserved their comeuppance.

He would make some enquiries straight away. Then when the damnable thing was safely in his chambers, he could contact

Allsop again, by which time he might be more than ready to find the wherewithal to pay.

Jay took a sedan back to the shop on Friargate. He tipped the bearers and strolled in through the double gates under the old hanging emblem of the three brass coins. It creaked a little in the breeze, for it was also a weathercock, the iron tail feathers swinging round to point to the west, the ever-open beak crowing eastwards. The weathercock had been his own idea. It was clever to make the pawnbroker's sign appear to be something else now the king had made such loans illegal.

The yard was full of people as usual. Everything was wreathed in a shifting mist that rose up from the nearby Thames to cling around skirts and ankles. Over at the far end of the yard were the hackney carriages of the moneyed clients, some tethered mounts and a few well-liveried servants hanging round the mounting blocks and trough, exchanging news and watching their employers come and go.

There was the customary queue of down-at-heel women with scraggy bundles, so many that the tail of the queue extended out of the side gate and into the road. Jay paused to wave to Dennis, who was issuing tickets above the lower stable door and passing the bundles back to where the two hired lads would sort and label them. With satisfaction he saw him draw the money from two bags nailed to the inside of the lower portion of the stable door, so as not to leave coinage or tokens on display.

Jay walked on, giving the dismal trail of women a wide berth, until he saw one of them staring fixedly at him. She looked familiar. He paused for an instant trying to place her, until he remembered. Ah yes, one of the piece workers in the wigmaker's. He dismissed her from his mind without a qualm, for she was of no account. She was not the winsome one, with the milky skin, who was making his peruke, but the ugly ginger-headed one. O'Malley, was she called? Anyway, the one the old boiler had tried to foist on him. Jay hurried his pace, blotting out the girl's stare.

The other girl, the pretty one with the wide-apart eyes and wavy hair, well, she could be useful. Women were like lodestones, drawing attention wherever they went. He had been looking out for the right sort of girl, and that girl looked simple, obviously from out of town, with a kind of fresh country charm. She was a bold one, he could tell. It was no good if they were too timid. A certain boldness was always needed for the selling and for what he had in mind. The wigmaker's girl might do.

He turned into the main warehouse. The double doors to what had once been a loading bay were bolted back to reveal what at first glance could be taken for an open market, laid out with trestle tables on which goods were displayed according to type. Brass on one table – warming pans, kettles and candlesticks. Linen on another – starched tablecloths, lawn and lace christening gowns, pillowslips.

Once a week the doors were thrown open so that people could buy, and today the place was warm with the press of purchasers. He squeezed past a table with every kind of pewter heaped high, closing his nose against the sulphurous smell of metal polish, then wended his way past more glinting cutlery, towards the back wall of the warehouse. He passed the tables without a glance, trying not to brush against anyone lest he soil his fine suit. He had no interest in these goods, for all the fine or valuable stock was in his father's quarters. All that is, except for the very best, the most exquisite. Of these treasures his father knew nothing – Jay hoarded them in his own secret hiding place in his upstairs rooms.

A notice above the stout iron-bound door read: *Walter Whitgift. Privatus. By Prior Appointment Only.* Jay pulled on a trailing rope. A dusty bell on the wall clanged. Its tone was peculiarly tuneless, as if the note had been squeezed out of it. The bell had once hung in St Stephen's Church but had been pawned against the more urgent roof repairs. It had been at Whitgift's four years now, and rang for a different kind of service.

Jay wished his father would make haste. At the table next to the door a barefoot woman was weeping over a pile of shoes, clogs and slippers. It was a common enough sight, but still he did not like the disturbance to be so close to him. He turned his back to shield himself from her tears, suppressing his natural urge to somehow make her stop. It made him uncomfortable, for he did not know where tears came from – they were mysterious and uncontrollable, and when women cried it made him angry. He felt it personally, as if he should be able to fix it. Women were always subject to these strange moods, he thought. Unlike men – you knew where you were with men. The fact that he could not seem to help these women, or understand their crying, only served to point up some lack in himself, a lack he could not exactly name, only feel, like a knot deep in the chest.

Impatient with the sobbing behind him, he tugged on the bell again. Its joyless noise rattled the rafters causing a sudden commotion and flapping overhead, followed by a shower of dust and droppings as the pigeons tried to find a quieter roost.

To his relief he heard the bar on the other side of the arched door shunt back and his father's wizened face appeared.

'It's you,' said his father grumpily, and stomped off into the darker recesses of his private quarters. 'Lock it after you.'

He did, and followed his father, stooping under the low lintels, for he was tall and this place had been used as a dairy long ago, in Bess's reign, when men were smaller. And even before then it had first been built for a small monastic order, now of course defunct on King Henry's orders. It was more than a century since any monks had chanted evensong here. They passed down a cloistered corridor, through several sunless interconnecting rooms furnished with a hotch-potch of locked cabinets – the gun room, the silver room and finally the gold room, which functioned also as an office. This was the only room with daylight; a thin stream of sun slid through the tiny round window and onto his father's desk. The walls were speckled with moving dots of light. His father was marking up rings and bracelets for sale, now that the owners had failed to buy them back by the due date.

He sat down opposite his father on a high-backed Windsor chair. The room whirred as if alive, a hundred pocket watches ticking away inside the cabinets.

His father did not look up but continued to examine a ring by holding it up close to his spectacles.

'Saw Tindall today, outside the Pelican,' Jay said. 'He looked a blaggard. His coat was that threadbare I'm surprised it holds together.'

'Nat Tindall the astrologer?' Now Jay had his father's attention. 'I've not seen Nat for years. Not in all of Cromwell's days. How does he, the old dog? Did you tell him to drop by?'

'He looked a pinchbeck. I tell you, Pa, we can't have the likes of him hanging around here.'

'Why, Jay? There's no harm in him coming in for a chinwag. He gave us good advice in the early days.'

'He'd bring the business down. He's naught but a leech.'

'Hold with your judgements now, son. It was on account of him I took this place – and now look at it, it's fair buzzing. He saw it in the stars, told me the date to sign for it and all. Happen we could do with a bit more of that advice.'

'Don't be soft, Pa. It's our own hard work has brought us all this, not any of his quackery.'

'We've had queer luck, though, haven't we, son? Though I

reckon 'tis you – you're my lucky talisman.' He smiled up at Jay, a smile that crinkled the brown skin on his forehead and around his eyes like an old leather glove. ''Tis uncanny the way the best stuff turns up here. Dear old Nat, he made quite a chart for it. Great big thing it was, took up half that wall. Baffled Bessie and me, it did, but he said our success was writ aforehand in the heavens. Insistent, he was. Something to do with Taurus, the Bull.'

'Bull, my backside. We've made our own reputation. And it's not lady luck, it's my hard graft – working my way through the stock every day and checking the gentry's lists in case their stolen goods turn up here.'

'And they always do. I'm telling you, it's uncommon fortune that brings them things through our door. Nat was right. Why, they could end up at any pop shop in London, but like as not they finish up here. 'Tis uncommon fortune, that.' He shook his head with an expression almost of reverence. Jay kept quiet. He knew full well why the goods always landed up in their establishment.

His father went on. 'Only last week, Justice Brinkley came by to ask after his missing portraits, and before a week was out, as if by bewitchment, here they were.' His father whistled softly through his teeth. 'No trace of where they came from, none of the lads can remember who brought them in, but the bugger paid handsomely to buy them back. Beats me why the constabulary never catch the villains – far too slow, likely. But mark me, if it weren't for us, Brinkley'd never have clapped ey'n on those portraits again.' His father's eyes watered. 'It was a ripe old time, when we first started. Yes, I miss Tindall. I had an affection for him, he had a wise old head on his shoulders.'

Jay remembered Tindall's knack of suddenly looming out of the shadows, like a living gargoyle, when Jay was about to do

DEBORAH SWIFT

something he shouldn't, like light-finger a watch from his pa's cabinet. As a boy it used to make him start, and feel guilty.

'But, Pa, charting the stars is old-fashioned. We've got to move with the times. The king made it plain he has no traffic with astrologers on account of the church, and we can't be seen to go against the king's wishes, 'twould be bad for business.'

Jay saw his father's lips press together in an expression he recognized well, a bull-headed stubbornness. This was the last thing Jay needed, to have some old charlatan noseying around the business, putting a muzzle on his activities. He changed the subject.

'Anyway, Pa, I've got an idea in my head that will really make us the talk of the town. Something new, that no one else has ever done.'

His father ignored him, bending over a pocket watch to tie on one of his labels. He penned a few marks with the quill, blew on it so the ink would dry, then looked up.

'Time for new ideas soon enough. You're too full o' them, if you ask me. Can't sit still a minute. Always got your finger in one pie or another. No staying power, that's your trouble. And put that down.'

Jay dropped a watch chain he'd been winding round his fingers back onto the table.

'Let the astrologer come,' his father said. 'There's more to life than we can see on the surface, son.'

You bet there is, Jay thought; just don't look too closely under your own two feet. He dragged his attention back to his father's words.

'You don't know what it's like to struggle. Times are uncertain. There's the war with the Dutch, and the last king lost his head, never known anything as cock-eyed as that in my life. Belt and braces, is what I've always said. That's why I had you schooled.'

66

Jay frowned. His schooling had not been a happy experience.

'Come on, Jay, please your old pa, eh? Look out for Nat Tindall, and if you see him again, tell him he's welcome. There'll be time enough for your newfangled schemes when I'm gone.'

His father always had that card – the one that made Jay feel as though he was standing over him, just waiting for him to die. That really was an ace, and he knew he could not trump it. But he had no intention of inviting that unwashed old goat Tindall anywhere near their premises, so he merely nodded. When his father had set his mind on anything and dug in his heels, it would take more than a coach and six to shift him. Unfortunately for him, Jay thought, his son was tarred with the same brush.

Chapter 7

One of Sadie's earliest memories was watching her father slump into sleep over the kitchen table. Ella said he was 'neither use nor ornament', and her face had been full of disgust. Sadie knew she herself would never qualify for the word 'ornament'. She grasped early on that she had better be of some use, that any advance she might make in life would come through skill and not looks, so she was adept at many small crafts. Hers were the neatest stitches, the sturdiest baskets and straw hats, hers the most mouth-watering lardy cakes.

So she had to bite her lip often, as Ella struggled to make Mr Whitgift's wig ready for his fitting. Ella wrested it this way and that, pulled and prodded at it, tugging on the hair, as if it were the wig's fault it would not go right. Once she saw Ella thrust the wig away in frustration and she went over to help, but Ella hissed at her.

'Keep out of my light.'

'Would you like me to do a few rows to speed it on?'

'Why? I can do it. He wanted me to do it, not you. Get out of it, you clod.'

And Sadie did not offer again, but watched Ella tussle with it.

She knew that fighting with the materials never made it easy – you had to respect the tools, let them help you.

When the day of the fitting arrived, the wig was finished just in time. Madame Lefevre had put it on a stand with the other finished perukes. Sadie was glad for Ella, because she had seen the effort she had put in. Granted, it was not as neat as her own work, but it would pass muster, and she was proud of the hours Ella had grafted, and excited to see how her handiwork would look. They heard the doorbell jingle and Mr Whitgift's slightly nasal voice in the lobby. Ella's cheeks were pink even before he came in the room. He wasn't exactly good-looking, his nose was too sharp and his chin too small, but there was a swagger about him that made you think he was. And he was dark, like a Lombardy man.

Madame Lefevre led him through and Ella smoothed over her apron and picked up the finished peruke, holding it out with pride.

'Ah,' Mr Whitgift said, 'it looks fine.' He plucked the dark curled wig out of her hand and twirled it round on his index finger.

'This way, sir,' Madame Lefevre said, holding aside the curtain as Mr Whitgift stooped under the lintel. She beckoned Ella, who dutifully followed. The door of the fitting room banged shut.

A few moments later they heard the door open and Madame Lefevre's whining voice. Ella reappeared, red-faced, and slumped into her seat. The girls stared at her, trying to catch her eye, until she pushed her tongue out at them.

'How did it go?' Sadie whispered.

But Ella continued to ignore them all, scuffing with her foot on the ground. Sadie's heart contracted for her. Something must have gone awry. Since arriving in London, Ella seemed to have lost all her customary perkiness. Sadie did not know exactly what had happened in Westmorland, why Thomas Ibbetson had died, but she often awoke at night to find Ella staring out of the window, chewing her fingernails to the quick.

Madame Lefevre's voice had lost its whining tone and now could be heard protesting loudly in the lobby. The bell jangled again as Mr Whitgift left, and a few moments later Madame Lefevre was in the room shaking the wig at them, for all the world like a dog with a rat.

'I have never been so humiliated.' She hurled the wig at Ella, who made no move to catch it. It fell to the floor at her feet. 'She reckoned it wrongly.' Drops of spittle flew from Madame Lefevre's mouth. 'He could have vouched for me all over the city. He has friends in the new theatre too. They need new perukes every month for their play-acting. The best client I have had for years, and she could not follow a few simple measurements.'

'If you please, madame, what's the matter with it?' Sadie asked.

'She sewed it too bloody tight, that's what.'

Ella was crimson. Madame Lefevre pointed to Corey. 'Corey Johnson. I want it set right by Monday.'

'Yes, madame,' Corey said.

Sadie wilted on her stool. She knew what to expect before the words left Madame Lefevre's mouth.

'And I warned you, you cannot gainsay it. You are dismissed. The pair of you. And you need not think I'll give you a wage. Look at the waste.'

Ella burst into life. 'That's not fair! Lay me off, but not Sadie. She's done nothing. 'Tis no fault of hers, she's a good worker.'

'No, Ella. I'll not stay. Not without you,' Sadie said.

'Don't be such a bonehead,' Ella said. 'We need the pay. No point the both of us being out of work.'

'Quiet!' Madame Lefevre approached Sadie, with a vestige of a smile. 'You may stay, but she goes.'

Sadie swallowed, and turned to Ella. What did she want her to do? 'I'm not doing it without you, you promised me. You said we'd always stick together.'

'Don't be a fool,' Ella said. 'You're grown up now, time to stop behaving like a biddy bairn. Keep your position, Sadie, if she's offering.'

'But what will you do?'

'Something'll turn up.'

'But, Ella—'

'Enough. Out, now, or she'll be with you,' Madame Lefevre said, grasping Ella by the arm and hustling her towards the stairs.

'I can walk out without your bloody help.' Ella wrested her arm away, and in doing so elbowed Madame Lefevre hard in the flat wood of her stomacher. Madame Lefevre reeled and staggered backwards, knocking over Ella's empty stool. The crash reverberated round the damp stone walls, round the cold bare ankles of the girls. The girls cowered down over their benches, anxious to keep out of trouble. A slam followed by the rattle of the bell announced Ella's departure.

Madame Lefevre was white-lipped. She primped and pinned her sparse black hair back into place and pulled the curtain tight to the wall. She stood with her back to it, as if to protect the girls in the event that Ella should return. Sadie sank down on her stool and stared at the space in front of her.

The other girls bent to their work, though the atmosphere was thick as gruel. Sadie did not dare look over at the empty space where Ella used to sit. If she did, she might cry. She tossed her hair forward over her face and continued to knot, even though her eyes ached and her head throbbed. It had been Ella who had always stood up for her against everyone's taunts. Now she was gone, who would defend her if they started calling her names? With Ella's absence, the room seemed suddenly cheerless, as if all the warmth and colour had been sucked out of it. A knot of fear tightened in her throat.

At home in Westmorland, she knew that if she was anywhere near trouble, the accusations would start. Folk would point and cross themselves, and whisper that Lucifer had left his mark on her. Sadie had kept herself to herself, taking in sewing and weaving, and never went out unless Ella was with her. When Ella was there she felt braver. Nobody ever dared to tease Ella, and she would brook no one taunting her sister either. Sadie hunched lower over the workbench.

She pulled a strand of hair until the knot tightened, and it brought to mind poor Mistress Ibbetson, the woman Ella said had been hanged through some fault of Ella's. She had heard rumours of these events when the milk boy came, and the man from the brewers for the empty jugs. But being closeted indoors had never heard the whole tale. And no wonder, she thought, as 'twas always Ella as brought the news. She had said Mistress Ibbetson wasn't a witch, but she had been hanged nonetheless. Sadie gripped tight onto the hook, pausing in mid-movement, a flutter in the pit of her stomach. What must that feel like, to know you had done nothing amiss, and to be sent to the gallows with not a soul to gainsay it?

She had been to one hanging, when she was five years old, just after their mother died, and she had clutched on to Ella's skirts, hiding her face the whole while, so she saw nothing. But she could hear, and that was enough. A man screamed his sins out loud for all to hear, with not an ounce of shame. The cries of the pedlars – the words that were not words but just sounds. Someone calling out in gulping sobs, 'My Georgie, my boy,' followed by her choked, 'Lord have mercy 'pon his soul.' She recalled the wind's ghostly voice, and the rain, the heckling crowd. The sudden hush as if the world had paused for breath. Then a creak like a gate swinging in the wind. She had pressed her palms over her ears but it did not drown the sound that erupted all around her. It was the snarl of a pack of wolves baying for blood.

The wig in front of her was a blur, her eyes were filled with water. She blinked it back, swallowed. Maybe she should have gone with her sister. But then Ella had urged her to stay. She looked over to where the stool was lying upended on the floor, and Ella's empty place. It seemed to mean something, like an omen.

At the end of the day there was nobody to walk home with. Sadie stepped out alone, although the streets were thronged with people. There were hundreds of youngsters like herself, all on their way home in raucous jostling groups. It was unnatural, she thought, there was not a wrinkled face in sight, and hardly any men her father's age in London. The days of shaking had seen to that. And what was it all for, all the bloodshed between the king's men and parliament? So many dead, so that in London the children roamed in packs. Madame Lefevre was the oldest person she had seen, not like in Netherbarrow, where the village was run by the elders.

When they had first arrived and were looking for work, they had to contend with crowds of urchins, all looking to make a little extra in good time for the Yuletide festivities. It had frightened her, she clung tight to Ella, terrified they might lose each other in the crush. And everyone was thin as if they'd not enough to eat, and quite a few with a harelip or withered foot, or other disfigurements. Sadie eyed these children with sympathy. Maybe she would not seem so unusual, there were so many odd-looking folk in London. Here people stared at Ella too, because of her smooth rosy cheeks and chubby arms.

Ella found out they were taking folk on at the wigmaker's,

and she had elbowed her way to the front of the herd with the aid of a bodkin from her pinafore.

'Show her your cap,' Ella said, pushing Sadie to the front of the crowd. She had taken it off and wordlessly pointed to the rows of almost invisible sewing, the neat smocked frill at the edge with its tiny cross-stitches.

'Are you quick?' Madame Lefevre had asked, eyeing Sadie's downcast face doubtfully.

'Like lightning,' Ella interrupted, her fingers crossed behind her back.

So they had been taken on. But every position could be filled four times over. Sadie dodged another group of dishevelled lads who scurried past with their heads down like rats. Now Ella would have no position, and her prospects of finding another employment must be thin. Sadie wondered if Ella had been out looking during the afternoon, and hoped for good news as she hurried back to Bread Street. Maybe she would have kindled a fire and have something hot waiting, for on the short journey from Friday Street the drizzle had already soaked through Sadie's clothes.

A mangy black cat, bony because of the wet, shot across her path trying to find shelter under the overhanging eaves. She knew she should spit to wipe out the bad luck, but she couldn't be bothered. With hunched shoulders she went to the darkest end of the alley, where there were three rickety doors set side by side. The rain was pouring off the roof in a steady stream. She had to stand under it to knock. She gave two sharp raps on the middle door and waited for Ella to open it.

No answer. She began to be worried. If Ella wasn't in, then where was she?

'Ella?' she shouted, banging hard on the door.

The door stayed shut.

She did not know what to do.

She had no key to the house, Ella had the only one. So she huddled under the eaves, as much out of the wet as she could, trembling with cold. She caught a whiff of something cooking in the house next door. It smelt like chicken broth. Her stomach churned from hunger. She had eaten nothing all day.

What if Ella was lost, or kidnapped, or drowned in the river? Sadie's thoughts began to run on, her imagination painting them into textures so real that she felt faint and had to sit down on the ground, made weak by what she had visioned in her head. What if Ella was inside the house, but had fallen down the ladder and hurt herself? Sadie jumped up and started hammering on the door and shouting for all she was worth.

'Shut your flamin' racket, for God's sake.' Mrs Tardy from the house across the way leaned out of the upstairs window. 'The babe's just got off to sleep and I won't have him woken.'

'Have you seen my sister?'

'Keep your voice down. No. I ain't seen no one.' The window smacked shut.

Sadie caved in and let herself sag back down onto the slimy step. Without Ella, London would swallow her up, like the whale did Jonah.

The great Bow bell had struck nine of the clock before Ella hurried into the yard. Like Sadie, she was drenched and shivering. Sadie was so angry she could hardly speak.

'Get that door open,' she said, half in tears.

Ella brought out the key and they ducked inside.

'We're having a fire, and that's that,' said Sadie. Ella sat down, bedraggled. She obviously had not been home since she left Madame Lefevre's shop.

'Where on earth have you been?'

'Shut it. Give us a minute, will you. Get that fire lit.'

Sadie began to break kindling and tear up rags to get a fire going. She did it in a fine fever, half wishing it was Ella's bones she was breaking.

She swore inwardly. The fire would smoke, for everything was damp and their chimney was just a hole cut into the roof. When it rained the damp seemed to stop the smoke rising. She sighed and piled on some wood from a broken old crate they had found down at the docks, and then a few hunks of coal.

Her sleeve steamed with the smell of wet flax as she tinkered to get the flame going. Ella looked on, but did nothing to help. Sadie fanned lamely at the smoke with her skirt.

'The least you could do is find us some supper,' she said, glaring at Ella.

'We've nothing in. Anyway I'm too tired with tramping after work.'

'Where'd you go?'

'I was that shamed. When he tried the wig on and it just sat on top. Feverface tried to force it down to his ears but he made such a face. She went into one of her thin-lipped rages.'

'What did he say?'

'He didn't get the chance. Madame Lefevre whipped it off his head and started laying into me, the scabby bitch. I don't know what he must have thought of me. Still, at least you got to stay put.'

'It's not the same without you.'

Ella ignored this and stood up and rummaged in the wall cupboard. She pulled down a paper bag and emptied the last few ounces of oats into a kettle to make a bland porridge. Sadie watched her stir it half-heartedly. The fire had taken now and was spitting and crackling. Ella looked comely, bending over in the firelight, her hair drying to curls, cheeks pink and flushed with heat.

Sadie wished she looked half so handsome. No matter how much she ate she was always thin as a stick, not rounded and curvy like Ella. And her hair hung straight as pondweed; she guessed she'd got that from Da.

'Did you get anything?' she asked.

'Nah. I tried the docks and the glassworks. Outside the glassworks I heard tell they were taking on at the bakehouse on Pudding Lane, so I belted over there. When I got there it were like a riot. No chance. So I've been downriver to the gunpowder works, that's why I were so late back – there wasn't another ferry till now.'

'No luck?'

'No. Come back next week, they said. But I'm not going back there anyroad. It stinks like hell. And there's explosions every week, a lad was telling me. Someone had his head blown off.'

'Oh, Ella.'

'No, I've decided. I'm on the lookout for a housemaid's place. Like I had before.'

Sadie felt a qualm of unease.

'Trouble is,' Ella said, 'I've no reference, so I'll have to blarney it. D'you want some of this?'

Ella ladled the thin grey porridge into two bowls and they ate silently, gazing into the fire as the embers died down.

'Will you give us a tale, Ell? Like you used to?'

'I can't think of anything.'

'What about one of the old ones? You know, one of Ma's – like you used to tell me in bed at home?'

'You don't want those old things. Don't tell me you still want Little Red Cap or Molly Whuppie now.'

'Oh, go on.' Sadie leaned forward. 'Oh, Grandmother, what big eyes you have. All the better to see you, maid.'

Ella smiled despite herself.

'Oh, Grandmother, what big ears you have,' Sadie said.

'All the better to hear you, maid,' they chorused together.

'Oh, Grandmother, what big teeth you have.'

'All the better to eat you up!' yelled Ella, jumping up and chasing Sadie round the room till she screamed. They fell back to their chairs laughing, the memories tugging at them like a hand on the sleeve. They sat quiet then, watching the embers in the fire.

'Do you remember her voice?'

'No, just her eyes. They were blue.'

'Grey.' Ella often snapped when Sadie mentioned their ma. Sadie knew better than to reply. Ella always contradicted her, as if she owned her memory and nobody else was allowed a part of it. Sadie had been only four when her mother died.

'What happened to her, Ella?'

'I told you. There was an accident on the sands with the coach. She drowned. She was trying to save me but the water carried her away.'

'But how? I've never understood it. How did she save you? Every time you tell me, it doesn't make sense. Tell me properly, Ell.'

'Leave it be.'

Sadie saw in her mind's eye a gentleman at the door. He had a row of very shiny buttons on his coat. She wanted those buttons. He was holding a bedraggled and silent Ella by the hand. And it seemed Ella was pulling her hand to get it away, but the man with the shiny buttons kept a tight grip on it. But it was so long ago and she was never sure if she recalled it straight or whether it was just imagination. But one thing she was sure of – her father's stricken face. It was like he was a lantern and the light just went out in it.

'Can you see pictures in the fire, Ell?'

'I've not looked,' she said. But after a while Ella said she saw gypsy musicians playing fiddle and drum and fine ladies stamping a dance in orange billowing skirts. Sadie looked into the heart of the coals, but could not find Ella's dancers. She only saw sunset on the ghylls, high peaks hung with cloud, and the lakes and rushing waterfalls of home.

That night Ella could not sleep, and finally gave up trying. She thought the days of nightmares and being unable to sleep were long gone. Sadie slept exhausted but restless, one arm flung out of the bed, the one blanket tangling round her thin frame. As Ella looked at her she had never felt so alone in her life. In the bustle of the day she could run away from herself, but at night there were no welcome distractions, just her and the dark. She lit a candle to push away the shadows flickering in the edges of her thoughts and stood it on the table. She gazed into the blue heart of the flame, shivered and turned to look behind. Even though she had thought she would feel safe in London, she could not help but always look back over her shoulder.

She had walked home from the gunpowder works and that was why she was so late home. She had made the journey there by boat, but it had made her queasy to be atop such a body of water, when you did not know how deep it was or what lay beneath. She could not bear to be near water after dark.

She hated the sound of it; it carried the memories, no matter how she quashed them. She had never told Sadie the truth – what was the use? No truth would bring Ma back; better for Sadie to believe Ma had done something to make her proud. Better to imagine a glorious heroic death. Sometimes the truth was just too much to bear.

The sound of the water lapped at her thoughts as she watched the flicker of the candle eddy round the walls. She was seven years old again. She absentmindedly balled her hem in her hand and crushed it, just the way she had as a little girl, standing on the shore all those years ago. She remembered covering her ears to the screams of the horses as the carriage overturned and they thrashed in their traces, spraying up salt water and wet sand. She remembered she was winded and it was a moment before she rolled over. The fine ladies sprawled on the ground, their skirts blowing and billowing, showing the tops of their stockings. One by one they sat up, rubbing at their backs, the gentlemen rushing to help. Ma's mistress was making a mighty fuss, groaning and a-carrying on. Ella cast about looking for Ma, but couldn't see her. A man came over to Ella and bounced her back onto her feet. She began to cry and it was then that she heard her mother's voice. 'Over here, help me.'

The men in their dark suits took a few steps forward but then retreated. They were talking in low voices. All Ella could make out were the words 'not safe'.

At first she thought her mother was kneeling down, but then saw she was buried in the sand up to her knees. The sand squirmed around her skirts like it was alive.

'Ma!' She ran towards her, thinking to join in the game, but cold wet hands grabbed her round the waist and pulled her back. At the same time, her mother shouted, 'No! Stay there, pet, stay with the gentleman.'

'Listen, the bore's a-coming!' A woman's panicky voice. Everything seemed to happen quickly after that.

Mistress shouted, 'Get the child, there's no time.'

Someone picked her up under his arms and began to run with her towards the shore. It made her teeth rattle in her head. She had a sideways tilted view of men uncoupling the horses and setting the ladies atop. They clung round the waists of the men, their bare legs showing as they were forced to ride astride. She began to howl. It was all noise and commotion.

The horses galloped up behind them, the three ladies from the carriage clinging onto the manes, skirts flapping against the bare backs. One of the gentlemen was riding up front.

'Get up,' Mistress said to the other man.

'What about the girl?' the man said, helping her up. The heavy bunch of keys the mistress always wore at her waist clinked.

'No room,' Mistress said, from the back of the horse where there were already two of them astride. 'Come on, we'll fetch hands from the village to deal with their own.'

'Wait there, maid. We'll go fetch help.' She remembered the sound of her own blubbering as he paused, looking at her in consternation as if he wished she would stop. Then he leapt onto the second horse so there were three riding together and they galloped away.

It was suddenly quiet. The sound of a gull screeched overhead.

Why didn't her mother come? But she could not. She stayed where she was, her skirts weighed with water. Her face was fixed on Ella. A little way off the carriage lay on its side, sticking out of the sand, one wheel askew.

There are those who say the bore that comes in from Morecambe Bay can outrun a man, that it moves quick. But Ella knew that to be a lie. That day it crept leisurely as you like, the fingers of the tide creeping slow up the bare leg of the estuary, filling the undulations until the crests of grey-yellow sand became just grey. Several times she called, but whenever she set foot on the sand her ma shouted, 'Get back, by Christ, or I'll get your da to leather you. Help's coming.'

So she waited, silent and shivering, the drizzle soaking her hair. When the flat expanse of water was up to her mother's waist she was like a small rock jutting out of the sea. By that time she had stopped calling, stopped saying anything at all. Ella waited until the rock was a tiny dot before she began to cry silently at her own helplessness.

Ella felt the hot tears on her face even now, all these years later. She stood as she had then, her hem tight in her fist. Ma's mistress did not come. Nobody came. She had waited there until it faded into dark and the wheel of the carriage disappeared and the sea and sky became one black void.

It was the constable who came in the end. 'It was too late,' he said. 'We couldn't have got to her. The water moves too quick.'

He had to drag her away for even at seven years old she knew that if she gave up waiting then her ma would really be lost. She fought with her fingernails and the metal tips of her clogs, but he was strong as wire and pulled her down the road till she had no scream left in her. He told her it would be a kindness to her father and to her sister to say Ma had died from hitting her head and been washed away. Ella had glared at him as he had told them, watched her father's face drain. She knew it to be another lie, but she had stayed dumb, that way it was bearable.

And now here was Sadie asking for the truth. She dropped her skirt and rubbed at her eyes, took up the candle and shut the shutters against the dark with a slam. In church they talked of the forgiveness of sins, God help her, but she could not forgive.

Chapter 8

The next morning when Sadie awoke, Ella looked pale and pinched. The rain was unrelenting – icy needles that pierced her cloak. Sadie scurried out of the door and hastened to work, dodging under the overhanging eaves to stay dry. Ella left at the same time for the streets around fashionable Whitehall, saying she would knock at back doors and see if she could be taken into service. Ella wore her best blue gown, but the hem was sodden even before she reached the end of the alley, and it was with no surprise that when Sadie returned from the perruquier's she was already sitting disconsolately at home.

'I must have knocked on a hundred doors,' Ella said. 'Some of them were so rude they shut the door in my face. Soon as I said I had no letter, I never got a look in. My feet are that sore.'

The rest of the week was no different. Ella's gown got more and more bedraggled, stained at the hem from walking the streets in the January wet. Her face took on a pinched and glum expression. One day she did not even bother making ready, just sat in her shift.

'Not going out?' Sadie asked.

'What's the point?'

'Come on. You won't get taken on tarrying here.'

'It's all right for you. You haven't walked all the streets of this bloody city till they're worn flat. You've got work in a nice dry shop.'

Sadie bit her tongue. She wanted to say 'But it's all your own doing', but she didn't. Ella was not beyond slapping her, even though Sadie was nearly as tall now.

'There's only one place left to try,' Ella said. 'The gunpowder works. They said they'd be taking on girls, I suppose I could go see if they've got anything.'

'Not there, Ella. You said it was dangerous.'

As if to spite her, Ella stood up and began to pull on her good dress. 'Well, I've tried everything else. How bad can it be?'

'Do you have to?'

'You got a better idea?'

Sadie watched Ella's back as she marched off towards the wharf to get the ferry upriver. The rain had eased at last and the dawning day was chill and grey. She wrapped the bulk of her woollen shawl over her head. At first she had been embarrassed about this rough grey garment, it marked her out as a country girl, but it was warm, unlike the fancy silks worn by the Londoners, and she was grateful for it. She rubbed her hands together and then folded them under her arms to keep the cold away.

Without thinking, she negotiated the maze of streets to the wig shop for the route was familiar to her now. When they first arrived in the city she had been horrified by the rotting piles of ordure in the road, the animal bones and vegetable peelings, but now she had become used to sidestepping it like a nimble goat. Some of the doors she passed were marked with the red cross, but there had been few reports of spotted fever in the last few months so her fear of it had somewhat abated. Nevertheless she still made a muttered 'God save us' as she hurried by.

Under the garishly painted sign showing a full-bottomed wig on a stand, she veered into the shop, then straight inside and down the stone stairs. She could have found her way blindfold, by the smell of it alone. Some of the younger girls were already there, sorting piles of horsehair from big sacks into colours and grades. The horsehair was used for cheaper wigs, or to bulk out the good hair when Madame Lefevre thought they could get away with it. The knotters were hunched over the work on their benches. Sadie took up her place next to Corey as usual and began work on the row of hair she had left unfinished yesterday.

The curtain rings rattled and they looked up to see Madame Lefevre arrive with another girl in tow behind her. She showed her to where Ella used to sit. Sadie and the others stared with frank curiosity.

The newcomer was a light-boned girl with a round pink face and thick gold-coloured hair in side bunches that jutted out from her cap, which was tied very tightly under her chin. She tripped in as though she already knew where she was going and settled down on Ella's stool as if she had been sitting there all her life. She sat very upright with her shoulders back and smoothed her hands over the folds of her dark skirts. Sadie did not like someone sitting in Ella's place.

'This is Mercy Fletcher,' Madame Lefevre said. She turned back to Mercy. 'Johnson will tell you where everything is and help if you should go awry.'

Corey smiled, and Mercy smiled back at Corey, a smile that did not show her teeth. Madame Lefevre nodded in satisfaction.

When Madame Lefevre had gone, Mercy turned to Corey, arched her eyebrows and said, 'I shouldn't think I'll need your help. I used to work for M'sieur Alphonse in Three Needle Street. It was a much bigger place than this, and we made all the new French styles.'

'If it was so fancy, why d'you leave then?' Betsy said, looking out of the side of her eyes at Corey, and getting in a dig.

'My brother had an argument with the proprietor.'

'Why was that then?' Pegeen asked.

'He couldn't get along with M'sieur Alphonse. Called him the king's fop. And the men used to sit round during fittings in their shirtsleeves exchanging lewd stories. Jacob didn't want my ears sullied with their filth, so he had a word with him about it. M'sieur Alphonse tried to make excuses, but Jacob won't take false talk from anyone, so he just put out God's fist at him. I've not been allowed to go back since.'

The girls stared and giggled, until Madame Lefevre put her head round the door.

'What's this "God's fist" she was talking about?' Sadie asked Corey later during the snap break.

'Jacob Fletcher's got a reputation on him,' Corey said. 'I'd no idea Mercy was his sister. He's a Puritan bully boy. He was the one roused a mob to torch the mercer's – on account of them being Catholics. The place went up whoosh! Like tinder, and the poor woman still abed inside. Terrible, it was.'

Sadie thought of Ella at the gunpowder factory. She hoped it wasn't true about the explosions. She didn't like the sound of Jacob Fletcher and she wished Ella was still working here at the wig shop, not Mercy.

After their dinner break, the girls knuckled down to their work under the watchful eye of Madame Lefevre, who was keeping a half-eye on Mercy Fletcher to see how she fared. Sadie could see Mercy's hands moving like quicksilver over the wig block. She was obviously an experienced knotter. Later in the afternoon, the bell sounded and Madame Lefevre clacked away to answer the door. A few moments later she appeared again round the curtain and pointed a finger in Sadie's direction.

'Mr Whitgift's asking after you.'

She stood up. All the girls paused in their knotting. From the way Madame said his name, it could have been the Good Lord himself.

'Says he wants to speak with the girl with the great red stain on her face.' Madame did not spare her embarrassment. 'Get a shift on, he's waiting.'

Sadie rubbed her hands on her apron and brushed the clinging hairs from her bodice as she went through into the shop. He was lounging against the wall, one ankle crossed over the other, his fancy hat in his hands. He held the door to the street open, with a long arm.

'Step outside with me a moment,' he said.

She ducked under his elbow, and smartly he shut the door in Madame's face. Sadie suppressed a smile, but was unsurprised when moments later Madame's dark shape appeared inside next to the window.

Sadie shivered; the air bit through her thin sleeves. He was trying not to stare, but he gave the sideways glances that people thought she did not notice.

He drew her away from the shop. 'Your sister does not seem cut out for the wig trade. Is it true she lost her position?'

'No, sir, I mean yes, sir,' she said, amazed that he should have come and asked for her. She clasped her hands and waited, her eyes cast down. It was safest to be quiet and keep her face blank.

'Tell her to call at my yard tomorrow after noon and I will arrange a new employment for her. Here is a bill with the address. If she points to my signature she'll gain admittance. Friargate.' He pressed a paper into Sadie's hand. She looked down at it but could not make out any of the words, it was fancy writing.

Sadie opened her mouth to tell him Ella had gone to the

gunpowder factory, but then thought better of it. Instead she gave a little curtsey.

'Make sure to tell her now. I'll expect her tomorrow.' He lifted his hat and crammed it back down on his head so that the three pheasant feathers bobbed and shivered. Then he gave a nod and turned on his heel.

Sadie hurried into the shop, the folded paper with its torn edge tight in her hand. As she went downstairs she was arrested by Madame Lefevre, who took her by the shoulder and spun her round.

'What was he after?'

'He was asking after my sister.'

'What did he want to know? Was it about me?' Madame Lefevre's eyes narrowed suspiciously and her fingers dug into Sadie's collarbone.

'No, madame, naught like that.'

'He gave her something,' piped up Mercy. 'I saw her stow it in the front of her apron.'

'Show me.'

She sighed, glared at Mercy and reluctantly brought out the paper.

'I'll take that,' said Madame Lefevre, snatching it out of her hand and holding it aloft. 'Gentlemen are forbidden on these premises unless they are buying, and you will not conduct personal business in my time. I won't stand for it, d'ye hear? You are not to leave your bench.'

'Yes, madame.'

She sat back down. During the rest of the afternoon she wondered about Mr Whitgift and the promise of work for Ella. He had said nothing about offering Sadie a position. She knew why, of course. It was because Ella was pretty and she was plain; she supposed it was too much to ask that he might find a place for both of them. She sighed. She couldn't cover the stain. When she was eleven years old Ella had tried to help by bringing home a powder to try to bleach it out. She'd got it from a travelling man who swore that when mixed with water it would make your skin soft and white.

'I'll tip it in and you stir,' Ella had said.

Together they peered into the basin whilst Sadie blended the powder into a thick lumpy paste.

'What is it?' Sadie asked.

'Don't know. He said just to mix it with water, leave it on. Said it would make anything white, that.'

'Here then, pass us the mirror.'

Ella held up their ma's old tin mirror for her to look, and Sadie scooped the mixture out of the bowl and daubed it all over until the livid red stain was completely covered.

It was a moment before she realized the paste stung and her face and hands were burning. She ran screaming to the pail, but too late.

The swollen eyes and blisters lasted weeks.

Just the memory prickled her skin like a nettle. And Pa had leathered them both. Even now her skin was likely to flare up if she put anything on it, so she was wary of soap, and would only wash with plain water, lest it bring the hives back. It was not Ella's fault, she'd only tried to help. But that's Ella all over, isn't it, Sadie thought. She never stops to think.

When her skin had finally healed, the mark was still there, redder than ever. So it was no wonder Mr Whitgift didn't want her serving in his shop. She would probably have to work in the wig shop for ever. She tried not to let the idea of Ella's good fortune bother her, picked up the wig hook and set to knotting again, but it gnawed at her insides, the sense of being looked over.

'Stop daydreaming!' Madame's tape shot out and caught

Sadie on the back of the wrist. Instinctively she withdrew her hand and put it to her mouth to suck it. The rest of the afternoon she sweated over her work in a high dudgeon.

She worried that she should have been quicker to put Whitgift's paper away. It was gone for good, and what would Ella do to her when she got home, if she knew she had let that old crow have it? Perhaps better to hold her tongue and say nothing about it. She did not like Whitgift, the way he lounged against the alley wall as if he owned every stone of it. Anyway, Ella might have got taken on at the gunpowder works, and what would a girl do with two positions? Maybe she need never know Whitgift had asked after her. She'd see how the land lay; could be that Ella was fixed with something by now.

'There was a great hollow chamber with, ooh, hundreds of us,' Ella said. 'They put me next to this lanky maid from Dulwich. You should have seen her – thinnest maid I've ever seen, like a taper. When she'd shown me how to do it, I picked it up right quick. The powder stank like rotten eggs. Can you smell it on me?'

Sadie inhaled, but shook her head. 'What did you have to do?'

'I were in what they call the corning yard, most dangerous place in the works. D'you know, we're not allowed aught metal in there, not even a button, case it should accidentally strike a spark and blast us to bits.'

Sadie stared disbelievingly. 'So you were taken on then? There's more work for you tomorrow?'

Ella shrugged. 'If I want it.'

Sadie thought guiltily of Mr Whitgift's paper.

Ella carried on. 'We'd to grind up brimstone, either coarse or fine, I had to mill it right fine. By, it was sweaty work, even in them barns. My arms ache from turning them millwheels. Look, you can see it under my nails, like black sugar. Mind, it were not as bad as the charcoal girls, black as sweeps they were. Honest, they were. I'm not going in that charcoal place, not for love nor money.'

'Why? What did they have to do?'

Ella leaned towards her. 'There was a girl there with only one arm. The other was just a stump. They say a spark from an iron wagon wheel fell on her grindstone, and bang!'

Mr Whitgift's paper niggled at Sadie's conscience. It was burning a hole in her bodice even though it was no longer there. She took a deep breath.

'Ella, when I was on my shift today, Mr Whitgift came by.'

Ella stiffened at the mention of his name. 'Oh, him,' she said dismissively, washing her hands in the pail. 'Was he collecting his new wig?'

'No. He came about you.'

Ella spun round, her hands dripping. 'What about me? What did he say?'

'He gave me an address, so he could offer you a position, but Madame Lefevre took it off me.'

Ella stared. 'You're jesting with me.'

'No, true as true.' Sadie told Ella the whole conversation.

'You let her get her hands on it?' Ella's face was a mixture of incredulity and rage. 'You fat-wit, why didn't you put it in your stays straight away?'

'I tried to, but Mercy Fletcher—'

'So how am I to know where his blasted shop is? And even if I did, they won't admit me without his letter.'

'You couldn't have read it anyway, you can't scarcely read. But his shop's on Friargate, he said so. So there. You can go there tomorrow. You'll need to get a new apron.' She carried on talking to Ella's back. 'It scares me, you working in that firepowder factory. Don't go back there, Ell.'

Ella turned round. 'Did he say what sort of position?'

'No. Serving maid in the pop shop or some such, I expect.'

Ella wrinkled her nose, then brightened. 'Maybe it'll be a housemaid's post, or even the housekeeper, after all, he's a single man on his own. Fancy that, me – a housekeeper.'

Sadie did not think this was at all likely, but she knew well how to keep the peace.

'Happen so,' she said.

Chapter 9

After several wrong turnings down dark ginnels, Ella eventually came to Broken Wharf and a sign showing a depressed-looking monk under a stone archway. This must be it – Friargate. She paused a moment and took a deep breath before going any further. She was nervous. What if Sadie had got it wrong and there was no position for her? But no, Sadie had always been sharp and good at remembering. She was like a little owl, always watching from a dark corner.

Ella had brazened it out, being laid off. Folk thought she was thick-skinned, but in truth she was not, just good at play-acting. It hurt her pride, made her feel good for nothing. But now Josiah Whitgift had asked for her. Asked for her personally. She lifted her shoulders and stepped out with renewed vigour.

She hoisted up her skirts to avoid them dragging in the icy wet, and hurried down the broad thoroughfare. When she spied the sign, she knew this must be Whitgift's, for the sign was an elaborate chair indicating a purveyor of furniture and wooden goods, but above the gates was a weathercock with three gold coins, the cipher of the pawnbroker. Of course pawnbroking was meant to be illegal unless you had a licence from the king, but nobody paid that much mind – London would grind to a halt completely if no loans were to be had.

The big iron gates stood open for the day's trade. Ella had to sidestep as a carriage turned in through the stone gateposts. What a place! It was a sprawl of old and new buildings, huddled together as if for warmth. The main part of it must have been a monastery once for it was built out of yellowish stone, now black with grime, inset with a series of arched windows with leaded glass. And it must have been a wealthy order, for there was proper stabling and storehouses, and a mounting block and churn stand alongside the gates. But leaning up against the main building was a jumble of sheds of wood and lath, like birds' nests on a cliff, so it was hard to see the whole extent of the place.

It was already full of bustle and activity, though it was not yet seven. A long queue of down-at-heel women snaked out of the gates, shuffling their way through the puddles. Ella hesitated and wondered whether to join the line, but decided instead that she had an invitation, so she had a right to be inside the yard. With a toss of her head she marched through the gates, the thrust of her chin daring anybody to stop her. Nobody did, but once through she looked around for some clue as to where she might find Mr Whitgift.

At the other end of the yard, the carriage was disgorging its fashionable occupants. She set off towards them, intending to ask for Mr Whitgift, but the liveried servants eyed her with disdain. Here, even the servants thought themselves above her. She baulked and turned back. Indecisive, she hovered in the middle of the yard.

'Hey, you.'

Ella turned, and saw that the voice had come from the direction of a stable door where a tousle-haired lad was brandishing a pair of fire irons.

'If you've anything to pawn you'll have to wait at the back of the queue,' he said, tying a ticket to the tongs.

'I've come to see Mr Whitgift. He's to offer me a position.'

A grunt indicated that he did not think it likely. 'Which Mr Whitgift? Elder or younger?'

'Don't know. Younger, I should think. Tall, wears a hat with pheasant feathers, a nice white smile. That one.'

The women near the front of the queue became restless, shuffling from foot to foot, impatient for the lad to continue their transactions.

'You got a letter?' the lad asked.

'No, he gave it my sister but she lost it. Look, if I could just see him, he'd know me—'

'We ain't got all day,' said one of the women waiting. 'You going to get the gaffer or not?'

The lad sighed, resigned. 'In through that door, cross the warehouse and pull on the bell. But don't dare say I sent you.'

Ella gave him a tiny nod, by way of thanks. She passed through the warehouse, wide-eyed, amazed at the sheer number of possessions displayed on the trestles. All of London must have their stuff in hock here. Along one wall was a row of stalls, once used for horses, but now each was full of different things – musical instruments, ironmongery, even a sedan chair. There was enough stuff in the warehouse to fill the houses of five Netherbarrows.

She rang the bell and the warehouse workers in their caps and brown fustian sleeves turned and stared. Pushing her shoulders back, she ignored them all. The door opened and there he was, taller and more rakish than she remembered.

'It's me, sir. From the wigmaker's.'

He moved away slightly, as if to get a better view of her. 'Ah yes,' he said, looking her slowly up and down, 'the little perruquier. Come with me.' He glanced behind him, as if to check nobody was looking, before leading her across the yard and in through a peeling door, where he pulled up two battered-looking chairs close together. He brushed his seat down with his fingertips before sitting. Ella took his signal and sat too, but she was disappointed. The room was like an old storehouse. It smelt of sour milk and there were cobwebs in the rafters.

'These are the chambers I have in mind for my new venture. A little fancy I have.'

Ella sat upright and looked up at him through her eyelashes. A new venture. She nodded, trying not to show how desperate she was to know what position he might offer her.

He looked around the room as if seeing some vision of his own, before clasping his hands in front of his chin and leaning forward. 'You are looking at the latest emporium for women to buy their beauty washes, skin potions and so forth. I have in mind to furnish it with comfort, like a bedchamber, so that ladies might rest awhile here, try out the decoctions, you know, whilst the gentlemen do their business with my father.'

Ella looked around the room. She did not understand. A bedchamber? She was wary. A large square box with a low-beamed ceiling with hooks for hanging meat, it had casement windows opening out onto the yard. A door ajar to one wall showed a set of narrow wooden treads leading to some upper rooms. Next to it in the wall was another door and a foot-square trap window to hold the churn scales when they were pushed through into the yard. She guessed it might have been the dairy once.

He continued. 'It does not look much now. But I have that well in hand. It will be furnished in the latest oriental style. Rugs from Turkey. Vases from the Ottoman empire and the east. Gilt chandeliers – forty candles on each, to give a radiant glow.'

Ella brightened and listened more intently. Turkey rugs, he

had said. She had caught a whiff of his enthusiasm and began to take more of an interest in her surroundings. The bare lime-washed walls stared back, but his words had begun to weave magic and in her mind the room had already begun a transformation. She did not know what the oriental style might be, but she could imagine herself as an exotic flower against a background of gilded leaves.

He was still talking. 'I need a girl with good skin. A pretty girl, one who will say to the ladies she uses only my salves and ointments.' She looked down, suddenly hot, nonplussed at this compliment. 'Someone forward, who can make a sale,' he continued.

Ella's dream dissolved. He was looking for a salesgirl. She mustered another nod to show her understanding, but she could not help feeling a pang of disappointment.

'The girl must look impeccable. Can you manage that, Miss . . . ?'

Ella thought quickly; she needed another name in case Titus Ibbetson was still looking for her. She said the first name that came into her head. 'Corey Johnson. Yes, sir.' Immediately she cursed herself. What a fool. She should have thought up a ladylike name, not the name of a common wig-knotter. She hoped Corey would never come here. Her face must have shown her awkwardness, for Mr Whitgift's eyes continued to range over her as if she were a horse being inspected.

'But I've never heard of aught like that,' she said, to hide her discomfort. 'Usually we take our baskets to the apothecary's to fetch the powders and then we mix up our own salves and tinctures at home.'

'Exactly. It's never been done before now. It's what you might call an experiment. But if it works, all the fine ladies of this city will flock to Whitgift's. It will be like a coffee shop but for ladies, so we must make sure the gentlemen will approve. You'll have to keep the ladies talking, and be persuasive.'

'I know I'm not used to London ways, society and that, and my manners might need a bit of minding, but I pick up quick.'

'Well, you'll need to grow a sweet tongue to tell the ladies how transformed they are and, above all, you must be discreet.'

Ella blushed. He was rubbing his hands together as if he was washing them. In one glance she took in his long pale fingers, the elegantly manicured hand, the lace cuffs, the gold signet ring. The hand of a wealthy man. Ella watched his fingers moving over each other and felt a burning sensation spread to her neck and chest. Her heart was beating wildly. She looked him straight in the eye.

He lowered his voice. 'Not every lady will want her husband to know that she has been here, that her beauty is the result of arti-fice. Men want to think a woman's charms are all natural. There are some that think these devices women use are evil, the work of Satan. So some ladies will require you to hold your tongue. But then, something tells me you are good at keeping secrets.'

'Yes,' she said, 'yes, I am.'

A flutter ran through her as their eyes met.

Jay Whitgift frowned and moved back in his seat. He steepled his hands. 'Then you can start the day after tomorrow. You will need something a little more suitable to wear, and your hair – it needs dressing.'

Ella swallowed. It was true, but she was still affronted; she put her hands up to her hair and tried to smooth out the parts that had been caught by the wind.

'I take it you know what is fashionable?' Mr Whitgift tilted his nose up and down, surveying her blue woollen dress. 'There are a number of good dresses in the clothing bay. Choose a gown with a tight bodice, and not too fussy. A damson shade might look well on you. Yes, a warm colour but nothing too powerful.'

He stood up and led the way back to the door. 'There is a closet there too where you can change every day when you arrive.'

'Yes, sir. Thank you, sir. And, sir, I'm right sorry about your peruke.' She wasn't, but it never did any harm to butter people. She lowered her eyelashes as if to apologize, hoping the effect would be pretty and demure.

'Never you mind, Miss Johnson,' he said drily, 'I am not looking for someone with manual ability. Just someone who can look winsome. This position will be more –' he hesitated – 'suited to your skills.'

He led her back out into what appeared to have once been the cloisters, but it was now divided into horses' stalls with wooden partitions up to where the vaulted ceiling began. There were no horses though, just rails hung with suits and hooks with lavender against the moths, and trestles piled high with every sort of garment.

'When you have chosen something, take it to Dennis, and he will sign it out for you.' He pointed to the stable door in the yard. 'And I expect you to be punctual. There is much to do. I have a whole army of people ready with the new wall-papering, and carpenters are already making up the cabinets. The rooms will be rendered tomorrow, and we will furnish them and put out the bills of trade the day after.'

'Yes, sir,' she said vigorously, to show her enthusiasm.

'Oh, and, Miss Johnson,' he continued, brushing a speck of dirt from his cuff, 'I expect you'll come across my old man sooner or later. He's a little behind the times and he doesn't approve. So if he's sharp with you, just smile and tell him to come to me.'

'That I will, sir. What a shame, that he don't approve.''

'He will though, soon enough, once he sees how it shapes up.'

'Pardon, sir, but what time?'

'Half after six. You can assist in laying out the chamber. I have persuaded one of my friends' mothers, Lady Horsefeather, to supervise how it is arranged. She moves in court circles – although it has to be said, very slowly.' He let out a spluttering laugh at this joke of his own. 'Afterwards, it will be up to you to maintain the standard she requires.'

'Very well, sir.'

Alone in the clothing bay, Ella hardly knew which way to turn first. She stared at the garments thrown together in great musty heaps, or hanging from bamboo poles strung from wall to wall. So many skirts to choose from, so many petticoats trimmed with gold point. She touched them reverently with her fingertips, half afraid to pick them up. She marvelled that people with gowns as costly as these could need to pawn them. But then, she guessed the wives had not much choice about it. Betsy from the wig shop had said that even the king used to pop a few things when he needed money for the war against the Dutch.

Some of the garments were stained and had probably never seen a buck tub, and one or two had a whiff about them that made her gag. But others looked new, as if straight from a French seamstress. There were a few sorters in the warehouse but no one paid her any mind, so she began to sift through the baskets and trunks of clothing, pulling out anything that looked likely. The air was damp and the cloth chilly, but Ella did not notice the cold or damp. She was in an agony of indecision over which gown to choose.

He had said to choose damson, but there was a scarlet silk suit trimmed with little bows that she kept returning to; there did not seem to be anything in damson that would fit. Red was almost damson anyway. To think, she might be wearing the gowns of duchesses or even the infamous Countess of Castlemaine, the king's mistress!

She reluctantly put the red skirt down and toyed with a stiff blue brocaded bodice. It was much more suitable for the cold season. But her fingers had a mind of their own, and when she lifted the scarlet silk skirt again, it swished gratifyingly over her bare ankles. The cloth was icy to the touch but then warmed quickly under her palms. She held the matching bodice up to her chest and it was light as a breeze, and though she could see it would be a close fit, the laces at the back allowed enough room. She had never had a bodice that laced at the back, because she had never had a servant to lace it for her. Perhaps Sadie might help her.

She felt a pang of guilt, picturing Sadie pulling the laces tight as if she were her lady's maid. But holding this volume of red silk in her arms and feeling its slippery weight was a sensation she did not want to forgo. This was the one. She would find a way to get it laced later. She picked out a green linsey riding cloak too, for otherwise how was she to keep the new gown dry? She thought of their tiny room in the rookery of Bread Street and tried to picture herself arriving there clad in red silk with the riding cloak swirling behind her. She could not imagine it. It was a leap too far. It was as if she had somehow stepped out of real life and into a fable. Reluctantly she decided she would have to leave the clothes at Whitgift's and come and go in her ordinary workaday garb.

She carried the cloak and gown to Dennis, the long-faced lad at the stable door. 'S'truth, you did have call to see him, after all,' he said. 'I thought you was fashing me.'

Ella looked at him haughtily. 'Mr Whitgift says I am to have these.'

Dennis took out a ledger. 'Just checking they've both a few more months to run.' He kept her hovering there whilst he painstakingly ran his long finger down the list, licking it to turn page after page, before he finally said, 'Ah, yes. Here we are. Fair enough, I'll put them to one side. Name?'

'Er, Miss Johnson. Corey Johnson.' Drat. She was stuck with that now. Dennis nodded. Ella watched him fold the garments and put them on a shelf behind. She could not help herself but give him a wide smile.

He smiled back. 'Address?'

She was momentarily nonplussed.

'Where do you live?' he said patiently.

'End of Bread Street. But we'll be moving soon, now I've got work. Somewhere better.'

'You looking for a room round here?'

'Why?'

'My ma sometimes lets out rooms. She's got one vacant now if you want to take a look. In Blackraven Alley.'

'Oh no, I don't think so. We're seeing a few tonight already,' she lied. Likely his lodgings would be some old fleapit.

'Suit yerself,' he said.

On the way home she spent a few precious pence on a bone comb and some hairpins so she could dress her hair. It felt good to go into the market and point at what she wanted and have it wrapped in a sliver of paper. She walked jauntily down the street in little steps, the way she imagined a lady might walk, repressing the urge to gallop to the wig shop to tell the girls of her good fortune. Of course she couldn't go back there. A wave of guilt hit her when she thought of Sadie, still hunched over her bench in the stink of the wig shop. Well, she could hardly have taken her with her, now, could she?

Ella tossed the little parcel in the air and caught it again, triumphant. Josiah Whitgift had singled her out. What a peach of a position – she would be paid handsomely to flatter fine ladies and show them how to look becoming. The only way to have security in life was to be a mistress, not a maid. And surely now her life had turned the corner, she was on her way. She could not wait to tell Sadie.

Chapter 10

Sadie saw straight away that it was good news. When Ella came in, her face was rosy and dimpled with smiles and she hugged Sadie hard, almost squeezing the breath out of her, something she had not done once since they came to London.

'What do you think?' Ella said. 'I'm to be in a parlour tempting ladies to buy belladonna and ceruse, and lavender oil, and morning dew.'

'A perfume seller?'

'No, not just any old perfume seller. I'm to be dressed up like a lady – Mr Whitgift himself picked out a fine gown for me, yards and yards of red silk, enough for . . . oh, six petticoats –' she danced Sadie round the table – 'and he said I'm as pretty as a poppy in a field. He wants me to dress my hair fancy, and—'

'Stop, I'm getting dizzy.' Sadie broke away from Ella's embrace. 'How much are you getting?'

'Nineteen shilling a month.'

Sadie gasped. It was far more than she got at the wig shop.

'I'm to start day after tomorrow. Won't get my first pay till the end of the month though.'

'Oh, Ell, what luck! We'll have to scrape till payday though, we've barely enough to feed ourselves. But there's still my portion from the wig shop coming in, that'll cover the rent.'

'We'll take on a better place as soon as I've got my feet under the table. I'll make myself necessary. There's an old Mr Whitgift too, the father. They don't get on. He's a crabbit old skinflint by all accounts. But I'm after twisting the old gent around my finger. I'm good with old men.'

Sadie felt a qualm of misgiving. 'You've hardly set foot in the place yet, don't start getting grand ideas. And don't go against Josiah Whitgift or you could end up back in the gunpowder works.'

'Oh, clap a stopper in it. I know what I'm doing. You always put a dampener on everything. Can't you just be pleased for me?'

'Course I'm pleased, I just worry in case it doesn't work out. We still have to buy barley for bread, and we're all but out of tallow for rushlights. I don't want you taking risks before you see a penny for your work. And I don't trust that Josiah Whitgift. Corey and Betsy told me there's shady things go on round his shop.'

'Lord love us, I've only just got the bloody position and you've got me out on my ear already. At least I'm bringing in a decent wage, not like your petty mouse droppings from the wig shop.'

'Don't. It was always good enough for you before. Anyways, I'm serious. Betsy says Whitgift's has gone downhill. There's rumours it's turned into a meeting house for all sorts – felons and highway thieves.'

'It's just a regular second-hand shop, with a pop shop on the side. But bigger, and grander. Lawks, Sadie, you should see it – great piles of pewter, cabinets full of gold plate.'

'Well, in that case, if we run short it will be a good place to pawn that gold and ruby seal.'

'We won't need to, now I'm working.'

Sadie changed the subject. 'What's he like, then, this Josiah Whitgift?'

'He's, well, he's . . .' Ella coloured. Sadie saw the flush rise into her cheeks, her eyes squirm away. 'He's just a man, what did you expect?' snapped Ella.

Sadie sighed. 'Have a care, Ell. I expect he only took you on because you're pretty. And good looks can be a blessing, but they can also be a curse.'

'And I suppose you'd know?'

The barb had been aimed precisely, and hit its target. Sadie felt the cut of it and cast her eyes downwards, but she held her tongue. Ella was obviously not in any mood to be reasoned with.

Sadie walked away and took up a cloth bag of sewing things from the trunk. With her back to Ella she sat down and began to darn her old shawl. She liked the texture of the wool, the oil of the sheep's fleece under her fingers. She wove the wool over and under, thinking of the green fells of Westmorland dotted with sheep. When this cold snap was over it would be lambing time, and the wethers would be growing fat.

A sharp knock at the door. Sadie gently put down her darning and backed away from the door towards the wall.

'You expecting anyone?' Ella said in a low voice.

Sadie shook her head emphatically.

'Who's there?' called Ella, her ear close to the door.

'Missus Tardy from over the way. Thought I'd best let you know, a gent was a-hanging round your front door today. He asked after you. Asked after a bonny girl, and a lass with a patch on her face.'

'Who?' Ella shouted.

'Open up and I'll tell you.'

Ella slid back the bolts and opened the door a crack. Mrs Tardy wedged her way in. She was a broad-beamed woman with a bare-bottomed toddler slung on her hip. Ella looked out through the door, then bolted her in.

'Tried to prise the door open. At least, he was till I came along, then he looked right guilty,' said Mrs Tardy, staring shamelessly round the room.

'What did he look like?' Sadie came out from the darkness.

Mrs Tardy walked round the room, taking everything in. Sadie saw her pause and look with interest at the trunk by the window, before turning back to answer. 'Bit of a paunch. Solid-looking.'

'What else?'

'I don't know – I only spoke with him a moment and our Jack was crying. 'Bout forty I should think, dark eyebrows. Shiny riding boots. Kept asking after you, asked if you'd been here long, who the landlord was, whether you paid cash.'

The two girls looked at each other.

'When was this?' Ella asked.

''Bout an hour ago, I'd say.'

Ella thanked her and pointedly shut the lid of the trunk. There were some silver-backed hairbrushes, the mother-of-pearl fan and a polished mahogany card box visible. Ella thanked her again and took hold of Mrs Tardy's elbow to steer her back to the front door. Mrs Tardy sniffed, she was clearly reluctant to leave, but Ella hustled her out, slamming the bolt after her.

Sadie fixed her eyes on the bolted door. It might be Da, she thought. He's missed me after all. Maybe it's my da come to fetch me home. And she was in one breath both overjoyed at the thought of going home to the wide open air of Westmorland, and terrified of her father's belt. She licked her lips, her mouth was dry. She slid her palm over the small of her back where the bruises used to be.

'D'you think it's Da?' she asked.

Ella took hold of her and shook her, reading her face. 'Listen here. It's not Da. More likely the law.'

'It could be. He could have come looking for us.'

'Don't hoodwink yourself. He never gave a cat's whisker for either of us, unless we could get him the price of a draught.'

Sadie put her knuckles to her mouth, blinked back tears.

'Don't greet. You know it's true. He'd shop us if he thought he could get summat out of it. Don't be fooling yerself he's any love left in him. If he ever came near us it would be that he's after.' Ella pointed at the trunk. 'He could buy a few jugs with that.'

Sadie looked over at the trunk. The pigskin was worn, but it was still a substantial thing. In the old year it had been full to bursting, but they had spent so much, sold everything for the next three months' rent, and there was not so much left inside it now, just a few bits and bobs Ella said she was keeping back for a rainy day. The expression had made Sadie laugh, seeing as in London it seemed to never stop raining. Now Ella hurried over to the trunk and threw back the lid.

'Get your things together. We're moving on.'

'What?'

'I've decided. We're leaving.'

'Just like that? You can't—'

'We've got to leave. Missus Tardy's got a mouth on her like an ox. She won't stop bellowing when she's had a few.'

'But we've paid rent up front.'

Ella shrugged. 'Can't be helped. 'Tain't safe to stay.'

'But I don't want to leave, Ella. I only just got used to it. And where will we go?'

'We'll find something. But if we stay here and Missus Tardy blabs on about our trunk, the game will be up. We'll have half of Westmorland after us for all we've thieved. It'll be the clappers for us, no question.'

'I'm not going. I hate London. But I feel safe in here. I can shut the door on it all.' Sadie's voice began to waver. 'This is my home now, and I'm not shifting.'

'D'you want us to end up behind bars?' Ella slapped her hard across the arm. 'Or would you rather hear your neck snap? 'Cos that's worse lodgings than any I could take you to. Gather your things. I'll go without you, else, and take the trunk with me, and then you'd have naught, except what coppers you can squeeze out of Feverface.'

Sadie chafed her arm to rub away the red marks of Ella's fingers, watching silently as Ella began to scrape together their possessions: the cooking pots, the wooden bowls, the tallow candles, the small sack of oatmeal. Ella dumped what she could into a bucket. Her face was sour as she bundled together the scraps of bedding from upstairs and thrust them into Sadie's arms.

'Hurry up,' she said.

Sadie pushed the things down into the top of the trunk, hardly able to see through her tears. Suddenly, the measly little room appeared to be familiar and comfortable, the crumbling walls homely and welcoming.

Both girls packed without looking at each other, because they knew that to do so would crack them both open. As Sadie shut the lid of the trunk, there was a hammering at the door. They startled, like rabbits.

Ella said, 'God alive, they're here already. Quick – out the back window.'

Sadie grabbed the bucket.

'No, leave that. The trunk.' Between them they lugged the trunk over towards the opening.

'Open this door!'

Sadie froze.

Ella paused mid-movement. 'God help us, it's the law.'

Sadie's knees turned to water.

'Push!' Ella said urgently, seeing Sadie weakening. They heaved the trunk up to the window. The thumping on the door grew louder.

The window opening was too narrow for the trunk – no matter which way they turned it, it would not fit through. They wrested it this way and that, in mounting panic.

'Open up. I just want to parley a while.' The voice had become more pleasant, the hammering less insistent.

'There's something familiar about that voice,' Ella whispered, 'but I can't place it. Quick, try pushing it this way.'

'Maybe we should just open the door, see who's—'

'Enough! If you do not open up, I will break the lock.'

Fear made Sadie lurch into action, clambering onto the trunk and hoisting herself through the narrow opening. 'We'll have to leave it,' she shouted, 'just pass the best things through.' She took the skin off her elbows as she went and landed heavily in the mud on the other side.

Ella hesitated. Sadie hopped from foot to foot. 'Please, Ella. It's the only way. It's too big. We'll never get it through.'

A fistful of spoons flew through the open window. Sadie tried to catch the objects before they hit the ground, but they shot out too fast for her to keep up with and she had to rake them up out of the dirt. She scraped them into a bundle with a blanket and twisted the smaller things into the folds of her apron.

A thud. The noise of heavy grunts interspersed with battering and splintering wood.

'Quick! He's breaking the door down.'

'Hang on whilst I get the good blanket.'

'No, you've no time,' sobbed Sadie, 'and we can't carry them all. Here – take my hand,' and she reached for Ella's wrist to pull her through the window opening.

But she had to pull her hand away as Ella tumbled out onto the ground in a pother of skirts and bedding, just as they heard the crash of the door giving way. They scrabbled like dogs in the mud, bagging together as much as they could carry in their shawls and aprons. Ella swooped down, anxious not to leave the broken string of pearls, the punch ladle and the few silver spoons glinting in the darkness.

'Stop!' A head appeared out of the window and Sadie caught a glimpse of angry bloodshot eyes and a tidemark of stubble, before she legged it as fast as she could manage down the filthy back alley, past the brewery and towards Thames Street and the river.

It was a moment before she realized her sister was not with her. She stumbled to a stop then doubled back to see the silhouette of Ella standing stock-still in the middle of the alley, staring at the window.

'Ella,' she shouted.

She saw Ella tiptoe towards the dark square of the window, and look in. A moment later she tottered backwards, her free hand over her chest. Why was Ella not coming? Something was the matter, she had to go back.

'What is it?' Sadie said, arriving breathless at Ella's side.

'It's Thomas,' Ella whispered. Her face was pinched, her eyes unfocused. Her hands fluttered at her throat. 'Sadie, he's not dead after all, he's come to find me.' She let out a huge sob and pulled away to go back to the house.

Sadie held tight on to her arm, restraining her. 'What are you talking about? Who is it?'

'It's not the law, it's my Thomas. Leave go!' She jerked her arm away.

A black shape hurtled round the corner and stopped right in front of them. He was a thick-set man in a heavy dark coat and narrow-brimmed hat. He paused, panting slightly, and his breath hung on the air as he looked from one to the other.

Ella dropped her blanket and the contents spilled back into the mud. She took a faltering step towards him, her hands outstretched. Sadie made a grab for her arm, but she was too late, she jerked away.

'Thomas?' Ella said, looking up at him, but then her hands stilled. They stared at each other for a beat, before Ella's hands went up to her mouth and she backed off, slowly at first, her eyes glued to his face.

'Which of you is Ella Appleby?'

'Run!' Ella snatched at Sadie's arm.

The man lurched forwards, swiping out towards them. For an instant Sadie felt his fingers catch on her sleeve, but she twisted away and sprinted after Ella for all she was worth.

'It's not him,' panted Ella, 'it's not Thomas.'

She looked back over her shoulder and saw him run out of the end of the alley and his change of gait as he spotted them. 'Hey,' he yelled, 'stop them.' But there was nobody nearby to hear.

They sprinted down the ginnel. Sadie clutched one hand to her apron, the blanket bundle banged against her back. The man laboured after them, his riding boots thudding loud in their ears as they fled.

With a supreme effort they reached the end of the street and threw themselves around the corner into the hubbub of Paul's Wharf. There were lanterns there hung by the taverns and crowds of tradesmen loading crates and chattels onto barges, and women carrying their wares on their heads. They elbowed their way between them to lose themselves in the crowd. But when Sadie looked back she could see his dark hat bobbing amongst the women's baskets and trays.

'In here,' she gasped. They dodged into the open doorway

of a ropery. Breathless, they squeezed behind a stack of colossal wooden bobbins.

Sadie's heart was beating wildly in her chest like the baby bird she had once rescued from a cat. She heard Ella's breath, shallow and fast. She was horrified to see her sister trembling. They cowered, pressed back against the wall, not daring to move, for the torchlights cast huge flickering shadows on the walls. In the ropery they could hear the clunk of the winding machines and the chatter of the women at work, and, once, a man's voice. They shrank back then, thinking it might be him.

They must have waited there almost one hour of the clock before daring to emerge onto the street. Sadie was on tenterhooks, looking around her, thinking to see the man's face loom up everywhere she looked.

'What does he want, Ell?'

'He wants his brother's chattels back, I should think, and to see me in gaol. Or worse. They say it's treason, stealing from your master.'

'What does that mean?'

'The penalty's death by burning.'

Sadie stopped dead.

Ella carried on talking even though Sadie had stopped responding. 'I thought it was my Thomas, but when he got closer I could see it wasn't. It must be his brother, Titus. He said they were twins, but I've never seen twins before. I never ever thought they'd look that close . . .'

Sadie was panicked now. 'Let's try to find somewhere to lodge, Ella, get inside. I'm scared out here. I keep thinking he'll see us.'

Ella was not listening. 'He's the very spit of Thomas. Just sharper round the eyes, and his face is thinner . . .'

Sadie put her hand on her arm. 'We'll go eastwards, to where

Corey lives – she says it's cheaper rents there, and there's plenty lodgings near the bridge with rooms to let. Come on, hurry, it's near six o'clock, and we'll need a bed afore long.'

'I can't get over it. They're like peas in a pod. He's not as broad as my Thomas. Thomas loves his food . . .' Ella's voice trailed away. Sadie heard her sniff, but she walked on quickly, pulling on Ella's arm, her eyes darting here and there in case the man in the boots should suddenly appear. They walked heads down, shawls pulled over their caps. Sadie cradled her full apron with one hand, the other held tight to the bundle. They saw neither hide nor hair of Titus Ibbetson, but his presence seemed to dog their steps. Ella was empty-handed, morose and silent.

Sadie stopped and rested the bundle on the ground a moment. Her arms ached.

'I suppose we could try Blackraven Alley,' Ella said eventually. 'Someone at Whitgift's said there was a room to rent there.'

Sadie nudged her to ask directions from a man with a milk cart and they were pointed down a cramped thoroughfare alongside the river. They looked for a sign with a bed and candle and knocked at the door. A tousle-headed lad with a long nose opened it, and by the light of his lantern she could see he had his shirt-sleeves rolled up and no boots on. A bare pink toe poked from a hole in his hose. He seemed to know Ella right enough for he said, 'Oh, it's you. You didn't find anything then?'

'Not yet. Thought we'd take a look at your room, as we were passing.'

'Is it for the both of you?'

'Oh, yes, me and my sister.'

'Pleased-to-meet-yer.' He ran all the words together into one long word. 'Come on up, I'll show you the room.' He led the way up the steep staircase and Sadie followed.

'What's your name?' he asked, turning to look at her.

'Sadie,' she said, hanging back to keep out of the light.

'Dennis,' he said.

He waved his candle lantern round a first-floor room with a tiny cracked stone fireplace, a leaking chimney hole and a creaking platform for a bed. The window jutted out over the river, and the stink of rotting garbage seeped through the sacking nailed over it to keep out the draught.

'It's not much, I know,' he said, 'but it's cheap.'

'How much?' Sadie asked. She clutched her bulging apron to her stomach, tried to toss her hair forward over her cheek.

'I can't live here,' Ella said, and then to Dennis, 'It's not suitable. We're after something bigger.'

Sadie's shoulders slumped. She would have been happy to settle anywhere as long as it was out of sight and had a bolt on the door. Ella walked out of the room and clattered down the stairs. Reluctantly Sadie trailed after her back onto the street, where a gang of rowdy boys emerged from an alley, kicking a dog for sport. It was yelping and had an old clog tied onto its tail. Sadie averted her eyes and they tried to walk by.

'Ooh, ladies. What yer got?'

Ella ignored them and made as if to sidle past.

'Not so fast, sweetheart, let's see what's in your swag.' The biggest boy jumped out in front of Sadie. He had a broken nose and wore a tattered man's coat with the cuffs rolled back, his hair grey with dirt. She guessed him to be about thirteen years old. They stepped past him, but immediately they were surrounded by about seven younger boys who appeared from the shadows. Individually, they would not have been any trouble, but as a mass they were intimidating. Sadie began to feel uneasy, her sixth sense telling her they should get away fast. The dog barked and skittered away down the road.

She looked around for a means of escape, but they were hemmed in. Even above, the buildings jutted out, blocking out the moonlight. The doors to the right had red crosses on them, peeling now, but obviously someone there had once had the pox. She shuddered. On the other side was a high wall, the side of the steelworks. No escape there either. The biggest boy had a stick in his hand; he held it out menacingly.

Ella untied her apron and thrust it onto the ground. 'Here,' she shouted, 'there's bread and cheese here.' The pack of boys fell onto the apron, fighting to get into the contents. Ella grasped Sadie's skirt and hauled her back through the door into the hallway they had just left. As she slammed the door behind them she could hear them shouting, 'It's empty! There's nothing in it!' A clatter, as a rain of stones hit the door.

'Back so soon?' Dennis reappeared, a look of amusement on his face. He nodded at the door. 'Ma won't be pleased that your friends have been making holes in her door.'

'They're not our friends, they set upon us on the street. We'd like to take the room,' Sadie said, aware that Dennis was staring openly at her.

'On a temporary let,' Ella added firmly, 'till we find something bigger. One week.'

'Not sure I should let it to people with friends like yours. And I can't let it for less than a month. Ma won't like it.'

Ella looked disgruntled. She opened her mouth, about to protest.

'One month, then,' Sadie said quickly, and she began to mount the stairs.

'Wait on! Are you thinking to move in now?'

'Our landlord died,' Ella said. 'They've put us out.'

'What about your things?'

'We'll fetch them over later,' Ella said, picking up the bundle from where Sadie had put it down. Dennis narrowed his eyes and looked to Sadie. She just dropped her head.

'I'll not ask,' he said.

'We'll take it tonight, if you don't mind,' Sadie said.

'Fair enough. I'll tell Ma and I'll call back tomorrow for the rental,' Dennis said. 'Six shilling. Get yourselves a good lock.'

'Ibbetson – he's still after us then,' said Sadie, when the door was shut.

Ella just nodded. There didn't seem to be anything else to say. She wandered round the room, fingering the old plank table and two odd-sized stools, and running her finger over the shelf in the larder alcove. There was a washstand with the wood all stained and ringed with watermarks, and a chipped jug half floating in a pail of water.

Ella pulled out a stool. 'Bring your bundle over, let's see what we've got.'

They put down their diminished possessions on the table. It made a sad sight. In Sadie's salvaged bundle of clothes and bedding, there was one cooking pot, a wooden platter, a silver punch ladle, a hand glass and a ticking pillow. In the apron, the mother-of-pearl fan, some fine lawn and lace napkins that had fallen in the mud, three spoons and two odd candlesticks that did not match.

'Is that all?' Ella asked.

Sadie nodded. 'I dropped the card box and the jug. Sorry.'

'You got anything else under your bodice?'

'Course.'

'Let's see then.'

Sadie held up her purse and tipped out the contents. A few coins rolled onto the pitted wooden surface. From Ella's, a broken pearl necklace and some lady's rings fell out amongst the coinage, followed by the seal on its slinking chain. Instantly,

Sadie was back in that cold, dark house, looking into the unseeing eyes of the man on the bed.

'Let's get rid of that,' she said, pointing.

'It's got his initials on it, look. I've a mind to keep it. It's pretty.'

'Can't we get rid of it, Ell? I hate it.'

Ella picked up the rings. 'We'll sell these first. We'll need bowls and a cookpot; we'll have to get down the fleamarket. Ye gods, I don't know how we'll manage till payday.'

'Dennis seems friendly.'

'Huh.' Ella's tone was scathing. 'It's a fleapit, just like I thought.'

'It's cheap though, we could do worse. And it's near to Whitgift's too.'

'I suppose.'

The rest of the evening Ella hardly spoke, but spent the time rolling and unrolling her hair, pinning it into elaborate arrangements and holding the hand mirror out at arm's length. 'I need some of them new bone curlers. Them ones you heat in the embers,' she said.

Sadie made up the bed and put out their meagre possessions. She felt safer being upstairs with people beneath. When she had finished she realized she was dog-tired and climbed into bed before Ella, leaving her still tying her hair in rags to coax it into side curls. She slept fitfully. Ella was late to bed and when she did come kept dragging the blanket her way. Besides, Sadie could hear sounds of a woman coughing below.

To her surprise Ella was up early for once instead of dozing and having to be prodded out of bed. When she brought the jug for washing, Ella was struggling again with her hair to secure it in a knot at the back, her mouth full of bone pins. Sadie scrubbed her face and rinsed her mouth. The water was that cold her teeth ached. She watched Ella from the corner of her eye, seeing the frustration etched on her sister's face as another loop of hair escaped from the heavy mass at the back.

Eventually Ella threw the comb down onto the bed. Sadie didn't want to be late for work, so she ignored Ella's huffing and puffing. But when she got home again that night she was surprised to see Ella was still there where she had left her. As soon as she came in through the door Ella wailed, 'It won't go right. And he said I'd to have my hair dressed. Properly. Not like our usual topknots and caps. I daren't go with it all hanging out like this.'

'Come here, let me see if I can fix it.'

Ella held out the pins on the flat of her hand. Sadie pulled her hair tight and twisted it, then pinned it hard to her scalp.

'Ouch! You're hurting.'

'It's your hair. It's too thick. I have to pin it tight or it will be out again in two shakes.'

She skewered some more wisps into the arrangement, leaving a few coils hanging at the sides.

'There. You'll pass muster,' Sadie said.

Ella picked up the glass and scrutinized her reflection. 'It's crooked.'

'No it's not, you can't see it properly in that glass. Don't worry, I'll tidy it again tomorrow, give it a last lick and polish before you go.'

'Wish I had a scrap of red riband to put in it.'

Sadie admired her handiwork from the back. It was fetching, even if she did say so herself.

The next morning when Ella was ready, Sadie stood with her by the door.

'You look lovely, Ella. It suits you. You look important, like you really are someone, not just our Ella from Netherbarrow.'

Ella frowned and grasped hold of her wrist. 'Look, I've never heard of Netherbarrow. No one must know where we're from. We're Londoners now, get it?'

Sadie nodded.

Ella released her arm. 'And I'm already someone. I'm Miss Corey Johnson, and I'm to serve in Whitgift's.'

'What?' Sadie stared, uncomprehending. 'What do you mean?'

'I'm calling myself Miss Johnson.'

'You changed your name to Corey's?'

'It's safer that way. They asked me at Whitgift's and I had to say something.'

'But that's daft. To call yourself by someone else's name. What if Corey finds out?'

'How will she? Unless you tell her? I'm not going back to that poxy wig shop.'

'It's still stupid. I can't call you that. Why did you call yourself that? Why not Peggy, or Susan or—'

'It was all I could think of in a hurry. And 'tis done now, so I'm stuck with it.' Ella pulled her cloak tight about her as if to shut Sadie out.

'Well, I'm not calling you that,' Sadie said.

'You can call me anything you like in here, but to everyone else I'm Miss Johnson – see?'

Sadie fiddled with the few remaining pins in her fingers. It felt strange, her sister having a different name. It bothered her.

'And I like it. It feels like a new beginning,' Ella went on. 'I'll make a success of Whitgift's, I just know it. We'll dine off oysters and cream pie yet. How will you like that, eh? I promised you silken sheets one day, and you're going to get them. And you know I always keep my promises.' She clattered downstairs.

Sadie was sceptical. But Ella had a way of convincing you, she thought. The stories she told you. From Ella's descriptions the silken sheets were almost tangible, their softness and scent. In some ways these imaginary sheets, steeped in lavender, light as clouds, seemed more real than the rough wool blankets they wound round themselves at night. For the sheets in their imaginations never wore out, always billowed fresh and new.

Chapter 11

In his room under the rafters, Jay went to his cabinet and unlocked the top drawer. Each drawer contained one of his collections. The bottom one housed a fine array of gold pocket watches; another drawer held a row of necklaces set with drop-pearls and diamonds, the next lady's daggers with ornamental handles. Others held bejewelled cloak pins, sets of gold buttons, cameos. This evening he took out his collection of snuffboxes and started to polish them to a gleam with a lint cloth. He bent to the task, his shoulders hunched, an action he had done so often it had left him with a slight stoop even when he stood up. This room held his baronetcy. These days a baronetcy could be bought – for a little over a thousand pounds. Every snuffbox was a bootstrap nearer to a title. He knew every single one, how much it was worth down to the last token, and he loved to feel the solidity of it, his wealth growing plump under his fingers.

He held one of the snuffboxes up to the pale light of the window. The box was engraved with cherubs and garlands, the metal moulded to make them stand proud of the polished surface. An exquisite piece of workmanship made by a craftsman long dead and buried, he had seen nothing so well wrought since. He brought it close to his face and smoothed his fingers over the surface. If only every beauty could be tamed, fixed in place like this – so that he could keep it locked in his cabinet until he had need of it.

At the strike of his timepiece he stood and walked over to the window. It was just growing dark, but he did not light the candles. Instead, he took out his brass telescope, swung the window ajar and pushed the instrument out. The familiar landmarks were brought close in mesmerizing detail. The spire of St Mary-by-the-Field, the barges on the bend of the Thames, the carriages of fashionable merchants. Through his spyglass, all of London was brought into his domain. He scanned up and down, looking for something.

Just coming around the corner into Friargate, completely unaware that they could be seen, were two familiar figures – Stevyn Lutch and Foxy Foxall, pushing a trundle cart. Or rather Lutch was pushing, and even from here Jay could see that Foxy was talking. He bent towards Lutch's ear as he walked, and gesticulated, waving his wiry arms in front of Lutch's face. Lutch replied with an occasional nod, and kept pushing. The cart jolted on the cobbles and almost toppled its load. The load was dressed to look like a pile of old blankets, but Jay hoped that what lay underneath might be a great deal prettier, given that he himself had given them precise instructions as to what to filch.

He closed the spyglass, folding it into itself and slipping it into its leather pouch. Now he lit the candles, preparing to let the men in. He hoped they had earned their wages this time. Recently they had seemed surly and reluctant, and the pickings had been miserable. Jay suspected they might be in the pay of someone else as well as himself. Well, it was to be hoped whoever it was knew what he was about. Lutch and Foxall were well-known hard cases. They only had to blow on a postern or a back door and it would open. They would crack your skull if you crossed them, and the blow would be silent and come from nowhere with no time to scream. When men like Allsop could not repay their loans, then Jay sent Lutch. When a gentleman asked him to supply a whore, then Foxy knew where to find one.

But Jay knew he needed to be on his mettle to deal with them, to be one step ahead. Foxy was a blabbermouth, and Jay was wary of Lutch, the dispatcher, whose face betrayed no emotion except mildness, but whose hands were muscular and pitted with knife scars. And his pa was right – belt and braces, always have more than one iron in the fire. And whatever you might do, never turn your back on them.

Outside, the dogs snarled and barked on the ends of their leashes and he heard the nightwatchman swear at them and open the gate. Jay went downstairs and swung the door open, just as Foxy had lifted his fist to knock.

'What did I say?' Jay said. 'No knocking. I don't want Pa woken.'

'Sorry. I think he's awake, though, I saw—'

'Never mind what you saw, just remember, that's all. Lutch, fetch it up to my chambers.'

Lutch carried the bundle up the winding stairs.

'Anything rare?' Jay said, hovering at Lutch's shoulder.

'Bits and bobs,' Foxy said. 'That big house – the one on Whitehall – that one was a proper sugarplum. Like you said, there was not a soul home, not even a kitchen wench. So we was straight in, easy,' Foxy said, 'and there was everything laid out for us. We only had to bag it and go.'

Lutch pushed the snuffboxes aside to make room and lifted the first bundle onto the table. He untied the flannel blanket and drew his blotched hands across the contents to spread them out, then stood back so Jay could take a look.

It was the usual assortment of small wares: gold and silver cutlery, watches, candle snuffers, card cases, sugar sifters. Jay leaned forward and, with a practised eye, picked out a garnet and diamond pendant winking from underneath a quill tray.

'This is the one I was after. Any more like this?'

'No. No more, the lady must have taken her twinkles with her to Richmond. Daft if you ask me, can't see why she'd need them in the country . . . but the pendant was hid at the back of a drawer, under these.' Foxy drew out a string of silk stockings from his pockets.

Jay frowned. 'I told you before not to take clothing. It's hard to shift, especially undergarments. They're no blinding use to me, they don't fetch enough. Not worth keeping, and my pa can't sell those back to the lady's husband, now can he? I've told you – don't waste your time with rags and scratchings.'

'They're not for you. They're mine. A little perk – my missus has always had a powerful craving for silk hose.'

Jay whipped the stockings out of Foxy's hand and wound them into a ball.

'No. What the deuce are you playing at? It is a dangerous enough game. I need to know exactly where the goods come from and go to.' He stuffed the stockings into his pocket. 'As long as everything comes here, and goes through me, I can keep my eye on it. There's no profit in nonsense like hose or kerchiefs. You get a decent cut that way for your trouble. If there starts to be a racket where every Tomfool and Harry are stealing for themselves, then I can't promise I'll be paying wages in the future. One mistake and it could be traced back to me. Any scent of that and our business is done. We don't want to end up in the Whit for the sake of a silk stocking now, do we?'

Foxy pouted. 'We deserve it. After all, it's us as does the houses, and us as takes the risks.'

'You'd still be on ha'pennies if it wasn't for me.'

Lutch was standing impassively near the door, flexing his veiny hands. Jay eyed him nervously.

Jay had a wide range of wily diversionary tactics to use when things got tense, for as a child he had learnt to his chagrin that he was not heavy enough to win in a proper fist-fight, nor for that matter brave enough. He wrangled his way out of difficulty by a combination of swagger and wit. He tried a different tack. 'Who gossips the most? Women, that's who,' he said. 'And when do they chatter? When they are all together, discussing the latest face powders, the modes and so on.'

'What's that got to do with it?' Foxy said.

'I've invented the perfect prattle shop. Of course I haven't called it that, it's to be the Ladies' Chambers. We can find out what jewels the ladies have. Choice little knick-knacks, or sentimental stuff they'll be sobbing to get back. You want information, this is where we'll get it. Come and have a look.'

Jay was itching to show somebody. He led the two men downstairs and across the yard, their heavy boots echoing behind him on the cobbles, and he opened the door into the new chambers with a flourish. He went round the walls lighting up the sconces.

'God almighty,' Foxy said.

Lutch stared blankly with his lower lip hanging.

In front of them was a bright red Turkey rug embroidered with paradise birds and peonies, curly-edged clouds and trees with fan-shaped leaves. Two walls were in the process of being lacquered entirely black, the other two were hung with frames of embossed leather wall-coverings in gold and mother-of-pearl. These showed willow trees and bridges and bald-headed men in robes walking in groves of bamboo or reclining in summerhouses. A long side table ran down one wall, on which was a row of looking glasses on stands. There was a powerful smell of varnish and rabbitskin glue.

'Enchanting, isn't it?'

'It's enough to make your eyes ache,' Foxy said. He pointed to a table laden with small glass bottles. 'What's all this?'

'Rose water.' Jay moved round the other side of the table and lifted one of the fragile stoppers, wafting it before them.

Foxy sniffed and made a face. 'Phaw. There's enough here to put out a house fire. What's it all for?'

'It's a boudoir. The ladies will sit here and wag their tongues. I've got a girl I'm going to train, she will report all the gossip to me.'

'What? A trull? Or a straight?' Foxy said.

'A straight. From the country by the looks of it, full of fresh country charm.'

Lutch did not look up from picking dirt from his fingernails with a penknife, but shook his head.

Foxy caught his meaning. 'Don't want to presume, boss, but it's common knowledge – the prettier the mott, the more trouble. That last one, fr'instance. I know Blanshard likes them wild, but we had a deal of trouble once she found out we'd duped her. Scratched like a weasel.' Foxy sucked on his protruding teeth, wiped his hands on the thighs of his moleskin breeches.

'This girl's not going to one of our gentlemen, and I've never had any trouble from any girl at Whitgift's.'

'What about—'

Jay flashed Foxy a warning look, and Foxy cleared his throat. At the sound, Lutch looked up from his nails.

Jay moved over to the table and ran his finger over it, holding the finger up to inspect it for dust. After a moment he said, 'I've said. There'll be no bother with this one. She's bright, and she'll tell us who's out of town, so we can be in easy. She'll see what jewels they wear and listen for talk of new purchases. If we're lucky we might even hear about the hidey-holes. She'll listen hard and ask the right questions and feed the answers back to me. We'll get a few bonuses as well as the business. Clever, eh?' Jay gestured round the room. 'And look at it. You can't tell me women won't flock here. It's pretty, isn't it?'

'It's a sight to behold, all right. No disrespect, boss, but I'd not trust aught with some chit.'

'She's new to London, sticks out a mile. Hasn't had chance yet to get caught up in any monkey business. You'll see. You'll be eating your words yet.'

'What does your pa make of it?'

'He doesn't hold with the idea. I asked him a while back about making a place for ladies to meet. Told him the better class of lady would likely browse in his warehouses, take a shine to some of the jewellery, trinkets and so forth. And then the gentlemen would open their purses. Didn't tell him she'd be a feed though. Anyway, he couldn't see the point. Women don't hold the pursestrings, see, and I couldn't make him see how it could turn a profit.'

'Has your pa been in here?' Foxy reached out a calloused hand to touch the wall-papering.

'Thought I'd make a few sales first, let him see the gents put their paws in their pockets, before he sees what I've done.'

Foxy looked around. 'Too right. I can't picture your pa in here. Be like seeing a muck cart in St James's Palace. And I'll bet it cost a ton, this fiddle-faddle. He won't like that, your pa.'

Lutch shook his head morosely. 'Nope,' he said.

'For heaven's sake, forget what my pa thinks, will you.'

Foxy shrugged.

'Anyway, you'll soon see how well it works. Few days' time it'll be the talk of London.' Jay started to snuff out the sconces.

'Come on, I've an errand for you. Rumour has it from my night-watchman there's a man called Jenks who has a little notebook I've been after. An ostler. He was in the Three Tuns trying to decipher what was in it. Make Jenks part with it and bring it to me. Don't care how you do it – bit of heavy if it's needed, the usual.'

'Is it valuable?' Foxy asked.

'Could be. It's Allsop's journal.'

Jay saw Lutch and Foxy exchange glances.

'What's in it?' Foxy said.

'How should I know? I've not seen it yet. Happen it could have our names in it, so I don't need to tell you how quick we need it back.'

Foxy said, 'Hang on, are you saying—'

Jay continued. 'Bloody fool Allsop – tried to put the screws on me. He's got a loan out already so go have a snoop round his house as well, see what pickings might be had there, find out anything else you can about him. I need to catch him wrong-footed in case he tries it on again. But more important – make sure there's nothing else in his house to link him to me. His sign's got a hawk and gauntlet on it. Trinity Lane, past St Paul's.'

'We're not to put the freeze on him, or take anything?' Foxy said.

'No, not yet. I'm holding off till I know how the land lies. It could mean a regular handout. And go easy, don't leave signs, he's not to get wind of it, do you hear?'

'If you say so.' Foxy raised his eyebrows at Lutch, who grunted his agreement.

'Everything else is set aside until I get ahold of that notebook. And here's a token in advance.'

Lutch moved over to lean on the lacquerwork table. Its spindly legs creaked under his weight.

Jay placed two coins on the table.

Lutch picked one up. He turned it over in his hand then gave Foxy a meaningful look.

Foxy swallowed. 'Sorry, boss, but we ain't best pleased with this.' Lutch held out the coin between his finger and thumb and looked sideways to Foxy, who nodded. 'Seems like we do all the work, but don't get much pickings.'

Lutch moved up to stand behind Foxy, who continued, 'Like last week we saw the Harper's gilt mantel clock with a ticket on it for eight pound. Dennis says it's already been sold – back to Harper. We nearly got caught for that, good job we're fast runners or we'd have been in the stone jug by now. Yet all we got for it was twelve shilling apiece. That ain't fair, and we're looking for better deals from now on.'

'Come on, Foxy, it's been a lean year. You and Lutch, well, you're the tightest rooks I know, but I can't give you more, I'd be squeezing myself dry.'

'Your pa would have something to say if he were to get to hear of it – that his business ain't quite what he thinks it is. It would be worth your while to give us a bit extra, if you see what I'm saying.'

Lutch looked up briefly then dropped his gaze.

'I saw him on the way through the gates, your father,' Foxy said, 'talking with a greasy-looking fellow in a long coat, he was. They went into his office.'

'What fellow?'

'Tall, stooping. Bit down-at-heel . . . I could go see your pa now.' Foxy beckoned to Lutch.

'Now then,' Jay said, 'don't go upsetting my old man, we can work this out. Tell you what, I'll cut you in on a percentage. How about five per cent?'

'Ten.'

'Seven, and there's my final offer.'

'Come on, boss. Be nice, now. I've got a family to keep.'

'Eight,' Lutch said quietly. Although Lutch was still looking down, something in his demeanour made Jay's stomach turn to water. He thought of all the necks those veiny hands had cracked.

'Done,' Jay said. 'Spit on it then.' He spat on his palm and Lutch did the same. When they shook hands Lutch's was a surprisingly gentle grasp, though his hand was rough as stone. Jay wiped his hand on his breeches. 'Now go after that notebook.'

When they'd gone he held the garnet and diamond necklace up to the candle. The light shone inside the gems like beads of blood. He swung it back and forth before the light. About seventeen pounds, eighteen if he was lucky. He opened one of the drawers with two other necklaces already pegged out on velvet. He laid the new one out with precision and pinned it down. From his window he could see his father's office and a candle still burnt within. It must be that snooper Tindall with his father. Nobody else matched that description. Damn. Now he would have to watch his step.

Chapter 12

The heat of the room enveloped Ella, after the bitter chill of the outside air. A smell of tallow assailed her nostrils, mixed with the sweetness of lavender and rose water. The light wavered and danced round the gold leaf on the walls. The small windows let in hardly any light, swagged as they were with thick gold-coloured drapery.

When Ella arrived, a little apprehensive as to what might be required of her, she could not believe the transformation from the dark square box. She could only stand and gape. She had never seen the like. So this was the 'oriental' style. She raised a finger to trail it over the embossed gold pictures on the walls; the raised texture of the leather clicked under her nails. She was hard pressed to believe it could be the same place at all – the dusty dairy had gone and now she was in an enchanted palace. She inhaled deeply as if to breathe it in. If the Netherbarrow lads could only see her now!

Earlier she had collected her gown and now one of the warehouse lads opened up and told her Mr Whitgift said she could change upstairs in the new ladies' chambers. She stopped short on the landing and saw that one door was ajar into some sort of storeroom, crates and punnets and baskets giving off the pungent aroma of lemon and herbs. She poked her head further round the door to see bags of French chalk and a crate of oil in jars. A quick glance over her shoulder to check no one was looking and she bent to pull out a cork. She inhaled the heavy sweetness of almond oil.

She was astonished to see that the other room seemed to be a bedroom. It had a small wooden bed, made of solid oak, with bolsters and ticking pillows. She stood a moment, looking at it, as if suddenly finding herself in the wrong place. She had not seen a proper wooden bed since leaving Thomas's house in Westmorland, and it made her feel uncomfortable. She remembered his inert figure humped under the white linen, the total stillness of his face. With it came the familiar suffocating impression of being trapped, of being locked into the wrong life by mistake.

The fear caught her unawares. She had the sensation of choking, as if a cold lap of water was rising up to her throat. She turned her back on the bed with a shudder and took a few deep breaths to calm herself. After a moment she felt able to lay out the red silk dress on the chair. Just the sight of it, the heap of scarlet silk, was enough to cheer her. The colour was the colour of life. She let her eyes drink it in. Then quickly, in case anyone should come, she wriggled out of her blue dress and eased herself into the red skirt.

She discarded her old dress with distaste. In Westmorland this dress had seemed the height of luxury. But now, next to the red silk, it looked like what it was – a servant's dress. She donned the red bodice and pulled at the strings of the back lacing, cursing under her breath, for she had to twist and contort herself like a cat to get it tight enough. She would have to get Sadie to lace it in the mornings – a girl could not get the right pull on her own.

When she had tied the laces in the best bow she could manage and tucked them inside the skirts, she stared out of the window at the activity in the yard. The queue at Dennis's window never seemed to get any smaller. From up here, it was a row of shuffling hats. Ella paid it no heed and instead treated the window as a mirror, checking her face for soot smuts and admiring her new hairstyle before going down into the shop.

'Ah, Miss Johnson.' His voice made her start. Jay Whitgift leaned back against the sideboard, raising his eyebrows. Then he laughed, showing his white teeth. 'Well, I suppose I did give you the choice.'

Ella looked down, confused, at her gown, smoothing it with her hands. 'It's a fine fit, sir. I made sure of that. Is it all right, sir?'

His mouth twitched. 'It will certainly attract attention. And your hair – it is most unusual.'

Ella was uncomfortable. She had a suspicion she was being laughed at but she did not understand why.

'You are not cold?'

'No, sir.'

He smirked again, but then his mouth tightened and he led her towards a stout woman dressed in a stiff coral-coloured gown.

'This is Mrs Horsefeather,' he said. Ella dipped her head as was expected of her.

She tried hard not to gape. There was so much lace on Mrs Horsefeather's cap and mantle that it gave the impression there was a wave breaking round her neck.

Mrs Horsefeather said, 'Come on, girl,' as if she was ten years old, and Jay Whitgift smiled and left them. Ella nodded, half an eye on his retreating back. He was easy enough on the eye and no mistake, she thought. Mrs Horsefeather coughed drily to gain her attention and proceeded to instruct her about the different items on display, keeping up a running commentary as she guided her through laying out the different stock ready for the opening. She showed her how to dab the perfume on the ladies' wrists and temples with the conical tip of the glass stopper, how to mix alabaster powder with egg white to make skin-whitener, how to use the belladonna dropper and, not least, how to stand respectfully to one side so that her breath should not fall on anyone's countenance.

Ella took it all in, in a state of excitement, as if she was drinking great draughts of the elixir of eternal life. She kept glancing at the glittering walls, the dancing candle flames, the displays of powder puffs and pomanders. She was dreaming, she must be. Miss Corey Johnson, of Whitgift's Chambers. She said the name to herself over and over, quashing the images of the other Corey bent over her stinking bench at Madame Lefevre's wig shop.

She learnt how to tally the coinage and put it in the drawer with the wooden compartments. She swirled her hand around the smooth wooden bowls and felt the coins trickling through her fingers. She could have stood there all day just feeling the weight and coolness of those coins.

The room soon grew hot, there were so many candles lit. She'd never seen so many. What an extravagance. Perhaps it was because ladies were careful of their complexions – not to get them in the sun, lest they turn brown, like any common labourer.

Ella licked the perspiration from her top lip. 'Beg pardon, is it always going to be this bright?' she asked.

'Mr Whitgift thinks candlelight more flattering to a lady's complexion,' Mrs Horsefeather said, patting her own cheek. Ella saw that Mrs Horsefeather's face was parched as a dried-up river-bed, her papery cheeks unnaturally rosy. She hoped she would never look as old as her.

Mrs Horsefeather poked Ella with a finger. 'Now give that table a dust, there is powder spilt all over it. And stop asking so many questions.'

But that's the first question I've asked, thought Ella. She took up the duster though, noticing that even the duster was a proper feather duster and not just an old rag or bobbit of clothing.

When Mrs Horsefeather went outside to talk with Jay about arrangements for opening day, Ella could contain herself no longer. She gave a huge whoop of joy and hopped round the room in a mad May-dance. In and out of the tables and chairs set out ready for the customers she went, picking up her red silk skirts and swishing them over her knees, until when Mrs Horsefeather returned she was pink-cheeked and panting with it all.

'You look a touch warm, Miss Johnson. It will not do. Mr Whitgift wants you to set an example. I suggest you take a few minutes to powder your nose.' She held out a small box.

Ella took it. 'Yes, Mrs Horsefeather,' she said.

Ella held her breath as Jay Whitgift inspected the chambers, now laid out with every sort of skin balm, glaze and herbal comfit. After moving the belladonna phials into military ranks on the counter, he turned to smile. 'Very good,' he said, strolling again round the counters and the displays. 'Tomorrow you will help Waley the apothecary in the back room with making up scented nosegays and salves. He will show you what to do.'

'Yes, sir,' said Ella, dimpling at him.

'If you're all ready, I'll get the bills printed up this afternoon,' Jay said.

'With what?' A ragged-looking gentleman in a flapping coat had come in behind them.

Jay frowned. 'Sorry, Tindall, gentlemen are not allowed in the Ladies' Chambers. Except for the proprietor, of course.'

'I know. But there's no ladies come yet. And there is not much coinage in that name, as far as I can see.'

Jay stepped away from him as if he smelt bad. 'Meaning?'

'Well, you cannot make a sign out of that. The newer coffee houses all have lively signs, ones that will stand out, attract attention. Like the Pelican or the Dancing Bear. You need something auspicious, attractive to ladies, like a powder puff or a fan.'

'I don't see any reason to complicate it,' Jay said. 'It's chambers where ladies will meet, so the Ladies' Chambers is good enough. I'll worry about the sign later.'

'Well, mark my words, it will fail if it has no proper signage.'

'I know what I'm doing, so I'll thank you to mind your own business. Oh, I forgot, you don't seem to have one.'

Tindall looked taken aback. Then he retorted, 'Well, yours seems a damnified business anyway, selling such pap and palter.' He picked up a creamware pot from the newly neatened pyramid and opened the lid to sniff at it. 'What is it Shakespeare said? To gild gold and paint the lily is a waste of time. I might not know much, but I know this: beautiful women have no need of all this –' here he held out the pot on his palm – 'and ugly women, well, whatever they do, they will still be ugly. No point gilding the lily then, is there?'

'At least my business is thriving, unlike . . .' Jay let the words hang there.

'Here, sir, I'll take that,' Ella said hurriedly, replacing the lid on the pot and putting it back on the pyramid. She wished Tindall would leave. There was an atmosphere in the room now, and she did not like him saying the shop might fail.

Tindall shook his head under his greasy felt hat. 'Only trying to be helpful, my boy,' he said, before turning on his heel and walking out.

Jay turned to Ella and Mrs Horsefeather. 'The bills for Whitgift's Ladies' Chambers will be put out tomorrow,' he snapped.

But when the bills came, they said, 'Under the Sign of the Gilded Lily', and when Ella next crossed the yard, there was the draughtsman drawing up a brand new sign with a golden flower in front of a red lace fan.

Chapter 13

Blackraven Alley

Sadie bent low over the table in the wavering shadow of a rush-light. She was darning her shawl again, using one of the wool fringes to mend a hole where she had caught it on a fencepost the day before. Her fingers were cold, the ends white and bloodless, for they had no wood. The bundle of faggots was finished yesterday. Last time she had gone to fetch wood she had scrabbled in the mud with the other scavengers for almost two hours, but gleaned only a small damp bundle of sticks and a few sackcloths fit for burning. It was hard to find enough fuel in the city, where there were no trees and there was no peat to be dug.

Smoke from other people's fires seeped in through the walls, although the heat did not penetrate through the damp. It was a drizzly night and the walls sweated like cheese. Sadie pushed her hair out of her eyes, put the shawl down on the table and rubbed her hands over her cheeks to warm them.

She looked up at the window. The sacking that was tacked over it was not quite big enough and gaped open to the sky outside. It was dark and Ella was late home. She wondered how her sister had fared at Whitgift's today. She seemed altogether taken with Jay Whitgift. It wasn't good to wear your heart on your sleeve like that, it gave gentlemen ideas. Sadie remembered the last time she had seen such a look on Ella's face. It was eighteen months ago, when she was describing Thomas Ibbetson's house. She remembered Ella's awed voice: 'Feather quilts in glossy satin covers, and the blankets – soft as lambs' tails, not like our thin rat-eared ones.' Ella's face had taken on the same rapt expression describing Jay Whitgift's clothes: 'Watered silk, Sadie, and cambric that fine you can see your hand through it.'

Sadie took up her needle and rethreaded it. The dreamy look she had seen on Ella's face meant trouble. To her mind Jay Whitgift was altogether too well turned out – like a tailor's dolly. When they had first arrived in London they had both chortled at the men in their ribands and bows and fancy curls, thinking it made them look like maids – funny how quickly she had got used to it. But Jay Whitgift's clothes fitted tight, as if they'd been shrunk to him, and he was spotless, right up to his pheasant-feathered hat and right down to his silver-buckled shoes.

The downstairs door clicked shut. She stood up and brushed the loose threads from her sleeve. She hurried to the landing and peered over the banister.

'Ella?'

It was not the top of Ella's head she saw, but the brown felt hat of Dennis from downstairs, listening at his own front door. Just as she was about to go back inside, fearing he would think her nosy, he turned his face to look up and caught sight of her. She withdrew hastily and turned away.

'Hang on,' he said in a loud whisper.

Sadie waited.

'Have you got a minute?'

She nodded, and he grinned broadly. He came up the stairs

two at a time in a kind of lope so that he made no noise with his boots.

'I think Ma's asleep,' he said, 'so I've got a few minutes before I need to see to her.' He had a large tied bundle with him, which he dumped on the landing at Sadie's feet. 'Last week's wash – from the wash-house down the way,' he said wryly, pointing.

'Oh,' Sadie said, uncertain whether it was a good idea to stand talking in the hall.

'If you've got the rent, I'll take it now,' he said.

'Oh, oh yes. Wait on.' She went inside to fetch her purse, and when she could not see it on the kitchen table she shifted her shawl, feeling for it until it was in her hand. When she turned again she was surprised to find Dennis standing just behind her.

She took a step away. He had taken off his cap and was scratching his head and looking at the shawl on the table.

'Blimey, that's neat,' he said, indicating the shawl with his head. 'When my ma does darning it looks like a drunken spider's made a web over the hole.'

'My sister thinks it's a fright and I should throw it away. Says it's not worth mending, but I like it.'

'It looks warm, that,' Dennis said. 'No point buying new if you can mend the old one. Don't know what's up with folk – we get them in Whitgift's all the time, pawning brand new stuff and wearing the old that's full of holes. Truth is, they can't afford to buy the new and end up pawning it. Then they finish up in their old togs just the same. Dunno why they don't just mend the old stuff.'

'Did Ell— I mean Corey come back with you?'

'No, it was that busy, it's been a madhouse in there. They don't let gents in either, so I can't say what goes on inside.' He spoke quickly, hardly pausing for breath, 'I've never seen that many fancy carriages with ladies in before. Looks like it's going to be a boon for Whitgift's. I like the name, "The Gilded Lily" – wasn't sure about the whole scheme to begin with, 'cos Jay Whitgift's a bit of a rum animal, but I've a lot of time for the gaffer. He lets me take time off if Ma's not so good, he's kind like that, he is.' He seemed to have run out of things to say. Then suddenly, 'Are you working?'

'I've got piece work at Lefevre's Perruquier's.'

Dennis looked blank.

'The wig shop round the back of Bread Street.' Sadie had been counting out the money whilst he was talking. Now she held it out to him.

'Thanks,' he said as he took it. 'I'm glad we've got one room let at least. The other one's been empty three weeks now. But Ma can't bear the idea of anyone directly overhead. She reckons 'twould stop her sleeping, you know, the noise and that.'

Sadie was surprised that after she gave him the money he made no attempt to go but continued to stand there. She started to move towards the door to encourage him, but he turned instead to the darning on the table.

'Show us how you do this,' he said, 'how you make it so neat.'

'You don't really want to see.'

'I do. Show us how it's done.' He patted the shawl.

Sadie flushed, embarrassed. It felt odd to show a lad how to sew. She picked up the needle and, feeling a little ridiculous, began to weave the thread.

'Over and under, see, then push it tight with the back of the needle. You have to keep the hole taut so that the weaving's even. It's simple, a child of three could do it.'

'My ma sure as hell can't. Let's have a go. I'm a bit older than three though. I'm seventeen. How old are you?'

'Sixteen this week.' She said it as if she could hardly believe it herself.

'Really? What day's your birthday?'

'Look, sit here and I'll pass you the needle.'

'Go on, tell us the day.'

'The twenty-sixth.'

'Thursday. I'll be sure to wish you many happy returns when the day comes. Now is this where it goes?'

He picked up the threads neatly with the tip of the needle, pushing the weft back against the warp. Sadie noticed how the tip of his tongue came out of the corner of his mouth as he concentrated, and that there was the slight shadow of a moustache on his upper lip.

'You've done this before,' she said.

He grinned up at her. 'I'll do a few more rows to make sure I've got it. You won't tell anyone, will you? 'Tis women's work, I know, but I've got that many hose with holes in, and I've stopped giving them to Ma, she can't manage them.'

She sat down opposite him at the table and watched as he completed the patch.

'Show us how to finish it off, now.'

She went over and he handed her the needle. She fumbled as she took it from him and it fell from her fingers onto the floor. They both dropped down together to search for it, feeling over the rough floorboards with their fingers. Sadie noticed how Dennis's wrists came a long way out of his cuffs as if his arms had recently grown too long for his sleeves.

Downstairs the door slammed and they both shot to their feet, looking guiltily at one another.

'That'll be your sister. And I'd better go. Ma might be awake and needing me.'

He fished his hat out of his waistband and, cramming it back on his head, hurried out of the door. Sadie heard his apologies as Ella tried to pass him on the stairs.

Ella breezed in, accompanied by an overpowering scent of lavender. She was wearing a bright red skirt and bodice cut very low at the front, under a dark green woollen cloak.

'What did he want?' Ella asked, wrinkling up her nose.

'Nothing. He came for the rental. My, Ella. You look right different. Where did you get that rig? From Whitgift's?'

'These are my working clothes. I left my others at the shop. You should've seen Jay's face when he first saw me in this. His mouth fell open that wide you could've stuck an apple in it.'

'I thought he picked the gown out for you?'

'Oh. Oh, yes he did.'

'Don't he mind you coming home in them?'

'Who's to know? I'll not tell him. Anyhows, I feel more like myself in these. Here – feel the weight of that. Gorgeous, isn't it.'

Sadie stretched out her hand to touch the fabric. 'By, it's fine. Watch it don't get dirty round the hem. We've not had chance to sweep today.'

Ella ignored her advice and sat down heavily on the bed, kicking off her muddy shoes. 'I'm glad to get the weight off my feet. I've been run ragged, fetching and carrying. Any supper?'

'No, Ella. We've nothing in. Have you not been paid yet? We could go to the bakehouse.'

'No. I've already said, payday's the end of the month. Two whole weeks. Never mind, I'm not fussed. Mrs Horsefeather gave me a currant muffin at lunchtime when she saw I'd got no bundle with me.' She flung her cloak down, releasing another cloud of perfume. 'What's that you're doing? Darning?'

Sadie nodded, staring at Ella's bosom, rising and falling out of the front of her bodice.

'Surprised you can be bothered with that old rag. It wants throwing away. Stinky old thing.'

'It keeps me warm. And it still smells of Farmer Pinkney's sheep. Do you remember him?'

'No. I'm done thinking on Netherbarrow now.'

Her words were like a door slamming. Ella looked different, bigger somehow. It wasn't just the yards of red material heaped up round her where she sat, or the pinned-up hair. Ella seemed to be growing, and she, Sadie, seemed to be shrinking.

Sadie wrapped up the darning things carefully, and put them on the windowsill. Ignoring Ella's scathing expression she wrapped the shawl round her shoulders. Out of the corner of her eye she caught a glimpse of the lights of the barges going by outside on the river. Their twinkling looked like hazy stars. She had a sudden longing to be on one of those barges, headed out on the ribbon of light, out towards the wide open swell of the sea.

'I'm lighting another rushlight,' Ella said, opening the tin box on the wall. 'It's right poky in here with only the one light. At Whitgift's there are chandeliers with dozens of candles, so bright they make your eyes smart. And a fire blazing in the grate, so's the ladies don't catch a chill. It's freezing. Is there no wood?'

'Not unless you want to go gather some.'

Ella sat down on the bed. 'What? In this gown? No, when I get paid, we'll have a good big fire, we'll buy a great dry bundle from Farrah's on the corner and heat up a boiling pan with a whole chicken in it.' Ella opened her arms to indicate a chicken of enormous proportions.

Sadie's mouth watered, her stomach was hollow. But Ella's optimism was infectious and she could not help but laugh. She sat down next to her. 'That's a bloody big chicken. More like a swan.'

'Oh, all right, milady, swan it is. Will you be having it stuffed with partridge or quail?'

'Oh, quail, I should think. Partridge is so common. And I should like some roast potatoes. About two dozen should be enough.'

'Two dozen? Why not three?' Ella mimed stuffing her mouth with potato until her cheeks bulged. They both fell into fits of laughter, clutching for each other so they did not fall off the bed.

'Sing a song of sixpence, a pocket full of rye, four and twenty turkeycocks, baked in a pie . . .' sang Ella.

Sadie spluttered with mirth. She caught a glimpse of the old Ella, the Ella before she went into service with the Ibbetsons, the Ella who used to keep her awake half the night with her play-acting and outrageous fairy tales. She squeezed Ella's arm and Ella tickled her round the waist.

Another noise at the door below made them both startle. Something about the quality of the knocking put them on the alert.

'Quick, get the bolt on,' Ella said.

The knocking in the hall below got louder.

Sadie pressed her ear to the door. She waved at Ella to extinguish the light. The room fell dark and silent. Down below they could hear the front door creak open.

'Is it that man again?' whispered Sadie.

'Shh. Be quiet so I can hear.'

'Come in,' said Dennis's voice. 'My ma's not so well, so you'll have to come into the back room if you want to speak with her.'

Footsteps walking on the flagged floor underneath.

'Yes?' Dennis's mother's voice, weakly, from somewhere under their feet.

Sadie and Ella pressed their ears to the door. A man's voice. 'We're looking for two girls. One quite a looker, the other with a red stain on her face. A lad thinks he saw them in the alley and told us they came in here.'

'Why? What've they done?' Dennis's voice.

Sadie gripped hold of Ella's hand.

'There's a reward out for them. Murder and robbery.' Sadie took a sharp intake of breath. He said murder. Surely that could not be true? She looked to Ella and saw the whites of Ella's eyes move, as she shook her head vigorously.

'It's the constable, Ma,' they heard Dennis say.

'Oh my. We did take in two girls, just last week, didn't we, Dennis? In the room upstairs.'

'No, Ma,' Dennis's voice insisted, 'it wasn't two girls. It was just the one.'

Sadie squeezed Ella's hand tight.

'Only one? I thought you said it was two? One that's a knotter, and the one from Whitgift's?'

'No, Ma. You're mistaken.' Dennis's voice was firm. 'It was just the one. She used to work as a knotter, but now she works at Whitgift's. She's very respectable. Shall I get her to come down?'

'Yes,' the constable said. 'I'd better have a word with her. Fetch her down, would you.'

Ella stood up, mouthing silently, 'What'll we do?'

Sadie shook her head.

'Miss Johnson?' There was a rap at the door.

'Yes,' Ella called.

Dennis said loudly, 'Two gentlemen to see you, the constable and his man. They're downstairs in the parlour.'

'What do they want?' Ella called out.

'Something about a burglary, you'd best come down.'

Ella threw her cloak over her shoulders and unlocked the door. She ushered Dennis inside with a frantic wave of her hand.

'They don't know about your sister,' he whispered, 'you'll have to go along with it.' Ella threw Sadie a glance, putting her finger to her lips, and started down the stairs, leaving Sadie alone with Dennis.

'Hide,' he whispered.

'Where?'

They looked round hopelessly at the box-like room with its single truckle bed.

'The other room?' Sadie said.

'No. Sorry. Key's still downstairs.'

'Dennis?' His mother's voice drifted up from below.

'Coming, Ma,' he called. He gave a rueful look, shrugged his shoulders and followed Ella downstairs.

Sadie knew that if they saw her, they would know who she was straight away. She struggled to drag the rough brown blanket further over the bed to give a hiding place underneath, but then tossed the blanket aside – it would be the first place anyone would look. In a panic she gathered together the meagre pile of belongings that had come from Westmorland and held them up in her apron. They would be recognized easily as Thomas Ibbetson's things. She would have to get rid of them, tiptoe down and out of the front door whilst Ella kept the constable talking in the back parlour.

She rushed to the window and peered out, thinking to throw the goods outside and collect them later. The banks of the Thames were below the level of the street and directly beneath, black oozing mudflats. She hesitated. What if their precious objects sank into the mud and she could not find them again? But she couldn't leave them here in the room. She'd have to carry them. She tied the corners of her apron to the waist-strings, secured it tightly and supported its awkward bulk in her arms. She tiptoed towards the door and out onto the landing, but paused mid-movement. She heard the downstairs door open, voices, and men's boots coming upstairs.

She scurried to the door of the room opposite and pushed it hard but, as Dennis had said, it was locked. There was nowhere to go. She shot back into the room. The window. It was her only hope. From the window she spied a small ledge running around the edge of the building, the ledge formed by the eaves of the room below – wooden rafters sticking out at intervals from the lath walls. She had seen seagulls perch there and heard their plaintive cries at night.

She hoisted herself up by the sacking at the window and clambered out. For the first time, she thanked the Lord there was no glass in it. The window frame was damp and rotten, but it gave her fingernails a good grip as she swung herself out over the black oily river beneath. The ledge was slippery with damp and bird droppings. She clung onto the window frame and edged herself sideways, out along the ledge, her bare feet skidding on the wooden parapet. She could feel the nailed-up cloth brushing against her fingers. With the other hand she found a beam from the half-timbered wall.

Someone opened the door inside and she heard Ella's voice.

'I've told you. There's no need to come in. I have never heard of Mr Ibbetson. You won't find anything here.'

'Get out of my way. We need to check this room, whether you will or no.'

Sadie heard the scrape of their boots as they looked around the room.

The curtain moved over her fingers, a delicate tickling touch, and Dennis's head poked out of the window. He saw her straight away. He raised his eyebrows at her in acknowledgement, then his head disappeared inside. Sadie sidled further out along the rail, reaching out to grip onto the half-timbering.

'What's out there?' said a man's voice.

'Nothing. Sheer drop to the river, sir,' Dennis said.

'Let's look then, boy.'

The curtain twitched and Sadie held her breath. It had started to rain again. A man's head in a grizzled wig appeared out of the window and he glanced briefly down towards the mudflats. Sadie clung tighter. But he did not turn to look sideways, just gave a brief grunt and pulled his head back inside. She almost wept with relief. She looked down to see what he was looking at and the height took her breath away. Far below her there was a curly-tailed dog scavenging among the fish-heads and slime. She felt faint and dizzy. She closed her eyes and clamped her numb fingers more tightly to the wooden framework. Pray God she might not fall. The water was thick as syrup; she did not know if she could swim or whether she would drown there in the mud. Her fingers were tired. The wind caught in her skirts and her apron was heavy, the contents threatening to overtopple her.

'There ain't no one else here,' said another man's voice. 'Sorry, miss, to disturb you. If you don't mind me saying, miss, it don't look like your kind of place, this. These two servant girls could still be round here. Slit your throat for your watch chain, they would, so I'm told.'

Sadie heard Ella say airily in her London voice, 'Oh it's only temporary. Till my new lodgings are ready.'

'Good evening, Miss . . . ?'

Sadie heard Ella reel off the name as if it had always belonged to her. 'Miss Johnson. Corey Johnson.'

'Sorry to have troubled you, Miss Johnson. Send us word if you come across these two girls. Here is the notice that's out for them. We'll be posting these up in this neighbourhood since we've been tipped off. As I said, there's a reward.'

'I sincerely hope I will never need to call you. Good evening, gentlemen.'

'See us out then, lad.'

'Right-o, sir,' Dennis said. She heard the door shut.

'Sadie?' Ella hissed. 'Sadie? Where the hell are you? Come out. They've gone.'

Sadie heard the rustle of Ella's dress as she moved about inside but she was powerless to speak. The apron full of the stolen goods dragged on her waist. She did not dare move, she needed all her concentration to keep her balance. The icy rain blew in her face and whipped at her skirts. She could not look down and she feared to move a single inch, so she pressed her back against the wall, gripping tight to the window frame.

She was dimly aware of noises within and then, suddenly, Dennis's voice.

'She's out here, help me get her inside.'

Ella's head appeared. 'You little fool,' she hissed, 'you could have fallen in! Come in quick, before someone sees you.'

'I can't,' Sadie said, hearing her own voice waver.

'You have to. They might see you, out there.'

'I can't move.'

'I'll have to help her,' she heard Dennis say. 'Bring the stool closer to the window so I can stand on it to reach her.'

Dennis's hand was dry and warm. It closed over her cold knuckles and took firm grasp of her wrist.

'Easy now,' he said, as if he was talking to a frightened horse. 'Just edge this way a little so I can take hold of you.'

She swallowed hard and felt with her feet for the slippery beams. Dennis's arms closed round her waist and she almost fell back in through the window. He swung her down to the ground. He smelt of leather and boot polish. She wriggled away from him in embarrassment.

'Sit down,' he said.

She did not need to be asked twice. She perched on the

wooden stool; her legs felt like duck down. Ella hovered, holding the door open, expecting Dennis to leave.

'Don't just stand there,' he said to Ella, 'lay a fire. She's frozen through.'

Ella stared at him, then at Sadie. Sadie dropped her eyes.

'Are you going to light a fire then, or what?' Dennis said, frowning at Ella.

'We've no wood,' Ella said.

He raised his eyes to the ceiling. 'Then give her your cloak. I'll fetch up a bit of kindling, and after I'll be needing to know the truth from you. Or I'll be calling them back.'

'It's none of your business,' Ella said.

'In that case I'll be claiming that reward.' He clomped down the stairs in his heavy boots.

Ella chased after him. 'Wait!'

'Keep your hair on,' he called, 'I'm only going to fetch up some wood.' His footfalls carried on down the stairs.

'Now look.' Ella burst back through the door and rounded on her.

'What? I haven't done anything.'

'He knows now, doesn't he?' Ella paced around the room as if it had got too small for her. Sadie found her legs were shaking under her skirts. 'Ssh, he's coming.'

Dennis carried in an armful of sticks and took a tinderbox from a pouch on his belt to begin making up a fire in the stone hearth.

'Own up. Who's going to tell me the truth? A murder and a robbery, they said.'

Sadie looked to Ella, who cast her eyes mutinously downwards.

'It's not true,' Sadie said. She shuddered, an image of Thomas Ibbetson's white face and fish-like eyes flashed into her mind.

'Did you kill someone?'

'Course not,' Ella said.

'So what did you steal?' Dennis's eyes were frankly curious.

Sadie made to untie and open her apron.

'No –' Ella took hold of her arm – 'don't show him. It's our business.'

Sadie wrapped the apron closer to her body.

'It's all right. I'm not interested in your things. Not as long as you can pay the rent. But it's going to be awkward now Ma thinks there's only one girl living here.'

'Yes, that was a daft idea and no mistaking,' Ella said.

'I thought it would help, if they thought there was only one girl living here. Sorry. But I don't think they'll be back – they're looking for two girls, not one. And best you keep out of sight,' he said to Sadie. 'They're after a girl . . .' He looked fixedly at the wall. 'A girl that looks like you,' he finished.

Sadie felt the heat rise to her face. Dennis continued, 'But I want to hear your side of it. I like to hear both sides of a story.'

Ella sat down, half turned away from Dennis and Sadie.

'Come on, you can tell me. You don't look much like killers,' Dennis said.

'Huh. You know nothing about us,' said Ella over her shoulder.

'They said you killed a gent.'

'He died all by himself.' She swivelled round. 'He just keeled over one day with the dropsy. Didn't need me to help.' Ella's voice had taken on a hard brittle edge. 'But I knew I'd be out flat – with no position and no reference. 'Tis always the same, the relatives toss you out with the old bedding. And I wasn't going home, not after being housekeeper in my own place. Besides, he owed me. A month's wages anyways.'

'I thought so. I trust my instincts. You looked that scared the day you first came, like the Devil and all the demons of hell were after you.' He manoeuvred another stick onto the fire, where it sprang into yellow flame. 'And anyway, I might not mind it if you were. Killers, I mean. It'd be interesting to meet a murderer. I read them penny chapbooks, but I bet yours is as good a tale.'

'Have they got pictures?' Sadie said.

'Some of 'em. I'll bring them up to show you. It's kind of dull round here. The last lodger was never in. I have to spend a lot of time with Ma, 'cos she needs looking after.'

'What's the matter with her?' Sadie asked.

'It's her lungs, some days she can't hardly breathe. She used to work at the wash-house, but she's too weak to lift the laundry now, and her chest can't cope with all that steam.'

Ella stood up and turned to face them both. 'Don't you understand,' she said, her voice rising, 'they're on our tail. I never thought he'd come after us this far. It's been months and the bugger's still chasing us.' Ella unfolded the notice the constable had given her and waved it at Dennis. 'You say you can read chapbooks. Well, can you read this?'

Dennis took it, looking embarrassed. 'Well, I can read a bit, but I'd need some help with this,' he said, holding it to the candle. 'There's long words. Old Tindall the astrologer's been at the shop a fair bit lately, talking with Gaffer Whitgift. He's the one for reading. I'll ask him if he can help.'

'No.' She snatched it back from him. 'What if it's got my likeness written on it? I don't want that anywhere near the Gilded Lily. Is there nobody else?'

'Can't think of anyone else with proper book learning. But I'll see what I can do.'

'We need to see what's written, who they're looking for,' Ella said.

'If them notices are up, I'll make sure to hide my face when I go out now,' Sadie said.

'You'll have to tiptoe past my ma,' Dennis said, 'now she thinks there's only one of you. She'd have you out quick as a lick of butter. She can't handle trouble, see. The least thing wears her out. I can't even answer back like I used to – it does for her, arguing. She never used to be like that, she—'

'Dennis?' A faint voice from below.

'Talk of the Devil. There she goes. I'll have to go. See you tomorrow.'

They listened to his boots thump downstairs.

Ella banged the door behind him so hard that the draught scattered loose ash from the fire over the floorboards. 'We're in a right old pickle now.'

'He won't tell,' Sadie said.

'I don't want to be beholden to some clod of a boy. He could put the screws on us, start asking for money to keep quiet.'

'He wouldn't do that.'

'How do you know?'

'I just know. He helped us, didn't he?'

'Don't be simple. Only because he wants a cut of whatever we've got. I can see straight through him. We've got to move on again, find a new place.'

'No, Ella. Not again. We can't keep on running. If we run, he'll think the constable was right. And we've no money for new lodgings, not till we get paid. We have to trust him, at least for a while. There's no choice.'

Ella sat down heavily, resting her forehead on her hands. There was a long pause before she eventually said, 'Do you think I want to risk my neck? Soon as one of us gets paid, we're off. But you'll have to come and go in the dark now. If anyone sees you, with that notice out, we're done for. You can't go back to the wig shop either. You're too easy to spot, and you speak like a country girl.'

'But, Ella, I have to go to work. We need the money. And if I don't go back tomorrow, and don't give notice, we'll get in even more trouble. You know what Old Feverface is like.'

'No. She don't know where we lodge, so you'll stay home, it'll be safer. If there's a reward out for us, every last beggar will be looking for a girl with a patch-face. You might as well have a bloody sign stuck to your forehead.' She sighed and threw out her hands in frustration. 'I shouldn't have brought you.'

Sadie bit her lip. 'Sorry, Ella.' A moment's pause, then, 'How will we manage for things if I don't go out?'

'You're not to go out, d'ye hear? It's too risky. What if they follow you and you lead them here?' She bent down close to Sadie's face. 'And if they find us, we'll burn.'

Sadie shoved her away with the flat of her palm. A slap came back instantly.

'Ow. That hurt.'

Ella walked away towards the window and looked outside before turning to say, 'It'll only be for a little while. Just till the hue and cry dies away. Six months from now, everything will be different, you'll see.'

Sadie's voice was small. 'But, Ella, what will I do, if I can't go out?'

'I don't know. Make yourself useful, I suppose, like always. Lay the fire, make clapbread. Mend.'

She tried to read Ella's expression. She couldn't mean it. 'Maybe that notice don't mention my face, maybe it don't give an image of us at all?'

Ella gave her a pitying stare and turned away without answering.

Chapter 14

The next day Ella was irritated to find that Dennis emerged from his downstairs rooms just as she was leaving. He stuck by her side all the way to Whitgift's, plying her with questions, where they'd come from, who their family was. She'd kept her lips tight-buttoned and let silence answer his questions. Eventually she turned to him and said, 'Look, whatever you think you're going to get out of me, you'll not be getting a bean. So we might as well make that clear.'

'I don't want nothing. What gave you that idea?'

'You know too much about us.'

'I'd say I didn't know enough.'

'Oh ha ha.'

Ella maintained a frosty silence to keep distance between them. She didn't want him tagging alongside her, heaven forbid. People might think she was betrothed to him. She marched past the tripe shop, which always smelt unaccountably of sweat, dodged round the stalls with fruit and vegetables, strode past the haberdasher's with its fluttering trails of ribbons and lace, but gave none of them so much as a glance. She was acutely aware of the ring of Dennis's iron-tipped boots just behind her.

She sneaked a look at him from the corner of her eye. His hair was pressed flat today with water under his hat, but it did nothing to improve his appearance. His nose stuck straight out from between his eyebrows like a drayhorse. As for his clothes, there were badly matched cloth patches on the elbows of his coat, and even they were worn to a shine. She could not tell from his appearance whether he was trustworthy. She'd have to be nice to him, though, or he might snitch on them. Her stomach churned. Titus Ibbetson must have sent the constable, so he was still after them, just when she had thought they were safe. She glanced round, looking for Ibbetson's dark hat in amongst the crowd. Each time she saw someone of his weight and build she felt her heart batter against her ribs.

The notices were something she had not bargained on. They were certain to have a description on them or they would be useless else. She could dye her hair, they'd not recognize her from the notices then, but what on earth could she do about Sadie?

Dennis was still keeping pace with her when they arrived at Whitgift's sign. When they reached the gates, she frowned.

'Can I trust you?'

'I won't let on where you are, if that's what you mean.'

'Will you take this to someone who can read? I don't know nobody who can.' She handed him the folded notice.

'I'll see what I can do.'

'Make sure it's no one that knows us.'

'What do you take me for?'

'Thanks, Dennis.' She made an effort to smile. He touched his hat a little too obviously and gave a mock bow, before moving off towards the offices. Pray God Sadie was right and she could trust him.

She paused a moment to look up at the brand new sign hanging from its wrought-iron bracket. It was artfully and brightly

painted with a gilt-edged lily and a realistic-looking glass perfume bottle in front of an oriental fan. She admired it a moment
before turning sharp right and pushing open the side door with
its frosted glass panels, hearing the tinkle of the little bell as she
shut it behind her. The wave of heat from the banked-up fire was
almost solid.

'Miss Johnson. You're late. Quick, quick.' Mrs Horsefeather
fussed around her. 'The doors will be opened at the next strike of
the clock.'

Ella hung up her cloak and smoothed her skirts.

Mrs Horsefeather scowled at her and heaved herself round
the back of the counter, where she took a list from a drawer. 'Today's callers. Lady Ireton, the Honourable Misses Edgware – they
are quite spoilt by their father, make sure you show them everything – Miss Rokeby, and the Countess of Maine. The Countess
of Maine never buys anything. She's a title but no money. She's
just paying us a visit to be nosy. The husbands and fathers all
have business with Mr Whitgift Senior, so don't let the ladies
leave until you have persuaded the husbands to open their purses
in the warehouses.'

Ella nodded, trying to remember all the names.

'I shall be positioned in one of the chairs outside in the vesti-
bule,' went on Mrs Horsefeather. 'The gentlemen may wait there
for their wives and daughters. Servants to wait in the yard.'

The door tinkled again and a small barefoot girl came in,
nearly tripping over the rug as she stared in blank amazement at
her surroundings.

'This is Meg,' said Mrs Horsefeather. 'You need a girl by you
to mend the fire, fetch refreshments and take messages to the ost-
lers for the carriages.'

'Meg, this is Miss Johnson.' Meg bobbed her head.

Ella was cock-a-hoop. Her own servant! Never mind that Meg

was probably only eight or nine years old and looked barely able to lift a coal scuttle. She smiled at Meg broadly, then pressed her mouth into a more ladylike expression.

Meg seemed to be well trained for she was already trimming the wicks in the wall-sconces.

'Ah, listen. That's the first carriage now. I'll go and see who it is.' Mrs Horsefeather puffed out of the door.

Ella hastened over to the lacquered table and picked up a hand mirror to check her appearance again, even though she had only just done so. The mirror was a glass one, not a tin one, and gave a very clear image. It showed a pale oval face with wide-apart blue eyes. She pinched at her cheeks a little and patted her eyebrows.

'Yes, they are a little unruly.'

Ella jumped. Jay had come in unannounced. She quickly replaced the mirror on the table, face down, her face scarlet.

'In London, heavy eyebrows are the sign of a labouring man. Ladies usually pluck them, with iron tweezers, to make them lighter. You may wish to do the same.'

'Oh.' And then, realizing it was clearly an order and something more was expected of her, 'Yes, sir. Indeed I will.'

'Good. But it may wait. I came to bring you this.' He held out a small notebook. 'You will find the inkwell and pen in the top drawer of the counter.'

Ella reached out to take the book. 'Thank you, sir.'

'I want you to make notes. If anyone tells you they are to be away from home, or that their house is to be empty, I would like you to write down the dates.'

'I can remember them, sir, there won't be no need to write them down.'

'I prefer the information in writing. So that I can advise them to put their valuables in our cabinets for safe-keeping, of course.' He smiled and caught her eye.

She wondered whether she could ask Dennis to write them down for her, but realized that it would not work. Mr Whitgift would recognize his penmanship. There was nothing for it, she'd have to tell him. 'Sorry, sir, I can't.'

Jay frowned.

'I can't write, sir. Nor read, 'cept my name and common stuff like figures on coins and inches on a yardstick.'

Jay Whitgift tutted. Ella was crestfallen. She did not want to disappoint Jay. Hastening to reassure him, she said, 'But there's naught wrong with my memory. I can keep the dates up here – in my head.' She tapped her temple. 'I might not be able to write, but I've not got cloth between my ears. I'm that sharp I'm almost a danger to misself.'

'Is that so?' He seemed amused again. 'We'll see. I'll come by at the end of the day and we'll try a little test.'

He strode towards the door, but then turned and gave her a smile that made her so flustered she brushed down her skirts again and tried to look busy with some pots of marigold cream. Her mind was racing with excitement. He was going to come back later. She patted her hair to check it was still in place.

The main door tinkled and Mrs Horsefeather ushered in two young ladies in mantles and muslin caps. Their faces were porcelain-white and their hair curled stiffly at the side. They ignored their surroundings completely and came straight to the counter. The taller one said, 'We want some eyebright. And it says on the billboard you have a skin balm that removes freckles.' She dropped her fan on the counter with the lazy air of one who is used to being waited on. Ella presumed these to be the Misses Edgware, with the rich pa.

'Yes, lemon and rosemary,' said Ella, reaching under the counter for the flat-lidded dishes tied up with ribbon. 'And the belladonna is in these phials, with the dropper. Here, let me show you a sample.' She put on her best accent. 'Would you like to take some refreshment?'

'I'm not sure we—'

'Meg, fetch hot chocolate.'

To Ella's great satisfaction, Meg hastened away and returned a few minutes later staggering under a laden tray. By this time, the door had opened twice more and two other young ladies had arrived.

The Misses Edgware sat over to one side, where there was a row of comfortable chairs upholstered in horsehair and leather. They chattered in high-pitched giggles. The two other ladies seemed to know them and the four were soon engaged in a lively conversation about a forthcoming concert. Ella listened hard – so hard in fact that one of the girls caught sight of her and turned her back, indicating to the others with her outraged glance that they should lower their voices.

Ella did not care. She stuck out her chin and continued to listen as Jay had asked. She had overheard by this time that Jay was going to the concert. She had never been to a concert, but she knew that she had neither the right manners nor the right clothes. Concerts were not for the likes of her. But it was a hard thing to hear them talk about it and know that she would never be invited herself. And she looked sideways at the Misses Edgware with their slender necks and thin, bird-like faces, and hoped that Jay did not find them attractive.

He was right, though. All the ladies had very scant eyebrows, like a line of single hairs, where hers appeared to be rough, like a man's. She was embarrassed about this. Why had she not noticed it before? She saw too that the other ladies all had very white skin. When she showed them the lemon and rosemary balm her arms were dark and brawny next to their white flesh. Their blood seemed to run blue, too. She saw the fine pattern of veins when she turned their arms over to put the lavender on their wrists.

She was able to convince them to buy quite a few items before they left, blanchinette for their complexions and ruby-red lip madder. She loved piling up the ribboned packages in the brown paper and tying the string into a handle. And even more, she'liked shouting Meg's name and hearing her reply, 'Yes, miss.' Then she would hand Meg the parcel to take to the carriages whilst the lady customer drew on her rabbitskin gloves. By lunchtime, the wooden drawers were heavier to pull than before and the pile of coins satisfyingly deep.

After they left, she hurried upstairs and slathered a good quantity of the lemon and rosemary balm over her arms and face, rubbing it in well. The bell on the door went again and she had to rub hurriedly at her arms to get the greasy white stain to melt and disappear into her skin. The shop was busy. The bills of trade had attracted attention and quite a few callers had not sent word in advance. At one point, there were so many ladies in the room that Meg had to be sent over to the pop shop for more chairs, and the assortment of furniture got odder and more mismatched with every visitor.

Everyone seemed to want refreshment at once and little china bowls with their slops seemed to litter every surface. Mrs Horsefeather's creaking voice drifted in through the door as she tried to calm the gentlemen who were waiting outside. Ella could hear her saying, 'But, sir, no gentlemen are permitted in the Gilded Lily. Let me go and see if your wife is ready.' And her perspiring face would appear round the door mouthing, 'Lady Ireton. Your husband is waiting.' But Lady Ireton was not ready to leave until she had heard the end of the story about her neighbour and her black manservant, and so the gentlemen became more and more impatient.

In desperation, at five o'clock Mrs Horsefeather rang a bell, there was a last-minute flurry of purchases and everyone was finally persuaded to leave.

'My dear! What a day.' Mrs Horsefeather sank into a chair that seemed to exhale under her weight. 'In a minute I'll bag the takings. Just give me a moment to rest my feet.' She fanned herself with her hand.

'I'll see to it, Mrs Horsefeather.'

'No. Mr Whitgift was most particular that I should do it and tally it against the items sold. Have you ticked them off on the slates?' Ella had. It had given her a sort of pride to notch each purchase with chalk on the small slate next to its display. She was a little vexed he had not trusted her to do it. She might not be able to read, but she could count well enough.

She knew, for example, that the lavender water had sold so well it had nearly run out of the door. But then, that was not surprising, given that Londoners were the rankest, foulest-smelling people she had ever met. It must be the air. People did not smell so bad in Westmorland.

She watched Mrs Horsefeather gather up the slates and count the money.

'Please, ma'am, will that be all?' Meg's voice was almost a whisper.

'Oh Lord, are you still here,' said Mrs Horsefeather. 'Well, judging by today, I guess we will be needing you again tomorrow.'

'Should I take them chairs back?'

There was still a collection of odd chairs stuck in the middle of the room.

'No, just push them up against the wall,' said Mrs Horsefeather. They watched her lug them over and line them up.

'You may go,' said Ella imperiously, when she had stacked the last one. Then she turned back to place the chalk in the box on the cabinet. Meg left silently, like a ghost.

'Sit here.' Jay had pulled up two chairs next to the cooling embers of the fire. He patted one of them, and Ella sat down.

'So, tell me where the Misses Edgware live.'

Ella thought. They had not said where they lived.

'They didn't say, sir.'

'Not good enough. Try to think of anything they said that would lead you to deduce where they live.'

Ella thought. 'They said they would need to hire a carriage to take them to the concert, and that the concert was in St Giles, Holborn . . .'

'Better.'

'. . . and one of them said it would take a quarter-hour by carriage to get there,' she said, with growing excitement, 'so they must live a quarter-hour from St Giles.'

'What else?'

'One of them said that they would only be at home a few more weeks, and this would be the last outing in town before they went back to the country. Oh yes, their father has to return to his country seat in Kent.' Ella had found this phrase puzzling, so she had recalled it well.

'When? Did they say when?'

'Yes, the tenth of next month, they said. Yes, I'm sure I'm right.'

'Well done, Miss Johnson. The Edgware family will be most appreciative when I suggest they should lock away their valuables.'

Lock up their valuables, my foot. Ella was not sure if he really expected her to believe him, so she kept her innocent face pinned on and sat up straighter in her chair. He was pleased with her. She had done well to remember it all, like he said. He was smiling at her now and getting something out of his waistcoat.

He handed her a sixpenny token, pressing his fingers against hers, then closing her hand round it. She was slightly disgruntled to be tipped like any common servant, but she clasped it tight. Sixpence! The leather was warm, where it had been next to his chest. His hand held her closed fist, and his other hand settled over it. His touch sent a shiver through her. She did not dare move.

He leaned in and whispered, 'There'll be a few extra pennies every time you help me.' He squeezed her hand. 'But it is our secret.' She nodded. 'This is business. A man has to look out for his business. You understand?'

Ella looked up into his dark eyes. 'Oh yes, sir. I'll do what I can.'

'Then you will be here tomorrow evening again after the chambers close.' He released her hand. She withdrew it, but remained sitting.

She toyed with a curl that had escaped from the tightly wound coil at the back of her head. He watched her, and she blushed, the air seemed to grow thick and cloying. Behind her a clock ticked. She saw him press his teeth into his bottom lip.

'Will that be all, sir?'

'Yes. Yes.' His eyes dropped away. He stood up sharply. 'Mrs Horsefeather has cashed up?'

She nodded.

'Then I will see you tomorrow.' He brushed some imaginary dust off his cuffs and hurried out of the door.

Ella smiled to herself. He must think her wet behind the ears to believe all that about locking away their valuables. He was a charmer and no mistake. But she knew that trick. He knew how to get away with bending the truth, just as she did herself.

They were alike. He'd be a catch, that one, but she'd have to play him right, after all she was nobody and he was heir to all this. And if he had any sense at all he'd be looking to better himself with a marriage into a high-class family, maybes even a title, so it wouldn't be easy. But she knew she was right for him – they would understand each other. If ever there was one, a match with Jay Whitgift was definitely a prize worth shooting for.

She hurried up the stairs, pulled her old clothes off the chair and tied them in a bundle. She would not wear them again. She was a lady now, and would have to learn to dress and behave like one, if she was to compete with the frail and slender beauty of the Edgware sisters. And she had sixpence now towards a pair of gloves to protect her hands. Soon her chapped fingers would be soft and white, like the Misses Edgware, not rough and red like Sadie's.

Chapter 15

Titus Ibbetson pushed his wig further back on his head, exposing his pale freckled forehead. He had bought a second jug of ale and it sat in front of him. He had drunk most of it, but he prided himself on being able to hold his liquor. He looked disapprovingly at the table next to him where a group of untidy young men were raucous with drink. They were armed with short swords and one of them had scars cut into his forearm in the manner of a sailor. They eyed him covertly and whispered and laughed amongst themselves. He ignored them, frowning into his tankard. Why was it that men of such a class were always so ugly? He stared morosely at one of the men with protruding teeth and a complexion pitted by the pox, before pouring more ale.

He took a draught of the thin yeasty liquid. He needed a drink. He still could not come to terms with the fact that Thomas was dead. When he had lost the trail of the Appleby sisters he had gone back to Coventry to fetch Isobel, and then returned to Netherbarrow to see Thomas buried. A bleak occasion with few mourners and the wind like a blade, whipping round the headstones. Afterwards, everything was made more complicated by the fact that the gaol could no longer account for the whereabouts of Alice, Thomas's wife, and there was no will that they could lay hands on. There was delay after delay. The inefficiency of the Westmorland legal system when they could give him no answers and seemed to be doing nothing angered him even more.

In the meantime he had spent long days sorting through the remains of Thomas's things, hoping to find some clue as to where Ella Appleby might have gone. It had shaken him that there was hardly an item of value left. No coin, no silver. Thomas's watch was gone, and his gold seal. On their twenty-first birthday their father had given them matching seals – rubies, engraved with their initials – and though he turned out every drawer in the house looking for the seal, it was nowhere to be seen.

When he opened the closet to search through Thomas's pockets, it had given him a peculiar sensation – the clothes looked so much like his own. Except that his own were hung in neat rows. Thomas's clothes were bundled together as if they had been hurriedly thrust inside. His dark working suit, almost an exact replica of Titus's own, drooped off its hanger, his two Sunday outfits crammed one over the other dangled lopsidedly from the hook. His shoes were discarded in an untidy heap of unmatched pairs. A mound of dirty undergarments and shirts had been jammed into a drawer. When he opened it the stench made him retch. It took him aback. No woman had cared enough to make sure his house was in order. A lump came to his throat. That slattern of a housemaid must be responsible. He closed the drawer again, unable to bring himself to touch it.

He sat down on the bed, now stripped bare of its bedding, and stared into the closet. Unused for some time, by the look of it, were Thomas's bespoke riding boots, the black and tan leather polished to a high sheen, their wooden trees still inside. They were too good to waste. He dragged them out, removed the trees and levered them on. They were a perfect fit. The soles were hardly worn; Thomas must have been saving them for some special occasion. And now that occasion would never come. Christmas had been and gone without him. Titus stood in his brother's best boots and bit back the tears.

'Damn you to hell.' He spoke to no one in particular, but strode out of the house with the fire of it still stoking his belly. He rode away, digging those boots into the horse's flank until it was galloping and foam flew from its mouth.

Now he wore the boots all the time. He glanced down at them under the table. They were scuffed and muddy, but he would wear them out before he gave up looking for those girls.

He would recognize the girls again if he saw them. The younger one particularly. Even in the twilight in the filth of Bread Street he had seen that raw patch on her face, like a map stretched over her eye. If only he had been younger and fitter, he might have caught up with them, but they slipped out of sight, and finding them in the stews of London was like looking for a woodlouse on a ship.

Tracking down the Appleby sisters was going to take time, he realized, so in the end he had fetched Isobel and now he was prepared to stay in London for as long as it took. Thomas's cook, Mistress Tansy, had helped him make an inventory of what was missing from the house so he could trace any goods that might be Thomas's. He glanced at the next table. He supposed he'd better get on with it, even though these men looked like they hadn't a peck of common sense between them.

'You seen two girls round here? One with a port-wine stain on her face?'

The men looked up, but then ignored him and carried on their conversation. Aggrieved, he placed a newly printed notice on the table in front of them and, following it with a finger, began to read it to them.

'*Reward*,' he said loudly, '*for the apprehension of two savage sisters, serving maids, who on the 28th October last, did murder their employer in cold blood,* and so forth . . . *Furthermore, they stole a quantity of silver plate, jewellery and other items –'*

He checked to see that his audience were listening to him. 'Have you seen them? Two serving maids from the northern counties, one with a great red birthing-mark?'

The men shook their heads, suddenly ill-tempered. 'No. Never heard of them.'

'They've not been in here,' the pock-marked man said. 'We'd have seen them, sure we would. We're in here every night. Have you tried asking in the tannery? They was taking on girls not so long back.'

'Yes,' said another, 'and you could always ask at Old Fever-face's. She has nearly twenty girls in her shop.'

'Fever face?'

To Titus's irritation they laughed raucously, sharing the joke between themselves.

'This is a serious affair. You have a duty to help me,' said Titus, trying to establish some order, 'it is a matter of the law.' But the men ignored him again and carried on whispering and nudging each other.

Titus felt anger rise up inside his chest. Stupid feeble-minded drunks. He picked up their jug and slammed it down on the table, so the dregs sloshed out. The men jumped and sat upright. The sailor stood up, his fists out. 'Waste our good ale, would you? I'll teach you to waste our ale—'

'The hell you won't,' Titus said, springing to his feet. 'Tell me where I can find this Mrs Feverface. If you do not, I will send for the constable and have him clap you all in the cells for drunken behaviour.'

'Now just hold on a minute, mister.' The cellarman appeared from behind the bar.

The sailor made a lunge with his fist.

Titus dodged it. He was panting now, in a great rage. 'I have warned you.'

'Don't, Ted, he might mean it. We can't afford to fight with the likes of him.' One of the others staggered to his feet and placed a restraining hand on his friend's arm. 'It's the perruquier's, sir. Madame Lefevre. Under the sign of the wig stand, round the corner.'

With that Titus swung back his fist and slammed it straight into the sailor's face. His knuckles made a satisfying crunch against the man's nose. The man swayed and toppled. Titus felt as if there was quicksilver running through his veins. He stalked out of the door, hearing his own blood pounding in his ears.

Chapter 16

The next day Sadie waited again till Ella had left before creeping down the stairs, carrying her clogs in her hand, so that Dennis's mother, Widow Gowper, would not guess there were two girls and not one. She had got Ella dressed and ready in whispers. Otherwise, Dennis's ma might think the girl upstairs was touched in the head – talking to herself. Ella had told her to stay indoors, but Sadie was determined to ignore that, she needed to say good-bye to Corey and Pegeen. Corey had been good to her since Ella left, sitting next to her in their snap time, sharing her bit of bread when Sadie had none. If she got there early she might be able to talk to them before Madame Lefevre arrived, tell them she would not be coming back and not to ask questions.

Once outside, Sadie shook her head so her hair fell over her eye and pulled her hood well down over her face. As she hurried along, it seemed as if everyone was staring at her. She hugged the buildings, walking under the overhangs, darting in and out of the shadows. She said a silent prayer every time she heard footsteps behind her, her shoulders hunched in case any moment someone might spin her round and see the stain on her face that marked her out.

Outside the fruiterer's was a mounting block with a rail behind it and she stopped short. There was one of the notices tied to it with string. It flapped slightly in the wind, but she was sure it was the same as the one the constable had given Ella. The sight of it filled her with dread. As she passed, she grabbed for it and ripped it down, crumpling it under her cloak. By the time she reached the corner of Cheapside she had a thick wodge of paper balled in her hand. But she knew it would be nigh on impossible to take them all down.

What if Madame Lefevre had seen one of the notices and the constable was already lying in wait for her there? Her palms were sweating as she squeezed the pieces of paper together, looking to her right and left as she went down the street. Just before the turning into Friday Street she saw Corey hurrying along, her head bent low against the biting wind. She stuffed the ball of paper into a crack between some shop shutters.

Several other girls pushed past her on their way to the wig shop, bantering good-naturedly. Sadie hurried over to greet Corey.

'Mornin',' Corey said.

Sadie took hold of her arm. 'Come away, Corey. I'm after talking with you.'

'What's the matter?' Corey's eyes searched hers.

'I'm giving notice.'

'Let's get inside into the warm then you can tell me.'

'No, I'm not coming in.'

'But why? What's up?'

'I can't tell you, but I just wanted to—'

Something caught Sadie's eye and she looked up. It was Mercy Fletcher, bouncing down the street in her black bonnet, and with her was a loutish-looking Puritan lad in a black wide-brimmed hat, likely her brother, Jacob. His face was set in a scowl. Mercy caught sight of Sadie and something in the way she stared just a fraction too long made the hairs rise up on the back of Sadie's neck.

She knows, Sadie thought.

'Look, Corey, I have to go now,' she said, flustered, unhooking her arm from Corey's.

'Wait a minute, tell me—'

At that moment she saw Mercy point and Jacob pulled off his hat and broke into a run.

'Sorry—' Sadie turned on her heels and ran as fast as she could back up Friday Street. She heard Corey's shout – 'Sadie!' But she did not stop. The street was busy and there were crowds of young folk going down to the brewer's and the lime-burner's, in groups of two or three, arm in arm or gossiping together, and carts and drays with the morning milk, but they were all coming towards her and it was like swimming against the tide. Her hood fell back but she put her head down and one hand over her face and, thrusting through the chests of those coming the other way, kept running up Wood Street. When she thought her lungs would burst she stopped and turned, scanning above the carriages and crowds for the blond head of Jacob Fletcher. But there was no sign of him. She slumped back against the wall of the vintner's and wiped her forehead.

Ella was right. They were all looking for her now. A dread engulfed her. She hauled the hood back over her head and retreated into its gloom. She took the long way home, in and out of the back alleyways, like a wary fox, eyes skinned for Mercy and her brother.

When she got to Bread Street she paused again to check nobody was behind her, looking up and down the street. It felt faintly absurd, to be skulking like a criminal. It was only then it dawned on Sadie that in other people's eyes that's what they were, for they had done nothing but run since the day they left Netherbarrow.

She swung the front door open and pushed it shut behind her, leaning against it a moment as she realized she was shaking from head to foot. Her legs were trembling as she dragged her way back upstairs. She turned the key carefully in the padlock to open the door, lest it should chink and alert Ma Gowper.

When she closed it on the world behind her she lay down on the bed and listened to her heart beating, terrified they might have followed her home. Titus Ibbetson, the constable, or Mercy and Jacob Fletcher. And now those notices were up, who else might be out there looking for a girl with a face like hers? Outside, a horn sounded from one of the barges and, startled, she leapt up. When she realized what it was she lay down again, pulling the shawl close over her face like a comforter, stroking the rough texture of the darned patch with her fingers, smelling the wet wool of Westmorland. Eventually she slept.

When she woke up it was dark and for a moment she was disorientated; she had forgotten what day it was, even where she was. When she remembered, a new wave of fear washed over her and in a panic she felt for a rushlight and struck a flint, blowing on the burning tip of the wax until it flared then settled into a tiny flame. In its meagre glow she splashed her face with water from the pail, ran her fingers through her hair to tidy it. On the table the mirror winked, left lying there by Ella, surrounded by a scatter of bone hairpins.

She brought the candle over and looked at her reflection, turning the mirror this way and that. Whenever she did this, she felt a pang of disappointment. The face that stared back always seemed to be somehow different from what she thought she was, more ordinary. Just a thin-faced girl with mousy hair. Tonight in the eerie shadows her face just seemed a little darker on one side. It looked just like anyone's face, yet everyone made such a fuss about it. Folk stared at her, and when they talked to her their eyes scanned back and forth as if they could not decide which side of her face to look at. Ella used to tell her that the red mark was the spot where God had left his hand just a little too long and the heat of it had branded her. She said it was a secret sign and that it meant God was looking after her. Sadie had stopped believing the tale a long time ago, knew it to be just one of Ella's fantasies, but she wanted it to be true, wanted to feel that there was someone strong to rely on, to watch over her. She set the glass back on the table, face down.

The cacophony of bells from the local churches tolled six. From habit, Sadie began to gather up her cloak for the nightly wood-gathering. She put on the cloak, but it was a full fifteen minutes before she moved. Dare she go out? There was a little oatmeal left to make flatbreads and she badly needed the cheer and warmth of a fire. Recently the weather had turned bitter. She could see her breath. Already there was talk of beggars dying from the cold, their clothes frozen into the mud so they had to be prised away before they could be dumped outside the city gates. The ground was too cold to dig.

Besides, Ella would not be back yet. Come on, girl, she said to herself, it's a moonless night, best chance yet to get a few sticks. She mustered the courage to go outside. On the stairs she shivered, half from cold and half from fear.

'Is that you, Dennis?' A querulous voice drifted up from the hall. Sadie halted and listened, rooted to the spot. She heard no movement from the rooms downstairs. Dennis had said his ma was bedfast, thank goodness, so she would not come out to the hall. A whisper of air sucked in as she opened the front door.

Outside, the world smelt of mildew and water. The Thames slid by like a cold black snake, with scales of thin ice that parted and re-formed, never quite solidifying. It had frozen over once, they said, and become a solid white road, turning into its opposite overnight. They said that in Bess's reign horses and carriages drove over it, while the ice creaked and moaned like an old lady with an attack of the croup. And London came to a standstill, its throat cut, with no trade able to get in or out of the city.

Today it was alive with the black shadows of wherries and skiffs and looming barges with oilskin-covered loads. In the darkness their moving lights sometimes made the ice fragments glitter so that the river became momentarily enchanted, before descending again into watery gloom.

On the banks there were a few other dark figures scavenging. Sadie had a length of twine wrapped around her hand to tie up anything she might find. She tucked her skirts into her waistband and looked for any jagged shapes sticking out of the mud. She pulled out a few claggy pieces of driftwood and tied them together. When she stopped to recover and looked up, her breath stood in white ghosts before her.

Over by the bridge was a group of silhouettes all pulling at something. Curious, Sadie moved closer so she could see what they were doing. There was a lot of activity with shouting and people running hither and thither carrying off loads in their aprons. Sadie saw a woman dash past, her apron full of something black.

Coal. A barge must have spilt its load of coal. Three lads stood up to their waists in the icy water hauling out the heavy sacks from the sludge. They cursed and yelled at those on the shore who had slit open the sacks they had already landed and were making off with it whilst they watched, helpless, in the current. Sadie did not even have to think. She ran towards the group, her small bundle of sticks banging against her back. A small curly-haired boy in oversized boots was trying to drag one of the sacks away, but it still had too much coal in it to move easily and he struggled to shift it.

'Shares?' panted Sadie.

The boy nodded. Together they dragged the sack up the bank. An old woman hobbled after them and tried to get her hands into the sack as they towed it by, but the lad kicked out at her legs until she tripped and skidded in the mud, tumbling away down the bank.

The boy was wiry and determined. She let him lead her, like a terrier dragging a hare. Hiding behind the shelter of a boathouse wall, they stopped and silently divvied up. A light spilled out of the tavern further up the street giving them just enough light to see by. The boy had a small pallet waiting there with strapped-on wheels. It was already loaded with a fish crate half full of sticks and rags, as well as a collection of metal horseshoes, clog irons and wheel bands. They shook half the coal into the crate, looking behind them all the while lest someone should hear and take it off them. That left Sadie with the sack, which was about quarter full.

The boy stuck out his hand. Sadie smiled and took it. He looked up at her, a gap-toothed grin splitting his face before it was replaced with a sudden look of puzzlement. Oh mercy. She had forgotten about her face. In a flash Sadie covered her head again with her hood. He had seen it. She wordlessly shouldered the bag of coal and hurried away.

She kept hobbling as best she could until the end of their street, where she stopped and put the load down for a breather, scanning behind her before turning into the blind alley. There was no sign of the boy, or anyone else. She broke into a half-run again, anxious to get safely indoors. She dumped the coal and sticks by the door and eased it open.

'Dennis?'

Blast. Ma Gowper had heard her again. She must have sharp

ears – she seemed to be able to hear a needle drop. Sadie paused, keeping still. The tap of footsteps behind her.

'Sadie?'

She whipped round to see Ella coming up behind her.

'Hush.' Sadie put her fingers to her lips.

Ella grasped Sadie's shoulders and shook her. 'What are you about? I said to stay indoors. You're too easy to get a fix on.'

'Sshh.' Sadie indicated the Gowpers' door. 'She's awake.'

'Good evening, Widow Gowper,' called Ella loudly. 'It's only me, Miss Johnson. Dennis will be along shortly.'

'Who's that with you? And what's with all the racket?' shouted Ma Gowper.

'No one, just me.'

'Come along in then, won't you, and give me the time of day.'

Ella raised her eyebrows. 'Upstairs,' she mouthed, before entering the Gowpers' rooms. A waft of stale urine filled the hall.

Sadie left her clogs at the bottom and carried her load up the narrow staircase. Even though she trod carefully, the sticks crackled against each other and the coal rattled in the sack. Ella's face appeared again from the door and glared up at her.

'There's nobody there, Widow Gowper, it's just the wind,' Sadie heard her call.

At the door to their room Sadie gently put down the coal and struggled to get the key out of her bodice, but stopped short. The padlock was twisted and hung loose on its haft. She touched it, not believing what she was seeing. Worried now, she unhooked it and stood for a moment with its weight in her hand. It would take a jemmy or a crowbar to do this. But she had only been gone a half-hour, maybe a little more.

She put her ear to the door. Nothing. She was dimly aware of Mrs Gowper's voice, below, 'What? What?' and Ella's high-pitched voice in reply. But not a sound from the room. She pushed the door gently with one hand, preparing to run. It swung open and she peered into the darkness. She let out her breath. There was no one there. Gingerly she stepped over the threshold, as if entering someone else's territory. As she made her way to the rush box to fetch a light, her feet encountered objects on the floor that shouldn't be there. She lit the light.

The room was untidy as if someone had left in a hurry. The bedclothes had been thrown off, the shelves emptied, and the one remaining basket was upside down, its contents strewn on the floor. Sadie picked it up and righted it. She knew already what she would find. There was no sign of the candlesticks, or the fan, or the silver punch ladle. They were gone, as she had known they would be the instant she had stepped into the room.

Ella's red shape appeared at the door.

'What are you thinking of, making such a racket?' she whispered. 'Mrs Gowper says there's been noises from up here –' she stopped mid-sentence, taking in the scene in front of her – 'since the last church bells,' she tailed off lamely. 'Sadie, what've you done?'

'We've been robbed,' said Sadie in a tight voice, folding up a blanket.

'What?' Ella seemed unable to grasp it.

'Someone battered the lock.'

'Who?'

'Well, how should I know? They didn't leave a calling card, if that's what you mean.' A picture of Mercy and her brother came into her mind. 'Whoever they were, they must've been dead quiet to get past her.' She pointed at the stairs.

Ella took another step into the room, but stood looking round helplessly.

'Come on, help me get things straight so's we know what's gone,' said Sadie.

'The fan . . . the candlesticks, the—?'

'Gone. There's not a stick left. Come on. Help me.'

Ella followed at Sadie's shoulder and plied her with questions. 'What made you go out? I said not to go out.'

Sadie ignored her and continued to pick things up from the floor.

'Did you go out to give notice at the wig shop? Sadie. Look at me. Why were you running when I got home? I said not to go out. And now this happens. Did anyone see you?'

'It could be Da,' Sadie said.

'No,' Ella said. 'For God's sake, will you forget about him. I'd know if he'd been here. I'd smell him. He would have waited as well, to see if he could get anything else off us. You know it's not Da. Did you tell Dennis what we'd got in here? You didn't, did you?'

Sadie shook her head.

'Did you tell Dennis?'

'Course not. Anyroad, it wouldn't be him.'

'I know. He's been at Whitgift's. But he might've told someone else. Gold's got a mouth on it once someone knows.'

'I didn't tell anyone.'

'Well, we can't exactly call the constable, can we?'

Sadie put the broken platter she was holding on the table and sat down, giving Ella her full attention. Her voice wavered as she spoke. 'What'll we do?'

Ella was pacing the room. 'Ma Gowper kept saying there was noises, but I thought she meant you. Why did you go out? We agreed. You weren't to go out. Not now them notices are up. It's too risky. What were you about?' Her eyes were accusing.

'I went scouting for wood. We'll freeze else. It were dark. Too dark for anyone to see me.' Her thoughts went back to Mercy's pointing finger as she ran down the street, and then to the look on the scavenger boy's face. She pushed the thoughts away. 'But

I had a stroke of luck,' she went on, 'I got coal. So's we can have a fire and a hot supper for once.' Sadie pointed to the door. 'The sack's there. There's kindling too.'

Ella sat down. 'Never mind the bloody kindling, we've just been robbed. That gold seal?'

Sadie nodded, biting her lip. She did not want to look at Ella.

'If they find out where that came from, we're in trouble. It's got his initials on it. He showed me. His twin brother will be looking out for it.'

'I know. I'm not daft. That's why I wanted to get rid before.'

'No. That's why I hung on to it. So's he couldn't trace it.'

Sadie raised her eyes. 'Too late now, anyways.'

She stood and went to the window. She was surprised how much all the objects had meant to them, and how quickly they had come to regard them as 'theirs' even though she knew full well where they had come from. Every now and then Ella would look up and ask, 'The snuffbox?', 'The mirror?' and Sadie would nod. Then there would be silence whilst they remembered the look and feel of the missing thing. Their small hoard had represented their future, the hope of better things ahead and their insurance against hunger and cold. They felt naked without them. And it was unsettling to think a stranger had been in their room. Sadie shivered to think of some unknown man's hands picking over her clothes, searching in their cupboards, seeing all their secrets.

The mirror particularly seemed to upset Ella.

'How'm I going to keep on at Whitgift's with no mirror?'

'I can tell you how you look.'

'Don't be stupid. It's not the same. We'll have to get another.'

'After we get a new candlestick. I can't sew with no light.'

'No, before. Because if I lose my position, we won't be able to afford anything else.'

'How long is it again till you get paid?'

Ella glared at her. They both knew the answer anyway. Ella turned away and drew her purse out of her bodice. She was about to open it, but then saw Sadie looking and pushed it back inside.

'How much you got?' Sadie asked.

'Three shilling, that's all,' Ella said quickly, fiddling with the drawstring round her neck.

'Just about enough for a new lock. A stronger one. Shall I light the fire?'

'Suppose so.' Ella went to the cupboard. 'Hey, will you look at that! They've even thieved our barley and cheese, and the bit of whey. Bloody jug's gone too.'

Sadie went and peered over Ella's shoulder. 'They must've been hungry.' A thought came to her. 'Bet it was those lads. The ones that were kicking that dog. They saw us bringing our load in here that first day. They looked hungry enough, they fair fell on your apron when you said it had bread in it.'

'The thieving beggars, they've even stolen our supper.' Then, more accusingly, 'They must have watched for you to go out.'

'There's a peck of oatmeal left. They can't have been that hungry 'cos they didn't take that.'

'I've a good mind to go after them,' Ella said, but she stayed where she was.

'And what would you do? We can't do aught. We stole the stuff ourselves.'

They lit a fire but it was a subdued meal, despite the heat. Sadie pushed on extra coal, as if to make up for what they'd lost. The room glowed in the light. But Ella sat away from the fire in case she should get smuts or ash on her fine new dress. She shielded her face from the heat with her hands.

Sadie handed her a plate. 'Why are you covering your eyes?'

'Because I don't want my face to be red tomorrow. Well-to-do ladies have very white skin. The Misses Edgware are white as milk.' She looked up at Sadie, the ghost of an apology in her eyes.

Sadie bridled. 'Maybe their rooms are not so draughty. You'll catch a chill sitting over there in that thin dress. Come in a bit and get cosy. Look, it's making my skirts steam.' Sadie wafted her grey woollen petticoat up and down.

But Ella remained resolutely away from the fire. Sadie cooked, tossing the flat cakes on the griddle plate, then flipping them deftly onto a cloth on the floor.

She wrapped the cloth round the cake and passed it to Ella.

'This is better'n bread and scrape, isn't it just,' said Sadie, biting into hers.

Ella looked at the plate sitting on her lap with distaste. She placed it on the floor untouched with a sigh that was meant to be heard. She was obviously still sore at her for going out. 'I had a muffin at Whitgift's,' she said.

'Really? You beggar. Did you not think to save me a bit?' asked Sadie.

'No, I was that thrang I didn't have time to think. Anyways, I don't think they'd like me taking stuff off the premises. It would be like stealing.'

Sadie contemplated this strange contradiction. Her heart was still beating faster than usual from the thought of someone taking their things. They'd been outraged to be robbed, but it was of no earthly use to tell anyone, not when they'd thieved the stuff themselves. And now here was Ella reluctant to bring home a bit of bread from Whitgift's.

'It would only be a morsel. Bet they could spare it. Try and bring me a bit next time?'

Ella nodded, but Sadie could see there was no intention

behind it. Ella seemed to be distracted, as if she were not there in the room but somewhere else. She kneaded the red silk in her hand, balling it and letting it go, over and over.

At length she turned to Sadie and said, 'Them goods can be traced easily if they're sold all of a piece. That seal's got his initials on. And they think I killed him.'

'It's not true.'

'Course it's not true. But when they find us we're done for. You do know that, don't you?'

Sadie did not answer. She pushed the poker into the fire, and the wood crackled and spat.

Chapter 17

⌐◦⦁⦁⦁◦¬

In Whitgift's Yard, the Gilded Lily had been open little more than a week, and it was thriving. A long cavalcade of gigs and carriages drew up every day, and the newly swept yard bustled with ladies coming and going on their little heels. Jay's father, Walt, was in his office, measuring some coin. He looked up from his magnifying lens and calipers. There was a commotion outside in the street, with posthorns blaring and horses whinnying.

He rubbed his hand over the dusty windowpane but it looked over the back wall towards the river and he couldn't see anything amiss. When the hullabaloo continued, he stood up and rubbed his aching back and, disgruntled at being disturbed, threaded his way through the warehouses. At the threshold to the yard he stopped. The yard was jammed with horses and carriages attempting to leave, but a gig was trying to press through the gates, preventing them. Walt hurried over to remonstrate with the driver, but when he got there the whole street was full of horses and carriages. And they all seemed to want to come into his yard. His mouth fell open. He stepped back inside, his eyes searching the throng.

'Jay!' he shouted, craning to see him above the moving sea of horses. He caught sight of Dennis, trying to persuade a driver to rein back his pair of greys.

'Where's Jay?' shouted Walt.

'Upstairs. In his chambers.'

'What's all this?'

'Jay's ladies, sir. Come to the Gilded Lily.'

'What?'

'Over there. In the old dairy. Where the new sign is.'

Walt looked vaguely around the yard. Dennis took hold of his shoulders and turned him round, pointing over the horses' heads to the gaudily painted sign. Walt set his jaw and forced his way through the jostling horses. He ignored the sign on the door that said 'Ladies Only' and shoved it open with a great push. Within a few moments he was hobbling back across the yard.

A moment later, when his father entered his attic chambers, Jay had the box of cameos out and was in so deep a trance that the sudden opening of the downstairs door made him shoot up out of his chair. In a trice he loped down the stairs to arrive just as his father had his foot on the bottom step.

'Don't come up, Pa,' he said.

'Come with me,' barked Walt, his face grey, bustling him out of the door.

Jay resisted. 'Hang fire. The brooches – I need to lock them away.'

'Later. First you'll sort out this mess.' Walt pointed to the packed yard, where a coachman was just baring his fists and a crowd was gathering, spoiling for a fight. 'Get those carriages out, then we'll talk.'

Jay looked out, amazed. Then he grinned. The coachman could take his chances. What a crowd! His idea was working. Why, there must be half of fashionable London here. He swaggered into the press of conveyances, nimbly manoeuvred himself past a sidestepping horse and dodged out of the gates. He strolled past the queue of carriages down the length of the street until he came to the last one. Apologizing profusely to the lady occupant and her maidservant, he told her that the Gilded Lily could be visited by appointment only, and instructed the driver to turn around. Proceeding thus up the line of carriages, Jay soon was able to free passage for those trying to exit the gates.

It had done him no harm to turn people away, he knew. It would just whet their appetites further. The more popular it was, the more exclusive he could make it. And when he had spoken earlier with the new girl, she had told him the book was full for three more days. She was sharp, that one, she'd picked up the ropes in no time. She was good for business too – the women envied her pearly complexion, so the apothecary's creams had flown off the shelf. It was all a lot of quackery he knew. Upper-class women were generally stupid, couldn't see a blind if it waved a stick at them, and he was right, they couldn't keep their mouths shut. Already he was reaping the benefit; they would be surprised to find out he had information about not only what new gimcrack their husbands had purchased, but also its value and even sometimes where it was kept.

Miss Johnson could be moulded into an asset – with her brows plucked and a little alabaster powder over her bosom, she could look picture-perfect. That is, so long as she was prepared to play his game. Trouble was – they always got meddlesome in the end, wanted to know more than was good for them.

Jay's musings were short-lived. As he approached the warehouse, he could see his father's bent figure waiting for him, his face sour.

'It's a circus,' said his father, leading him into his office. 'I told you before, we'll have no dealings with women's business. When I'm gone, you can do what you like, but I'll not have it.'

'But we've turned over nineteen pounds in less than a week's trade, and that can't be bad. Just give it time to settle.'

'Settle? Settle you say? I'll never live it down. It looks like a strumpet fair – all that gilt, that brazen girl in scarlet with her hair coming down. You can't tell me it's a respectable business. It stinks like a midden.'

'But I'll wager the gentlemen have stayed longer in the warehouse . . .' His father did not answer, but from his expression Jay could see that they had. 'They have, haven't they?' His father opened his mouth to protest, but Jay pressed on. 'And I'll bet your takings are up too. Show us the figures, Pa, come on.'

Jay riffled through the papers on the desk looking for the big leather ledger showing the day's accounts.

'Leave it be!' his father shouted. 'I don't dare ask you where the money came from for all that show and tackle. There'll be time enough for you to juggle with the figures when I'm cold and gone. You're not cock o' the roost yet. But for now you will repay me if there's even a single farthing down. Those rooms are to be closed today. Do you hear?'

Jay frowned and stuck out his chin. 'I can't. We've appointments booked till the end of the week.'

'If you don't want to abide by my rules, then by heaven you don't have to stay under my roof.'

'What about the appointments?'

'Cancel them.'

Jay took out a leather pocket book and pulled his finger down the page. 'Let's see . . . yes, Thursday is Lady Waltham, and Lady Jane, you know, Sir John Bickford's wife. Friday is Miss Lucie Almoner, and Miss Catherine Holmes, milliners to the queen . . . I suppose there would be time to send a message . . .' He paused to see if his words were having any effect.

His father sat down heavily in his captain's chair and swivelled it round with a creak so he had his back to Jay. Jay stood fast, letting the names sink in.

At length his father sighed. 'Well, I suppose you had better honour these few appointments. But no more. There's a deal goes on around here that I don't know about, and I'm telling you, I don't like it. I'm not beyond putting you out to make your own way. A son should have respect and do his duty by his parents, and well you know it.'

'Quite right.'

Jay turned at the voice behind him, and saw that Tindall had appeared in the doorway. He looked as odious as ever, his cuffs grey and his eyes watery above his hooked nose. Jay glared at him. What right had he to just walk in on their private conversation? But his father turned back in his chair and beckoned him into the room.

'Ah, Tindall, my friend,' said his father, 'just the man. You can help solve a little problem we have. I need advice. Maybes you can tell us whether this new-fangled idea of Jay's has any firepower in it or whether it's a damp fuse.'

'Yes, I'd noticed the increase in activity. I told you the sign would be a good idea. But it's "painted lily", the Shakespeare quotation, not "gilded lily".'

'I don't care if it's a daffydilly, will it be good for business?' Walt said.

Tindall took a piece of paper from his moth-eaten leather bag, and a piece of lead. 'You'll need to tell me the day you first conceived it, the exact time, if possible, and the precise time you opened the door for business.'

'I don't know. I can't remember when I thought of it,' Jay said.

Tindall tutted and looked to his father.

'Then you'd better think on,' said his father. 'I trust Nat's judgement. He's always spot on. So if he says it's right, then I'll give you six months. If not then I'll tear that wretched papering down myself if I have to.'

The next day, Jay humoured his father by giving him the dates he asked for. When he dropped the parchment on the desk in front of him, his father had smiled and rubbed his hands together as if it had been a royal writ. Gullible old fool. Astrology was a dead end. The only way to make a fortune was through your own craft and cunning, and knowing the right people in society. By the time he was thirty he wanted that big house in Whitehall he'd set his sights on, and a baronetcy to go with it.

Jay walked across the yard to check on the Gilded Lily. He hoped the dates he gave Tindall were auspicious, it would be less trouble if they were. He didn't want to argue with his father and lose the business he had been grooming for so long. There were rumours that the king was to grant a dispensation to pawnbrokers, and the millwheel of his father's ramshackle yard could be sold on for a pretty penny as soon as he did. Meanwhile, he could build up his collections, hive off the most appealing trinkets ready for his new house and offer judicious loans to gentlemen in hard times who would pay him a fine fee. As for his future in the stars – it was all nonsense. Old ideas that should have died with the old king. But he sensed trouble – he suspected that Tindall would say the stars were opposed to the Gilded Lily just to put the wind up his father.

Sometimes when he saw his father crouching at his desk, his papery skin stretched over his dome-like skull, he wished he would get on with it and die. Once or twice it had even crossed his mind that he might hire Stevyn Lutch to do the deed for him. But so far, he had been too squeamish. And his father deserved a gentler end than that, the old fool. Besides, he did not want to risk the taint of blood anywhere near him. Too many people he knew had ended up on the triple cross at Tyburn.

He opened the door to the Gilded Lily and inhaled the slightly sickly smell of face powder. As he passed the counter he straightened the row of neatly labelled bottles of lily-of-the-valley and stood the evergreens up more stiffly in the vase. Miss Johnson was leaning over the counter showing some velveteen patches to a lady in a broad-brimmed hat. Miss Johnson was wearing a patch herself, on her cheekbone. Her face was very white and she had plucked her eyebrows. Her breasts rose and fell as she talked; she waved her hands in little expressive gestures, like a fluttering moth. Her features were animated. The ceruse would soon crack if she carried on like that. He hoped she was listening as well as she was talking.

He went straight upstairs to the attic above and sat on the bed. A routine had become quickly established. She knew now that if he came in, she should go up straight away. He heard her footsteps clatter on the stairs. She launched straight in with a breathless report on the young woman in the hat.

'Her father's come in to get his carriage clock out of hock. He's won a wager with his brother, over a bantam fight. She says the clock sits on top of the spice cupboard,' she puffed. 'Fancy that!' She suddenly remembered to lower her voice. 'You'd best be telling him that don't sound like a fitting place.'

'Good. Anything else?'

'No. Not that I can think of.'

'What about that brooch she had pinning her cloak?'

'I don't know, I didn't notice.'

'Diamonds, with a drop pearl. I pay you to notice these things, Miss Johnson. Next time, be more observant.'

'Sorry, sir.' He saw with satisfaction that she was deflated.

'Her address, Miss Johnson. We'll need her address to send our handbill.'

'Oh yes, that's easy,' she said, brightening. 'I've got a ledger, like a visitors' book. Mrs Horsefeather fetched it for me. I get them all to write in it afore they go, those that can, with their name and where they live. They likes to see who else has been in, and when they ask I tell them what the others bought.' She smiled. 'Well, truth be told, I tells them they've bought the dearest goods, so that will push them to buy.'

'Miss Johnson, that is very well done. And might I say that the powder and patch become you. Though it finishes a little abruptly. It is permitted for you to take more powder for your . . .' He patted his finger lightly on her chest.

She blushed, a flush that was visible only on her neck, which became inflamed with colour. He stepped away, brushing his hand down his coat. He did not like the thought of Miss Johnson's blood rising to the surface of her skin.

She looked confused and lowered her gaze to the ground.

'You may return to your customer now, Miss Johnson,' he snapped.

'Yes, sir,' she said, and hastened away.

He must send her for some more suitable footwear. The noise of her wooden soles gave away her background.

As she went, he heard someone else coming up the stairs and muffled exchanges of apology as they passed each other. He went to the landing to see who it was. It was Foxy Foxall.

'Was that her? The girl?' he asked.

'Yes, it was. What are you doing in here? It's ladies only.'

'She don't look bad. But I bet she's still a bit rough round the edges to be set up here, with your kind of folk. Her feet don't half make a clatter.'

Jay found himself on the defensive. 'I'm employing the girl, not marrying her. She's forward enough to make a sale, and she's biddable enough that I can mould her manners.'

'Biddable, is she?' Foxy looked relieved.

'She's given us some addresses, and the dates the occupants are out of town. It's working like a dream, just as I said it would. Tell Lutch your next job will be on the fourteenth. If all goes to plan, next outing will be Friday. The Rowlands' house in Ham. The family are attending a concert I'm inviting them to. There'll be servants about. But the house is a large one by the river, and by eight of the clock the first floor should be empty. You can get there by boat. Go for the ladies' jewellery. In particular, there's a gold cartouche with a sentimental inscription on it from the husband. The girl told me she was wearing it when she came in yesterday. When it ends up here, they'll pay over the odds to buy it back – oh, and anything else small and valuable – those new-fangled tea caddies, silverware, porcelain, the usual.'

'Remind me never to dine with you,' Foxy said, with a grin.

'I'd never invite you, that is, unless you had the Crown Jewels.'

'Huh. Next on your list, are they?'

'So?' Jay raised his eyebrows in question.

'We've got our hands on that book you were after. The calf-skin diary.'

Jay held out his hands but Foxy slipped his own hands into his pocket and shook his head.

'No, I didn't bring it with me. Lutch has it put safe by.'

'Why did you not bring it?'

Foxy shifted his weight uncomfortably. 'Thing is, we reckoned it might be worth more than you're telling. Being that you're so keen to have it, like. And we thought it best to protect ourselves. We're thinking on having it read.'

'What are you saying?'

'Well, if our names are in it, we need to know.'

'Do you think I don't know that? We're all in this predicament together, aren't we? Once it's in my hands it'll be safe with me.'

'It's awkward. You could put the press on Allsop, and if he don't play ball, you could sell it on, and we don't want that. Not if it has our names in it. We need a bit of warranty, so it seems to me safest we hang on to it till we've had it read. If we're clean, then we'll pass it on to you, but if any business is to be done with Allsop, then we'll expect a decent cut.'

'We've had this out before, Foxy. We made an agreement. Seven per cent.'

'It was eight,' Foxy said sharply. 'Happen we'll go to the gent ourselves, and do our own deals.'

'If you do that, then a little bird might tweet about your activities,' Jay said. Seeing Foxy's face darken and his mouth open to protest, Jay carried on. 'I'll send word to Allsop today. Come back tomorrow, Foxy. And next time bring the book. Haven't I always done right by you?'

'Maybe, and maybe not. But times is hard now, right enough, and a man's got to look to his own.' Foxy squared his shoulders. 'I'll be on my way. Lutch and I will drop by at lighting-up time tomorrow. Right?'

'Tomorrow it is,' nodded Jay. He watched Foxy leave, with an uneasy feeling. Something was out of kilter. He did not want to bargain under the looming presence of Lutch. And anyway, it should be him setting the times, not Foxy Foxall.

Ella pulled absently at the lace on her cuffs; she was on tenterhooks. The notices were up everywhere. She recognized the words at the top of the bill now. *Savage Sisters*, it said. Dennis had asked the curate at St Margaret's to read it for him. Earlier, Mrs Horsefeather had been disgruntled when Dennis had called at the Gilded Lily door to speak with Ella.

'I've had it read,' he said, 'and it don't look good.'

'What? What does it say?'

'At the top it's got the words *Savage Sisters* in great big letters. He's offering fifty pounds reward.'

Fifty pounds. Ella's heart fell. 'Does it say what we look like?'

'Not half. It gives a good description.'

'Does it say about Sadie's face?'

'It says you robbed and murdered Thomas Ibbetson. Curate told me it said he was a "squire of gentle manners and good standing".'

'It's a lie. I'm telling you, we just took a few bits and pieces, that's all.'

'Well, there's one of them notices pinned up on the *Si Quis* door of St Paul's – saw it this morning, so look after your sister.' He had stared at her then as if she were some curio from a sideshow. 'I'm not sure what to make of you,' he said.

'Naught,' she said. 'Unless you're after claiming that reward.'

'Course not,' he said. 'You trust me, don't you?'

She was forced to nod and smile at him then, until she was interrupted by Mrs Horsefeather's disapproving cough from behind, whereupon she had turned her back and gone inside with her head held high.

After that she fretted every moment about the notices. It confirmed her worst fears: Titus Ibbetson had not given up looking for them, even after all these weeks. Ella had not forgotten the look of fire in his eyes when he had caught up with them in Bread Street. The memory of him was odd, as if he were somehow her own Thomas turned evil against her. And what if Jay were to read one of the notices and remember her sister from the wig shop? He'd soon put two and two together. Whenever the doorbell tinkled, Ella looked to the door in a panic, but so far it had just been well-turned-out ladies and their dowdy chaperones, eyes greedy for potions, patches and paint.

Later in the afternoon she had nearly bolted out of her skin when a redheaded man came in. He'd come in when she was up-stairs, but she heard the door go as she was on the landing and she had paused mid-step, her heart in her mouth. Next moment he was halfway up the stairs to the storeroom. He must be a cheeky cobber to ignore the 'Ladies Only' sign – or most likely couldn't read. She'd tried to stop him as he passed, but he introduced him-self as Mr Foxall and said Jay knew him well and would let him up.

She wondered what he wanted, but warmed at the thought of Jay's approval that she had let him by. Not that she could have stopped him, anyroad. The redheaded man didn't look the type Jay would give time to, though – too rough. But he hadn't left yet, so they must be doing some business.

Her thoughts swung back to Jay. Even when she wasn't think-ing of him, his presence seemed to shadow everything she did. She said his name to herself under her breath, though she was ever careful to call him Mr Whitgift to his face. Ella Whitgift. It sounded fine, like a proper lady. Johnson was too plain, and Appleby reminded her too much of orchards and Westmorland. She could not rid herself of his image, which bit into her thoughts the way frost gradually creeps over glass, its ferny patterns ob-scuring the view.

She replayed their last meeting. He had praised her, hadn't he? And she could still feel the spot on her chest where his finger had lingered, a slight warmth on her cold skin. She hoped he had not noticed her blushes, and she recalled how he had pulled his hand away like he shouldn't have touched her. Perhaps he did not want to offend her, and this thought, that he might be considering her feelings, brought another rush of heat so that she had to pat her brow with the back of her hand. Though she was embarrassed that he had said her powder stopped too short; her front would be powdered more thoroughly next time she saw him.

'Are you awake, girl?'

She jumped to attention and fixed a smile to her face.

'Give me a sample of that.' An elderly woman in a dark green suit pointed to the row of pots behind her and Ella absent-mindedly passed her a jar of marigold cream. Another customer was tapping her fingers impatiently on the counter. The elderly woman gave Ella a sharp look and raised her eyebrows at the woman who was waiting. She pursed her mouth and swept up the jar, and both women crossed over to the mirror where two more of their crab-faced cronies were already peering disconsolately at their creased reflections and trying to tease their greying hair into side curls.

Ella listened out for Jay coming downstairs. She had been certain he found her attractive; after all, he had come back to the perruquier's and asked for her on purpose, hadn't he? When they had been upstairs earlier, it had all been proceeding beautifully. She thought he might embrace her, but then she had caught the sudden retreat in his eyes. She did not like it when he blew hot and cold like that.

Footsteps on the stairs made her look up, with a ready smile on her lips, but it was the male visitor who came down first, hurrying by with his cap in his hand and his gingery head down, as if afraid the ladies might bite him.

Ella tucked a stray strand of hair behind her ear and came out from behind the counter. But Jay passed by frowning, as if intent on his own thoughts, and he merely glanced at her distractedly as he passed, without even a nod. Ella watched his tall frame go, admiring the swing of his navy coat, the length of his stride. He cut a fine figure in his dazzling white lace neckerchief and flowing cuffs; her heart constricted with longing. Thomas Ibbetson had been portly and solid, full of aches and pains, not like this handsome young man at all.

Shortly afterwards the last of the cluster of customers left, and Ella hurried upstairs, a porcelain pot in her hand. A glance into the yard showed two carriages leaving, and no new arrivals. She stood in the centre of the room. It was silent. She walked over to the bed. There was a slight pressure mark where Jay had sat down, the cover was a little ruckled. Ella ran her hand over it, but did not straighten it. Her fingers lingered there a moment on the warmth of where he had been sitting.

She opened the pot and trailed her fingers into the cool white cream. Slowly she smoothed the white over her collarbone and further down over her breasts. She picked up the hand mirror. Her skin bloomed white under her moving touch. As she watched, the backs of her hands appeared brown next to her white bosom, as if they did not belong to her. For a moment she imagined these were Jay's hands slowly caressing her, and her lips parted. She would have him – him and his warehouse empire. He had worked his way up from the gutter, same as she – it was the perfect match. No matter what it took, she would be Ella Whitgift.

She surveyed herself with satisfaction, her skin bloomed pale as the moon. She wondered whether the pearly cream would be heavy enough to make Sadie's face white too, and hide the red stain underneath. Well, she would take it home and try it on Sadie's face tonight. Nobody would know if she slipped the pot into her basket when she left.

Chapter 18

When Sadie heard the noise of the door latch, she patted down her skirts, half hoping that the friendly lad from downstairs might come upstairs again. But then she chided herself. Why would he do that? He had taken the rent money already, so there was no good excuse for him to come up. She heard the door into Widow Gowper's chambers opening and let out a small sigh. The room was neat as a pin, the empty shelf scrubbed clean. In a rush of enthusiasm she had spring-cleaned the whole of their lodgings for something to do, not that you could call it 'spring'-cleaning in the freezing sleet of the last few days. She had washed and combed her hair. He seemed good-hearted, the landlady's son, it would have been nice to have a little company. She missed listening to the banter in the wig shop already, any small noise echoed in the room – after the perruquier's it was just too quiet.

She had tacked the curtain across the window and lit a fire ready for Ella coming home. A bundle of rushes from the store cupboard lay on the table. When the fat was melted she dipped the rushes in one at a time, twirling them so they were well coated before leaving them standing in a ewer to set. Might as well make a goodly stock – Ella seemed to want to burn more and more. It was extravagant, this sudden need for light. It was almost as if Ella was afraid of the dark. First thing she asked for when she came in from the Lily was always more light.

She had made about a dozen rushlights when she heard his footsteps on the stairs. She knew it was not Ella because of the heaviness of the tread, but she was still surprised to hear a polite knock on the door. She smoothed her hair and went to open it. It was him. She smiled and waited.

His hands were full of white pamphlets. He struggled to pull out something from amongst them. 'The rent agreement,' he said. 'Ma likes to know what's what, so one of you will have to make your sign on here.' He waved a folded parchment.

'Best be my sister then, she's the eldest and she can make a better sign.'

'Today's the twenty-sixth, isn't it. Your birthday. See, I remembered.'

She smiled; she had forgotten all about it.

'Many happy returns of this day,' he said in a strangely formal tone. 'I've brought you a few of my penny chapbooks, thought you might like to choose one as a gift, like. I've been collecting them since I was a nipper.'

'Oh, I couldn't take one of your books. And besides I can't barely read.'

'Go on.' He held them out. 'There's all sorts here. Some have pictures and all. I'll show you.'

So she opened the door wide and let him in. He put his nose over the boiling pot and inhaled, grimacing.

'What are you cooking?'

'I'm not, it's tallow – for the rushes.' She stooped to take the pan off the fire and cleared a space on the table.

'Look,' he said, spreading out the dog-eared booklets, 'there's tales here would make your hair stand on end. My father started this collection when he was at sea. To while away the hours, like. All the villains are here – the cut-throats, the highway robbers, the bezzlers. See here, this one's about James Hind, you know, the highwayman?' He picked out a crumbling-edged pamphlet and handed it to her. It showed a line-drawn portrait of a swaggering royalist next to a prancing horse.

'He was a master of disguise. Folk say he even hid the king,' Dennis said. 'What a rogue – fair terrified the ladies. No one dared take a coach up Ludgate whilst he was abroad – you had to take the long way round till they caught him. And here, oh, you'll like this one – Mull Sack.'

'Is that his name?' asked Sadie picking up the pamphlet and staring at the black-faced man on the cover.

'He was called that because he liked a tipple, and they say he was often bamboozled with it and all.'

'What did he do?'

'Pickpocket. But very clever. Used to be a chimney sweep. This one's from Newgate, shows him in his plumed hat. He was famous for that, just look at them feathers.'

Sadie scanned the table as Dennis talked, telling her in his lively voice about heroes and robberies, booty and plunder. She listened as he wove his tales, thought it was strange to hear these stories of thieves and cut-throats, for were not she and Ella thieves too? But these thieves were heroes, they were fearless. When they were caught, they broke free of their fetters, scaled prison walls, took on fantastical disguises and led the constables a merry dance.

It was nothing like real life, she thought, as he chattered on, nothing like looking over your shoulder all the time, like waking every morning afraid you might not see another. Nothing like running through the muck of London with your chest so tight it might burst.

Dennis was pushing another pamphlet towards her now. 'This is one of my father's. It's nigh on sixty year old. There were nineteen pirates, all hanged at Execution Dock, you know, at Wapping. There's the date, see, 1609.' He patted it reverently to point out the figures. 'For seamen, they take them there, not to the triple cross at Tyburn. They string them up over the water, and three tides have to rise over them afore they can be cut down. My grandfather was there, actually there on the dock that day, and he passed the pamphlet on like, and now it's mine.'

Sadie felt faint. The illustration showed a man dangling by the neck, his feet dragged sideways by swirling water. She sat down heavily on the stool, her ears buzzing like flies, and put her head low to her knees.

'Oh, I say. Are you all right?' He squatted down to look at her, eyes full of concern. Then a look of realization dawned on his face. 'It's me, ain't it? I've upset you. How could I be such a dolt? I don't think of you like that – I mean, you and your sister, I believe you. I mean, I know the constable's after you, but—'

'It's all right, I know you didn't mean anything by it.'

'Here, let me get you some ale.' He hastily piled all the pamphlets together face down into a heap and taking a cup from the shelf, hurried to the jug.

She sat up again to take the cup and shakily took a sip, seeing him watching her.

'I'm sorry,' he said. 'I always was bunglesome. Always putting my big feet right in it. It's just – well, I thought you might like a present on your birthday, and that's all I've got. My chapbooks. I never thought—'

'It's a fine collection. Thank you for showing me it.'

He smiled, relieved. 'Are you feeling better?'

'A little.' She wiped her face with her sleeve. 'Fancy you remembering my birthday. Sixteen! I would never have thought this time last year I'd turn sixteen in London.'

'Born under the sign of the water carrier you are. I'm born under the sign of the lion. Pa Whitgift's friend the astrologer says it makes me quick-tempered, but I think my temper's fair worn to a slither with seeing to Ma.'

They laughed. He stood up and put his cap back on, pressing the brim down towards his nose. 'Well, I guess your sister will be home soon, to wish you many happy returns too. I can hear Ma coughing again and she'll be after her treacle. She thinks I've popped out to get some more, so I'd best go down the shop afore they pull the shutters down.' He scooped up a pamphlet and held it out.

'This one's pretty. It's Barbary Bess. Keep this one.'

Sadie had never heard of Barbary Bess, but she took it from his hand. 'Thank you,' she said. 'She's a fine-looking woman.'

'You needn't worry. They transported her.'

'Oh, I see.'

Something about his earnestness made her smile. He gathered up the rest of his booklets and stood awkwardly by the door. 'Sorry if I upset you. I hardly ever get these out now,' he said, 'but they're grand tales, it's good to share them with someone. You're a good listener. My father always used to say a tale's naught without a good listener.'

'You could tell me a bit more about your father,' she said, emboldened by his compliment. 'I like to hear stories, and I lack company all day now I can't go out.'

'I'll call another day then, after work, if I might,' he said, as if suddenly aware of the proprieties. And then as an afterthought, 'Your sister could sit with us too, if you like.'

Sadie was touched at his attempt to provide her with a chaperone, but she did not want Ella to be there. Ella would scoff at him, at his bright-eyed interest in the sensational crimes of the day. She would not find his enthusiasm endearing as Sadie had, she knew.

'This time suits me,' she said, instantly rewarded by his pleased expression.

'Aye, your sister's at Jay Whitgift's beck and call, so I guess her hours will be a bit irregular. Happen it'll calm down after the first few weeks. Every lady in London seems to want a gawp at the Gilded Lily, 'cos it's new. And Jay Whitgift's got an eye for the decorations, it's fair decked out like a palace inside.'

'Yes, Ella told me.'

'You know she told me her name was Corey.'

'Yes. It's just, she didn't want anyone at Whitgift's to know her real name, because – well, you know why.'

'But Sadie's your real name, ain't it?'

'Course.' She blushed. To hide her embarrassment, she said, 'Dennis is an unusual name. You don't get many Dennises.'

'Dennis Edward Gowper. Dennis after the French saint. My ma's idea, guess she was hoping I might turn out to be less trouble.' He chuckled. 'No chance. Edward after my pa.'

'Pleased to make your acquaintance, Dennis Edward.'

They smiled at each other.

After Dennis had gone, Sadie sat at the table and turned the pages of the chapbook slowly. She felt different, special. Sixteen – a grown woman. She did not dare to think he liked her. He was just being kind, that was all. Nobody could like a girl with a face like hers. He hadn't stared though, like other people did, at least not at that part of her face. He seemed to have been watching her lips as she spoke. She contemplated the picture of Barbary Bess, a woman dressed as a man, swaggering, her drillscrew curls floating out to the sides of her head.

The door banged and Ella was home.

'What's that?' she said, whipping it off the table. Sadie's hands flew up after it but it was too late. 'Where did you get this folderol?'

'Dennis from downstairs brought it, when he brought the agreement.'

'What for? You can't read. Only your name and that. Not worth much, these. But maybe you could sell it on for a farthing.'

'I'm keeping it. Give it over.'

Ella tossed it back onto the table. Sadie put her hand over it and pulled it into her lap. 'He brought it up special. He had a whole pile of them, from his father.'

Ella wasn't listening, she was unloading her basket and kicking off her shoes. 'It's turned right chilly. My feet are freezing. Where's this agreement then?'

'He brought it on account of it being my birthday.'

A pause, during which Ella looked discomfited. 'How did he know it was your birthday?'

'I must have said something last week.'

'To him? What on earth for? Anyway, I've got you a present. Didn't think I'd forgotten, did you? Look, here. Better than that old thing.' Ella brought out a pot tied with a yellow ribbon from the basket.

'Face-whitener,' she said.

'Oh.'

'It'll cover everything, I've tried it. Don't I get a "thank you kindly", or an embrace?'

'Course you do.' Sadie stood and squeezed Ella round the waist. 'Thank you, Ell.' Ella's stays made it feel as if she was embracing a wooden bucket.

'Come on then, open it up.'

Sadie took a deep breath. 'Sorry, Ell, but you know I won't use it. Remember.'

'Go on – look, this is different. It's made of starch. It will cover everything, make you bonny as a babe, honest.' She licked her finger and circled it in the paste, then rubbed a patch onto her arm where it glowed like a small coin on her skin. 'Sit down. I'll do your face.'

'I don't want my face doing.'

'But them notices give a good description. I'll bet half the world's looking for a girl with a mark on her face; he's offering fifty pound.'

Sadie was stunned, she could think of nothing to say. Ella carried on. 'You want to get out of here, don't you? Maybe get a position someplace like me?'

'No. I don't want my face covered in that stuff. Besides, it will rub off, and then where would I be?'

'All the ladies are wearing it. I see them every day at the Lily. And I'm telling you, nobody will even look twice at you.' Ella held the pot out towards her.

Sadie stood up and backed away, tucking the chapbook into her apron. 'No. I told you, I don't want to. It's all very well for you – you have a pretty face and a fine gown. You look like you should be wearing it. But I can't walk round here like that, not in these clothes. I stick out too much. I can't have a white face gathering wood or working at the wig shop, you know I can't. I'd look like a whore. I can't have a white face and a mud-spattered apron.'

'D'you know what, you're right. Why didn't I think of that? You're going to need a proper gown like mine. I'll have to save for one from my wage. I could see what Whitgift's have got in the rag market next sale day though. We'll dress you up so fine, and do your hair, and nobody will guess what's underneath the white. I promise, you'll look like a queen when I've done.'

'And then won't we stick out, two fine ladies living in a damp rats' nest in Blackraven Alley.' Sadie could not keep the bitterness from her voice.

'What's got into you? Is it that boy? Don't forget it was you wanted to live here. And now we're stuck with it. But I might be able to put a bit aside to buy a new gown.'

'Bet you won't.'

'I will. Cross my heart.'

Sadie just stared.

'Mind, there's not a deal left after food and lodgings and such, so it might take a few months.'

'Months. Oh.' Sadie picked up a dishcloth, wrung it out in the pail of water and wiped the table. She was unsure if she was disappointed or relieved. When she was small she had wished and wished for some sort of magic, that someone would wave a wand and she would wake up and find the stain gone, but now the magic was here in the room it terrified her.

Ella was talking about the cream, how Waley the apothecary made it, but Sadie was scarcely listening. Even if she dared to try it she still could not imagine going out with her face exposed like that, with only a layer of cream between her and people's stares. Yet it was what she had always wanted – to go abroad and for no one to single her out. But she had misgivings somehow. She wanted folk to accept her as she was, not to be always in disguise. Besides, she was not Ella, did not have her nerve.

An image of Dennis came to mind; she remembered his lively brown eyes as he watched her explain the darning, and his contrite expression when he thought he had offended her. What would he think of her if she painted up her face? What would she do if it went wrong and she came out all in blisters?

'Come on, Sadie. Give it a try. It's perfectly safe. It'll make you pretty.' Ella held out her hand, the back of it pasted white.

'I said no. Just leave me alone.'

Ella pursed her lips and pulled on her gloves. 'Fine. Next time it's your birthday I won't bother. I'm going out. I'll come back when you're in a better temper.'

Chapter 19

Sadie had stayed hidden away in their room now for four days. Ella said the notices were up everywhere, so she was mortal afraid to go out in daylight. Dennis had only called again once, and then only to say his ma was taken poorly again and he had to sit with her. And right enough she could hear Ma Gowper's cough from the room below day and night, and guessed he must have been kept busy ministering to her needs.

The weather was chill and the room as cold and dark as ever. The January sun was hidden by cloud and fog; in London there always seemed to be both. After doing the chores, Sadie pulled her wool shawl over her arms and leaned her elbows on the windowsill, watching the river slide by in the haze. There were gulls, swooping down onto the mud, pulling out the remains of a rotting fish or squalling over the barges as they passed. Sadie watched their antics with something approaching envy. It could have been worse, she thought, at least there was a view – the window could have backed onto a wall.

She could not see the street, but she could hear it. Out there the vendors were plying their trade, the milk asses brayed as they were led door to door. The howl of the ragman and the high-pitched yelp of the belt and laces boy made her restless. She sighed and turned back into the gloom.

At first she had busied herself scrubbing and cleaning, but the besom made a scraping noise on the bare floorboards, so she stopped. She had heard Ella call goodbye to Widow Gowper and she did not wish to arouse her suspicions or scare her. She would be afraid, poor woman, down there all alone. No wonder she listened out so hard. She was helpless down there in that bed, just as she, Sadie, was helpless up here.

It felt strange, not making up her snap bundle or dodging the stray dogs on the way to the wig shop. In the countryside, dogs were used for hunting or for bringing back the game. They had a use and a purpose. Here they ran wild like wolves.

When Ella had departed for Whitgift's that morning after much fussing with her hair, Sadie had laid out all their remaining possessions on the table. Ella had bought basic cooking pots, second-hand blankets and other necessities from Whitgift's. They had hardly anything left to sell.

'Right,' Sadie said to herself, 'let's see what's what,' and she tallied on her hands, making a rough calculation. They might last two months, that was all, if she couldn't go to work.

They could have been running out on the fells of Westmorland, the fresh wind in their faces, the pale green-edged frills of the first snowdrops just beginning to brighten the woodland verges. Sadie knew well enough they could not go back. And what would they do, if it did not turn out well for Ella at Whitgift's, and Sadie could not work? She quaked at the prospect of relying on Ella. Yesterday she had asked her to buy taters and onions, but Ella had come home empty-handed. What was more, there had been a fratch about it.

Sadie had been grating a knob of suet into a basin of flour. She was making a pudding. When she heard the door open, she had called out to Ella straight away, 'Let's have them taters and onions then. I'll soon get supper ready.'

Ella shook her head. 'I haven't got any.'

Sadie paused, her hands rimed with flour. Ella looked different. Her face was powdered, so that her eyelids appeared red and raw in contrast, and she had a new pair of white lace-edged gloves on.

Sadie could not take it in. New gloves. And no taters.

'You beggar,' she whispered. 'Did you use our money to buy new gloves?'

Ella pulled off the gloves and dangled them from one hand. 'Course not. Jay gave me them. He said it's too chilly to be out without gloves.'

'Let's have a deek then.' Sadie tugged them from Ella's hand. She turned them over and held them to her nose. They were fine white lambswool, fragrant with cloves, a delicate lace crochet at the cuff. Sadie flung them on the table.

'I don't believe you. Them are not warm gloves. Them are trumpery. Don't you tell me someone pawned these. They're too good. They're not second-hand, are they? They're new.'

'So what?' said Ella, pushing her nose into the air. 'Jay *bought* them for me.' She picked up the gloves. 'From a *shop*. A ladies' outfitters. So there.'

'Show me the rest of our money then.'

'I can't. I haven't got any. I had to pay Dennis to get the notice read.'

'He never asked you for money?'

'He did.'

'The whole three shilling?'

'He did, so.'

Sadie turned away. She was impatient with Ella's tale, it seemed unlikely Dennis would have asked for such a large tip.

It made her cross when she couldn't get at the truth, as if it was she getting it muddled, not Ella. But she could not go down and ask Dennis about it without alerting his mother to her presence, even if she had the courage to do so. She sighed in frustration.

'What are we going to do, then?' She waved the pudding cloth at Ella. 'How am I supposed to make a pudding with no vegetables?'

Ella had shrugged her shoulders and said they would eat plain pudding. And Sadie had retorted that if she, Sadie, was not able to go out to market to buy, then Ella must do it. Ella had looked sulky, and sat in the corner all evening cleaning and pushing at her fingernails with a pointed stick.

So this morning as Ella was getting ready to leave the house, Sadie said, 'Ask Jay for an advance, won't you? We can't live off fresh air. If he'll buy you them gloves, he'll surely not grudge us a few onions. Get some vegetables in, won't you? Please?'

Ella's thin eyebrows lowered and her mouth took on a stubborn cast. 'It's difficult. It's one thing to be given a gift. Another kettle o' fish to ask favours.'

'Just try it, won't you. It's not a favour. You're owed a week's wages by rights already.'

'Oh, give up grizzling. All you have to do is laze about here all day.' And Ella dragged her cloak off the back of the chair and made a great noise of going downstairs. So all Sadie could do was wait, and hope Ella would bring something home. But it was a long wait every day, and Sadie found it frustrating to have so little to do. The little pot of white cream still sat on the table where Ella had left it. She lifted the lid and looked at where Ella's finger had poked in and made a well in the cream. Her birthday present. She blinked back tears, tied the lid back on tight, picked it up between her finger and thumb and dropped it into the jug with a broken handle. Then she pushed it to the back of the shelf out of sight.

Ella must have talked to Jay, for a few days later she did bring home a half-dozen pigeon eggs and some breadcakes. But as the week passed, she was erratic with her purchases, there was no rhyme or reason to her buying. Often the ingredients would not make a meal, for Ella had no proper practical knowledge of cooking. After all, there'd been a cook at the Ibbetsons that did all that. She'd not had to fix for her da every day like Sadie.

Da. Sadie thought back to her life in Westmorland. There she had lived in the terror of Da's belt, but now that fear was like a phantom. She could not feel it any more, but it still haunted her. Would he still be thinking of her? Surely he could not forget his own flesh and blood. If they were caught, would he come then? Ella said they would be sentenced to burn if they were found, and she imagined him coming just too late. She scrubbed hard at the table again until it was bleached white, tried not to remember the woodcut images of Tyburn, where the pyre provided another noonday's entertainment and guaranteed immortality in one of Dennis's chapbooks.

The next night Ella came home with a pot of lye and a tiny paper twist of saffron and dyed her hair a dull yellow. Perhaps it was a good idea to disguise herself, but the colour looked strange to Sadie's eyes. Ella's hair had lost its lustre and shine.

Every day Ella went off in her fine red dress and green cloak, leaving Sadie behind in the tiny box above the river. Within a week, Ella had grown impatient with Sadie's questions about her day, and when Sadie asked her with a simple, 'Well?' she said, 'Just the usual. Rich old magpies and their gossip.'

Sadie was agog to hear all about fashionable London and

pressed Ella for tales of what went on at the Gilded Lily. She asked about Jay Whitgift and about Dennis, and loved to hear of Mrs Horsefeather and her frowzy gowns. Ella had always loved to be the first to tell of all the goings-on in Netherbarrow, but here it was like the cat had got her tongue. Sadie knew better than to ask too much lest they get into another fratch.

Spring was still a long way off, the weather worsened, the wind howled through the window despite its sacking covering, and oft times Sadie was reduced to pacing up and down to keep warm. She put on all the clothes she had, one on top of the other. Her usual skirt and bodice, underneath her flannel nightgown, with one of Ella's too-big grey gowns over that. It did not matter what she looked like in the day, for she never went out, and there was no one to see her. She dare not wear her clogs, in case she alerted Ma Gowper, so she wrapped her feet in rags in the day-time to keep the cold at bay.

At night, though, she tidied herself and sponged down her good brown dress in case Dennis should come by. She combed her hair until it shone. He had been up twice, to tell her tales of his father's ship, his voyages across the seas to the Barbary Coast, and to share a cup of warm skemmy with her. She did not tell Ella of these visits – they were private, something she could relive in the tedious hours whilst Ella was out at work.

The first time Dennis asked her if she might like to walk with him to fetch his mother's physic, but she had said no. She daren't go out, she said to him, in case someone followed her home. She would not want Ella to be caught on her account. It had felt bad to turn him down, and afterwards she went over to the cupboard to fetch the pot, with the idea of painting her face. But in the end she left the paste in the jug. The smell of it was enough to give her gooseflesh. And without a gown to wear with it, she would look preposterous. And whereas Ella and all the fine ladies would only need a light touch over their peachy complexions, she would need it thick as curds.

But the next day Dennis turned up again as usual with more of his chapbooks in hand, and she grinned with pleasure that her refusal had not offended him. He sat close to her as they pored over the pictures together. She always made sure she sat with her good side next to him. He had a way of telling that made the stories come alive in the room, like he was weaving a vast tapestry before her eyes. She enjoyed his lively expressions and the way he moved his hands like a conjuror.

They were yarns his father had told him, thrilling tales of pirates and slave ships and a giant fish that nearly swallowed the ship. She asked him whether his father had been involved with the fighting in the days of shaking.

'No,' he said. 'He went back to sea. Never could stand the fighting. Told me a story about it once, and it made me think he was right.'

'Oh, tell me it, Dennis, I'd love another tale. Especially one from your father.'

He pressed his lips together trying not to grin. 'Wait whilst I think on it a while,' he said, 'I need to get it set in the right order.' Then he began, his eyes rolling up under his eyebrows as if he was bringing the story from the realms above him.

'There were once two villages,' he said, 'and there had been haggling over the land that lay between them for many generations. Finally the arguments got so hot that they decided the only way to settle it was to raise armies and fight a war over the land.'

Sadie propped her elbows on the table and put her chin in her hands, settling down to watch Dennis's face as he talked.

He glanced to check she was listening, then continued. 'Now each village had a standard-bearer who carried the emblem of the village on a flag, and these two men were the most guarded men in the village because they each carried the symbol of their village's honour. When the signal was given, the battle began. But both sides were equally matched, and all around them men were falling –' he mimed thrashing to and fro with a sword – 'and many fell,' he said, 'but these two standard-bearers were protected. Day after day, the war was fought, first with one side having the upper hand, the next day the other. The terrible slaughter waged on until the men of both armies lay either dead or wounded, and eventually at the end of the seventh day only the two standard-bearers remained. "We will duel," said one, "and finish this dispute for good."'

'Oh,' said Sadie, caught up in the tale. Dennis smiled before resuming.

'"Very well," said the other, "but we have been fighting all day. Let us sleep first and fight at dawn when we are fresh."

'"I agree," said his enemy.

'So they lit a camp fire and sat one on either side. As the night wore on, and it became dull just to sit in silence, one of the men began to talk. He told of his wife and child, and life in their village. About how the last year's harvest had been bad.

'"Ours too," said the other man, and began to tell of life in his own village, of his parents, and his son's difficulty in learning to ride a horse. So they shared the little details of their lives with each other, the things that were the same, the things that were different.

'When the sun peeped over the horizon both men were ready. The standards were shoved into the ground behind them, the flags flapped in the wind. Their comrades were dead, they stood alone on the plain facing each other. Before the first man could even touch his hilt, the second drew his blade, but then slowly, he sheathed it again. Seeing his enemy unarmed, the other knew he could finish him and whipped out his sword, but he too could not strike the blow, but returned it unused to its scabbard.

'Ever since then,' Dennis went on, 'the villages have met once a year on the anniversary of the battle to celebrate their kinship one with another and to light a beacon together, and both villages lived in harmony and happily ever after from that day forth.'

Sadie clapped her hands together. 'Oh, that's lovely. I haven't heard that one before.'

Dennis grinned. 'It's one of my favourites. I used to ask for it again and again when I was a boy. I used to want to be a standard-bearer. It sounded grand. What's your favourite story?'

'I don't know,' she said, 'I'll have to think.' Though immediately the tale of Snow White and Rose Red had come into her mind. It was the only one she could remember her mother telling, such a vague memory really, just the names, and her mother's hopeful expression. But somehow she didn't want to tell Dennis, it gave too much away.

'You know,' Dennis said, 'when my father told me that tale he used to say, "Always remember, you can't hate someone if you know their story." People sometimes used to call my father a coward when he wouldn't fight for king or parliament, thought he was running away. It hurt him that, and it hurt me to think they didn't think well of him. But I knew him, and the story, and knew the thought behind it.'

Sadie could feel the emotion in his voice. 'He sounds like a good man,' she said quietly. She placed her hand on Dennis's arm where it lay on the table.

'The best. One day, you must tell me about your family,' Dennis said, looking into her eyes. He did not move his arm, but left it where it was.

A vision of her da, his face twisted with anger, came into her mind. 'Perhaps,' she said, glancing away, knowing she probably would not. It made her ashamed to think she was related to such a person.

'Look, I brought you something,' he said, withdrawing his arm gently as the clocks chimed.

'Another chapbook?' she asked.

'No,' he said, looking embarrassed. He brought out a piece of lavender ribbon and held it between finger and thumb. 'I thought 'twould suit you, the colour. And you could use it to tie up your hair.'

'Oh you shouldn't have. It's not my birthday now.'

'Take it, won't you?' He dangled it out towards her.

'All right,' she said, and she reached out to take it. 'I look forward to your visits,' she said shyly.

'Me too,' he said.

And she had tied the piece of ribbon into the neck of her shift, next to her skin, for she did not want Ella to see it. She might laugh, and Sadie knew she could not bear that. And as she did her chores, she treasured his words over and over, reliving the story.

The next day, the snow came. They woke to a tangible hush as the clattering hooves and cartwheels outside were muffled by a thick wad of white. Sadie pulled open the curtain and saw the swirling flakes falling down onto the drift below. The river was a streak, like a black scar, through it.

'Snow,' said Sadie, with great excitement.

'Oh bother,' Ella said. 'What a nuisance. I'll have to wear my clogs. It'll be slippery walking in those. Wish I could take a carriage.'

'Fat chance,' said Sadie. 'Bet even the gigs can't go far in this. It's thick as thatch.'

For the last week Ella's feet had been shod in dainty leather bootees. Sadie had not asked where they had come from, but the thought pained her that they must have been dearer than the cost of a new gown. Ella was late, and flustered enough already. Ella put on her clogs and began to wrap her bootees in Sadie's shawl to carry to work.

'What are you doing?'

'I'll need to carry my boots.'

'Not in my shawl, you won't.' She took hold of it to take it back, but Ella dug in her nails and clung on.

'It's not fit to be worn, that. Leave go.'

'No. It's mine and you're not having it.' She wrestled it free and Ella's bootees spilled onto the floor. 'Carry them in your own.' Her eyes were hot with tears.

When she had gone, Sadie hugged the shawl to her chest, rocking it back and forth for comfort. Later, she scoured the corner of the room for any remaining sticks. She scraped them together into a bundle – not enough to have a proper fire. Somehow she could not see Ella scavenging for wood. Not now she was so finely dressed.

Sadie went to her usual vantage point at the window and pushed her head out to inhale the snow in the air and to catch a few stray flakes on her fingers, where they melted into glistening drops. The river was unusually quiet, only a few row boats, and the snow had almost stopped falling. She longed to touch the soft white crust below so much that she ached with it. Why had Ella grumbled about the snow? Even London looked beautiful, veiled like a bride.

She heard shrieks of glee from below. Two lads were throwing snowballs at each other. One of them she recognized straight away as the little lad who had helped her lug the coal up the bank, the other was obviously his big brother, for they had the same curly hair and flattened features. She watched with interest as the younger boy squashed a pie of snow in his hand and hurled it inexpertly at his brother.

The brother ducked and yelled, 'Nah! Missed!'

He was ready with his own snowball prepared, and lobbed it hard at Sadie's friend, who caught it full on the chin.

'Ow. That hurt.'

Wiping the snow clumsily from his face he blindly gathered more snow for a second shot and threw it haphazardly back. By some miracle, it hit his brother square in the face and he staggered backwards and tripped over an upturned skiff, landing on his behind in the snow. Before she could stop herself Sadie let out a whoop, and the boy shot a curious glance at her window.

Sadie pulled instantly inside, her heart thudding.

She must be careful – no one must know she was here. If she had to go on the run again, perhaps they would not find it so easy to hide next time. Everyone would be looking out for them, all the booty hunters. Nobody would care that they were innocent, just so long as they could claim the reward. They would be fodder for the scaffold and someone would line their pocket at their expense.

She shivered and tied her shawl in a tight knot in front of her chest. It would do no good to dwell on it. Happen, good things might be round the corner. She could go out at night, like she had last night, to stretch her legs and breathe in the fresh air. And feel the snow crunch under her feet, and maybe suck on an icicle from the eaves.

She had got used to walking at night now, her hood over her face, creeping in the shadows of the alleys lest anyone should see her. It was risky, and it made her chest pound and her palms sweat, but it was worth the fear, just to get out from the four walls. She never talked to anyone. It was this that was the hardest, the lack of company.

She missed her work. She was unused to having idle hands,

and had asked over and over for Ella to bring her something to do. Maybe labelling up bottles, or mending – anything to while away the time. But Ella brought nothing home, and it was plain she'd never leave Whitgift's – her heart was set on sweetening Jay, and she was that stubborn. Except once, the button had come loose on Ella's boot, and Ella had arrived with needle and thread to mend it. Sadie had it finished in no time, and used the thread to repair all the clothes she owned, until all her clothes were stitched with brown thread, even her chemise. She had even begun a small sampler on a scrap cut from a petticoat.

She had painstakingly embroidered *Sadie Apleby. Borne 164*— but the thread finally ran out, and her hands lay still again in her lap.

She imagined all the girls bent over their wig stands at Madame Lefevre's. Little Betsy, Alyson, Pegeen, plain-faced Corey. Even Madame Lefevre did not seem so harsh. She thought almost fondly of her black crow-like presence now. She remembered when Ella and she had walked to the wig shop together, and they had all sat whispering at break suppressing giggles over one of Ella's outrageous anecdotes.

Sadie sighed and sat down at the table, and ran the scrap of beeswax and the polishing cloth over it for the hundredth time, her thoughts still with the girls at Madame Lefevre's. When her thoughts were not with the girls, she stared at the cover of Barbary Bess, with her tumbling curls, imagining a life for her full of swash and daring.

Chapter 20

Madame Lefevre banged two wig blocks together to get the girls' attention.

Corey jumped and sat up obediently like the rest of the girls, curious about the visitor who had just come in. He was a stout hunch-shouldered man, with a large pale forehead, jutting eyebrows and a mouth that appeared too small for his face. She noticed dried spittle at the corners of his lips.

Madame Lefevre introduced him as Mr Ibbetson, but before she had finished telling them why he had come, he interrupted her and pushed his way to the centre of the room. He must have ridden there, despite the snow, for he was still in his heavy wool mantle and riding boots.

'The good lady here tells me there were two sisters that worked in this establishment up until a few weeks ago. Country girls from Westmorland. Ella and Sadie Appleby. You remember them?'

The girls nodded mutely. They had smelt his authority as soon as he opened his mouth.

'Have you seen them recently?' he said.

Silence.

'Do any of you know where they live?'

The girls shook their heads. His manner was one of a chastising schoolteacher. It made Corey reluctant to speak, even if she knew the answer.

'Not one of you? No?'

He marched round the bench looking into their faces as if he wanted to read the contents of their minds.

'There is a reward,' he said, 'for information that will lead me to them.' He peered at Alyson, who, embarrassed, dropped her chin to her chest. 'A substantial reward.' He drew the words out as if to emphasize them.

Mercy smiled politely at him. Madame Lefevre frowned.

'Do you know where they live?' Sensing Mercy's interest he addressed her directly.

'Oh no,' Mercy said, tossing her blonde curls, 'I'm afraid not. My brother and I caught sight of Sadie Appleby just up the street. We tried to catch her, but she ran like her heels were on fire and we couldn't catch up with her. We'd heard about the notices at church, someone told us they were looking for a girl like her.'

Corey glared at her.

'When?' Madame Lefevre asked.

'More than a week ago. But she's never been near us since, has she?'

Mr Ibbetson narrowed his eyes and closed his mouth until it was a tiny hole, sucking in his breath. 'If I find out that any one of you is concealing information as to their whereabouts, then I will have you clapped in irons for assisting a known felon.'

Mercy turned and whispered, in a voice clearly intended to be heard, 'Told you so. Told you there was a notice out for that Sadie and her sister, but you'd none of it. Marked by the Devil, she is, didn't I say so?'

Corey was impatient with Mercy, but she bit her lip.

'Yes, Mercy said Sadie put a hex on us,' said Betsy.

Mercy scowled at her, and Betsy blushed and closed her mouth.

'What have they done, sir?' asked Alyson.

'Don't be impertinent,' Madame Lefevre said.

Mr Ibbetson answered. 'Suffocated a man to death.' Although nobody spoke or moved, the words hung in the air. 'Then they took every last penny from the house. Can you imagine? Even his watch out of his pocket. What sort of a person would do that?'

Mercy nodded her head up and down. Corey took in the words, but somehow could not make them sit sensibly with the girls she had known. She stared at Mr Ibbetson trying to weigh him up.

'What about the reward?' Mercy interrupted. 'How much is it?'

'Fletcher!' Madame Lefevre said.

Mr Ibbetson turned to Madame Lefevre and almost put his hand on her arm before withdrawing it. 'He was my brother. My twin brother.' His mouth twitched with emotion. 'Have any of you got brothers at home?' But then he clenched his fist, sweat had broken out on his forehead. 'Nobody seems to be doing anything. The Netherbarrow constable sent me an urgent message last week to say he had some news of them, so off I went, haring up there. What a waste of time. He was only telling me what I already knew, that they had been sighted at a tavern here in London somewhere. Bloody useless. And now, all this snow . . .'

He sat down heavily on one of the stools and wiped his mouth with a kerchief drawn from his breeches. 'I'll see justice done and those two on the gibbet if it's the last thing I do.' He mopped his face again. 'I caught a glimpse of them near to here in Bread Street, but they ran off. For anyone who can lead me to them, the reward is fifty pounds.'

The girls gasped.

Corey looked at Alyson. The gibbet. It was serious, someone was going to hang. Whatever Ella and Sadie were supposed to have done, she did not fancy their chances against this man if he was wealthy enough to offer such a reward. Fifty pounds! It was a fortune. And he already knew they used to lodge in Bread Street. Madame Lefevre was staring at her. Corey lowered her head.

'I am residing temporarily at the Blue Ball on Aldergate,' Ibbetson said. 'I am sure that there must be some kind soul who can find out their whereabouts for me.' He looked round the room. 'In the daytime, I will be pursuing various lines of inquiry, but I can be found at the Blue Ball after dusk, should any of you think further and wish to lay claim to that reward.'

'The Blue Ball, did you hear that, girls?' Madame Lefevre said.

'Yes, Madame Lefevre,' they chorused. She showed him out, but was back moments later, her eyes sharp.

'Corey Johnson. You walked home with Ella and Sadie some nights. Where do they lodge?'

'Don't know, madame. Ella said their father was after them to take them back to Westmorland, so they left their lodging house and moved on. I don't know where to.'

'Their father? More like the yeoman constable. Where did they used to live?'

'Somewhere round Bread Street, like he said. But I only ever walked to the end of the road with them, and that's as much as I know.'

Madame Lefevre gave Corey a withering look, as if to indicate the useless nature of her answers before retiring into her office.

Madame Lefevre rummaged in her drawer searching for something. She was sure she still had it somewhere. She pulled the whole drawer out and sat with it on her knee, riffling through it in her black lace fingerless gloves. Ah, yes. She extracted a printed piece of paper from underneath a greasy felt pincushion and a yellowing sheaf of bills. She smiled to herself and held it up in front of her spectacles to read the small print.

Whitgift and Son, Purveyors of Goods to the Gentry, Goods valued and Charitable Loans offered. Jewellery a Speciality.

There was a cramped-up signature made with a scratchy nib, *Josiah Whitgift*. The 'i's had the dots very precisely aligned. She looked at the bottom corner: *Friargate, London.*

Moments later she had her cloak and bonnet on and was out of the front door, trudging eastwards through the snow, leaving the girls unsupervised in the shop.

Corey and the rest of the girls heard the bell go and felt the draught from the door, and for a couple of minutes they thought it must be another customer coming in for a fitting. But strangely they heard no voices from the front shop, not a sound. After a few moments Mercy stood up and tentatively hooked open the calico curtain with her finger. The shop was empty. There was no sign of Madame Lefevre.

'She's gone out.'

'Out?' Alyson whispered. 'She can't have gone out.'

'Well, she's not here, so she must have.'

'What, and just left us here?' Betsy said.

'Let's have a ganders,' Corey said, getting up to look through the doorway. 'It's true – she has gone out.'

'Why?' Alyson said.

'She must know something,' Mercy said, 'about the Appleby girls. There's notices out all over London. We nearly caught her, me and Jacob. It's our bounden duty to clamp down on sinners.'

Betsy nodded.

'Fiddlesticks. I don't believe it. I don't think they did it. Who else agrees with me?' Corey said.

'Course they did. They're on the run. Why else did they walk out like that, one after the other?' Mercy said.

'By all the saints, that's right,' Pegeen said.

Mercy looked smug. 'And anyway, a gentleman like that wouldn't put out a reward unless their guilt was certain.'

'Well, they might have been in trouble, but they wouldn't have done for anyone. You never met Ella. She left before you came. She liked to play a part, and she could be a vain little madam, she might even have done a bit of thievery, like the rest of us when we're short, but I can't believe she's killed a man.'

'How dare you. I've never stolen anything in my life,' Mercy said.

'Ella was a bit above herself, but not Sadie. Sadie'd never hurt a fly,' Alyson said.

'I'm telling you, my thumbs are pricking, I can tell evil from a hundred paces,' said Mercy in a pulpit voice, 'and Sadie Appleby is the Devil's child.'

'At least she would never browbeat another girl to do her knotting.' Corey looked directly at Mercy.

A pause.

'What do you mean?'

'You know well enough.'

'Are you calling me a bully?'

The girls looked down at their work stations, sensing trouble in the air.

'Well, you are, aren't you?' Corey said. 'I saw little Betsy coming in this morning and handing over a night's worth of horsehair knotting.' She turned to Betsy. 'You do her knotting for her, don't you?'

Betsy quailed, and stammered, 'No, well, I . . .' She looked helplessly at Mercy.

Mercy took hold of Betsy's arm and said, 'She doesn't. You don't, do you?'

'No,' Betsy said in a small voice.

'Let go of her arm,' Corey said.

Mercy held tight.

'Let go, you vixen, or I'll make you.'

Mercy made a face and waggled her head. Corey lunged for Mercy and grabbed her hair.

Mercy aimed a boot tip at Corey's ankle but she dodged it neatly, still clinging to Mercy's hair. Mercy pushed Betsy roughly away and scratched her fingernails in a long stripe down Corey's cheek.

'Devil fetch you,' Corey said, putting one hand up to her face, while with the other she wound her fingers into Mercy's hair, pulling her forwards.

By this time the girls had formed an unruly circle around them and were shouting, 'Clubs out,' and stamping their clogged feet. Mercy shoved Corey hard so that she fell back with a crack against the bench, her spine bent backwards, but Mercy overbalanced and fell with her, and the two scrabbled to get away to get enough space to hit each other.

'Let go, you beggar.' Mercy bit hard into Corey's hand, but Corey held tight.

Mercy brought her fist down hard onto Corey's nose. Corey yelped, as blood oozed from her nostril. Corey reached out behind her on the bench. Her hands closed around a pair of scissors.

There was a flash of metal and the girls fell away in shock.

Corey backed away and wiped her nose, holding the yellow hank of Mercy's hair in her hand. She let it drop, astonished to see it there. It was one of Mercy's bunches. The curls lay on the wooden floor like a heap of wood shavings. Mercy stared at it a moment, before pressing her hands to her head in horror.

'My hair.' Her voice was thin and small. She stooped to gather it up, her face screwed up and white. The other girls parted silently as she made her way to the door. Corey's nose dripped blood through her fingers.

'Betsy?' called Mercy, from the door. But Betsy did not move.

Chapter 21

Jay was outside the gate again in the thinning snow, turning away carriages. Wednesdays were particularly bad, and this one was no exception, even in this weather. As he strode back towards the gate he saw a crowd of louts hanging round.

'Clear off,' he said.

One of the larger lads came forward. He was filthy and had a nose bent to one side with fighting. He wore a tattered man's coat that was turned back at the sleeves, and his hands looked red raw with cold where he clutched the neck of a heavy sack.

'You work at Whitgift's, mister?' he said.

Jay ignored him and set off towards the nearest carriage.

'Begging pardon, sir, you want to see some trinkets?'

Jay paused, but then shook his head and carried on walking.

'Nice little fan, silver thimbles, an' a ruby seal . . .'

Now Jay was interested and when he slowed the lads gathered round.

'Is it chored?' Jay asked, knowing the answer by the look of them.

'Niver. It's my granddam's. She died an' left it to me.'

'And my eye's a pie. Let's look, then.' Jay positioned his back to the wall, his hand on his sword. You could never be too careful.

The lad held out the grubby oat-sack and rummaged inside. It looked weighty, and clinked as the lad brought out a pretty fan, mounted in silver and mother-of-pearl.

'How much?' Jay said.

'Sice for that,' the lad said.

'A penny, and no more. What else?'

'A few bits and pieces.' The lad pulled out a gold and ruby seal. Jay tried not to let them see he was interested. 'Oh, another of those,' he said. 'I've got similar ones already. I could take it off your hands for –' he thought a moment – 'a shilling, a shilling for the lot.'

'But I bet it's gold,' the lad said, holding it out in front of him. 'And there's a load more spoons and plate and that in here.'

'Look, it's got a moniker on it. They don't sell. A shilling's my final offer.'

'Give it over then.'

'The goods first.'

The boy dropped the seal into the sack, put it on the ground and stepped away. 'My shilling,' he said.

'Here,' Jay tossed the coin over their heads so they had to chase after it down the street. Then he swept up the bag and loped back inside the yard, grinning to himself. The coin he had tossed had been thrupence.

He went up to his chambers and tipped the sack onto his desk.

The beggars. The sack contained only the fan and the seal, his desk was littered with sticks and cobbles.

He picked out the seal from the debris on his desk. It was not something he would keep, he decided. He knew he must be hard on himself, sell a few things on. This one was finely made, but he had others much finer in the drawers. He looked at the letters chased into the ruby, T.W.I., wondered if he knew of anyone with those initials he could sell it to. The edge of the design was blurred, worn from use. He wanted only perfection. It could go down into the yard. He'd maybe get six or seven pounds for it.

In the office on the other side of the yard, Walt Whitgift leaned over the chart on the desk in front of him, his nose barely a foot from its surface. Though he had wanted an education for his son, he had little book-learning himself, and the chart was covered in tiny spider-like ciphers that filled him with bafflement. He watched carefully though, as Tindall's bony finger continued to point out figures and squiggly lines as he talked.

'Here we have a conjunction of Venus and Saturn – a sure harbinger of dissent. I'm afraid the influence will last for several months, but then again, see that square to the trine? We can see foreshadowed here the fire of Mars, which would seem to indicate rapid growth and expansion. Of course I cannot discount the effect of the comet – as cited in Lilly's Almanac.'

'Is that good?'

'Well, last time it passed, we went to war with the French, so no, I would think not. But see here.' Again he stabbed a cracked and yellowing nail onto the parchment. 'There is fame coming, that's the influence of Leo . . .'

'Fame, you say? That's good.' He stood up and shook another shovel of coal into the fireplace, where it hissed damply and belched smoke.

'Well, it could be good, but look at this, there's a shadow over Venus.'

'Look, Tindall, I'm not much of a one for map-reading.' He patted Tindall on the shoulder. 'My eyesight's not what it was, and it tires me. Tell me plainly, will my son's new business be a success?'

'Oh, undoubtedly.'

'Will it make money?'

'The stars are favourable.'

'Then that's all I need to know. I don't want to fall out with my son.' He sat back down.

'But, Walter, I've said already, there's a shadow over this chart somehow, and a death. It doesn't add up. At the end of this month there's a conflagration of planets. Look at Saturn again.'

Walt sighed. He did not want to know if it was going to be bad.

Tindall began explaining again. 'There are elements which seem to show—'

The bell on the back of the door jangled loudly. Walt breathed a sigh of relief.

'Ah, sorry, Tindall, looks like I'm needed in the warehouse. We'll talk further later, shall we?'

Walt stood up again and limped to the door. These days his legs seized if he sat still for too long. He opened it warily.

A pinch-faced woman dressed entirely in black was standing there stamping the snow off her boots.

'Come in,' he said, opening the door wide. She was obviously in mourning. Perhaps she needed money for the funeral. She marched in, and refused a chair with a vigorous shake of the head. She did not look as if she was grieving. She peered at him over wire spectacles.

'Where can I find Josiah Whitgift?' she said.

'Oh, it's Jay you're after seeing? He's over at the Gilded Lily, the ladies' chambers at the other side of the yard. I'll get the boy to show you.'

'No need. I'll find it,' she said, and turned smartly on her heel. The door shuddered in its frame as she shut it.

'A Puritan killjoy,' said Tindall. 'I've seen the likes before.

These griping widows, always wanting to stir up trouble where there's none. Probably come to make a fuss, accuse your son of popery and such.'

'Don't fret, Tindall. Jay'll not have any trouble with her. He can handle it, can my Jay. He can sweet-talk the sourest lady. They all come round in the end.'

'Would you like me to escort her, check what she's about?'

'Would you, Nat, save my legs?'

'I'll come back later, tell you what she was after.' And Tindall hurried out through the door into the slippery yard.

Ella was looking out of the window, watching the men scraping the snow to clear a space for the carriages to turn, when Madame Lefevre crossed the yard. She recognized her stark black silhouette straight away and instinctively stepped back to the edge of the window. Maybe she had come to pawn something. But when she stopped to talk to Meg, and Meg pointed in her direction, her heart sank. She was looking for her.

She had to hide. The old crow must have seen the notices. She was lettered enough to read them for herself and would be chasing that reward. Without a thought for the customers she rushed upstairs and into the storeroom and shut the door behind her. To her surprise Jay Whitgift was up there. There were a lot of blocks of soap all lined up in rows on the table. He dropped the bundle he was holding up to his nose and looked embarrassed. 'Just sorting these soaps,' he said. 'Is anything the matter?'

'No. I mean, yes.' She heard the door go below, and her heart began to pound.

'Are you unwell?'

She did not answer.

'I take it the hounds of hell are after you?' He laughed.

'No.' She was unable to smile at his jest. 'Look, the woman

who's just come in. She knows me. I mean, it's Madame Lefevre, you know, my old employer from the wig shop. I don't want her to know I'm here, working for you.'

'Why not?'

'I just . . .'

'Good day?' The hollow impatience of Madame Lefevre's voice came from beneath their feet.

'Please, sir, would you tell her I've moved on? I don't want her to know where I work.'

'This is inconvenient – I don't expect to employ a salesgirl then have to go down myself.'

'Mr Whitgift? Is there anyone there?' echoed Madame Lefevre.

'Please, sir?' Ella kept her voice steady.

'Downstairs, Miss Johnson.'

Ella did not move. She shook her head and clung tight to the latch lever on the door.

Jay gave her a hard stare, frowned and pushed past her to go downstairs.

Ella leaned out onto the landing so she could hear their conversation. She dare not move nearer in case a floorboard should creak and give her away. Her mouth was dry. What if Madame had one of the notices with her? Jay Whitgift would recognize her straight away and she would be finished. Her thoughts tangled in her head. She forced herself to listen.

She heard Jay's voice. 'Ah, good afternoon, madam. I trust you are well.'

'Quite well, thanking you. I have come about Ella Appleby – the girl who made such a sow's ear of your wig.'

'There is no need to apologize further, madam . . .'

'No, no. I am trying to locate her.'

'Hold on, what did you say her name was?'

'Ella Appleby.'

There was a pause. Ella's fingernails bit into her palm. Pray God she would not tell him what they had done.

'Well, I am afraid I cannot help you. I have no idea where she is. Devilish weather, isn't it?'

'But the little girl in the yard told me there was a girl of her description working here.'

'Well, I'm afraid the little girl is not very well informed. I let your girl go. I'm afraid she did not suit.'

Ella loosened her grip on the banister rail and sat down. She craned her head so as to hear better.

'Where is she now?' asked Madame Lefevre.

'I have no idea, madam, nor do I care. She was a bad lot.'

Ella felt a stab at being referred to this way, but she was relieved he had not given her away.

'You have no idea where she lives?'

'I take no interest in the personal lives of my employees, madam, so no.'

'If she should come here again . . .'

'She won't.'

'But if she does, will you tell her to drop by the perruquier's?'

'Why should I?'

'There's some money owed to her. A considerable sum. She might be glad of it, now she has no position.'

Ella dropped down to a crouch. The crafty old stick. She'd got wind of the notices and seen the reward.

Jay's voice floated up.

'If I see her again, which I sincerely hope I will not, I will tell her no such thing. If you owe her money, then I should keep it. She certainly did nothing for your business.'

'That's true, but I feel that would be uncharitable. Let me

know if you come across her. Her or her sister, you remember, the girl with the birthmark on her face.'

'Whilst you are here, may I interest you in some calendula cream? It is very efficacious, so I am told. All the ladies swear by it for keeping wrinkles at bay.'

The slight pause told Ella that Madame Lefevre had registered the veiled insult.

'No, no,' came her voice. 'Just, I'd be interested to hear any news—'

The door jangled again.

'Ah, Jay. You are here after all.' Another man's voice.

'Oh it's you, Tindall,' said Jay. 'Would you escort Madame Lefevre across the yard, she's just leaving.'

'So you found him then,' said Tindall's voice. 'Here, take my arm. The yard's damned slippery, the cobbles are thick with ice – nearly came a cropper myself.'

Ella positioned herself behind the curtain. Dusk had fallen quickly. She watched as the shanky figure of Tindall led Madame Lefevre across the yard in tottering steps. They were talking as they went. She could see Tindall bend to listen, and once they stopped and seemed to be deep in conversation. Ella's stomach churned, wondering what they were saying and whether Madame Lefevre was telling him anything about her and Sadie. Eventually he raised his hand to Madame Lefevre and she turned out of the gate into the gathering darkness of the street outside. Ella released the fabric of the curtain which she held gripped in one hand. Her palm was sweating, her nerves jangling. She heard Jay moving downstairs and then the door to the stairway creak open.

Her stomach sank. Now she would have to face Jay and she was afraid. She had thought London to be safe. And it would have been. Were it not for Sadie, and her disfigurement. She could have disappeared quick, were it not for her. Two girls were much more conspicuous, and if one had a mark on her face – well. The city was tightening around her, twisting like the twitch they used to control an unbroken horse.

His heels rang on the wooden stairs. She steeled herself, took a deep breath.

'Are you going to tell me what this is about?' Jay reappeared grim-faced on the landing. 'You deceived me, gave me a false name.'

Ella curtseyed to him. 'Beg pardon, Mr Whitgift, I wanted a fresh start. I didn't mean nothing by it.'

'Why would you do that? She says there's money owed to you. Don't you want to lay claim to it?'

'That's lies. There's no money. She just wants to know where I am.'

'But why?' He moved closer to her, a glint in his eye. She felt hot suddenly, her tight-laced bodice was constricting her.

'Do you want the truth? She's after me because I owe her,' she lied, opening her eyes wide and looking into his.

'How much?'

'When she sacked me I was angry, so I robbed the petty cash drawer. But it was only a few farthings. Don't give me away. It weren't much and they'll brand me if you do.'

He scrutinized her a moment. 'I'm not sure I believe you, Ella Appleby. I was brought up in the backstreets of Whitechapel, and I tell you – I can smell something fishy from a hundred yards, and you're a good deal nearer.'

Ella looked down at her shoes.

'If I find anything's gone missing from the Gilded Lily . . .'

Ella thought of the second pot of alabaster cream she had tucked in her apron and was disconcerted to find the heat rising to her cheeks.

'You minx! You have, haven't you?'

Embarrassed, Ella brought out the pot of cream and held it out on her palm.

'What, this?' He let out a great snort of laughter. 'You pinched this?' She did not know why he was laughing. 'A ha'porth of cream?'

'Sorry, Mr Whitgift. I'll pay for it. 'Twas only a borrow, till I get my pay purse next week. I wanted to look more—'

'You've been using it?'

'Yes.'

'Come here.'

She approached him with her head bowed. He put his hands under her chin and tilted her face up and to the side. She thought she might faint, the blood beat at her temples. She held her breath.

'You could do with a little more. It would make you less ruddy.' He took hold of a wisp of her hair and lifted it between his finger and thumb. 'Lady Lucie Edgware has her hair styled very fetchingly, don't you think?'

'It is that. Very well done,' said Ella, quashing the feelings of envy that threatened to show in her face, and staying still as he fingered her hair.

'You could do worse than copy her style.' He released her hair and turned away saying, 'You may keep the cream. I expect you to recompense the business, though, from your next pay packet.'

Ella fumbled to put the jar away. He was looking at her with his black eyebrows furrowed and his lips pressed together. She crossed her fingers he believed her story about thieving from Madame Lefevre's.

'Miss Appleby, if that is truly who you are, I will keep your secret. I will not tell Madame Lefevre you are here. But I expect you to be obedient in return. You understand me?' He stacked the soaps in a neat tower one on top of the other. 'You may remain as Miss Johnson here, but the slightest whiff of trouble and I shall send for the wigmaker myself.'

She nodded. She dare not let the relief show on her face.

'You may go back down. Oh, one thing before you go. Walk with smaller steps, and daintily. When a gentlewoman enters, it must be silent, I should only hear the rustle of her skirts.'

'Yes, sir.'

Ella turned and made her way stiffly to the shop, slowly picking up her feet, placing them silently on the stair treads. She was mortified. He must think her a clumsy cluck, even in her new dainty boots. She made herself walk slowly, even though it made her feel strange to be creeping thus and not romping from one task to the next in a terrible hurry like she had when she was a housemaid. But if it was what Jay wanted and it stopped him asking any more questions, then she would oblige him. He followed her down, and she could feel him staring at her as she descended, an almost physical sensation of his eyes on the nape of her neck.

When he left her alone in the shop she almost fell to her knees in gratitude. She still had her position. But it had been frightening, Feverface appearing in the yard like that, and now Jay knew her real name he might read about her on the notices. She'd passed one on her way to the Lily, nailed to the shutter of the pudding shop. They must be on every street corner by now, and how much longer could she keep Sadie out of the public eye? She tussled it in her thoughts. Curse Sadie. But for her, she would have been invisible.

Chapter 22

Sadie opened the door to greet her sister.

'Brrr! Let me get inside!'

Ella dumped her basket and shrugged out of her cloak, shaking it at arm's length to dispel the snowflakes from its shoulders before depositing it on the hook on the back of the door.

Sadie drew back, surprised to see that Ella was dressed in another gown, this time an elaborate bright green and gold velvet, with lace point on the sleeves and a swathe of embroidered leaves and flowers on the front panel. Ella crossed the room carefully, as if treading on eggshells, and sat down stiffly on one of the hard stools. Her hair was dressed in a tight new style with a froth of lace ribbon wound around the topknot.

She looked sheepish as though she was expecting a comment from Sadie, but none was forthcoming. Sadie sat down again silently, her mouth set in a line, and carried on cutting up bacon fat to make lardy cakes. So she had another fine new gown, did she? And she, Sadie, still in her Westmorland woollen.

After a few minutes' strained silence, 'Been to Cornhill?' asked Sadie.

'No. I didn't want to trudge all the way up there in this snow.

Look, my feet are frozen. Can't wear my good leather bootees in this.' She wriggled a foot free from her wooden clog.

Sadie looked at Ella's reddened toes. They did not look like they belonged to the rest of her.

'It's turned slushy now and I did not want this dress to spoil,' Ella continued. 'I came straight home instead. I'll get the corn-meal tomorrow.'

Sadie made no comment, but got up and threw the bacon bits into a basin.

'Did you get your pay?'

'Yes.'

At last. Sadie threw up her hands. 'God be praised. So you can go to the flesh market as well, and get some ribs and maybe a bit of brisket. I'm that tired of patties and puddings.'

'Hmm.' Ella arranged her skirts on the stool and eased herself to upright.

Sadie sat down opposite her, wiped her hands and said, 'Let's have a deek at your pay. We'll count it out and put the rent aside. Then we can make a reckoning of what's left, for food and fuel.'

Ella did not open her purse. 'There's no need, I've paid the rent already. I called in on Ma Gowper on the way up.'

'That's good. How is she?'

'What do you think of my new suit?'

'Very fine.' Sadie's words were clipped.

'It's from Whitgift's Yard. You know, another one from their closet. He gave me another, picked it out on purpose. Sorry, I've not enough put by yet to buy one for you and I can't pinch one – they watch me like a hawk.'

Sadie could scarcely bring herself to look at it, but when Ella came in she had noticed straight away the hem was perfectly clean, despite the snow, as if it had never been worn. She must have held it up, all the way home. The green lent Ella's face and chest a slightly unhealthy cast. The new dress was much less becoming than the other. Ella's face was deathly pale, her chest white and heaving, as if the stays were making her breathless. There were two spots of bright red cochineal on her cheeks. Of late her eyes had slid away from Sadie's face whenever she asked her anything about Whitgift's.

Sadie cleared a space on the table and patted it with her hand. 'Shall we count it now?'

Ella paused a moment before pulling out her purse and dropping it with deliberate carelessness onto the table. Sadie began to comb the coins across the table one by one, making neat piles. When she had finished she looked up in concern.

'Is this right? Did the Whitgifts dock your pay?'

'No, he never. I told you, I've paid the rent.'

'Even with that, there still looks to be a shortfall.'

'I've told you. It's right. The old baggage put the rent up. She's that narrow she'd skin a flea for a ha'penny.' Ella scooped the coins and tokens off the table and crammed them back in the purse. 'Anyway, you don't have to keep account. I earn the money and I'm the one trailing the markets every day.'

'Oh, Ell, that's not fair. You know I'd be out that door in the shake of a tail, if I could.'

'But you can't. Your blasted description is all over those notices. Every last beggar in London is searching for you. Woe betide any other girl with a port wine stain on her face. A few days ago even that old crow Madame Lefevre was asking at Whitgift's after you.'

Sadie stood up. 'You never told me that. Why didn't you tell me?'

'It's all right. Sit tight. He sent her away. Said we'd moved on.'

'How long do you think, before it dies down?'

DEBORAH SWIFT

'God knows. It's like a bloody beacon, that face of yours. I was daft. I should have thought on it, left you safe in Netherbarrow. But I can't send you back. If they caught you they'd fetch it all out of you somehow.'

'How do you mean?' Then realizing what she meant, Sadie bit her lip and reached out her hand tentatively towards Ella's.

'Ella, don't be like that, give us a squeeze like we used to do.'

Ella stood up and moved away. 'You're too old for that soft nonsense now, Sadie. You have to stand on your own two feet, you can't be hanging round my skirts no more like a bairn.'

'I'm not. I just want us to stick together, that's all. Like you promised.'

'You could go out. If only you'd see sense and whiten your face.'

'I need a gown first.'

Ella shook her head wordlessly, then looked away towards the window.

Sadie picked up the dishcloth and wrung it. Her hands were trembling. 'Why didn't you tell me Old Feverface came to the yard? Everyone's chasing us. I'm scared, Ell.'

Ella turned back and snapped, 'Do you think I don't know? But there's nothing I can do about it, can I? I can't turn back time, we just have to sit it out. Wait for the dust to settle.'

'It's been a long time settling. And we need another wage; I can scarce make a meal with what we've got.' She stood up and paced the room, thinking at home she'd be taking in mending. Surely she could do something like that. 'I know, how's about you bring me some piece work, Ell?'

'For Christ's sake, I'm too busy to be running round after you. I've got responsibilities now at the Lily. Somebody's got to put bread on the table.'

'But I could help,' she said. 'I could fill scent bottles, or make up nosegays or baskets. I'm good at that, I've a right neat hand. I could do that without going out.'

'Don't be a goose. People would ask questions, wouldn't they, about where they'd come from. And if there was trouble, we can't shift from here again. We'd never get another place to stay, you would be spotted straight away. You and your stupid face. You've not touched that cream. I can see you've not.'

'Stop it.' She put the dishcloth down gently on the table. 'Don't start on me again.'

'I'd be clear and free if it wasn't for you. I'm that scared someone'll spot you, and then we'll be done for.'

'That's not true, stop saying such things.'

'I only brought you with me 'cos I was sorry for you. I couldn't leave you there with *him*, could I?'

Sadie felt a lump in her throat. Ella's dress creaked as she spoke. Sadie saw that some of the lacing was agape and a small roll of Ella's white flesh was swelling out. Ella was still speaking. 'It's hard looking out for you, I'm sick of having to worry myself to a fray. I don't know what to do if you won't even help yourself.' Ella stopped short. Her chest rose and fell as if she could not catch her breath.

Sadie felt her voice waver. 'I didn't make the trouble. It's your fault we had to run away, not mine.'

Ella moved towards her, pointing a finger. 'And whose fault is it that it keeps coming after us?'

She couldn't mean it. And yet from her expression Sadie could see that she did. 'That's it. Why are you being so spiteful? It's not my fault.'

Ella stared at her poker-faced, playing with the gold points of her laces. Her calmness made Sadie want to hit her. Perhaps Ella really meant it. A sob bubbled up from Sadie's throat. 'I've had enough. I don't care if they do catch us, I don't care if I burn, there's no one cares enough to bother anyhow.' She was crying now. Great tears rolled down her face. She had to get out. She turned and clattered blindly down the stairs.

'Oh Christ,' Ella said. She stood uncertainly on the doorstep looking right and left up the street. Sadie was nowhere to be seen.

'Miss Johnson,' came the quavering voice from behind the Gowpers' door, 'is that you?'

'Oh, put a gag in it,' Ella shouted and thumped her fist loudly at the door panel. 'Bloody stupid old hag.' Behind the door she heard the old woman cry, 'Help, Dennis!' Ella aimed a few vicious kicks at the door with her clog.

She sat on the stairs to organize her thoughts. She had a bad feeling pricking in the pit of her stomach. She knew that when she got angry the bile took over, that she'd say things she'd regret. And maybe she'd been a bit harsh with Sadie, but she'd only spoken the truth. It would be foolish to go haring after her, the safest thing was to keep separate. She'd come back anyway, there was nowhere else she could go. The snow was still slick on the ground so she'd be bound to come home.

Ella ignored Widow Gowper's querulous calls and went back upstairs to wait. The room was oddly empty without Sadie there. Sadie had become as much a part of the furnishings as the dealwood table and the oak stools. Ella went to the window. The landscape looked milky and pale, divided by the black Thames. As time went by and Sadie still had not returned, she began to fear that her sister had been caught. If she had, how long would it be before the constable came for her too? She imagined she could hear shouting, footsteps coming up the alley. Her hands started to sweat. The room seemed to grow smaller, to hem her in.

She peered out of the tiny window at the narrow ledge beneath. How on earth had Sadie balanced on that? She did not fancy her chances of escaping that way, if they came for her; there was a sheer drop below, and no way down to street level. Fear snaked up her spine. She grabbed her cloak and threw it on, not caring it was inside out, and half ran, half tripped down the stairs again. She looked quickly over her shoulder, to check she was not being watched or followed, then ran pell-mell, skidding down the dark alley.

Sadie huddled under the jetty, where it was thick dark and there was a little shelter. It was sleeting now, stinging icy water. She sat on a broken stone pillar from an older wharf that must have been washed away in years gone by. Melting snow dripped through the gaps between the boards, and every now and then a wash from a passing ship threatened to swamp her feet. She picked up a stick and stabbed through the snow to the mud, feeling the crust of ice break, over and over until the stick snapped. She scraped the mud into furrows and swirls with the broken stump.

She shivered in her thin sleeves, she had not picked up her cloak. Best stay in the dark where nobody could see her. It wasn't her fault she was born this way, she thought. What had happened to Ella? She didn't seem like her sister any more. When had she turned so hard and mean? Sadie thought back to when they were small, and Ella slapping the baker's boy when he dared to taunt her about her face. At night Ella used to kiss her on the head, rumple her hair, tell her she was God's favourite, and they had curled up close together under the knitted blanket in the big creaking bed. She had fallen asleep listening to some tale of Ella's, like the one about a beautiful girl who had married a monster. But then the monster had turned into a prince, so he wasn't a monster after all. In stories ugly people always turned into beautiful people in the end; there were no stories where the ugly person just stayed ugly.

Sadie's shoulders heaved and she wiped a tear on her sleeve. She remembered her da, and the way bitterness seemed to have wormed into everything he did. Until she was eight, her da was kept busy gardening for the squire. He took out his sorrow and anger at Ma's death by digging and hefting and lugging. Then as if it had suddenly shifted out of kilter, the world turned into a darker place. Cromwell came with his parliament, and there was to be no May merrymaking, and people were to be sober and quiet. The squire's house had been ransacked, and her da was told there would be no more garden work for him. He put away his yellow jerkin and began wearing temperance colours. Then somehow in their house the darkness and sadness had turned inwards, and like many folks, they hid their troubles behind closed doors.

Da changed, and he'd leather them for no cause at all, but on account he'd had a skinful, had nothing to do and felt like it. And Ella's pinching had started. Sometimes Ella would be blithe and happy, but other times she would suddenly turn on her, scratch her or pinch her as if she hated the world, and Sadie was the butt of it. Ella was like two people at once. Sadie had tried to be good and act small. She had tried to keep Ella merry, watching her face for any sign of a shadow. And if the shadow came, to dodge out of the way of her nipping fingers.

Despite this, when Ella had gone into service with the Ibbetsons she had missed her so badly. She prayed Ella would come for her, take her away from Da. She had forgotten about the pinching. But now it came back to her in a wave of self-pity.

Sadie looked at the river. The surface of the water fluttered with the currents of all the different craft and glassy flakes of ice floated on its surface. It was deep and black underneath its moving skin; it would be easy to walk into it and disappear. Then Ella would be free. They would both be free. Her da had not bothered to come looking. She stood up and walked towards the edge where the snow had melted into streaks and the mudbank fell away. Fragments of ice in the wash slapped with a strange chink against the posts of the jetty. She stared at it in a trance.

A wash from a passing skiff slopped icy water over her ankle. The next wave came up to her knees. It was so cold it burnt. She shuddered and jumped back. A tall ship was approaching, gliding slowly, its masts like glittering fingers in the light of the ship's lantern. The wash made the surface ripple outwards with a tinkling sound as her skirts began to float up from her ankles. Her feet were already numb. She took a few steps back to the shore. She wondered again what it would be like to wade in . . . just a few steps, she mused to herself, and it would be over, and Ella would be free of her. What happened when you died, she wondered. How did Saint Peter decide who was fit for Heaven?

The bottom was uneven and the stones slippery. Suddenly she lost her footing, her arms flailed and her legs struggled to stay upright. She felt her body instinctively clinging to life, desperate to right itself, not ready to give up. She staggered to stand.

Just then the ship unfurled its sails. Sadie gasped. The noise was like a gunshot. A crack of sailcloth and the ship pranced forwards. The great expanse of canvas, like a rolling cloud, pulled the ship through the water. She turned her face towards it, her heart jolted in her chest.

She stood in the muddy water up to her knees, her skirts dragging heavier and heavier, but she could not move. She was entranced by the ship, ploughing its way downriver, its white sails filled with wind. She thought of Dennis's father, his adventures in foreign lands. The pictures swam in front of her eyes, all the colour and drama. And then she thought of Dennis, his slightly furrowed eyebrows as he pointed to the pictures in his books. The ship was right opposite her now. It filled her with a sense of joy and freedom. It moved fast, slipping away through the water towards the open horizon.

Sadie staggered up the bank. She hauled on her wet skirts, plunged noisily back towards the shore and the lamps of London, cursing her stupidity. She wrung out the dripping material as best she could. She watched, shivering, as the ship's sails became a mere pinprick in the dark, before turning her face and running hell for leather towards Old Swan Stairs and Blackraven Alley.

Chapter 23

Sadie paused just inside the door, her teeth chattering, hearing the sound of crying and coughing from the Gowpers' chambers, and the murmur of Dennis's voice soothing her.

He's a good son, she thought to herself.

She took off her clogs and tiptoed upstairs, where she was surprised to find the door was ajar but Ella's cloak gone from the peg. She checked all round the room, but there was no sign of it, so Ella must have gone out. But the door was unlocked. It was unlike her to leave it open; she hoped it did not mean the worst. What if Ibbetson had tracked them down? She closed the door but left it open a crack to listen out for Ella, and took off her sodden skirt and boots and put on some old petticoats. She rubbed her feet hard until they began to tingle and the toes lost their pallor and turned red. The smell of the Thames seemed to fill the room. With a pang of guilt, Sadie reasoned that perhaps Ella was still out searching for her, and by now she must be worried to death.

A rap at the door. Sadie jumped, and turned round.

'Can I come in?' said Dennis's voice.

Oh no, not now. 'Wait on.' Sadie hastened to the trunk and wrapped an old apron around her waist to hide her petticoat, though she knew she looked dishevelled and her hands were still muddy. She swirled them in the pail and dried them on her sides. She hoped her eyes were not too red – she did not want him to know she'd been crying.

Dennis sidled in, looking uncomfortable. He held his cap in one hand, and the other plucked nervously at the seam of his brown tweed breeches. He gazed down at the space in front of her feet, as if addressing the floorboards,

'I got home and found my ma in a right old state. She's that upset it's taken me near on an hour to quieten her. Someone's been a-hammering at our door and shouting at her.' He looked into her face in appeal. 'I told you, she can't stand trouble. She says it was Miss Johnson from up the stairs. Is that right? Was it your sister?' He paused. 'Or was it you?' His eyes rested on her face briefly but then flicked downwards again.

'It wasn't me. I'm sorry. It must have been Ella. She's upset. We had a disagreement.' She avoided his eyes, aware that this hardly described what had passed between them.

The pair of them paused, both staring ridiculously at the floor. Eventually Dennis looked up and said, 'Sorry, Sadie, but I can't be having it. I said – if there's trouble, then you'll have to find somewhere else.'

'Oh, please, no . . . don't say that. It won't happen again, I promise. I'll talk to her, honest.'

He looked doubtful. 'No. When I first said you could have the room you looked like nice country girls, and I was sorry for you because them lads were after you. Then I finds out you're on the run. I should have turfed you out there and then. But I didn't. God knows why not. Now this. Sorry, but Ma says the girl's got to pack her things and go.'

'We can't. You know we can't,' Sadie said, tears starting to prick in her eyes again. 'There's notices out all over London. If

I'm seen, then we'll both hang. Have a heart, don't put us out, Dennis.'

Dennis squeezed his cap between his hands and shifted from foot to foot. He cleared his throat. 'Ma's already suspicious. She says she can hear noises and shouting from up here. She thinks your sister's entertaining menfolk and she'll not stand for it. I didn't think you were like that.'

'I'm not. You know it's not that. I try to be quiet as I can, but it's hard, cooped up here every day. I'll talk to Ella, we won't be no more trouble, I swear. Just give us a bit more time, till the hue and cry has gone. Then we'll move on, if you like, I promise.'

'I don't know. She was right upset, thought it were some beggar breaking in again, till she heard a girl's voice shouting through the door.'

'Sorry if we upset your ma, Dennis. We'll be quiet as the grave. But please don't put us out. Where could we go?'

'Sorry, Sadie.' Dennis twisted his cap in his hands and hurried to go out of the door.

'I'll do anything.' Her voice broke as she called after him. 'I'll do all your mending, or anything. Just let us stay.'

'No,' he said, turning, anger flaring in his eyes. He softened. 'You don't need to do that, I mean . . . if you stay, there's to be no more fuss, and no more bothering Ma.'

'There won't be, I promise. Please, Dennis?'

'Well, I . . .'

'You'll let us stay?'

He inclined his head with a barely perceptible nod. 'Don't know what I'll tell Ma.'

She rushed towards him as if to hug him, but stopped short and mumbled instead, 'Beg pardon, I mean . . .'

'I must be mad,' he said. 'But if you went, I couldn't stand to hear you'd been caught and hanged and be thinking it were all my fault.' He turned to leave, but she followed him to the door.

'Thank you, Dennis. You won't hear another sound, promise.'

'It's a big favour I'm doing you, so I hope you're mindful of it.' His face creased into a smile. 'Keep safe now, and tell that sister of yourn I expect her to come apologize to Ma.'

'I'll tell her,' Sadie said, knowing there wasn't a hare's chance. 'Sorry' wasn't a word generally in Ella's vocabulary.

When he had gone Sadie tiptoed down to look out of the door to see if there was any sign of Ella. But the street was empty, the night was frosty and most sensible folks were inside by a warm fire. She came back up the stairs shaky from the strain of it all. She put her hand to her chest, felt the scrap of lavender ribbon there and the reassuring thump of her heart. She was ashamed that Dennis had had to come up, uncomfortable that he should think ill of her. She could still see his rueful expression in her mind's eye, and it pained her, a sharp ache in the pit of her stomach.

She roused herself to make a tin cup of watered ale, added a pinch of allspice and heated it over two candle flames until it bubbled. Then she sat with it cradled on her lap, keeping the scalding metal moving in her hands, waiting for Ella's return.

At length Sadie found her head nodding. She sat up with a start. Still no Ella. Befuddled with sleep, she closed the gaping door. She pushed away the thoughts that Ella might have been recognized, or something untoward might have happened to her. She was just too tired to worry about her any more. Her legs were leaden, her eyes smarted and her head ached. She took herself to their shared bed and pulled the covers up to her chin. She stroked the lint of her shawl between her finger and thumb, the way she had when she was a child, and when she fell asleep, she slept for a long time.

Some time in the night Ella must have returned, because in the morning Sadie awoke to find that there was a bowl on the table, with the remains of some millet gruel, and a bone comb lying there. Sadie let out a great breath of relief. Ella must have been back and gone out again to work as usual. By the fire stone was a tiny poundweight bundle of kindling such as you might buy from a shop. These signs of normality lifted her spirits and she happily washed Ella's platter, as she was wont to do, and when she found Ella's dirty chemise cast onto the floor, she picked it up and put it in the buck tub along with her wet things from the night before. She moved slowly, so as not to make a noise, and she was leisurely with these tasks, for she knew time would hang heavy on her hands through the daylight hours, and she could not risk going out until after dark.

That day she lit a fire, taking cheer from the crackle and spit of the wood. Widow Gowper would never know, she never went out. The wind whistled its hollow song through the chimneys and spires of the city, and the water began to melt in the jug. She trimmed the wicks on the rushlights, boiled down the saved candle-ends to make soap and gazed out of the window at her friend, the river. There were plates of ice now stretched out from the bank, like ragged shelves. The sea birds were standing on them squawking their hunger to each other. She could not wait for nightfall – to go out, feel the fresh air nip her nose and go back to the water's edge to watch for tall ships from the jetty. She might find more fuel too; the fire was like a beast, always needing to be fed.

She knew the hours between four of the clock and dusk always felt the longest; it was at this time she began to get restless. She put on her cap and shawl and her hooded cloak, long before the dark. Standing by the window, impatient, she watched the setting sun bleed into the sky, saw the few buildings on the opposite bank flame and then fade to featureless shapes, becoming blank holes in the landscape.

She watched the night ferries go by, rejoicing at each passing lantern. When she could see a dozen lanterns, surely then it was dark enough for her to venture outside, though she worried about the reflected light from the snow. When night finally fell and she turned back into the room it was darker than she anticipated, but she did not bother with a taper as she knew every inch of the space. She wrapped her shawl tight about her head and face, cowled the hood of her cloak into a deep cave.

She felt for the door and found the thin metal latch that served as a handle. She pressed it down and pulled the door.

It wouldn't shift.

She fiddled with the latch, thinking it must not be fully disengaged. Another hard pull. It was stuck.

Perhaps it was frozen. She knew this was unlikely. She tugged even harder, but it still didn't open. She could hear the hasp rattling on the other side. Frustrated, she went to light a stub of candle. She held it up to the door to see where it might be jammed. But she could not see anything, just a thin sliver of darkness. She leaned back on the latch with all her might but it did not give an inch. She dare not rattle it too hard, and she could not shout to anyone for help.

She paced the room, hoping that when Ella came home from Whitgift's she would be able to get it open from the other side somehow. But as the night grew on, there was still no sign of Ella. She went to the window again, drawn as always by the view of the life from which she was excluded. The odd flake of snow drifted past on its leisurely journey to extinction in the river. Shortly after the bells struck eleven of the clock, she heard a noise outside.

It was the sound of clinking metal as if someone was fiddling with the lock. Sadie went over to the door and, half fearful, put her ear to it. She could hear someone shuffling outside.

'Ell, is that you?' she whispered.

'Course it's me,' came the short reply.

'Is the door still stuck? What's the matter with it? I can't open it.'

Just then the door swung open and Ella came in.

'It's not stuck,' she said. 'I locked it.'

Sadie was dumbfounded. 'With this,' continued Ella in the low voice they always used at home. She held up a new iron padlock, from which a large key protruded. Sadie stood aside to let her pass, still a little confused.

'Where did you get that from?'

'The ironmongery. Last night.' She lifted it up and held it out. 'Four shilling, it cost me.'

Ella kicked off her snow-crusted clogs onto the floor where the snow began to pool in a dark stain. Sadie noticed her lips had been smeared with a red paint. 'You mean . . . you mean you locked me in on purpose?'

'Well, I couldn't have you roving all over London.'

Sadie looked at the lock in disgust. 'Four shilling for that? You're mad. Fancy locking me in. What if there was a fire? I wouldn't have been able to get out.'

'Then you'd have been warm for a change!' Ella giggled at her own joke. 'There won't be a fire. I reckoned someone might recognize you and follow you home. And then they'd have us both by the necks. So I took precautions.'

'Well, I won't be locked in again, d'you hear?'

'Stop bellyaching. It was only a few hours. Look what I've brought us.' She held up a basket. 'Peace offering,' she said, pulling back the cover to reveal some cold pasties.

'I don't want any. Where were you last night?'

'I went back to the night market by the bridge. Stayed awhile to listen to the ballad singers. You were snoring like a horse when I got home.'

'I was not.'

'Please yourself. I'm going to bed. I'm that tired I could sleep for a hundred years.'

Neither of them mentioned their falling out. Ella washed her face then made a great fuss of getting undressed, struggling with the lacing of her bodice, unable to twist to undo the points in her stiff busk. Sadie did not offer to help as she usually did, but let her curse and strive. In her shift Ella looked like the little girl Sadie used to know, with her calves and ankles showing like they did at haymaking when the weather was hot and they cooled off their feet in the trough. Sadie watched her gather up the folds of the shiny gown from round her feet before hanging the whole rig from the back of the door. Ella wrapped herself in a blanket and climbed into bed without a word.

'Night,' Sadie said.

Ella ignored her, pulled all the blankets and the knitted coverlet up to her chin and shut her eyes, leaving the bare palliasse at the other end. Sadie wondered how her sister could sleep like that – she slept upright now, stiff as a scarecrow, lest her hair spoil.

Chapter 24

The next day the weak morning sun filtered through the window as Sadie watched Ella, mirror in hand, apply white paste to her skin. She must have brought that home from Whitgift's, Sadie thought, wondering how much it cost and how many vegetables it would have paid for. But she said nothing. Ella was quivering with cold and looked tired and wan even before she started. It was as if she was trying to obliterate every trace of her natural self.

'Is that the same cream you gave me?' Sadie asked as Ella's cheeks disappeared under a coating of white. 'What's in it?'

'It's ceruse. White lead.' Ella dabbed blots of cochineal paper onto her cheeks so that they flared suddenly pink.

'It smells like metal. Who'd want that on their skin?'

'Oh, for heaven's sake. Everyone does. There's no harm in it. I wish you'd bloody do it. Instead of sitting here your whole life. Pass me that comb, will you.'

Sadie handed it to her, feeling a stab of guilt. 'Sorry, Ell,' she said, 'about the other day. Let's be friends, shall we?'

'Who's not friends?' But her voice was cold.

Sadie took a deep breath. 'Dennis was up. He wanted to give us notice. Said you'd been shouting at his ma.'

Ella did not look up from her ministrations to her complexion. 'Poxy old crab. She yaps at me every time I pass. I can't bear to listen to her droning on. She collars anyone who goes past her door.'

'Happen she's lonely, on her own all day.' Sadie knew how that felt. 'She only wants a bit of company.'

Ella ignored this and, drawing out a brush from her muslin washbag, began to paint in fine lines where her eyebrows used to be. 'You told him we're staying, right?'

'He was serious. Said you'd to go and beg pardon. If we make any more noise, we're out.'

Ella gave a small snort.

'He really meant it. Won't you call on her on the way down? Smooth things over, like?'

'Hmm.' Ella's voice was non-committal. She bundled her pots and potions back in the bag and threw it down on the bed. She brushed down her skirts. Her face was like a mask, her painted eyebrows lacked the expression her real ones had and the ceruse seemed to make her face stiff. Already there were fine cracks around the nose and lips.

'Right. I'm going to work,' she said, sweeping up the padlock from the table.

Sadie saw her pick it up, realized what she was doing and leapt after her. 'No,' she whispered, 'no, Ella. Not again, don't lock me in.'

But Ella was already on the outside of the door.

'Ella!' Sadie grabbed hold of the edge of the door with both hands, wrestling to keep it open as Ella tried to pull it shut.

'Be quiet. Do you want to wake Ma Gowper?' Ella hissed.

For a moment there was a wordless struggle as both girls pulled at either side of the door. Sadie could not get a grip on the dusty floorboards and she scuffled to keep her footing, her fingers clamped round the door. It began to creak shut, but still

Sadie clung on, trying to keep it open. The iron padlock cracked down hard on Sadie's hand. Sadie instinctively let go and brought her smarting fingers to her mouth. In an instant Ella had shut the door smartly behind her, and she heard the rattle of the hasp and the grate of the key being turned in the padlock.

'It's for your own good,' Ella's low voice said from the hall.

'Please, Ella, don't lock me in,' whispered Sadie, 'I'll stay here, honest.'

'Then it don't matter if the door's locked.'

'But, Ella –'

'I said I'd be back, didn't I. After I finish work.'

'What time's that? Ella?'

But there was no answer, just the noise of Ella's feet tapping downstairs. She heard Ma Gowper's faint call from below. Sadie listened to see if she could hear Ella knock at her door. But no, moments later she heard the creak of the front door and the click as it shut.

Ella walked as quickly as she could to Whitgift's, given the icy conditions. Sadie was safe indoors now, out of sight. Dennis would already be at work, so there was no one to know she was locked in. And Ella could breathe easy for now. She tried to walk with small steps, and kept away from the overhangs of the buildings, where the icicles were sharp as teeth and snow slid off the roofs to land on your head and shoulders in an icy shock. She jostled for the wall with the other pedestrians, picking her way over the slippery cobbles in her new heels. Although she hitched up her skirts, the hem still got soaked by a passing cart spraying slush from the drains, where the horse dung, peelings and other refuse made a permanent midden in the middle of the street. Swearing at the departing tailgate, she tried to brush off the worst of it with her fingers just outside the yard.

Still, she felt a pang of pride as she entered Whitgift's. Not for her the snaking queue of women in homespun fustian, pawning their only pair of shoes to buy a few loaves. She knew she did not look like a serving maid any more. She had gone up in the world. It would be hard for anyone to recognize the girl from Westmorland. She was yellow-haired 'Miss Johnson' now, of the Gilded Lily on Friargate, not plain 'Appleby'. She threw back her cloak and held her head up high, noting with satisfaction the sullen stares of the bundled women standing in line.

As she reached the door, a flutter of apprehension seized her and she paused to take a deep breath and compose herself, in case Jay should be about. He was in her thoughts all the time. She had stopped calling him Jay, or even Mr Whitgift, because there was only one man ever in her thoughts, and to call him by his name to others seemed to give away too much about her feelings for him.

The image of him seemed to sit in the back of her mind, burnt there like a brand with a white-hot iron. It gave her a kind of pain, the same kind of pain she had when looking in the glass, a sort of nameless longing. The way he walked – with his slightly swinging gait, the narrowness of his long fingers when he rested them on the counter. The image of his face loomed behind all she did, the thin lips with his slightly wolf-like white teeth, the impeccable cut of his clothes.

Yesterday he had implied she was a little too wide round the waist, so when she got to the Lily she had Meg haul on the laces of her stays, and now they were so tight she was almost breathless.

'It is important,' he had said to her, 'that you set an example. Fashionable ladies are already looking to you. Not for breeding or manners, for they already have those, but for your appearance. You are the living example of every pot and potion the Gilded Lily has to offer. So you must take pains to be immaculate. Gain their confidence, for we must keep them coming, the ladies of quality.'

'Yes, Mr Whitgift,' she had said, blushing furiously beneath her ceruse, because he had called her beautiful.

'Perhaps take a little less refreshment with the customers, though, and tighten your stays, I think your waist is thickening a little.'

She had nodded, but it had hurt. She had steadfastly refused all food and drink since, and it made her feel a little light-headed. But the tightened stays pushed up her bosom even higher and gave a satisfying curve to her hips, so she supposed it was worth it. And if he wished her to have a narrow waist, then she would have a narrow waist.

It was true, though, that since she had taken her appearance in hand, the customers were more inclined to ask her advice, and items she recommended were racing out of the door. She had imitated the refined way of speaking as much as she was able, learnt to talk of music and painting and whist, merely by repeating another's words to someone else. She had never painted or played – never touched a spinet or sat down to cards. It was lucky, she thought, that she had always been a good mimic. And she had learnt to talk of their jewels. Jay's eyes lit up whenever she talked of these.

So today the chambers were thronged with young ladies, all of them wanting to know which skin whitener she used, which shade of red on the lips, how she had such a smooth complexion. Of course she could not tell them it was because she was brought up in the country where epidemics of the pox were rare, so she pointed to Whitgift's Rare Elixir and told them it was guaranteed to keep the pox away, and smiled sweetly and wrapped the little jars in paper and straw, and felt the delicious cool coins run through her fingers. Whilst Mrs Horsefeather puffed back and forth with messages for the gentlemen, Ella was kept busy – showing pomades and hair restoratives, demonstrating how to crush rose petals into a kerchief to provide a pleasant scent, and telling ladies how much better they looked since buying the Lily's Patent Skin Dew.

An instinct, a slight jump of the heart, alerted her to Jay's presence almost before he opened the door. He arrived just after midday, followed by the ruffled silhouette of Mrs Horsefeather.

Ella was attending to the Misses Edgware, back again for some arrowroot tooth-powder and a nettle hair rinse. When they saw him saunter in they looked as if they might swoon at any moment, scooping their purchases hurriedly into their bags lest he should see them. They cracked open their embroidered fans, hiding behind them with a flutter of their charcoaled eye-lashes. He smiled and raised his hat to them, occasioning more flurrying.

Ella stood to attention as he approached, and breathed in so that her waist should appear smaller. He waved Mrs Horsefeather to behind the counter and indicated Ella should follow him up-stairs with a twitch of his eyebrow. She followed, waving for Meg to accompany her, aware that the Edgware sisters immediately began whispering behind their fans.

'I am expanding the business,' he said, not bothering to sit down. 'I talked my father round and he has agreed to it.'

Ella smiled and nodded.

'It has been a runaway success. His takings are up. So I am going to have the Lily open at night, as well as in the daylight hours. It seems there is a demand. Several gentlemen have said their wives would like a place to feel safe in town whilst their husbands play at cards or do their business. But I know men, and I know that often their business can go on until all hours. And Mrs Horsefeather is no earthly use in the evenings. So I will need to take on another hand, because one maid cannot be lively all that time . . .'

Ella felt her face fall. 'Oh no, not another maid. You don't need anyone else, Mr Whitgift.' The words were out before she could prevent them. 'I mean to say – I can do all those hours. Let me work the evenings too.' Another maid? In her shop? Not if she could help it. The new maid might be pretty.

Jay twirled a signet ring round and round on his little finger, and then shook his head. 'You have done well, started to make a reputation as a beauty, and the women confide in you. And that means you are able to give me the information I need.'

She nodded. She knew that when he asked about the women's jewellery – what gems they wore, what new purchases they had made for their houses – his consuming interest was not in securing its safety, but she played his game with an unspoken understanding.

He sat on the bed, his long legs pushed out towards her. 'You may sit,' he said. 'I wish the current situation to continue. It is good for business. No, we will need extra help. You will start to look tired if you are at the counter all that time, and besides, a little variety . . .'

'I'm sure I can manage it. And I'd like the extra hours. It wouldn't tire me, I know it wouldn't—'

'Enough. I have decided. You will work afternoons and evenings, when we are busiest. The new maid will work the mornings when our customers are, how shall I say, less well-to-do. In exchange for working evenings, and for convenience, you will lodge here in this room.'

'This room?' Ella was dumbfounded. Was he really telling her she could live here, at the Gilded Lily?

'You will be on call in case we require extra help in the Lily. I always had it in mind, but I was not sure whether you would be satisfactory. But now I know for certain you will not let me down. After all, I know you would not wish to return to the per-ruquier's. We understand each other, do we not?'

He looked directly into her eyes. She flustered, and fiddled with the lace at her neck. He was leaning on her, she knew. She felt hemmed in, trapped. But she shook the sensation away, for surely he did not mean it in that way. He only meant to compliment her, surely.

'I would never let you down,' she said, 'but it's a bit awkward. There's my sister, you see.'

He brushed this aside. 'Naturally, you may have arrangements to make, notice to give and so forth. You may move in immediately if you wish. Here are the keys. Mind them well. The main gate is always kept locked outside hours, you will need to ring the bell for admittance, but these are for the chambers at the Lily.'

He held them out to her. She stared at them as if they were a manifestation from heaven above.

'No money will be kept on the premises overnight.'

She coloured.

'The Lily will be open tomorrow evening,' he continued, 'and I expect you to be there. One of the delivery carts will be at your disposal tomorrow afternoon for you to bring over your things.'

Ella did not know how to react. She opened her mouth to ask if she could do the work but still live at home, but then she shut it again. She didn't want to live in the tiny damp box with Sadie, she wanted to live at Whitgift's, in these warm dry rooms, and more than anything she wanted to be close to Jay. She didn't know how it could be done, but she was not going to give away the chance.

He dangled the keys on his index finger. 'You don't look taken with the idea.'

She leapt to reassure him. 'Oh, don't say that, I am. But it's bowled me over. I never expected it, that's all.' She held her hand out for the keys. He dropped them into her palm from his pinched finger and thumb.

'Good, then it's settled. And by the way, that green dress is something – very *à la mode*. It is more subtle than the red. Who did it belong to?'

'Me, sir.'

'You? It's not from the clothing bay?'

'No. I bought it myself. With last month's wages. Chose the stuff and all.' She brushed her hands proudly over the folds at the hips. 'I went out in my snap time and had a draper make it to fit.' Then she added, 'I didn't want to be beholden to anyone no more.'

He smiled, seeming to find this amusing. 'I see. Very laudable. Turn around, so that I can see the back.' She turned, and heard the clack of his shoes as he came up behind her. He placed a hand on the small of her back. She tried to swivel around to face him, but he turned her away again by the shoulders.

'It is pretty well done. The fabric is not top quality, but it is very neatly sewn.'

To be this close to him gave her a shiver of anticipation. His breath was light on the back of her neck. She waited motionless, hoping he might embrace her, but instead he took hold of some of the hair that had come loose from her topknot. She felt the slight tug as he twisted it around his finger and tucked it into one of the hairpins, before turning her back to face him.

'Very good,' he said. 'I have ordered a pair of looking glasses from Venice – picture-sized glasses – for the Lily. Beautiful things with very fine gilded frames. I have half a mind to install one of them up here, as well as in the shop downstairs, so that you may make sure you do not have mud on your hem.' He looked pointedly at her feet.

'Beg pardon, sir. It's difficult to stay clean and all, when I have to walk here in all weathers. But when I live here, I'll be spotless, I promise.'

'Spotless, is it now?' He laughed, looking down his long nose at her. 'I somehow don't think so.'

She laughed along with him as they went back downstairs, although she did not really understand why he seemed to find her so amusing. She didn't want to be thought of as amusing, she wanted to be taken seriously. He did not laugh at the young lady customers who came into the Lily, he treated them with deference, even respect.

During the afternoon she contemplated this, worrying it over in her mind. She barely listened as her visitors spoke, but handed them the phials and ointments with an absent smile. She thought back to the day she first set eyes on Jay in the wig shop. She knew straight away he was a man of consequence by the way Madame Lefevre treated him. But it was different now she was in his employ. She felt the weight of his authority now, his ability to dispense with her. She felt the press of power in him, and she did not like it. If someone told her what to do or gave her orders, it set off the urge in her to do the very opposite. Contrary, they had called her in the village. But she also sensed the hot flicker of her heart whenever she thought of him. She wanted to have a chance with him, to bring his power to herself, and for that she would bear anything. They were alike, she and him. He ran deep, just as she did. She could beguile him, if she lived here at the Lily, for she had never failed with a man yet. Men needed persuading a little, that was all. It was a question of willpower.

During the afternoon she found several excuses to pop upstairs to see her chamber. She was already thinking of it as her chamber. The chamber with the proper wooden bed and the lime-painted walls, the long low windows with the stuff drapes, the washstand with the pretty blue and white basin and ewer. And fancy – now she was to have a fine looking glass with a gilded frame.

She had no idea what to do about Sadie. Lord knows, she couldn't bring her here, but nor could she send her back to Westmorland – either way she would be spotted in a moment and their lives would unravel. Yet she could not leave Sadie in the Gowpers' lodgings; who would keep an eye on her? It was clear that she couldn't be trusted to stay indoors. Hadn't she warned her, plain as plain, not to go out? And then at the very first sign of an argument, what had she done – she'd run off into the street. It wasn't even full dark. What if someone had seen her? It did not bear thinking about. Sadie didn't understand, maybe did not feel death snapping at her heels. The world was a ruthless place. Sadie was weak, would probably blab if they pressed her. No, she must stay where she was, safe out of sight.

Chapter 25

Madame Lefevre pointed to the empty stool.

'Where's Mercy Fletcher?'

Corey carried on knotting, focused intently on the work in front of her, but sharply aware of the other girls' embarrassment and Madame Lefevre's probing look.

'I don't know, madame,' Alyson said. 'We haven't seen her.'

Madame Lefevre tapped the measuring stick on her hand and walked between the benches. 'Does anyone know where she is?'

'No, madame,' Betsy said. 'Maybe it's the weather.'

Corey breathed a sigh of relief, they weren't going to tell on her.

'Been in a fist-fight, have we?' Madame addressed Corey.

'Fell over, madame. Slipped in the snow.'

Madame Lefevre narrowed her eyes, and sniffed to show her disbelief.

When she had gone Corey turned to Betsy. 'Thanks, Betsy, for keeping quiet.'

Betsy didn't say anything, just smiled a rueful smile, and they all continued to knot peacefully in silence.

Mercy did not return to work for the rest of the week. But the following Monday they heard the noise of boots on the scraper inside the front door and felt the sudden icy draught. When this happened the girls paused in what they were doing, to listen and see who the customer might be and what they wanted. Already they had overheard Madame Lefevre accept an order for four more footmen's perukes, even though she had made a great fuss about orders only that morning, telling them they were over-stretched with one less girl. They had looked at each other with raised eyebrows and shaken their heads.

This time the voice was easily identified as Mr Ibbetson, the man who had been enquiring after Ella and Sadie. Last time he had been, Alyson said his slightly nasal voice sounded as if his mouth was full of false teeth. Fortunately for the listening girls, it was also the sort of voice that carried.

'I was passing so I thought I would call. Is there any further news of the Appleby sisters?'

'I'm afraid not,' Madame Lefevre's voice replied.

'You did not think to make further enquiries with the girls?' He said it as if it was Madame Lefevre's fault.

'Have there been no sightings then?'

'On the contrary. I had to go down to Newgate Gaol yester-day. There was a half-dozen waiting for me there. They kept the folk who'd brought them in waiting in the alley beyond, as well. Vultures, all of them. Some unscrupulous people will try anything for money. None of the girls in the cells was she. In fact I've never seen such a crowd of hapless cases. Would you credit it – there was even one poor soul languishing there who was sixty years old.'

'Really? Well, I am afraid, Mr Ibbetson, that as far as I can see the trail is completely cold. Despite my best efforts on your behalf, it seems they are vanished into thin air.'

'I shall not give up, you know.'

'I'll let you know, sir, if there's anything further I can do . . .' A draught caused the calico curtain to swing, and then the shop door closed.

Madame marched into the room. 'If anyone here knows anything, or sees hide or hair of Sadie or Ella Appleby, you are to come straight to me. Not to the Blue Ball, but to me. Do I make myself clear?'

'Yes, madame,' they chorused, having no intention of doing any such thing.

Corey hoped that Sadie was hidden safe somewhere and not one of those poor girls in the pits in Newgate. She was uneasy to think that old Feverface had been out sniffing after Sadie and Ella. All afternoon Corey could not shift Sadie and Ella from her mind, wondering what it felt like to have the spectre of the noose hanging over you.

No wonder Sadie had shot off so quick when Mercy set her brother on her. And it must have taken some courage to come say her farewells. But oh my Lord, she sure and certain hoped Sadie was feeling brave now, with that cold fish Ibbetson out looking for her, and that killjoy Mercy Fletcher, and Old Feverface intent on claiming the reward and bringing her to the gallows.

That night when Corey got home, she helped her mam get supper ready as usual before she went to work. Her mam worked in the Fox's Brush tavern of a night, so Corey was always left in sole charge of the children. Three of them, Tom, Harry and Benny – all little terrors that'd test the mettle of a saint. When she had rounded Tom and Harry up, taken off their wet mitts and got them to the table, she shouted outside again for Benny, the youngest, to come in. He was always the last, couldn't bear to leave his friends in case he missed something.

When he finally did come in, hands and face filthy as always, he said, 'What's in the pot, sis?'

'Beet and barley soup, same as usual. Now wash your hands.'

'Good, I'm starving. Hey, there's some new notices up by the wharf. I just seen 'em. There was a few folks gathered round so we went up for a look-see. A man was nailing them up whilst we stood by. He told us to sling it, but we hung round anyways. There's one up asking after two maids. "Savage Sisters", the man said. What's "savage"?'

'Ooh,' said Tom, the eldest. 'What've they done?'

Corey turned from adding salt to the pot. 'Savage? It means sort of fierce, or cruel maybe. But maybes they're not really like that. Do you know aught else?'

'Nah. Only what the man said. Said one of them's got a great red stain on her cheek. That they're evil and round here some place.' He looked round the parlour as if one of them might materialize any moment from a dark corner.

Corey stirred the soup. Those notices must be about Sadie and Ella. It made her angry, her friends being hounded like this. Not that she really knew the truth of it, but no mistaking, Sadie and Ella were in trouble up to their necks. She tapped the wooden spoon briskly on the edge of the pot. 'Less of your nonsense now, soup's ready,' she said.

Benny ignored her and carried on chattering to his brothers. 'After we come away Simon says he's seen one of them, but we don't believe him. He makes up porkies all the time. Anyhow, he said she was on the shore a-gatherin' coal. Well, that's cuckoo, ain't it?'

There was laughter round the table. Corey ladled the soup into his bowl as he talked. 'Catch one of them gatherin' coal! No, she'd be out slitting people's throats with her other half. Peter says they've done all sorts. There was another washed-up body by the bridge only the day afore yesterday, all bloated, and Peter says he bets it's them as strangulated her.'

'Who are Simon and Peter?' Corey said. 'Do I know them?'

'Yes, sure you do, the costermonger's sons. Peter and Simon Reed. Peter's the eldest, and Simon's his brother—'

'Are they in the ginnel now?'

'Yep, I asked 'em to wait up whilst I had this.' He was already sliding off the stool, his bread and dripping still in his hand, anxious to be back outside playing with his friends.

'Hold on, Benny. If you bring Simon and Peter inside, I'll give them a currant patty to share.'

'I'll get 'em.'

A few moments later her kitchen was even more full of grubby children. She soon picked out Simon and asked him if he'd wait and tell her about what he'd seen.

'It were only one of 'em,' he said, 'but I'm sure it were her because even though it were dark I could see she had a great big patch on her face. Like Uncle Seth's dog it were – from here to here. She seemed friendly-like. Course then I din't know she was savage and she'd cut your heart out, so I din't know to be scared.'

'Where was this, Simon?'

'Not far. Just round the corner. Old Swan Stairs, near enough. On the shore there. She was pretending to be an ornary girl. And I've seen her again since. Looking out a window, and laughing at me. That's twice I seen her. But I ain't going back.'

'If I come with you now, will you show me which window?'

'No. Not on your life. I was just lucky the first time that she was acting friendly. But that might have been to trick me. She stared at me last time and then she laughed. It gives me the creeps now when I remember it, that laugh.'

'You'll be safe with me. I would really like to see where you saw her – because once I had a friend with a patch on her face, and she wasn't savage at all. I've lost track of my friend and I'm still looking for her.'

'I know. Peter says everyone's looking for her. But he says not to tell, 'cos she might come after me and slit my throat.'

'Where was this, Simon?'

'I dunno. I can remember it, I think. But what if she sees me? She might come and get me. Peter says she can shift shape like a witch and fly in your window at night.'

'I'll be with you, so you needn't be scared. I'll hold your hand if you like.'

'Nah,' he backed away, 'don't need nobody to hold my hand.' Corey could see he was not keen, but an offer of a few more currant buns soon tempered his resistance.

'Tom, pass me my togs from the hook.' Tom reached behind him and passed her cloak and hat over.

She shouted back through the door. 'I'm just bobbing out a while. You'd better all be washed up and said your prayers by the time I get back, or there'll be trouble – you hear me?'

Silence.

'D'you hear me?' she yelled.

A chorus of mumbles from the other children.

'Come on then, Simon.'

He ran ahead, looking back over his shoulder for reassurance she was still there, whilst they hurried towards Old Swan Stairs.

When they got to Thames Street they turned off down the alley to the shore and the lad hid behind Corey and pointed. The window was on the upper floor, and black, like a hole in a tooth. The house looked like any other, a rickety jumble of timbers and beams part suspended over the water. Icicles hung in festoons from the half-timbering. Corey led him across the frozen boards of the wharf and up the side alley of the house so she could get a better look. There seemed to be nobody at home, the house was lightless.

'It's all right. There's nobody home.'

'Phew. I was scared she'd see me again – three times is power-ful bad luck.'

'Can you find your way home?'

Simon nodded. 'I used to come here a lot, with Dad's bogey, getting washed-up pickings from the barges. It's only a step or two.'

'Thanks, Simon. Run along home then.'

He hesitated a moment. 'Please, miss, what about my currant patty?'

She laughed. 'Oh yes, come along tomorrow for your share.'

She watched him run off, fleet-footed as a rabbit, racing past the upturned boats, dodging the ropes and quay stones with nimble leaps.

When Simon had gone she looked at the front door of the house and was surprised to see it was open, just a crack, propped on the latch. She touched it with her hand and it creaked open. Unable to resist, she went in and looked around. There were two doors off the hall, one opposite and one on her right, open, with a staircase leading to an upper floor. The doors were dusty and the walls crumbling with flaking limewash. Though it looked un-kempt and deserted, she could smell the soot of a fire so she called out anyway.

'Hello?'

A woman's voice came from the door opposite. 'Come in, Corey.'

Corey started. She thought she had used her name. She put a foot on the stair but it creaked loudly.

The woman's voice called out, 'Who's that?'

She stopped guiltily. 'Sorry to bother you, my name's Corey Johnson, I'm looking—'

'I thought it was you. Well, don't stand about out there, come in. I want a word with you, about the noise.'

Corey hesitated, but the voice said 'Come on in' again, so she pushed open the door and went in. The room was warm, the remains of a coal fire glowed in the grate giving a little light. On the other side of the room was a wooden fourpost bed with the curtains drawn back and a confusion of blankets and linen piled over it. A middle-aged woman swathed in knitted shawls was perched there, pale as the sheets, her cheeks hollow and grey. She broke into a hacking cough the minute she saw Corey. When she had her breath back, she looked at her out of red-rimmed eyes.

'Who the Devil are you?'

'Corey Johnson, I—'

'Don't be funny with me. Corey Johnson lives upstairs, and you're not her. What do you want?' Then more weakly, 'I'm warning you – my son will be home any minute and he's got a knife.'

'I *am* Corey Johnson. That's my name, honest. I don't know another Corey Johnson. I'm looking for two girls.'

'What about them? There was a constable round here looking for them before. He talked to Miss Johnson from upstairs. But you're confusing me. You said you were Miss Johnson. You're not Miss Johnson.' She started to struggle in the bed and become more agitated. 'Dennis!' she cried, 'Dennis!'

She must be lost in the wits, thought Corey, backing away. 'Beg pardon, mistress, please don't take on so, I'm going now.'

'Help!' the woman said weakly, her frightened eyes peering over the scrambled bedclothes. But before she could call out again, she burst into another fit of racking coughs.

'Oh please,' Corey said, 'don't upset yourself, I'm going now. I'm so sorry to have bothered you.' She retreated rapidly into the hall. Inside the coughing continued. As Corey went out of the front door she nearly bumped into a tall, long-faced young lad in a felt hat and knitted muffler.

'Dennis?' came the faint voice from inside. The lad stared at Corey questioningly, as if to ask her what her business was, but she lowered her head and pushed past him. If this was Dennis, the son with the knife, she had no desire to linger.

Sadie stood at the window, staring out. She had heard Dennis's voice from below and his mother's cough, but Dennis had not been up, perhaps he was still sore at them for disturbing her. She had hoped when he saw the lock he might persuade Ella to take it off. It wasn't that she'd go anywhere, but it was galling to think Ella did not trust her. Earlier she thought she heard Ella's voice, talking with Mrs Gowper, but then nobody had appeared. It must have been her imagination, she thought. So the next time she heard Ella's footsteps on the stairs she did not move, even when the door opened and the draught from the hall blew in.

'For God's sake, what are you doing in the dark?' Ella said.

A pause, during which Sadie heard the slight hiss of Ella's skirts brushing the boards.

'And look, the breakfast things are still unwashed,' Ella said accusingly. 'I've been hard at work all day and you've not even tidied yourself up or lit a fire.' She must have found the flints for the room wavered into light.

Sadie held herself very tightly with her arms folded over her chest. 'I have tidied myself up,' she said.

'I said, what have you been doing all day? The dirty dishes are still here.'

Sadie swivelled round. 'You didn't fetch in any water. So there's none for boiling or for washing,' she said.

'Sorry, I forgot. Never mind, I can go in a minute. What are you looking at out there?'

'Ships. I'm watching for tall ships.'

'Come on, Sadie, get supper started. I've bought some herrings, and a big fat bloomer from the bakery. And I've got good news.'

Her heart leapt. 'Have they stopped looking for us?'

'No. No, not that.'

Sadie sighed, and turned to the window again. 'Better fetch the water from the pump,' she said, still looking out. 'Go on. And you'd better lock me in. You never know, I might go running into the street shouting, "Look at us! We're the Savage Sisters!"'

Ella made a noisy fuss of fetching the bucket and disappeared downstairs to fill it from the pump well in the yard round the corner. When she came back she held it gingerly with both hands so it swayed and slopped as she carried it.

'Why are you carrying it like that?' Sadie said.

'The rope tears my hands. I don't want them to look like working girl's hands. And I forgot to put my gloves on.'

Sadie lifted her hands in mock horror. 'Oh my, milady, we can't have that.'

'Look, Sadie, let's get a fire lit and supper on. You're just hungry. You'll feel better when you've eaten.' Ella set down the bucket and rubbed at her palm with her fingers. She began to pull out sticks one by one from the kindling, dragging them at arm's length so the whole pile came with it. Unable to resist, Sadie hurried over to help.

'Not like that, look – it makes it untidy. Come here, I'll do it.' Sadie crouched to make up the fire.

Ella drew out a waxed paper packet from her basket, opening it so the salty smell filled the room. 'Get a skillet on, there's enough for two portions each.'

Sadie sniffed. 'Did you say there was bread?'

Ella held up the chubby loaf with a flourish. 'Tan-tara!'

Sadie smiled, though she wasn't really ready to. She cleared the table and coaxed the fire with the remains of the wood, and as she did these practical tasks she felt in better cheer. Soon there was the pungent smell of frying fish. She bent over the skillet with concentration, turning the fish gently with a wooden spatula so as not to break them. Ella watched, a safe distance from the spitting pan. Fish smoke was renowned for lingering in hair and clothes, she said.

Sadie said grace. She did this on purpose because she knew Ella had no time for it. Ella shuffled on her seat whilst she did so. Happen Ella did not like her inviting the Good Lord in to watch them and see what they were doing, but it made Sadie feel safer somehow. They ate in silence a while, giving their full attention to the food.

'It's good,' Sadie said, with her mouth full. 'It was a fine idea to get herring, Ella.' She was trying to apologize for her earlier sulkiness. 'Tell me about this news, now.'

Ella took another small mouthful, but then put the bread down.

'Well, I've been promoted.'

'Oh, Ell, that's gradely. Does that mean you'll be getting more money?'

'Yes, a bit more, but it's different hours. I'm to work afternoons and evenings now.'

'Oh.' Sadie tried to take in what that would mean.

Ella went on, 'It'll be late evenings, because Whitgift's is going to stay open till gone midnight.'

Sadie put down her plate. 'Ella, can't you turn it down? It's awful lonely here at night. Now I don't go out, the nights on my own are the worst.'

'I've already said yes. It's a big compliment, it would have been insulting to the Whitgifts to turn it down.'

Sadie sighed. 'I can see you've made your mind up, and you'll go your own way as usual. Well, I suppose we'll just have to make the most of the mornings then.'

Ella trailed the fish heads round her plate with her knife, before looking up. 'The thing is, Sadie, it's a live-in position,' she said, and then hastily, 'It's only temporary, just for a few weeks whilst the Lily gets up and running . . .'

Sadie stared a moment, then stood up and threw the platter down on the table so the knife clattered to the ground.

'What about me?'

Ella's hand stopped halfway to her mouth.

'What about me, Ella? Is there a place for me at your precious Whitgift's? Oh, I thought not. I can't sleep nights because the whole of London's out looking for me. For me, Ella. For something you've done.'

Ella took her plate off her lap and set it on the table. She wiped her mouth on her kerchief with irritating slowness. 'You came with me, when we stole those things, you knew what we were doing.'

'Yes, but I didn't know it would mean this. I didn't know then that you'd murdered him.'

'I didn't kill anyone, do you hear.' Ella's hand shot out and slapped Sadie hard across the face. Sadie did not flinch, though the blow made her cheek sting.

'I don't believe you,' she retorted. 'I would never have thought that my own sister would lock me in a room whilst she went out whoring every day, but look at what you've come to.'

'You cat. You know that's not true.'

'Widow Gowper thinks it is.' Sadie knew it was nonsense, but she wanted to hurt Ella back.

'That old witch. How are we supposed to eat if I don't work? I have to work at the Lily. It's not my fault you look the way you do. You could cover it up, use the cream I bought you.'

'Get off to your precious Lily then.'

Ella did not reply.

'Go on. You make me sick. You dragged me here, and now you're going to leave me flat. So bloody get on with it. Get to your fancy-man at Whitgift's, I'm not going to stand in your way. I can do without you, so help me I can.' Sadie picked up Ella's cloak and hurled it at her. 'Get out, now. And don't come back either.'

Ella bent over stiffly and retrieved the wrap from the floor. 'All right. If you're set on being like that, I'm going. I'll come see you every day, I promise. You'll need me to fetch for you, get the water, buy food. If you won't cover your face I can't let you go out, you know I can't.'

'What?' Sadie struggled to grasp the implications of Ella's words. 'Wait a minute, you're not going to lock me in again—'

'It'll only be for a few weeks. Just until they stop looking for you and it's safe for you to go out.' Ella was shouldering her cloak and preparing to leave.

Sadie's eyes suddenly filled with tears. 'No. Don't leave me locked up like a dog. Don't go, Ella. I didn't mean it, I'm sorry. You're all I've got left. Don't leave me here. You promised we'd stick together. Please don't go.'

'Then why won't you wear the bloody cream? Don't tell me it's because of that stuff I bought in Netherbarrow. That was years ago. You can't still be blaming me for that now.'

Sadie looked at her. A great sob arose in her throat. Tears began to pour down her face. She couldn't answer.

'Well, what is it? I don't think it's the cream you're afraid of. It's life, that's what it is. You're afraid of anything good happening. And you hate it if anything good happens to me.'

'Don't,' Sadie said, 'you know that's not true,' but even as she said it, Ella swept up the empty basket and stepped outside the door.

'No, Ella!'

'Well, I'm taking whatever Whitgift's offering. I'll not let you hold me back. I'll be back tomorrow to bring provisions.'

'Where are you going? No, Ella, I'll stay inside I promise, please—'

Even as Sadie said the words the key was turning in the padlock, and Ella was gone.

Chapter 26

To Jay's great relief Foxy and Lutch had delivered Allsop's notebook as they had agreed. 'We didn't dare take on a reader,' Foxy had said scowling, 'in case he couldn't be trusted. Better the Devil you know.' After a little haggling and parting with a larger sum than he had deemed proper, Jay now had the notebook in his possession. He banked up the fire in his chambers and settled down to read it.

By the time he had read the first close-packed page he knew why Allsop was so desperate to get the book back. Each page was dated, and each page detailed in exhaustive particulars Allsop's encounters with the filthy doxies from the gin houses of Blackfriars. Jay pored over the document, turning the pages in growing disbelief. It was all here – how Allsop had bribed the gaoler of Newgate to supply him with brutish condemned women for a fee, until the gaoler was replaced with someone younger and, it seemed, less corrupt. How he was bereft of the wild company he sought until striking a bargain with one Josiah Whitgift, described to Jay's intense annoyance as *a rogueish dandyprat, who puffs himself up beyond his station.* It told how Jay's men supplied him with rough-hand whores from the stews of Southwark, and what was more, it showed in figures how much Allsop had won and lost at cards, and described Jay's loans as extortionate. *The blaggard has me by the hamstrings*, Jay read.

Jay closed the book with a snap. There was enough knowledge in here to hang him three times over. He'd have to put the screws on Allsop, make sure he did not sing. But it was awkward. It would need delicate handling. Allsop might turn the tables on him, was not beyond a bit of blackmail himself if he was in a tight corner. Jay stood up and paced up and down the narrow space in the room, stooping to avoid the eaves, mulling over what to do next.

Should he burn it? Well, it was safest that way, but then again, there was knowledge in here could be used to sink more than one ship. That gaoler, for instance. What fine gold or plate might he have in his house? And who knows what other gentlemen may be mentioned therein? Then he smiled. Of course – he could take out the pages that referred to him – or better still, pay Togsy the forger to set it right.

As for Allsop, Foxy and Lutch had broken into his house like he had asked. He had to pay the pair a sweetener to extract the information, but eventually they let drop that Allsop had an extensive collection of wrought silver, enough fancy swords and daggers in a purpose-built armoury chest to start a rebellion and, what was more, a collection of fine paintings including some twenty miniatures painted on glass. And yet that coxcomb Allsop had been mealy-mouthed about paying back the interest on his loan.

Foxy had said the miniatures were laid out on top of the French writing desk in Allsop's private chamber. Jay's fingers had begun to itch as soon as these were mentioned. He owned many fine collections, but his favourite items were always the small things that could be squirrelled away in a drawer, away from all prying eyes. Jay unlocked the Chinese cabinet on his desk and slid the diary inside. He sat for a moment before turning the key. He could not resist those miniatures. He would take Lutch for back-up, and if Allsop would not play, well, there was always the cane.

After reading the diary, he had sent a runner the next day to tell Allsop he would be calling, and at nine in the evening he was admitted by a bland-faced manservant into Allsop's newly built house in Whitehall. He had detailed Lutch to wait for him with the coachman outside, and to come in if he had not reappeared by the time the clock struck the half-hour.

'You have my notebook?' Allsop was awaiting him in the overstuffed hall, a look of nervous expectation on his jowly face.

'Yes.' Jay patted his waistcoat.

'Are you a lettered man, Mr Whitgift?'

'If you mean have I read it, then yes, of course I have. It is best to know exactly what I am dealing with. So yes, even a dandyprat such as I can understand its implications.' He raised his eyebrow at Allsop, who visibly paled. 'Now, send your manservant away.'

'Don't try any funny business with me, Whitgift.'

'I'm doing no deals unless he leaves.' Jay wanted no witnesses to this particular conversation.

Allsop thought a moment, then nodded to the manservant. 'Wait below.' He kept himself close to the door, Jay noticed, and his face was very pink. He must be rattled.

'You will keep it to yourself, won't you, Whitgift, once we have agreed a fee?'

'That depends on the fee,' Jay said, walking through to the drawing room and sitting himself nonchalantly on one of Allsop's mahogany chairs. He crossed one long slim leg over the other.

Allsop was sweating. 'What figure did you have in mind?'

'Well, as I said, ten pounds. That seems a fair price, as I went to considerable trouble to locate it for you.' Allsop was about to protest, but then sat down heavily, pinching his fleshy eyebrows between finger and thumb. Jay continued, 'But then, I had not read it. Now I find there is still the matter of my discretion. It is of value, is it not?'

'You mean I must pay you to keep quiet?'

'I prefer to think you might wish to offer me a gift. You know I am a connoisseur of fine painting, Mr Allsop. Particularly miniatures. Have you anything like that?'

'You devil. How did you know?'

'I have my informants. It is my business to know.' He leaned back comfortably. 'I believe the miniatures are on your French escritoire across the hall.'

Allsop blanched. He rubbed his face, confused. In that moment Jay knew it would be all right. He had been right to get the knowledge about Allsop's house. Now he had the upper hand, Allsop was on the back foot and both men knew it. His puzzled face showed he was trying to work out how Jay could possibly know the details of the inside of his house.

'I'll have to think about it. Those miniatures have been in my family for generations. Give me a few minutes to fetch your fee. I'll be back.'

'Oh, and by the way,' Jay said, 'my men are just outside. So I wouldn't try to go anywhere if I were you.'

Allsop cast his eye out of the window, and Jay saw the flicker when he caught sight of Lutch.

'Ask your manservant to fetch your purse.'

Allsop poked his head into the hall and gave instructions.

'I'll help myself to a drink then, as you did not offer,' Jay said. He took off his open cloak and muffler and strolled over to the glass decanter to pour a draught of port wine. He held up the glass to look at its chased stem before sitting back down and taking a large swig.

Allsop stood awkwardly by the door until the servant returned. When the servant had gone Jay put down the glass to take the leather bag Allsop offered him. Allsop stepped away from him as if he might burn his fingers. Jay tightened the drawstrings and tucked it away.

'Aren't you going to count it?'

'No, we made a gentleman's agreement. You know better than to gull me. I trust you know what's good for you.'

'My notebook, then.' Allsop held out his hand.

'In a moment,' said Jay, patting the bulge in his waistcoat pocket. 'Now, shall we take a look at your miniatures?'

'I don't see why it's of interest. It's not a very good collection, not valuable – just a few trinkets, mostly from my father.'

'I'd still like to take a look, I have a few myself.'

Allsop frowned. 'This way then, but I've told you, they only have sentimental value. Family portraits.' He went ahead of him into a smaller, well-furnished chamber; it was hung with green moiré paper, with a window, not yet shuttered, looking onto the street. The fire blazed under a stone mantel. Jay glanced outside again to see the solid-hewn figure of Lutch still stamping his feet on the hard-packed snow and rubbing the horse's nose. Jay smiled. Seeing his accomplice always gave him confidence.

Turning to Allsop, who was fidgeting with discomfort, he said, 'It's not the value, though, that interests me, but their beauty, don't you think? Some things just set up a flutter in here –' he pointed to his chest. 'They can be worthless, but the sight of them still makes me long for them.'

Allsop did not reply. They had stopped in front of a table with brass claw-and-ball feet. On the inlaid surface lay about twenty portraits, each no bigger than a pennyweight. The colours glowed through the domed surfaces of the glass.

'Take this one,' Jay said. 'This portrait is particularly appealing, with the embroidered ruff. Look at the quality of those brushstrokes, sharp as needles.'

Allsop grunted. Jay held up another and grimaced. 'Now this is valuable. But ugly. I won't have ugliness in my personal chambers. My father will deal in anything, as long as it's worth a bit. But I like to think I have taste,' Jay said. 'Can you bring me more light?'

Allsop reluctantly brought over a branched chandelier and lit it. The pinpoints of light fell on the domed glass surfaces. Jay smiled. Good, Allsop had fallen to doing his bidding like a lapdog. Jay homed his gaze on each painting in turn, while Allsop hovered, his hands pressed together.

'I'll take this one, and this one too with the pretty lady in ermine. It's by the great Cooper, if I'm not mistaken.'

'One alone would serve my dues, surely?'

'I thought you said the miniatures were of little value?' Jay smiled.

'What about taking this one instead?' Allsop picked up a larger one in a brass frame. 'It's a portrait of the Duchess of Albemarle, my father thought her a great beauty.'

'Really? She looks a little homely to me. But then I suppose beauty is in the eye of the beholder. No, I'll take those two and these ones.' He pointed to four more.

'Just a minute, Whitgift, those are the best in the collection, I'll have nothing left.'

'I can see we both appreciate fine things. But if you give me all six you can be assured that my lips will be forever sealed. The journal was most illuminating. Your financial affairs are fascinating, not to mention your little arrangement with Newgate Gaol.'

'Four, Whitgift. Four is surely enough.'

'With four or five, well, you may hear a few rumours. Nothing definite, mind, but rumours.'

'You dog.' Allsop turned away, as if to wash his hands of the whole business. 'Take the six,' he said tersely, with his back turned. 'And then, do I have your word?'

'My word as a gentleman. And then there will only be the original loan owing. Thirty pounds, was it not? Let's shake hands on it.' He offered Allsop his hand, and Allsop's damp white palm enclosed his briefly for a fraction of a second before falling away.

Ignoring the sweating Allsop, Jay drew the six best miniatures into a group and lined them up precisely in a circle on the veneered table, his long fingers picking up first one then another to arrange them in a pleasing order. Then he stepped away. 'Have your man wrap them for me, will you.'

Allsop rang for a servant.

Jay walked ahead of Allsop back to the drawing room as if he lived there. Allsop followed him a step behind.

'Well, Mr Allsop, it has been a pleasure doing business with you again,' Jay said. 'Sit down, do. You may be assured I have never set eyes on any notebook. Discretion is a part of my service, so be sure to call on me, should you require anything further.'

'My notebook. Give it over now.'

'That? Oh no, sorry, Allsop, I haven't got it with me.'

'But I thought—'

'What, this?' Jay drew a folded broadsheet out of his waistcoat. 'It's just the latest news. I had a little article I was going to publish there if things did not go to plan with a certain client.'

'Damn your eyes! I've given you the fee, haven't I? Give me my book!' He lunged for Jay, who sidestepped neatly.

'I wouldn't do that, if I were you.'

'I'll call the constable!'

'Sit down, do, Allsop. You know as well as I you can't do that. It has been an easy matter to take out the pages of the book that refer to me. But whilst I have the book in my possession . . .' He let his words sink in. Of course he hadn't yet removed those pages, but it was safe enough locked in his cabinet.

Allsop sat down heavily, the chair creaked under his weight. He put his head in his hands.

'Now here is my offer,' Jay said. 'I have many contacts, and can supply just about anything in London, and I see no reason why we should not continue our little business. You need a particular kind of girl and, as you know, I can obtain them. There must be many other well-to-do gentlemen such as yourself who will pay for that sort of service. And then again, I suppose there may be other gentlemen who may require a loan in these hard times. I expect you to supply me with some names.'

'Are you blackmailing me?'

'That's an ugly word. I told you, I don't like ugliness. No, just a little business arrangement. Call the journal my insurance. I would like to meet some of your friends, Allsop, particularly those who are received at court. What could be wrong with that? No reason why we should not grease each other's palms.'

Allsop wiped the back of his neck with his hand. 'And if I should decline to do business with you?'

'Oh, I wouldn't do that. After all, I'm offering you what you want – your reputation – and you are giving me what I want in return. What could be better?'

'I need to think,' Allsop said, pressing a palm to his temple. 'My man will see you out.' He rang the bell.

'If I were you, I would not be too long thinking about it. I'll be back tomorrow.' Jay put on his gloves, easing each finger into its leather pocket, then interlacing his fingers. He took up the cloth bundle containing the miniatures from the manservant, bowed slightly to Allsop and bounded down the steps to his carriage.

Behind him, Allsop shut the shutters tight and slammed the bolts on. He summoned the servant and told him to double-check the windows and doors, make sure they were locked. He went over to the desk and tried to rearrange the few inconsequential miniatures that were left. They looked lost without the rest. Impatient, he opened the lid of the desk and thrust them inside out of sight. Then he poured himself a measure of sack and sat ruminating for a long time, before going to his collection of wrought silver and lining it up along the shelf in the cabinet.

He picked up the silver sugar-shaker and turned it in his palm. It had been commissioned by his father and had been his mother's pride and joy when the new craze for sugar had begun. And now it looked like he would lose it. That snake Josiah Whitgift would bleed him dry.

He had the diary, there was no doubt of it. Trouble was, Whitgift was surrounded by his henchmen. Allsop shut the cabinet door with a slam. Why had he started that bloody journal? He didn't want to end up in a dark alley with his throat slit. Even if he knew someone to call on, he would not fancy their chances against Whitgift's men.

Chapter 27

Sadie turned over in bed and stretched her legs and arms. The last few days she felt stiff in the mornings. Partly it was the withering cold, but she guessed it was also because she missed her busyness and exercise, and now her hands were too often idle. Her world was drained of colour and warmth, had become washed out, faded like curtains left too long in the sun.

When she looked around the room it gave her no cause for cheer – the blackened grate, the chipped earthenware pots, the grey moth-eaten bedcovers. Out of the window the snow had melted and then refrozen; the sullen Thames cut the landscape in two, a faint mist rising from it to pall over the mudflats. Dennis had not been up at all and it bothered her. She was lonely. She wondered if he'd seen the padlock on the door and thought they were out, not thinking to knock. But at least she felt safe. Nobody knew she was here; it was almost like she did not exist.

That day Sadie was surprised to hear the jangle of the lock even before ten of the clock. Ella pushed open the door, bringing with her the usual overpowering fragrance of lavender and rose oil.

Sadie took a step back. Ella seemed to take up too much

space. She was clad in her stiff green velvet gown with the green riding cloak over it. A scarf of squirrel fur was wrapped around her neck. Her hair was rigid as if carved of wood, her face white and expressionless, except for her lips. She no longer looked like Sadie's flesh and blood, or for that matter flesh and blood at all. Ella did not notice Sadie staring, but held the back of one gloved hand to her nose, toying with the key to the lock in her other.

'It stinks in here. It smells like a midden. Must be the river.' Ella put her basket on the table. Sadie unpacked the basket whilst Ella prowled round the room as if unable to settle.

Sadie took out some onions, a turnip and some wilting leeks, but pounced on a little greaseproof paper bag at the bottom and sniffed it.

Anxious to mend the bad feeling between them, Sadie said, 'Oh my word, bacon. I can't believe it. That's top, Ella. I've got some flour left for lardy cakes, so I'll be right well fed. And what's this?' She drew out another little package, wrapped in brown paper.

'It's silk, and needles. You said you were bored with nothing to occupy your time. So I thought you could knit us stockings. You've always been neat with a needle.'

Sadie could hardly speak. She was choked. After their fratch the other day she could not believe Ella had bought her a present. Tears threatened to well up in her eyes.

'Thanks, Ell.'

She opened the package wonderingly, and brought out a pair of fine bone needles and a ball of silk so light the threads were almost transparent. She made as if to hug Ella, but Ella stepped back, saying, ''Tis naught. Is there enough silk? For a pair of stockings?'

Sadie held the silk up to the light. 'By, it's like spider-silk.

I'll likely need another skein, three more for two pairs. Oh, Ell, they'll be finished in no time. I love knitting.'

Ella nodded stiffly. 'I'll get some more silk when I pass the haberdasher's again,' and she turned and rustled her way to the window.

Sadie ran the thread between her finger and thumb. 'What news, Ella? Are the notices down?'

'Not yet. But maybe it won't be long now.'

'How is it at Whitgift's? How are you getting on with saving?'

'Saving? Chance would be a fine thing on what I get.'

Sadie dropped the silk and needles onto the table. 'But I thought they'd promoted you. Don't you get better pay now?'

'No. They take for board and lodgings. And I have to share my room now. There's a new girl. Polly.'

'What's she like?'

'She's pretty, in a common sort of way, but she's a bit of a prattler.'

'Come and sit down and tell me all about it. It's been that dull here at home. Have you seen anything of Dennis? Is Ma Gowper better? I haven't heard her coughing the last few days.'

Ella drifted back towards the table, but did not sit.

'He's taken her off to the country to his auntie's. They'll be there a week. Ma Gowper had a funny turn, he said to tell you.'

'When was this?'

'Monday? Day afore yesterday, maybes?'

Sadie opened her mouth to chastise Ella for not telling her, but Ella continued, 'Sorry, Sadie, I can't stay long, there's a sedan waiting for me outside . . .'

'A sedan? But you promised!' burst out Sadie. 'You promised you'd stay longer today, and I've been looking forward to it.'

'I know. But Polly's sick, and there's nobody to look after the

Lily. He said I could just pop out for a minute, but I have to hurry back straight away.'

Sadie looked at Ella's mask-like face and her heart sank. Although it sounded reasonable enough, an instinct told her Ella was not telling her the truth. Sadie slumped on her stool, bit her lip and returned to her silent protest.

Ella shifted from foot to foot. 'Sorry, Sadie, but I have to get back. There'll be longer tomorrow, promise.'

Sadie did not react, she could not bear to look at her, standing there in her stupid little lambskin gloves.

'I'll try to bring more silk too.' Ella's voice held a slight note of appeal. She went back to the door and opened it, turning to face into the room in order to fasten the lock. 'See you tomorrow then?'

Ella was framed in the doorway, a painted wooden figurehead without a ship. Sadie deliberately looked away.

Chapter 28

Foxy sat on the front seat of the boxwagon rubbing his hands together through his knitted gloves. The nag was restless. A rangy bay with a balding mane, it seemed to be able to pick up the dark and distress that always accompanied this wait in Tannery Row – the gloomy alley with its smell of the river.

Tonight the passage was quiet as usual. During the day it teemed with wagons bearing the carcasses for the tannery from the slaughterhouse in the next street, with dogs snatching after scraps as they passed.

Lutch was longer than usual and Foxy was cold, anxious to be off for their usual ale supper and to have a gamble on the skittles. And he knew, the longer he hung around the more suspicious it would look. This was the second time in a week he'd drawn the closed wagon up next to the ginnel to the river. He hated it when it was silent like this. He didn't know what was going on, whether the girl was gone or not. He preferred to hear them struggle and plead. It was with relief that he saw Lutch round the corner, unaccompanied, his bamboo stick dangling from his hand.

'All right?' Foxy said as he climbed up beside him.

'River's running slow. There's patches of ice near the bank.'

Foxy clicked and the nag shied and jerked into motion.

'King's Head?'

Lutch nodded.

A few minutes later they trotted into the yard at the King's Head. The horse knew its way and headed for the trough at the back. Foxy hung up the reins.

'You were a while, back there.'

Lutch shrugged.

'That was the second mott this week. The more we do, the more risky it is. I don't like it. It was better when it was just the burglaries, wasn't it?'

Lutch grunted.

'Does it not bother you?'

'Depends. These ones pay more.'

'I know. But don't you ever feel sorry for them?'

'Sorry?' Lutch looked at him with incomprehension.

'When you – I mean, when they go.' Foxy was embarrassed to have started on the subject at all. 'I mean, even doing the Christmas goose gets to me. Such a waste somehow.'

'Plenty more, though, ain't there. We don't have no trouble finding them.'

'True enough.'

'All of 'em after something for nothing. Eating out of our hands soon as you say the name "Lord Allsop". Change their tune after, though, don't they? You've seen 'em. He breaks 'em somehow. Reckon I do them a service.'

He was right. That last girl for example. When they'd picked her up she'd never stopped talking – feverish with it, she was. But after, well, she was pale as a wraith, in a kind of stupor. She'd gone with Lutch and his throttling cane meek as a lamb.

'Trough's frozen,' Foxy said.

Lutch jumped down and stabbed at the ice on the surface of

the water with his cane. He rubbed the horse on the forehead as it dipped its nose. It brought its head back up and shook it, before lowering it again. Lutch knew what it wanted. He fondled its ears. 'There, Titan. Who's a handsome fella-my-lad, eh?'

Tindall was late working in Walt's office. Walt had long gone up to his bed. These days he grew tired sooner and he was grumpy about all the comings and goings at the Gilded Lily. The chattering in the yard made it hard to concentrate on his reckonings.

'Can't get no peace, no more,' Walt said. 'I'm sick to death of women's prattling. Don't know how our Jay stands it.'

After Walt retired at night, Tindall often found an excuse to work on, partly because he enjoyed the act of writing up the day's ledgers, but mostly because Walt's office was always warm and it was a shame to waste a good fire. He had not told Walt his own billet was a grim room in the rotting sheds of Whitechapel, shared with an itinerant preacher who was nearly always drunk and two Irish tinkers who treated the room as their slophouse.

So when Walt went up to bed, Tindall penned on for a while, toasting his bare bunioned feet in the hearth, enjoying the companionable sound of the ticking watches and relishing having the chamber to himself. After he had finished, he blew out the candles and took off his hat, preparing to lay himself out for his sleep by the fire. Cockerels would wake him long before Walt got down here, and he could be away for a wash at the pumphouse and then back at opening time as usual. The dogs were used to him, and he knew to wake the nightwatchman as he passed, so that he knew Tindall was going 'off duty'.

The yard was quiet after the last of the customers had left the Gilded Lily, though sometimes the noise of their comings and goings went on until two of the clock. So it was with surprise that just before dawn he heard the noise of hooves and wheels outside.

He peered out of the back window and saw a closed boxwagon draw up outside the gates. He pressed his nose to the glass.

Jay Whitgift came out and asked the nightwatchman to open the gate. Tindall saw the two men climb down and come inside, leaving the carriage in the lane. One was a wiry red-haired chap he had seen about the yard before – usually headed for Jay's chambers. The other was a barge of an individual clad in a thin coat and leather vest, with no cloak or gloves despite the bone-cracking cold. Jay must have been watching out for them. As he passed he looked sideways at the office window as if to check his father was abed. Tindall withdrew. He did not want Jay Whitgift to know he was still there, he would tell Walt. Tindall had no wish to reveal his embarrassing circumstances.

The heavier man brought a small parcel wrapped in dark cloth and passed it to Jay. Jay was still fully dressed, despite the hour, and unwrapped the parcel there and then. Tindall caught a glimpse of something glittering in the moonlight before Jay covered it again and put it down on the frozen cobbles. He nodded, and counted out a large sum of money from a coin bag. The two men fished their pockets from their breeches and tucked the money away. Not a word was said, so this must be a regular occurrence. He had not noticed it before though, likely he was asleep. Tindall was curious. Who were these men, and what were they doing skulking in Walt's yard at this hour?

'Everything all right?' Jay's whispered voice drifted up. 'Next one's Saturday – Mr Wolfenden again, Allsop's friend. Don't forget, he likes them young – and maidenly. Though I know that's asking some. The younger the better – he complained to me the last one was too old.'

'Same price then, if you want them tidied up afterwards. And what are we bringing?' asked the shorter man, setting off towards the gate.

'Two pair of silver-mounted ladies' pistols. Don't leave Wolfenden's without them.' Jay's voice was faint now as they traversed the yard.

The men walked to the gate, where he saw them have a few more words before the watchman locked up, and Jay walked back towards his chambers, glancing once more at the window where Tindall ducked out of sight.

Tindall lay down in front of the greying embers, blew on them a little to bring back the glow. What sort of transaction was that, then? His instinct told him it was some scurvy business Jay did not want his father to know about, so he was even more determined to get to the bottom of it. Jay Whitgift had always been a two-faced weasel, even when he was small. But poor Walt couldn't see it; Tindall was always astonished that his friend thought Apollo himself rose in his son's eyes. Even now, despite Walt's outward huffing and puffing about Jay and the blasted Gilded Lily, Tindall could see the ridiculous light of pride in Walt's expression whenever he talked of it.

But just last week, the perruquier from Friday Street had been over asking for Jay. She said she had reason to believe Jay had hired a young girl who had robbed and killed her employer. Well, that would not surprise him one jot. She said Jay had sent her away, telling her the girl had been dismissed. But Tindall was not so sure; the woman in the Lily, Miss Johnson, she had that country look, not grey like those raised in the smut of the city. He'd like to find out more about her background. He knew that, like everything about Jay Whitgift, the Gilded Lily would have two sides to it – like Gemini, the sign Jay was born under. One side all sunshine and light, and the other – well, Tindall meant to find out all about the other. He owed it to Walt.

*

Titus Ibbetson did not approve of the rough banter in the bar of the Blue Ball, so now he and Isobel sat in their chilly upstairs chamber, forgoing the warmth of the fire, whilst they planned what to do next. Willetts the maid sat in a corner, hemming one of Isobel's black crepe shawls.

'Can you believe it, the wigmaker was no help at all!' Titus shook his head.

'It beggars belief. After you told her what they'd done.' Isobel leaned forward in her black wool mourning-gown. 'And what about their father? He showed no interest at all. You would think a father would have wanted to know what had befallen his daughters, wouldn't you?'

'That sort'll do anything for money. He wouldn't have told me a thing, had I not rattled my purse at him. It's hard to fathom it – he said the elder one had been living in with Thomas for a month or more. She brought a few coppers out of her wages home every week to make sure the sister was provided for. The sister must have been a bit simple. Didn't go out much. And no wonder, with that great red stain all over her face.' He sighed. 'But Appleby would say no more, even for another half-shilling, so I guess we will have to rely on the wigmaker for help with our enquiries. Straight after, I sent the constable round to arrest the father anyway. He knows more than he's telling, and maybe a spell without a drink will loosen his tongue.'

'What next?'

'Constable tells me a few more girls have been brought in to Newgate Gaol. I expect I shall have to go and look them over.' He sighed. 'God above, the whole task is so wearisome, what with the stench and the noise.'

'Perhaps we should go back home. It's been a bootless state of affairs, and you are wearing yourself thin with the worry of it.'

Titus flapped his hand at her, dismissing the idea. 'Hogwash. I shall go over to the gaol in the morning.'

'And what will I do?'

'You may accompany me in the carriage. Do not fret, you need not come inside.'

'But if you do not really need my assistance, surely it would be better if I went back to Shrewsbury and made sure our house is in order. We have been away too long, and the smoke in this tavern is making me ill.'

Titus frowned. Isobel was always complaining about something. 'It will not be for much longer. I need you here. A wife's duty is to be with her husband. Have patience. The notices will turn them up sooner or later, London is full of grasping beggars looking to get rich. They'd hand over their own mother for a groat, most of them.'

'But—'

'Don't make me shout.'

Willetts looked up briefly, but Titus's look made her bow her head, and prick her thumb with the needle.

Chapter 29

Scratch, scratch.

There it was again. Sadie turned but couldn't see anything. She carried on with what she was doing, rolling out the last of the oatmeal to make clapbread. A few moments later she saw it – a little brown mouse. It pattered across the floor and rested under the inkblot shadow of a stool. She held herself very still. Perhaps if she was quiet enough she would be able to watch it a while.

The mouse washed its whiskers unconcerned. Sadie hunkered down, lowering herself to the floor, and as she did so the mouse stopped what it was doing and fixed her with its shiny bead-like eyes. Sadie returned the gaze. The mouse was beautiful. Its coat was a soft velvety brown like the inside of a mushroom, and its little sides vibrated under the fur. Such a fast-beating tiny heart, she thought. After looking back at her for a while, it cocked its head then made a skittish dash for the stray oats under the table before returning to its place under the stool.

'Hello, little fellow,' whispered Sadie. 'Are you hungry?'

The mouse watched her steadily as it nibbled at the oats, its tail sticking straight out behind, its half-moon ears quivering.

''Tis cold out. Bet that's why you've come indoors, hey?'

She held out a bit of the oatmeal in her floury hand.

'Come on now,' she said, 'don't be scared.' She reached a bit further, but her arm knocked the table and the rolling pin fell off and clattered to the ground. The mouse zigzagged away in a flash and disappeared into a small knothole in the wooden floor.

Sadie tiptoed over, put her eye to the dark hole, but the mouse was gone. She had enjoyed their small moment together, fancied that in their wordless conversation the mouse had understood something of what she was saying.

'You daft beggar,' she told herself. She knew well enough that mice were vermin. Back in Westmorland she'd have chased it out with a besom. But here she could not help remembering the story of the Ash Maid, where the little mice became footmen and a fairy godmother came along to say, 'You shall go to the ball.'

She pictured Ella in her green and gold, but she did not want to look like Ella. Ella used to be all soft curves, rosy-cheeked, her hair an unruly mass down her back. Now she was all hard edges and frowns. She closed her eyes and imagined herself dancing in a beautiful flowing gown, and when she looked up it was Dennis's face smiling down at her.

If only she could be transformed, like the Ash Maid. She went to the jug and looked in at the pot of whitening cream she had hidden there out of sight. She picked it out and held its weight in her palm. Her hands were cold, so she blew on them a little before she untied the ribbon and lifted the lid. She fetched the mirror over and tentatively dipped a fingertip into the paste. Bringing it to her nose, she inhaled, smelling the whiff of grease and tang of metal. After waiting a while and seeing that her finger did not itch or burn, she spread a little on the back of her hand. Still nothing. Should she use it? What would Dennis think of her when her face was all white? She didn't want him to think she was loose. But without it she would never be able to go out. Her stomach fluttered with nerves. There had been no visit from Dennis, not since he had been up to tell her they must leave because of the noise. Trust Ella to forget to tell her he had gone away. And she let her think he had fallen out of sorts with her. Curse Ella.

Her sister's sharp words came back to her. Ella was right. She was afraid of not having the birthmark any more. She'd had it her whole life. The stain gave her a reason to hang back, a reason to hide, to stay in the shadows whilst others stepped forward.

She stood up and went to the window, pondering. Hadn't she always hated being singled out? But now she was unsure. It was complicated. On the one hand she loathed the stares and the name-calling, but how would it feel if no one gave her a second glance? Who would she be without it? She had heard of players who, once they had the greasepaint on, were afraid to go on the stage. Stage fright, they called it. Except for her the whole world felt like a stage. She sighed, went back and sat at the table, turned the mirror face down, pushed the pot away. Then she leaned forward across the table and buried her head in the crook of her arms.

It had not taken long for Ella to feel settled living in at the Gilded Lily. She loved to draw the tapestry curtains when business was done and then to take the embers on a shovel from the downstairs fire and put them into her own hearth. Any candles in the chandelier that were not burnt as low as the others, she took those upstairs too, and lined them up on the table so she could see to wash and powder her face before sliding into bed. But then she left them burning all night, to cast away the shadows in the room.

Her reputation as a beauty soon spread, and she revelled in it. She could scarce believe it – fashionable ladies exchanged her secrets, her opinion on powder and paint was sought out and whispered at elegant soirees. Sometimes, when they asked her advice, she told them nonsense just for the spite of it. Just last week she had told two ladies that they should wash in the urine of puppies to improve their complexion. She watched their eyes widen and, nodding sagely all the time, she watched them whisper together as they left. Chuckling to herself, she knew they would be onto their servants straight away to see if there were any nursing bitches to be found. Afterwards, the thought of it made her laugh until her ribs ached and she had to press her stays with her hands.

She loved the new hours. She had always been a night creature, and she found working in the evenings exciting. The atmosphere was livelier – more young ladies in fashionable silks and velvets with sparkling jewels, and not so many old dowds with moustaches.

The morning girl was a vivacious brunette called Polly, but she had a sharp face and eyes that seemed to be set a bit too close together. Ella had made a quick assessment and deemed her to be less pretty than herself, and from then on had treated her the way she treated Meg.

Polly was younger than Ella, and a little in awe of her, which suited Ella well. The coachmen had begun to hang round the door of the Lily trying to catch a glimpse of them both, and she found it flattering, but also, she thought, no more than she deserved. And besides, she had no interest in coachmen, she had bigger fish to fry.

Of course she had not sent for her things from the Gowpers', because she knew it would only upset Sadie, and besides, their possessions were mean enough, and would be more so divided thus. She bought what she required from Whitgift's on sale day. But she had been back to Blackraven Alley several times, taking provisions, and to take out the slops. Sadie looked even more down-at-heel now that Ella was not there and that daft Dennis was away. Stupid, stubborn girl. She still had not got used to the idea of the lock, could not see it was for her own good. Last time Ella went, she refused to speak to her, so Ella had to satisfy herself by leaving the basket on the table.

One day Meg came to tell her Dennis was at the door of the Lily, asking for her. She panicked, thinking he must have been home and seen the lock, talked to Sadie. Reluctantly, she went to the door, her open fan before her face like a fence between them, but she was surprised to hear him say, 'You owe me. Tindall's just told me you're living in. You should've told us.'

'Yes, I'm working more hours now,' she said guardedly, wagging the fan.

'Why did you not tell me? You should've given Ma more notice,' Dennis went on. 'It's not good to leave an empty house, and we'll have trouble finding some more tenants now. And Ma's been taken right bad, taken a turn for the worse, that's why I've not been over for the rent. The air in Epping's better for her cough. I've not had chance to get back home, only come back to sort things out with the gaffer.' Ella exhaled with relief. So he had not been home.

'Oh, we need the room yet,' Ella said. 'My sister's still living there. She can't go out you see – well, you know why not.' Ella closed the fan, and looked round behind her in case anyone should be within earshot.

'Are you telling me Sadie's still living upstairs all by herself?'

'Yes. Well, not exactly. I go there every day, make sure she's got everything she needs.'

'She was there all last week? On her own?'

'Well, I call every day.'

Dennis pursed his lips and frowned. 'It must be mighty dull, cooped up there alone all day.'

Ella bristled. 'Better than being swung on the end of a rope. Anyways, I go there every morning to keep her company, and I took her some knitting to do.'

'That's good. I'm glad she's still there. I thought she must have moved on when you did, and I worry if the place is empty. Ask her if she'll keep an eye on the place for us, would you? I've got to stay in Epping a while longer, Ma's right bad. I thought it'd only be a day or two, but I've just come to ask the gaffer if I can have another week. He were right kind about it, says he'll keep my position till Ma's better. What shall I tell her? Ma, I mean, about you moving out?'

'Nothing. It would make her suspicious. She don't need to know anything. I pay the rent, don't I? There's still one girl living there. She'll just think it's me.'

Dennis frowned and looked like he was about to speak, but Ella continued, 'It's temporary. I told you that from the beginning. But just give us another month or so. I'll see you set right – a bit of extra for your trouble.'

She wedged the fan under her arm and fumbled in her purse. She didn't want Dennis poking his nose into it. It was clear he did not approve of Sadie being left on her own, and he might let Sadie out, then she might try to run home, causing all sorts of mayhem. She couldn't keep her there for ever, she knew, but maybe in a week or so the notices would be down.

'Here,' she said, holding out a handful of coins, 'this is for last month, and this month too.'

Dennis took it, saying, 'Well, at least you've not asked for credit. You've been good tenants that way.' He held out the change.

'No, keep it. It's a bit spare for your trouble, you know, for keeping quiet about us.'

Dennis looked taken aback. 'No, I can't accept that. It's only what any friend would do.' He tried to thrust it back into her hand.

Ella stepped away. She did not want that threadbare Dennis to be a friend. 'You take it. For physic for your ma. I can afford it. I've been taken on proper now.'

Dennis looked down on the coins askance, but Ella folded her arms. Eventually he withdrew his hand with a shrug and put it away. 'Well, thanks. I guess you're right, I'll need this for the apothecary. It's this bloody winter. Ma's cough's a deal worse in this cold, and she's feverish.'

Ella turned to go, but he followed her. She stopped, irritated. He rubbed his hands through his bristly hair. 'I dunno what to think. I'm afraid her mind's gone. She says you went in to see her last Monday afternoon, insistent she was, made a big song and dance about it. I was in half a mind to give you notice, but then I remembered. I saw you here serving in the Lily, Monday. So I know it's all rank nonsense she's talking. She keeps raving that you're not the same girl you were. It must be your hair. I noticed it's different. When we get back from Auntie's, happen you'll call in on her, it might help.'

'Hmm,' said Ella, nodding but knowing she would not.

'Say hello to Sadie. Be sure and tell her we'll be back Friday. I'll call then, bring her some more of my penny books, tell her all about it.'

Ella smiled. She was pleased he was staying away. An instinct told her he certainly would not like the idea of the lock. If the Gowpers were away, she would be able to come and go as she pleased, without hearing a shout from downstairs every time she so much as breathed. And Dennis was far too meddlesome, she didn't want the likes of him befriending Sadie. The great cart-horse, what did she see in him anyway? She pushed away a twinge of jealousy.

Ella returned to the counter. Looking at the customers all morning in their fine jewellery set off a hankering for something with a bit of sparkle, something to catch the light – and Jay's attention. It was sale day today – she would buy earrings.

Later she went to the warehouses and soon found the section with the cheaper jewellery. It was staffed by several young tough-looking lads, to deter anyone who dared to think they might pilfer something. Whitgift's was locktight to thieves. If anyone tried to leave with goods they had not paid for, the alarm was raised and the gates shut and the constable called. Walt Whitgift had built his reputation on fair trade, they said, and he came down hard on those who broke the law. She doubted that his son was quite so scrupulous.

She wandered along the tables, looking into the small trays with the cloak pins and watch chains laid out. There was a whole section of jewellery with knots or tresses of human hair woven into elaborate miniature plaits and pressed into rings or brooches. It reminded her of Madame Lefevre, and of her time in the dank basement of the wig shop. Thank the Lord she didn't have to put up with the stench of greasy hair any more. She shook her shoulders as if to rid herself of the memory, and moved swiftly past, looking for the section with the earrings.

She averted her eyes as she passed a wooden tray containing gold and ivory teeth on wires. Did people really pawn these? And who would buy them? As if to answer her question an old woman in a stained serving-smock came up and began to turn them over, obviously looking for a tooth that would fit. Shuddering, Ella moved along, until she saw the glint and twinkle that had always fascinated her. Five minutes later she was back again, carrying a small twist of paper with her new earrings inside. The barber-surgeon would pierce her ears the lad had said, and he was open until dusk. It would be painful – she would have to bite on her folded glove – but worth it.

She felt a little guilty about buying the earrings. Jay had agreed to advance her two pounds for the alteration of a new velvet gown from the warehouse since she was to be working evenings too, and she had collected the gown only yesterday. Now her conscience needled her. She knew she was supposed to have spent that money on a gown for Sadie, and now she had been tempted by new earrings too. But the little glass pendants had been irresistible.

She wandered over to the clothing tables and picked out a serviceable gold-coloured holland gown, just a little worn on the bodice. It had matching sleeves too, with the laces and all. It wasn't silk or velvet, but surely it would do for Sadie. When Sadie got a position she would be able to save, like Ella had, for a better one.

Ella knew in her heart this was a myth, a story she was telling herself. She knew that in a way Sadie was right, that she would be too frightened to go out into the world the way Ella had, the stain was too raw, and she would be scared of someone unmasking her. Even if Sadie agreed to wear the ceruse, Ella herself was not sure she could bear the worry of it, wondering what she was up to every day. It was hard enough to keep herself out of trouble. She sighed. Why was everything so difficult? But Ella had no other plan; the thought of ministering to Sadie for ever was a thought she could not brook.

Ella turned the bottom of the yellow dress to look at the quality of the stitching. The hem was worn to nothing in some places, but the bodice was the right size.

'How much?'

'Five shilling.'

'You've naught cheaper?'

'It's a good 'un, that. Quality.'

'Look at the wear on that hem, I'm not paying that. I'll give you two.'

'Don't know as I can—'

'I work here in the Lily. Jay Whitgift says I can have it cut-price.'

'I know. Miss Johnson, ain't it? I've seen you about.'

There was not enough in her purse to pay for it, but she flashed her eyes and talked sweetly to the warehouse lad and finally he let her have it on the slate. He wrapped it for her, staring all the while as if she were a sideshow. She pandered to him just for the fun of it until the poor lad was quite red in the face. If only she could have that effect on Jay Whitgift.

Chapter 30

Sadie leaned her elbows on the windowsill. Outside the window the river was silent and shiny, the surface still as a mirror, reflecting the grey sky and the buildings and cathedral of Southwark on the other side. For a few days now there had been no traffic up and down, and it was unnaturally still. The river frozen was a different creature altogether.

The frost had papered the wooden sill with white fingers of ferns, and when she hitched back the curtain to look out that afternoon she saw that the glassy water was dotted with little black coals. At least that was what she thought they were, until she saw one fall from the sky. It landed with hardly a sound. And then she realized. They were starlings, the blood frozen in their hearts even in flight.

Their chambers were quiet without Ma's cough from beneath. It was surprising just how much comfort was to be had from knowing there was another person downstairs.

She picked up her knitting and wound the silk slowly round the needles. She was knitting slowly, partly because her fingers were cold and stiff, but mostly because she wanted to make the activity last a long time. The bone needles clacked and she pulled the silk taut, feeling it slide through her fingers. They were smooth now she was no longer working at the wig shop. She sighed, wondering how Corey and Betsy and the others were, and whether Mercy Fletcher still ruled the roost.

One pair of stockings lay folded on the kitchen table; they were the pair for Ella, long in the leg with tiny feet. Now she knitted her own – her feet were larger and her legs shorter. She did not know if she would ever have chance to wear them, or even finish them, because there was only one skein of the silk left and each pair took three skeins.

When Ella arrived this time with the provisions, Sadie did not look up but smelt the perfume that hung on her clothes, saw her lace-gloved hands place a small bag on the table.

She carried on knitting, ignored the parcel.

'Oh, are those my stockings – let's have a deek.' Ella picked up the finished pair and hung them over her palm. 'Oh, Sadie, they're right fine, did they take you long to do?'

'There's nothing else to do in here but knit.'

'I'll think of you every time I wear them,' Ella said, wafting the filmy stockings back and forth.

Sadie gritted her teeth; she doubted it. She squashed her ill-temper by stabbing with the needles more intently.

'Today it's sausage and some apples, and a few other bits and bobs.' Ella unloaded her basket piece by piece. She did this without bending; the stiff blue material of her dress rustled. As usual Sadie could not resist standing up to take a look in the basket. She was slightly pacified to see more skeins of silk as well as some string and a block of beeswax to make candles. Ella lined everything up on the table and Sadie knew she was expecting her to admire it and compliment her on her choices, but she just nodded.

'Are them notices still up?' she asked.

'Stop asking me that. I'd tell you, wouldn't I, if they weren't.

But I've brought you something.' Ella pointed to the brown packet on the table. 'Hair dye. It's black. I thought 'twould suit your colouring better than the yellow. And it will look fine, with your complexion made-up—'

Sadie began to speak but Ella spoke over her. 'And there's something else. I don't want you to say no until you've seen it.'

She lifted a big flat box tied with string onto the table.

'What is it?'

'It's a gown.'

'You're jesting.'

'It is. Told you I'd save for one.'

Sadie did not move.

'Aren't you going to open it?'

'You do it.'

'Here then, bring us a knife for the string.'

Sadie went to the shelf and brought back a knife, passed it to Ella handle first. Ella sawed through the string and pulled open the lid. A mass of heavy gold-coloured damask was revealed.

'Go on, bring it out.'

Sadie put her hand into the box and drew out a handful of the stuff. It was a full skirt, cold to the touch and there was a slight rancid smell to the cloth. 'Where did you get it?'

'Whitgift's of course. Had to save my wages for it.'

Sadie hefted it up and put the skirt aside on a chair before pulling out the bodice, holding it out at arm's length. It was a little creased, but finer than anything she had ever worn before. She flicked her hair forward over her face, the gesture she always made when she was uncomfortable. She could not imagine herself dressed in this gown. Even with her hair dyed black and her face hidden beneath a plaster of white. She was not Ella. She dropped the bodice onto the table.

'I can't wear that. You'll have to take it back.'

'Why? It will fit, look, there's plenty of room in that bodice.' Ella stretched the seams between her hands.

'I'm not wearing it, I wouldn't look right.'

There were two patches of bright red on Ella's cheeks now. 'But you'd be free, you could go out, you'd be able to look out for yourself, get a position, you wouldn't need me any more to help you.'

'So that's it. Sick of looking after me are you? I never asked you to. I never asked you to lock me up in here.'

'I had to. To save your skin. Oh come on, Sadie, it was for your own good. Just say you'll think on it. Dressed in this and with the face powder you could go anywhere. Honestly, the face powder's gentle enough for a baby's behind, you could just try it—'

'Who'd take me on? I wouldn't dare smile in case the paint cracked. I'd be found out in no time. Madame would know me straight away.'

'You wouldn't go back to Madame Lefevre's, fool – they know you there. No, you'd have to go someplace else – another big city. Bristol perhaps, or Plymouth, get a job in service. We could both go. Make up some tale.'

'In service? With a painted face? How many places do you know of where they want painted servants?' Sadie stuffed the mound of fabric back into the box. 'No, Ella. I'm sick of doing your bidding. It seems wherever you go, trouble follows. I don't want to make up a tale and be forever thinking I'll be caught short.'

'Just try it on. There's no harm in trying it, is there?'

'I'll not wear it, I've told you – I'd rather die.'

'Then you probably will. Those notices are still up, and I can't take care of you for ever.'

'Then stop. What do I care? You're not like my sister any

319

more. I don't want a sister like you 'cos the crows on the windowsill pay me more mind than you do, with your fancy airs and graces. Look at you. You're not respectable no more. I don't want to look like you, like some trumped-up whore.'

Ella opened her mouth to speak, but Sadie shouted her down. 'I'm ashamed you're my sister. What would our ma have thought if she could see you now, painted up like a jilt?'

Ella stood stock-still. 'Leave her out of it.' Then she snatched up the empty basket and went out, shutting the door with a slam. Sadie heard the key turn. 'Stay there forever and rot, then,' hissed a voice from outside. On the table the box lay open, where Ella had left it.

'Don't you dare speak to me like that,' Sadie said to the shut door, 'your face might crack,' but even as she said it the sound of Ella's feet died away.

It took nearly the whole day for Ella's anger to subside. She served the customers with a scowl and was glad when the last one left. It was only the thought of Jay that cheered her. That night she dressed with more than usual care for the evening shift as he usually called in at the end of the evening to harry out the last customers and check the takings. She had bought clay hair curlers to heat on the fire, and now her yellow hair was dressed fashionably in stiff side curls strengthened with sugar water, her topknot pinned with lace and ribbon. Her earlobes had hardly stopped bleeding, but she was determined to wear her new purchase straight away, and the new glass-stone earrings twinkled in the light. The stays of her bodice were laced extra tight, thanks to Meg.

During the evening opening hours she was complimented many times, and two different women asked for the address of her dressmaker. She did not tell them, for she did not want to see copies of her dress all over town, nor, if truth be told, did she want them to know it was altered in a tiny backstreet cottage, and not at a fashionable tailor's. She made light of it, said she had several and could not remember, and watched the expressions of envy flicker in their eyes.

Whilst she was here at the Gilded Lily she could forget all about the flight from Westmorland, the notices, the freezing room at Blackraven Alley, the fratch with Sadie. She was another person here. Every now and then, though, a shiver ran down her spine, as if her body was ahead of her thoughts and was afraid. At such moments she could do nothing but take a deep breath, smooth down her new gown and fix a smile on her face, being careful not to wrinkle her forehead or cheeks lest her ceruse should crack.

'I hear old Tindall's been bothering you,' said Jay, when the door had shut that day for the final time. They were alone in the shop now, except for Meg who was silently sweeping the floor.

'That's right. He was asking where I used to work and that. I told him same as I told you. Why?' she said, warily.

His eyes flicked to her new earrings, but then back to her face. 'He told my father you're bad for business. I don't see that you can be, not wearing that dress anyway. It looks very well on you. Though I think you may need a little more rouge – the colour is a little . . . icy.'

'Oh.' She was crestfallen. 'Does it not suit me?'

'I'm not saying it doesn't become you. It's just that the shade is somewhat cold, and in this weather it has the effect of making you appear older and harder.'

'I thought you liked blue. You said it would suit me – to match my eyes.'

His mouth turned down at the corners. 'I do like blue. But there are blues, and blues. This blue is a little harsh.'

'I see.' Deflated, she sat down on one of the salon chairs. Blasted Tindall. That cozener had set him against her.

'But I suppose it is quite a fetching style,' he said grudgingly, 'and it does show off the whiteness of your skin.'

Ella pouted as she mulled over his words, knowing she had spent money she had not yet earned on a dress he did not even find becoming. She watched him, with the familiar ache just below her ribcage.

'I take it you have a warm cloak? There's talk of a frost fair. There are already stalls on the river upstream, and Mrs Horsefeather has gone to see if she might arrange a booth for the Gilded Lily. All the ladies will be out to parade in style. You will serve there in the afternoons, and perhaps in the evenings if we can supply enough light.'

'Thank you, Mr Whitgift.' Ella hoped the linsey riding cloak would be warm enough for a whole afternoon outdoors in the bitter wind. He continued to pace a while, seeming distracted. He did not dismiss her, so she sat tight.

'We've had a turn of luck,' he said. 'A gentleman friend of mine, Wycliffe, has expressed a desire to meet you. He heard of you through Lord Allsop, one of my clients, and Sir Sedley, whose cousin you served here. Wycliffe is a member of the Wits club. The Duke of Buckingham is a member, and Buckhurst and a few other thespians. I would like you to impress some of these other gentlemen; they have connections at court. Charles Sedley is a personal friend of the king, so it is a great honour for you to meet his acquaintance Wycliffe.'

Ella could not believe her ears. Her mood changed in an instant, but she tried not to let her delight show. She could not take in all the names, so she simply said, 'Beg pardon, sir, but what do they want to meet me for?'

'Wycliffe has a fancy to get involved with the new theatre

on Vere Street. Women on the stage are the latest fad. The new playhouse is bursting at the seams with people wanting to see a woman tread the boards. I thought a short spell in a play might bring us in even more business, so I have persuaded him and his actor friends to take a look at you.'

'You mean me? In a play?'

'If you suit. It will be up to Sedley and his friends to decide if they have a role that befits you.'

He sat down opposite her. 'I'll take you over to Sedley's to-morrow night. I expect you to be nice to him and show him every favour. He has very wealthy and influential friends. I want him to recommend me to his fashionable set, tell them they can send their rich wives and daughters to the Lily.'

She was cock-a-hoop.

'And wear the red.' He reached over and touched her arm. 'It'll make you stand out, give you the dramatic look for the stage.'

'I will.' She smiled at him, looking up through her eyelashes, a seductive smile of encouragement. His nearness to her was almost a torture, so much did she want him.

He patted her arm and stood again. Her heart contracted with disappointment.

'The new looking glasses are on their way,' he said. 'The shipment from Venice has docked, but there's trouble getting carriers. Everyone wants them now the river's frozen. I've paid extra to guarantee delivery tomorrow. The glasses are the best money could buy. I commissioned an Italian woodcarver – such a feeling for wood, he has – to fashion the frames. You will be able to take more care over your appearance. After all, you are rapidly becoming the face of London.'

Ella basked. She was somebody now – the face of London.

*

Jay went upstairs to his eyrie. The cabinets were gradually taking over the floor space. He liked things to be tidy, so they were all labelled and piled up in size order, but he had to squeeze sideways down a narrow gap to get to his desk. Visitors used to come up here to do business with him, but not any longer; he did not want anyone else to view his collections. And besides, there was simply no room.

Partly this expansion gave him great pleasure, for his collections were visibly growing under his feet, but partly it caused him consternation, for he knew he would need more space soon. The house in Whitehall could not come quickly enough. He unwrapped the latest parcel from Allsop; it had been sitting on his desk a few days. It was the small pair of silver goblets and the sugar-shaker he had asked for. Foxy had brought them over. Foxy had been griping about the weather again, and he was right – it was damned difficult to keep to his appointments and obligations in these icy conditions.

One of Allsop's friends, the pox-ridden Wolfenden, had demanded another whore, and Foxy said it had been hard to find someone young enough, the weather was keeping the doxies indoors. In the end, though, Foxy had found one who'd pass for a maid, and she'd been no trouble, Lutch had despatched her as usual.

He picked up one of the goblets and stroked its stem. They were charming, he thought, but given the lack of space, perhaps he had others in storage that were prettier and he should sell these on. He took down the top three crates from a pile near the door, cursing as he tried to find somewhere else to put them. Finally he had the crate labelled 'drinking vessels' on his desk.

He unpacked the items from the straw one by one, and stood them side by side. Astonished, when he had done standing them, he saw that there were nearly forty. And he knew there was another box full beneath that one. He looked at them with a critical eye and picked the likely goblets up one at a time, feeling their cool metallic weight in his hand. By the time he had examined half of them, and found a good reason to keep every single one, he knew that he simply could not let any of them go.

He sighed. Bags of coinage were not the same as having the actual objects there before him, to see the workmanship, the texture, the sheer weight of it all. He hoped his father would not last too much longer. He needed that house in Whitehall. Just think how many rooms he could fill then! He would not need to stint, he could keep thousands of goblets. He would have his baronetcy and the world's finest collection of silver.

The river was now the widest street in the city. For the past week Ella had not had time to go down to the riverside, though she had been told by Polly that the freeze extended as far down as the abbey on Thorney Island. The sight that met her eyes that afternoon was extraordinary. The water had set solid into a grey glacial surface, in parts smooth, in parts jagged where the tide had upturned thick plates of ice. Downstream from the bridge a huge sailing ship was embedded in the surface, its mast listing at an angle, its rigging stiff with icicles. The ice had expanded to crush it, and the hull was staved in where it joined the water. By the banks, white boulders of ice burst from the smooth surface and a set of wooden steps had been set there, guarded by a dour waterman determined to eke a living somehow from the unrecognizable water.

'Where do you think the Lily's booth is?' asked Polly.

'Over there I expect.' Ella pointed to a snaking row of covered stalls, colourfully arrayed with flags and signs and bunting. Ella was reluctant to set foot on the ice. She knew that the water was still underneath, making its slow surly journey to the sea. But she did not want Polly to see her fear, so she pretended nonchalance, despite her fluttering stomach.

After paying their pennies to the waterman, she and Polly picked their way down the makeshift wooden steps and onto the river. Ella hung tight to the stair rail as she stepped out onto the frozen surface. Her throat was tight, she felt her breath come shallow and fast. And it felt like blasphemy, that any highway felon might walk on the water just like Jesus had.

'By, this feels strange,' Ella said shakily, watching her feet as she walked.

'Look,' said Polly. There were several horses pulling boats that had been fitted out with wheels and were taking well-to-do families for rides up and down the river. One of them held a corpulent gentleman and his equally fat wife and children.

'Suppose if it will hold them up, it must be all right then,' Ella said and Polly giggled.

Gaining confidence they hurried down the main thoroughfare, nicknamed Freezeland Street, surprised to find that it was not as slippery as they might expect, as somebody had thoughtfully strewn a layer of straw underfoot. About halfway down the row they spotted the hastily painted sign for the Gilded Lily, a sad-looking thing in comparison with the proper one at Whitgift's, thought Ella. But there was Mrs Horsefeather, wrapped up in a foxfur hat and cape, unloading a crate of bottles from a sled. A number of watermen were vying with each other for the work as they dragged more goods for the Lily across.

'Thank goodness. I am quite worn out with all this bending,' Mrs Horsefeather said. 'You girls can do it now. If you need my assistance I will be at the rum and gingerbread booth. I need something to warm my old joints.'

'Come on then,' said Polly when she had gone.

Ella began to relax. Everyone else was treating the hardened river with calm acceptance, so she began to stack the trestle with the goods and bring out the slate for chalking. Her feet tingled from the cold. From a distance the Frost Fair had looked charming, with its tented row of stalls and bright bunting, but now the reality of having to stand out in the cold for several hours bit home.

'Wish I had her furs,' Ella said, pointing at a lady in a rabbit-skin muffler.

'Or a pair of sheepskin gloves,' Polly said. 'When Miss Woodward came in last week she had on such a pretty pair. But best keep moving, that'll keep the cold away.'

They set to work unloading the crates. Business was brisk and the crowd grew thicker by the hour. All of London seemed to be here. On the ice, lords mingled with labourers; Freezeland Street belonged to everyone. Nothing could go in or out of London, so many treated it as a holiday. Stiltwalkers and jugglers roamed up and down stopping to create a crowd, who were enjoying a festive atmosphere fuelled by much medicinal use of hot ale or spirits.

Around lunchtime Ella spotted a familiar figure walking down the ice, the distinctive hat with its three pheasant feathers marking him out. He was with a group of other young dandies, all in tight-fitting coats with cloaks a-swagger. 'Look lively,' she said to Polly, 'here comes Jay Whitgift.'

Polly immediately straightened her skirts and pulled down her hood so that her hair was showing. Not to be outdone, Ella did the same, but also undid her cloak to show more of the lace chemise.

The men paused outside one of the tented alehouses, with a wooden crown atop, and Jay laughed at some jest before clapping one of his friends on the back. The others disappeared inside, and Jay sauntered down the row, pausing at the goldsmith's and the printing booth where you could have a souvenir ticket printed by the heavy iron press.

When he got to the Lily's tent, he said, 'Ah. I see by the slates, I was right to set you up here. You've done well. Who has been in?'

'Miss Woodward and her friends, Miss Almoner, with her mother. Oh, and Lady Edgware. But mostly folks I've not seen afore.'

'There was Miss Hunter,' said Polly pushing her way forward.

'Oh yes, Miss Hunter –' Ella glared at Polly – 'but she don't count 'cos she didn't buy anything.'

'Have you enough stock?'

'Yes, sir, there's plenty,' Polly said before Ella could reply. 'Ain't it grand, sir! There's boys skating on the ice, in proper skating shoes. They must be Dutch, 'cos we ain't got nothing like that over here, and over by the ship there's a man set up a stage to dance jigs—'

'And we saw a spit outside the tent called the King's Head and it were roasting a whole ox,' interrupted Ella.

'Is that right? Where is the King's Head?'

'Turn left at the end of this row,' Polly said, as Ella opened her mouth to tell him.

'Very good,' he said, smiling at Polly. 'I'm partial to a roast.' He looked at Ella. 'I should fasten up, if I were you, the cold can soon go to your chest. Can't have you sickening for anything before tonight. Have you no muffler?'

'Yes, Mr Whitgift, but I did not think—'

'Wrap up, then. My carriage will call for you at nine. Make sure you're ready.'

'I will be.'

'Keep up the good work,' he said, throwing a smile at Polly. Then he turned on his heel and headed back towards the Crown. They watched him duck under the awning and disappear from view.

'I'll take one of these,' said a red-nosed woman, swathed in a woollen shawl.

'Eleven pence,' Polly said.

Ella took her coins and Polly began to wrap the item.

'What's this about him coming for you in a carriage?' Polly said, handing the woman the package.

'He's going to take me to meet his friends. One of them's a knight of the king's bedchamber.'

'You never!'

'Cross my heart. They're all earls and lords. And one of them bides with the duke's players. They're after a pretty girl to go on stage. They asked after me particular.'

'Can't think why. Anyway, play-acting's only for whores.' Polly's face was sour.

''Tis not. Jay says the king and everyone goes to the theatre now. You're behind the times.'

'Jay says, Jay says. Bet he only wants you to open your legs.'

'Don't be coarse. Just 'cos he asked for me and not you. You're jealous, that's all.'

'Am not.'

'Yes, you are. 'Cos you know what it means when a man takes you out in his carriage.'

'No! You're never betrothed.'

'I'm not saying anything.'

Polly huffed through her nose and turned her back on her. A few moments later, she rejoined with, 'I don't believe you. He'd never in a hundred Sundays wed you. Pa Whitgift's trying to get him set up with Miriam Edgware.'

'I'm saying nothing. You just watch me, that's all.'

Chapter 31

As she walked back to the Gilded Lily from the Frost Fair, Ella kept thinking about Sadie's words, that her mother would have thought she looked like a whore. There was an unaccustomed pain in her chest that would not go away. Sadie had become awkward. Time was, she was as docile as a kitten. Ella did not know what she would do if she had to mind her much longer. If Sadie would not help herself by doing as Ella suggested, then what would happen? She couldn't stay locked up there for ever. She had provided nothing whilst Ella was out working at Whitgift's, all she'd been able to do was to make a measly pair of stockings. It had been weeks since Sadie had been able to work, and Ella had to pay all Sadie's rent out of her own wages. It wasn't fair.

She walked as fast as she could given the icy streets. The air was swimming with tiny snowflakes that melted as they touched her face so that she had to shake her hood to keep it from getting wet. She gritted her teeth and pushed her head forward as she walked.

She nodded to the nightwatchman, and opened up the Gilded Lily. A wave of warmth hit her – Meg must have banked the fires. She lit a candle and, seeing a large square parcel in the shop, hurried upstairs. The second parcel was there in her chamber – the new mirror. Carefully, so as not to waste the moment, she sawed through the string with her nail-paring knife and peeled back the oilcloth wrapping. Her mouth fell open in an expression of incredulous delight. She let the cloth fall to the ground, where it buffeted a cloud of dust that swam in the stuffy air.

Nothing had prepared her for the vision of the other world she saw before her. It was a window into another room. She saw a young woman, dressed in a wash of blue, a white lace fan dangling half open from one arm, standing before a set of low windows, each criss-crossed with lozenges of glass panes, and each bearing a panel of brownish-green stained glass in the centre. She could see quite clearly the slightly distorted snow on the roofs of the other buildings outside the window, and even the smoke from the chimneys moving against the night sky.

Of course she had seen looking glasses before – but they had been small pocket glasses or hand glasses. Women wore them hung from their waists, and men flashed them in their hats, or showed off their carved glass-cases at the card table. Other looking glasses of this size were made of polished metal, and the reflection was like looking through a gauze or an insistent mizzle of rain.

Tentatively she moved closer to the seamless surface of the glass, and the woman in the gilded frame moved closer too. A curvaceous figure, with slender arms, leaning slightly forward from her nipped-in waist. The brass eyeholes on the front-lacing of the dress, the fine dentelle of the lace on the chemise, even the rise and fall of the bosom. Ella looked, delighted. Sadie was wrong. The woman she saw there was a fine lady. As so could Sadie be too, if only she would see sense.

Ella brushed down her skirts and posed some more, turning this way and that, looking over her shoulder at the back lacing of

331

her dress. She moved closer to the mirror and slowly raised her head until, startled, she met a pair of blue eyes, fringed with thick dark lashes, looming from a marble-white face.

She recoiled.

The picture had been alluring at first, from a distance, like a painting in a book. But as she looked more closely, the image grew more disturbing. She hurried to light more candles. At first she was curious to see the dull lifeless hair, crimped and tonged with sugar into stiff yellow side curls, the eyebrows uneven painted lines over rough stubble. Was this the woman renowned throughout London for her beauty? As she looked into this new harsh reflection her expression turned to one of fascinated horror.

Her hand came up to touch her hair, and with shock she saw that the skin on the back of her hands was crinkled, the fingers bony. Tentatively, she peered closer. The Spanish cochineal she had applied to her lips had bled into the white powder of her skin, and her upper lip was a mass of tiny fissures, crazed like a second-hand chamber pot. Unable to take it in, she brought her face right up to the glass, until she could see that there were certainly cracks in the paste around her nose, and that her forehead had all the appearance of a limewashed building ravaged by the weather.

She examined the surface of her skin with growing nausea, until a mist from her nose softened the definition of the features before her and she withdrew to let the bloom on the glass clear.

She thought of the forthcoming evening. Jay had made it plain he was expecting her to make a good impression on Wycliffe. Wycliffe was used to the company of the gentlemen at court. She was actually going to be in the same room as someone who had dined with the new king. Perhaps Jay had given her the looking glass before she was introduced on purpose. She squirmed with shame. A hot flush of embarrassment rose around her neck, creeping upwards to her cheeks until they glowed damson. Ella observed the patch of colour flare, then fade until her complexion returned to its usual pallor.

A means must be found somehow to perfect herself before Jay's carriage arrived. She twisted the cord of her fan round her hand until the fingers turned white whilst she thought what to do. There was nobody in the Lily. She hurried downstairs.

Two hours later when the door opened below, Ella did not hear it. She had moved her dressing stool before the glass, and now stood behind it dressed in scarlet silk. Her face was illuminated by two torchères ablaze with lighted candles set either side of the frame. Before the mirror was the side table, with a scatter of open pots and phials, its surface smeared with white and pocked with powder.

'Miss Johnson!' The call came from below.

Ella turned slowly, holding her own gaze, until she was standing side-on to the glass, examining her profile, a look of intense scrutiny on her face. Her face was motionless.

Only her eyes moved, liquid in the dry shell of her face.

Jay's carriage and pair were outside the door. The horses' flanks steamed in the night air. Ella swirled on her cloak over her red dress and braced herself against the thickening snow. Jay nodded his approval, and Ella dipped her head. She dare not smile lest her carefully applied lip paint should bleed. She looked across at Jay from behind her fan as they jolted through the cobbled streets. His hat was on his knee and the ridge of ice crystals on the brim melted into a puddle of water which dripped onto the floor of the carriage. He stared steadily out of the window, as if he were travelling alone. Her eyes took in his profile, his aquiline nose, the slightly furrowed brow, and the familiar longing twisted her heart. She did not dare to speak, for in polite society, the gentleman must always speak first.

She vaguely thought that he should have arranged a lady's maid for her, if she was to meet with Wycliffe. She had become confused now as to where her station was in life. Before she worked at Whitgift's it had been very clear. Now she was unsure if she was a servant or a lady. She was expected to behave like a lady, keep a tone of reserve, even rudeness. But now it was becoming clear she was still a servant, since he did not think her yet worthy of a chaperone or of a lady's maid.

The carriage took them through the narrow streets towards the centre of the city, and the buildings passed in a blur of candle-lit windows and intermittent snow. The streets were empty of night-time hawkers and whores, for it was already after curfew. Just the usual assortment of ragged and yelping dogs that owned the streets after dark.

The carriage drew up at an imposing stone house and Jay descended, his boots sinking in the snow. He walked ahead, whilst the burly coachman helped her out. She picked up her skirts to lift them clear of the ground and tiptoed as quickly as she could in the slippery conditions. A servant opened the door and ushered him up a staircase into a stuffy retiring room and Ella followed, hands gripping tight onto her fan. She walked with her back rigid and her head up, playing the lady, ready to make an impression on these famous gallants of the king's acquaintance.

The four gentlemen in the room were playing cards and barely glanced up from the table. Ella was disconcerted to see she was the only woman in the room.

'Ah, Whitgift. Good,' said one of the men, smiling at him and beckoning him over. 'Filthy weather, isn't it?'

'Is that the girl?' asked another, giving her a cursory glance. He was dressed in an oriental robe and a soft turban-like cap. Jay started to speak but before he could answer he shook his head. 'Well, she won't do. A yellow-haired maid is no good. Not for the stage. The fashion is for *les brunettes*, dark girls. They look more striking from a distance.' He looked at Ella as if she was something distasteful. He turned impatiently back to his cards. 'Why did not anyone tell me that she was blonde,' he grumbled.

'You didn't ask,' Jay said.

'Don't heed Mohun, you can join us for the next round. Here, have a drink,' said a corpulent gent, raking a pile of coins towards him on the table. 'Buckhurst's brought a cask.'

One of the other men looked up from his hand of cards to stare at them both, then winked at Jay. Buckhurst was a younger man than Jay, she guessed, with a crop of black curly hair tied back with a large bow, and a lovelock dangling over one eye.

Jay helped himself to a glass of wine. He waved Ella to the upright chair near the door. She sat down, hot with humiliation. She sat still, unsure what was expected of her, and wondering how long she must watch them play cards. The room blazed with the heat of the fire and a number of dripping candlesticks, both free-standing and on the table. The table was a delicate item of expensive polished wood, but the surface of it was marred by great pools of wax from the candles, and numerous drinking cups sitting in wet patches of wine.

The men continued to play, all except Jay, gambling for larger and larger sums of money. Ella sat upright on the chair, whilst the men ignored her, as if she was an unwanted item of furniture. But before long she became engrossed in following the game. The amount of the wagers horrified her. They were betting their gold, their horses, even their land. At one point the corpulent man, whom they called Sedley, was on a losing streak, and she heard him say to Jay, 'Bridge us a loan, won't you, Whitgift?'

Jay nodded, and brought out a fat purse. 'Two shillings to the pound, by the end of the month,' he said. He counted out the coins and they shook hands, the game continuing until the gentleman with the lovelock, Buckhurst, who was obviously the worse for drink, bet his entire stable. Ella could not imagine how anyone could do such a thing. She was mightily relieved when he won, and his horses were saved, to much rowdy cheering from the men.

'Hey, fellows, did you hear about Winstanley?' Sedley said.

'No, what about him?' said Mohun.

'A few years ago he gambled his estate away to Lord Wessex in a dispute about a horse. They played dice. The one who won got the nag and the house. Winstanley lost, and he had to pack his wife and family off, send them to the back of beyond – Kingsbridge I think it was, to live with his sister. About a month ago he persuaded Wessex to play again, and guess what? He won it back!' There was much laughter.

Sedley continued. 'He's turned simple since though. He's had the emblem of the winning card, the Ace of Clubs, included in the family crest and now it's everywhere – on the border of the tapestries in the hall, above the front door, even on the caps of the chimneys. Wouldn't be surprised if there's a club on all the piss pots too!'

The men laughed uproariously.

'Good old Winstanley!' said Buckhurst, glancing at Ella to see her reaction.

Ella pretended to laugh, a small sound from the back of her throat, but privately she was appalled. To think of the poor wife! That her home, everything she held dear, all her precious things, could be lost overnight on the mere throw of a dice! And yet she must live under his roof again, knowing that everything she owned might be lost on a whim, with no warning at all.

Jay laughed along with the rest of them. He seemed to find it all a cause for jest, and suggested that all the men might like to include some fanciful item in their family crest. Many lewd suggestions were made until Jay coughed and they all looked round at Ella, still sitting politely in the corner.

'Another round. My deal,' Sedley said.

'Hey, where's old Wolfenden these days?' Wycliffe said.

'Back on form,' said Buckhurst with a grin. 'You know he was months having treatment in the tubs for the French pox. And his face has rotted so much now that he had to get a silversmith to fashion him a new nose.'

'Is it really that bad?' Wycliffe asked.

'He tried everything. Last I heard he was on doses of quicksilver. Made him retch for England, and cost him that fine racehorse he had. He was mighty cast down with it all. Still, it seems to be working, which he's mighty glad about. Says he can't afford much more treatment. Blames that French jilt on Lukener's Lane.'

They carried on playing, engrossed in the game, until Mohun said, 'I'm out,' and the rest threw their cards down on the table. Buckhurst raked in the winnings.

'Pass us another drink,' said Mohun. 'Let's talk about this idea we've got for the new play at Vere Street.'

Wycliffe stood up, filled a glass and passed it over, and said to Ella, 'My apologies, madam, I have offered you no refreshment. Would you like some wine?'

Wycliffe was a short, slight man with a girlish voice. Ella was aware of all the gentlemen suddenly watching her, and she felt uncomfortable. Wine reminded her of her father and it made her retch. She did not really want any but thought it rude to refuse it, and she could not ask for ale – not in this company anyway.

'A small glass, thank you,' she said in her best accent. The men looked amused, and Wycliffe poured a thimbleful into a cup. 'Is this enough?'

Ella nodded, and they all laughed.

'Only jesting,' said Wycliffe, sloshing a generous measure

into her cup and handing it to her. His hand was unsteady and it slopped into her lap. She hastily brushed it away, but there was a stain spreading on her borrowed red gown and nobody offered to fetch a cloth. There were no servants, they must all be abed. The tart smell of the alcohol catapulted her thoughts back to Nether-barrow, and her father.

'Drink up,' said Wycliffe. Ella obediently lifted the cup to her lips and, holding her breath, took a small sip. 'Your good health!' he said. 'Now, how would you like to be on the stage?'

'Beg pardon, sir, but I don't know anything about it.'

'Can you recite anything for us?'

'I don't know.' She looked to Jay in appeal, but his eyes were on Wycliffe.

'Come on, you must know something. Any little ditty. What about a song?'

Ella felt her stays digging into her ribs, she did not think she could sing. 'I don't know . . . I could try reciting "Maid in a Garret" . . .' she said.

'Fine, go ahead. Stand there.'

She stood where he pointed, in the middle of the room, pain-fully aware that this was not at all what she had in mind when she climbed into the carriage on Friargate. She was not sure what they wanted but she began, hesitating over the first few words:

'I was told by my aunt, I was told by my mother,
That going to a weddin' is the makings of another.'

They were laughing uproariously already. She felt as if she were shrinking, getting smaller every moment like Hop o' my Thumb. She hesitated.

'No, no, go on,' spluttered Wycliffe. 'She's priceless,' she heard him say. She rallied herself by speaking a little louder.

> *'And if this be so then I'll go without a biddin',*
> *Oh kind providence won't you send me to a weddin'!'*

They sniggered and whispered one to another the whole time she was reciting. Wycliffe was crying with mirth, his hand clapped over his mouth. In a desperate attempt to salvage herself she tried making some gestures, as she declaimed:

> *'Come rich man, come poor man, come fool or come witty,*
> *Come any man at all! Won't you marry out of pity?'*

When she stopped they stamped and whistled, but fell to laughing with each other, not applauding her. She felt two inches tall.

'I'll marry you myself! Sure I will! How about you, Whitgift?' Wycliffe said.

He gave a tight-lipped smile, at which the rest of the company exploded into guffaws.

'Still don't think she'll do, the fashion in the theatre is for dark girls – not yellow,' said Mohun.

'Shame,' said Buckhurst. 'It would have been a good advertisement for that knocking shop of yours, Whitgift. You got any dark girls?'

Jay had no time to reply before Wycliffe said, 'Hey, Sedley, did you see Fanny Gurney at the old tennis court?'

'What legs!' Sedley said, pointing his toe in mimicry.

'I'd give her one!' shouted Buckhurst.

Ella seemed to have been forgotten already. She went back to her chair, relieved to escape the focus of their attention. But it was short-lived.

'Hey, you're not drinking,' Buckhurst said, spotting her half-empty glass. 'Drink it up now, like a good girl.'

Ella took a deep breath and drained the rest of the cup. The smell of the liquor made her feel ill. It tasted sour on her tongue. Wycliffe took the glass out of her hand and refilled it, passing it back to her. She looked down at it helplessly, unable to drink it.

'Oh, fellows,' Mohun said, 'I've just had a snappy idea. It's Allsop's birthday next week and we're meeting him in the King's for a few. Wouldn't it be a caper to have your yellow-haired girl recite her poem. A bit of entertainment. If it goes down well, you never know, I might reconsider, put her in my new play,' said Mohun.

'I'm not sure she will be to Allsop's taste,' Jay said, looking discomfited.

'Fiddlesticks. Of course she will. What could be better?' Wycliffe said.

'I don't think Allsop cares—'

'Oh, don't be a spoilsport.' Wycliffe turned to Ella. 'That's settled then. Jay will bring you over in the carriage and we'll drive you over to Allsop's later to surprise him. Get her to wear something pretty, Jay. Mr Allsop likes ladies to look pretty.'

'I will make sure she is suitably dressed,' said Jay tersely.

Ella brushed at the stain on her skirt again. She was nervous. She had never heard of Lord Allsop, but the men of the Wits club had a reputation. Buckingham had set it up, and he was known as a rakehell. People had lost count of the number of mistresses he had. One of them had even been set up in a house of her own, but there had been wild talk of kidnappings and rape too.

It would not be wise to refuse, and half of her was curious. After all, Allsop was probably a wealthy man. But a part of her warned her to be wary. She looked over to Jay for reassurance; she sensed he had not been so keen on the idea of her meeting Allsop. It gladdened her that he was protective of her reputation. After all, he was likely taken with her himself. She cast him an alluring glance. But Jay was staring morosely out of the window into the dark, a glass of wine at his lips.

The wine had started to go to her head. She couldn't think straight. She reached as if to put the wine cup down on the side table, but Buckhurst saw her and said, 'Not wasting it, are you? Here.' He took a great swig from her cup, before passing it back to her.

'Sorry, sir,' said Ella, trying to push it back to him, 'but I've had enough wine.'

'Enough wine! One can never have enough wine, isn't that right, Wycliffe?' Buckhurst said.

'Quite right,' Wycliffe said.

'Mr Allsop will expect you to drink with him, make sport and be merry. He won't want sour-faced abstainers at his party. We had enough of all that in Old Noll's day,' Sedley said.

Jay was looking at her, frowning. Ella coloured. She was already too hot, and the powder she was wearing made her face feel tight. She fanned herself with her other hand. Her head was swimming. Nauseous, she gritted her teeth and drank the cup to the dregs through barely parted lips.

'There you are, see,' said Buckhurst.

Jay smiled thinly. Ella sat very still, feeling her stomach heave and the bile rise to her throat. She swallowed it down. She heard Sedley say, 'Thanks for the loan, Whitgift. You'll get it back when my new play is produced. I've brought you that chased silver salver we talked of. It's on the console in the hall.'

'Very good. Nice to do business with you. It will be part of my private collection. I already have a silver salver in a similar style. Embossed with a hunting scene – a stag at bay, and hounds, most lifelike.'

'A stag, you say.' Wycliffe smiled at Jay, a complicit smile that was not lost on Ella. Jay looked down, a faint tinge of pink washed over his face. He busied himself pouring another drink. Wycliffe moved to the cask too and wound his arm around Jay's waist before tilting his head up to kiss him on the neck. His lips lingered there. Jay's hand moved slowly around Wycliffe's back, hitched up his coat and rested on his buttock, where his fingers traced long slow circles.

Ella dabbed her forehead with the back of her arm. She felt sick and faint. Her brow was clammy. The point of her wooden stomacher pressed into her belly so that she shifted uncomfortably on the chair. There was a humming in her ears and the candle flames turned hazy and began to swim before her eyes.

'Excuse me,' she said. She stood up shakily and hurried out of the room onto the landing, where she tottered down the stairs to the chilly hallway. There she clung to the newel post of the staircase and gulped great breaths of cold air.

Jay did not follow her out. A manservant, who must have heard the bang of the door, appeared from downstairs. His demeanour was frosty.

'Is anything the matter, madam?' he asked.

'I feel faint,' she said. 'Get us some water from the kitchen, will you?' She did not bother to disguise her country accent.

The servant glared at her, bowed and went back down the dark stairwell. Ella tasted his disapproval though he had not spoken. He thinks I'm a jumped-up bitch, she thought, and who can blame him? Having to wait on the likes of me. I'll bet he's straight downstairs to tell all the kitchen staff.

She longed for the companionship of being in service. She pictured the chats around the kitchen table, the easy gossip, the sense of camaraderie. She had a sudden urge to follow him downstairs. She imagined loosening off her tight stays, sitting comfortably with the rest of the servants over a jug of well-watered ale. But she had put herself above all that. Or perhaps beneath it, she did not know.

She held more tightly to the banister. Her sickness was fading and her head felt clearer, but she did not want to let go. She was stuck, caught between the glittering fashionable world upstairs, where she was evidently an object of derision, and the world downstairs where she had betrayed her class.

The servant handed her a chipped earthenware cup of water. He had not bothered to put it on a tray. It was a deliberate insult. She took the cup anyway and drank it down in one. The cold water revived her determination.

'That will be all,' she said, in her best clipped accent, thrusting the empty cup towards him. The man took it, but looked up at the sound of footfalls upstairs. Above, she heard the door open and voices saying goodnight as the men prepared to depart. Her shoulders sank with relief.

'Turner. Have the carriage brought round,' shouted Wycliffe.

'Yes, sir.' The servant melted back downstairs.

'Here,' said Jay, thrusting Ella her cloak, 'get in the carriage.' She put it on, her eyes downcast, and went outside onto the street. The carriage rolled up in front of her and she climbed awkwardly in.

A few moments later Jay joined her. She could not see his face in the darkness and he did not speak. She moved away from him in the carriage until her shoulder was jammed hard against the door. Only when they arrived back at the chambers did he say, 'It is a shame you were unable to impress my thespian friends. Mr Wycliffe is generous to those he favours. If you do not please Allsop and my friend Wycliffe is disappointed again, then I am sure I can persuade the wigmaker to take you back on.'

The sun crept in with a watery glow through the window, and Sadie threw back the sacking to let in more of its light. The river was empty of boats this morning, of skiffs and wherries and barges, and there were none of the usual hoots and bells and whistles. It was icy too, the sky a sudden unexpected blue. Yesterday, when the scavengers walked along the shore she could hear the crunch of ice breaking under their feet. The sounds were clear and sharp. She heard the cries of the milkmaid and the aleman too and licked her dry lips. She had taken nothing to drink since Ella left. There was no ale and even the pail was dry; she had looked at it countless times.

She had eaten well, the bacon and bread had been tasty, but had only added to her thirst. She went over to the door and pushed against it, in case by some miracle it might open. Of course it didn't. Ella had locked it as she said she would. Sadie began to get concerned. She roamed the room, unable to settle back to her knitting.

By afternoon there was still no sign of Ella. What on earth would she do if Ella did not come back? She had not even heard any noises from below, and she missed the constant barking of Ma Gowper's cough. What if Ella had been discovered somehow and caught, and was in prison unable to get a message to her? In her mind Sadie pictured the bouncing girl with the brown hair, rosy face and a cheeky grin. The sister she knew from Westmorland. Sadie shook her head, as if to rattle that picture free. She replaced it with the picture of the white-faced Ella in the blue gown.

'Oh, Ell,' she whispered, 'where are you?'

Chapter 32

Ella had overslept. Usually the light woke her, and the distant crowing of cockerels. Then she would stretch her bare toes in the soft warmth of the blanket and have a few moments wallowing in bed before getting up to begin her vigil at the mirror.

Today, however, she was woken by a sharp hammering on the door.

'What is it,' she croaked, half asleep. Her voice didn't seem to be working properly.

'I'm off now,' shouted Polly.

Ella did not reply, just turned over in bed, hugging a bolster closer to her chest.

Polly shouted again. 'Corey, Jay Whitgift wants to see me in his chambers. I've turned the notice on the door, so you've got a few minutes before he does his rounds.'

Ella was confused. She jumped up and ran to the window in her shift. The sundial on the wall showed after noon! She looked at it again. That couldn't be right. Downstairs the frosty yard was full of carriages.

'Christ almighty,' she said.

She ran over to the mirror. The picture was all too clear. She looked dishevelled, like a harlot. After the disastrous evening at Sedley's she had fallen into bed at four in the morning without bothering to wash her face or tidy her hair. Now her hair was like a stook of straw, her face smeared with black soot where it had run from around her eyes. Her head throbbed as if a hedge-layer wielded a mallet inside it.

'Meg,' she cried, throwing on her petticoats. Where on earth was she? She rang the bell.

'Yes, mam?' Meg's face appeared round the door, a shawl tied round her head and shoulders.

'You stupid girl. Why weren't you here earlier?'

'You didn't ring, mam.' She was staring at Ella's face with curiosity.

Ella lashed out, slapping Meg a stinging blow on the arm. 'That's for your cheek. You know I always need you to lace me up at nine o'clock.'

Meg gulped as if she might burst into tears.

'Don't just stand there, get on with it. No – not the red, the blue. The blue! Over there, you maggot brain! And hurry.'

Ella fidgeted as Meg struggled to lace her into her dress, and when Meg took a comb to her hair screamed at her when it snagged. When she next looked round, Meg had slunk away. 'You'll be out, my girl,' she muttered fiercely under her breath.

Ella leaned towards the mirror, hastily slapping on another layer of ceruse. She had a pimple coming on her chin, so she covered it with a heart-shaped patch. Her hands shook. Her eyes were bloodshot and still half closed. She dropped some of the stinging nightshade into each eye and was rewarded by her pupils becoming enormous. It made the room slightly blurred, softer round the edges. She finished her toilet hurriedly, scrubbing salt over her teeth to take away the rancid taste in her mouth. In case the smell of liquor lingered, she dribbled cologne over her chest.

By this time the shadow on the dial had crept to half after twelve. 'Oh God – Sadie,' she said under her breath. There wasn't time to go to Blackraven Alley now. She'd have to go at night, after work. She glanced out of the window to see Jay walking across the yard as he usually did, making his lunchtime rounds. The sight of him made her shrivel inside with shame. To think, she had set her cap at him, when the signs were written all over him, plain as plain, that it wasn't the girls he was after. The vision of being Ella Whitgift crumbled into dust.

She shot downstairs, turned the notice on the door to 'Open' and took up her place behind the counter. She mustn't lose her position. It came to her in a flash that her charm would be no use in a tight corner – not with Jay Whitgift. Why had she overslept? Stupid Meg should have woken her.

It was a bad start to the day, like waking to find the fire had gone out. The fear of losing her position made her light-headed. Her thoughts slid back to Sadie waiting for her at Blackraven Alley. Surely a few more hours wouldn't matter. After all, she had plenty to keep her occupied. With any luck, by the time Ella arrived, she might have finished the second pair of stockings. But even this thought discomfited her.

She felt bad about her arguments with Sadie, it rankled like a broken bodice-bone. She had thought her younger sister's opinion of her to be of little account, but now she was surprised to find that it mattered. It was not something she was used to, Sadie calling her names. She pictured the small damp room above the Thames and Sadie's expectant face. Unaccountably, it made her feel angry. It's not my fault, she thought; she'll have to wait.

She uncorked a jar and applied a little more madder to her lips, brushed down her skirts and waited behind the counter, pretending to arrange a display of pots of marigold cream. Jay's silhouette approached behind the single pane of glass in the door.

347

She felt slightly sick, and swallowed; the taste of wine still lingered on her palate.

The door opened and he strode towards her. He carried a rolled-up paper in his hand, probably a stock list or a roster of orders. She forced a smile to her lips, pushed away the image of his hand tracing the shape of Wycliffe's buttocks. She hoped he would not notice her hastily applied face. Jay stopped directly before her and glowered under his thin eyebrows. It crossed her mind that perhaps he also was feeling under the weather after the evening at Wycliffe's. But something in his demeanour made the back of her neck prickle.

Wordlessly he unrolled the paper and spread it out on the table to face her. She took a sharp breath. He smoothed the paper flat and picked up four pots of salve to hold it open and weight it down, standing them with mathematical precision on the corners. Ella could not read the paper, but it didn't matter. She had recognized it as soon as he unrolled it. It was one of the 'reward' notices. She stared at it, her mouth dry. She could not speak so she just waited.

'Tell me why I should not claim this reward,' he said.

She decided to try to bluff it out. 'Beg pardon, sir, I can't read.'

Jay laughed, but it was a laugh without merriment. 'You know well enough what it is. Someone at the Corn Exchange was telling me that there was a reward out for two maids. As soon as he said one of them had a piebald face, I thought to myself, now then, I've seen someone with a face like that, now where was it?'

Ella was watching him warily. He did not seem angry, just puffed up and full of himself.

'Of course!' he said, hitting his forehead in mock frustration, 'it was at the perruquier's. Your sister. I was about to dismiss it as a coincidence, but then I got to thinking – how Madame Lefevre was so keen to find you. And you spun me that yarn about pinching from the till. I thought it mighty odd then that you wanted your whereabouts kept secret.' He leaned towards her, resting his forearm on the table. 'No wonder – you're wanted for murder.'

She clutched at the front of her bodice. The game was up. There was no point in denying it.

'I didn't do it, sir.'

'It matters not an ounce to me whether you did or no. But you have to understand, it's a risk to me you working here. Either they'll think I'm stupid, or they'll think I'm protecting you. Neither is an option. So I'll have to hand you over, you know that.'

'Please, sir, don't do that. They'll hang us.'

Jay moved away, tapping his hat against his thigh, as if weighing it up.

He's enjoying this, she thought, with a sudden realization.

'You thought to take me for a simpleton, Miss Appleby. That was foolish. Now tell me, where is your sister?'

Ella shrivelled inside. 'Don't know, sir.'

'What do you mean, you don't know?'

Ella thought quickly. 'When I moved in here she couldn't pay the rent. She was angry with me and moved out of our lodgings.'

'Where is she now?'

'I've told you. I don't know.'

Ella glanced at the door. Even if she got past Jay, there was not a cat's chance of escaping through the throng of carriages. Jay saw her look.

'Oh, my man Lutch has instructions not to let you leave the premises.'

She looked again and saw the dark silhouette of a man just outside the door.

'Wycliffe was very keen for you to provide a suitable – how shall I say – *divertissement* for Allsop, and I see no reason for that to change.' Jay laughed at some joke of his own. 'A day here or there will not matter. Ibbetson will wait.' He turned back to face her, smiling his wolfish smile. 'Perhaps I may reconsider if you please my friends. But if you wish to be of value you must look attractive,' he went on. 'There is white powder sprinkled on your bodice, and your lips need repainting.' He looked at her with distaste as though she were a dog with fleas. The door tinkled and Polly hurried brightly in. She stopped short of the counter, evidently taking in the odd atmosphere in the room.

'As we discussed, Miss Johnson is not to go out of the Lily without my say-so. She will stay indoors and you will not mention her name to anyone. Do you understand? Get your warm cloak and bonnet on, Miss Bennett. You will be on duty at the Frost Fair to assist Mrs Horsefeather. The boy will come for you in the gig at the quarter bell.'

'Yes, Mr Whitgift.' Polly simpered and tossed her brown curls at him, before giving Ella a triumphant look.

Jay went to the door. 'Chaperone Miss Johnson until I get back,' he said shortly. 'Don't let her go anywhere on her own.' He disappeared into the yard.

'What's going on?' said Polly.

Ella shook her head. 'Mind your own. I just need a few minutes to fix my face. You can give me a few minutes for that, can't you?'

'He said I've not to let you out of my sight, or I lose my place.'

'Oh, for God's sake. Come to the top of the stairs with me then.'

Polly looked doubtful, but she followed Ella. Ella walked up the stairs like a doll, as if her legs were not her own. Her mind was racing. She just needed some time to think. At the door to the room Ella said, 'Look. I just want a few minutes alone to fix my face, all right?'

'What's up?' Polly said, trying again.

'Nothing.'

'I'll be listening at the door. If I hear anything funny, I'll bring Mr Whitgift.'

'Do I look like I'm going to turn bedlam? I've told you, I'm only going to fix my face.'

She closed the door on Polly's curiosity. She had to try to think, make a plan. She looked directly below and saw the bulky head and shoulders of a man standing just outside the door. She hurried to the windows, ran her fingers over them, but they were sealed with layers of caulk and had no handles. Damn, they didn't open. And they faced the yard, where everybody came and went. So there was no way out from up there. She knew there was a tiny window in the back downstairs, but it wasn't even big enough for a cat. The rest of the windows faced the front where Jay's man was on guard.

She went over to the mirror, and her reflection stared back at her, impassive, as if nothing was amiss. A wave of anger came over her at her naivety. She had thought herself and Jay to be alike. She wondered how she could ever have thought him attractive. She loathed him. She hated his sloe-black eyes, his pointed nose, his almost fleshless fingers. She hated the immaculate cut of his clothes, his too-clean cuffs, the way he swaggered from place to place, ignoring all the customers queuing in the yard as if they were invisible.

And she had caught the look between Wycliffe and him. The intimacy of that look had made her wince with shame at her own stupidity. Whatever she looked like on the outside, she was still just so much chaff to him.

A great rage filled her. She grabbed a wet muslin cloth from the ewer and scrubbed at her face. The white lead came off in big streaks, the cochineal from her lips stained the cloth red.

The door opened with a creak and Polly's curious head came round the corner.

'Get out!' yelled Ella with venom, turning her dripping face towards her.

Polly's eyebrows shot up and she retreated back behind the door. A few moments later Ella heard the noise of the gig outside and Jay Whitgift's voice. Then the sound of the door banging to, as Polly left. Ella went over to the window again and was disconcerted to see the big-shouldered man still stationed outside.

She sat back down and scrubbed at her face until it was red. When she looked up again she saw the wide-eyed country girl that had first come to London, breathless with hopes and dreams of a better life. The face reminded her of someone. She paused in her rubbing and stared. And then she saw it. The wide mouth, the snub upturned nose. It was Sadie.

It was the first time she had ever caught a family resemblance between herself and her sister. And more, it reminded her of her ma. Her eyes turned glassy, but she wiped them roughly with the muslin. Ella remembered how Sadie had tried to hug her the last time she had gone to see her, and the ache in her chest grew stronger. With awful clarity she remembered seeing Sadie holding out her arms, and then her face fall, as Ella ignored her and stepped away. The vision transformed, was replaced by a picture of her hand in its fine lace glove, turning the key in the padlock. Her eyes were streaming now, and she wiped them roughly not caring that it stung, to punish herself.

Sadie would be waiting for her, would need her to fetch food and water. The thought of Sadie waiting patiently by the locked door, her stomach hollow with hunger, made a small moan escape from the back of Ella's throat. She would wait, and nobody would come. In a panic, Ella groped for the solid metal shape of the key to the padlock, hung beneath her skirts. She let out a sigh of relief. It was still there. She must get out of here. She was suddenly hot, on fire with hatred for herself. Sweat broke out on her forehead and she scraped it away with the cloth. She felt for the key again and stood up.

The room was stifling, airless. Meg had banked up the fire and it crackled now. It had blazed away even when she was out of the room. It had seemed like luxury, but now it seemed wasteful and needless. She thought of Sadie scavenging her few sticks for a fire for cooking and remembered her promise, made all those years ago in the big bed in Netherbarrow, that she should dine on sweetmeats and sleep on silk. She knew where Sadie was now – sitting silently in her old petticoats, her feet wrapped in rags, looking at the empty shelf. Ella moaned. She had tried to leave Netherbarrow behind, but it was as if the river Nether flowed in her veins instead of blood.

Slowly and deliberately she pasted on a new layer of white ceruse. This time it was to hide herself, hide the old Ella, so that she might appear to be still Miss Johnson, when she knew as sure as the sun rose each morning that she could never be anyone but Ella Appleby of Westmorland. She plastered the white paste over her neck and bosom. Deliberately she drew in blue veins with a crayon, and rubbed the blue over her eyelids. She made her lips even redder, and her eyelashes black with soot powder. Her emotion manifested as a sort of deliberateness, an icy control. She would not be beaten. She would find a way to get out of the Lily, for she must go to her sister.

She whisked away the powder at her neckline with a hogshair brush, and smoothed her skirts. The process made her calm. She picked up her fan and sat down to fathom a plan.

Sadie had been two days without food or water. The air was sharp. The night had been remorselessly cold and Sadie had hung a small jug out of the window, hoping to catch a little moisture or dew inside it by the morning, but when she hauled it back in by its string, it was still empty but rimed with frost. The skin of her fingers stuck to it. She breathed onto her fingers to warm them, frightened she might tear them without, then saw as she did so that her breath clouded on the outside of the jug forming little beads of moisture. She breathed onto it again and a trickle of water ran down the green glazed surface. Sadie licked at it eagerly, and spent some time repeating this, before tiring of it and hanging the jug back outside.

On the third day she woke parched, her lips chapped and sore. She dragged herself out of bed and checked the jug. Still empty. She prowled the room looking for anything that might hold a little moisture, but the room was dry. She had made it so by burning anything small that would catch – fearful she might freeze in her sleep and never wake. Now she had no wooden bowls, no stool, no box for the rushlights, no shelf on which to put her last glazed pots. There were dry oats in the food press – too heavy for her to lift; her cloak on the back of the door was rough as sand to the touch.

Sadie saw that her hands looked wrinkled, her tongue felt too large for her mouth. Good Lord above, she would die if she were left here without water another day. Where on earth was Ella? Please God she was safe.

Desperate, she took up a metal skillet and banged with all her might on the floor, listening for a reply from downstairs. She kept this up for an hour, but no one came. The clattering was hollow through the empty house, as if she were the only person left in the entire world.

There was nobody on the bank today, no mudlarks or other scavengers. The river stood still, stopped in its tracks. Sadie shouted to try and attract attention, but her voice was hoarse and the bitter wind carried it away. Her stomach clenched at the sight of the ledge she had stood on when the constable came. She quailed at the idea of venturing onto it again. The wind would blow her away, and beneath her the ground was set into jagged black furrows by the frost. But it was her only option. That, or die here in this desiccated room. What had become of Ella? Three days, and not a sign of her. But if she was safe, why had she not come? A tear trickled down her cheek. She let it fall. Did not even stretch out her tongue. Perhaps Ella really had tired of looking after her and was never coming back. Out of the window the sky darkened, a squall of snow and wind flapped the curtain. Angrily, she stuffed a blanket into the gap so the room fell dark.

Sadie shivered and came away. The dress Ella had bought was still on the table. She had burnt the box last night, to give a few moments' heat and cheer. She held it in front of her. It was no use to her, trapped in here. She would burn it; God help her, it would warm her one way or the other. She went to fetch the one good knife to cut it to shreds. The desire to rip it to pieces warred with her fear of wasting anything. She picked up the yellow fabric and shook it out. A faint smell of dust and stale perfume tickled her nostrils. She laid it down.

It was no use waiting. Ella was not going to come. There was nobody in the house, only her. She had to get out. Why waste her strength on the dress? She grabbed the knife and approached the door. She began to dig the point into the wood over and over with grim determination. Perhaps if she could gouge a hole she might be able to pick the lock from the outside. Heaven only knows what the Gowpers would make of her ruining their door. But there had been no sign of Dennis or his mother and there was no telling when they might be back. Sadie dug patiently at the door as the wind whistled, the splinters sticking to her sleeves, not noticing that outside the snow had begun to fall heavy and deep.

All day she scraped at the wood until her hand was blistered from the knife. It was a small triumph when the knife finally burst through the door, but then the hole was too small for her hand to go through and she had to gouge at the wood for another hour to make the hole large enough. Once through she felt for the padlock and manoeuvred various kitchen knives to try to get the lock to open, but it was no use, it would not budge. She wept with frustration, hurled the knife to the ground.

It would have to be the window after all. She looked out and was amazed to see how much snow had fallen, and that it was still falling, more quietly now, in big lacy flakes. Below, the snow had formed into drifts along the riverbank. Directly beneath her the wind had shaped it into a soft mattress of white. She picked up the knife again and dropped it out of the window. It disappeared into the mound of snow, leaving a deep hole behind it.

Sadie put on her grey woollen cloak, tied her Westmorland shawl tightly round her head and shoulders, gathered up her purse and tucked it into her bodice. She dragged the blanket clear, hitched her skirts and clawed her way up onto the windowsill, her clogs kicking against the lath walls. Teeth chattering with cold, she edged out onto the ledge. The flakes floated icy on her eyelids, dissolving into a blur of rain. She gauged where the thickest drift of snow lay. Please God, she could jump that far. Her heart hammered in her chest.

Sadie took a deep breath and leapt.

When she looked up she seemed to see stars, but then realized it was only the patterns of snowflakes eddying above her. There was a weight of snow over her face. She struggled to sit up and was relieved to find that everything was working. She scrubbed the snow from her face. A wave of euphoria hit her. She could scarce believe it, she had done it. The snow was deep around her, she was lying in a well of white. She scrambled to her feet, staggering up to her knees in the compressed snow. She sucked the moisture from a handful of the stuff before brushing herself down. She did not look up to the ledge from where she had jumped but pulled her shawl closer round her face and dived for the dark shadows of the alleyway.

Chapter 33

Mercy Fletcher waited out of sight behind the cobbler's on the corner, her eyes fixed on the entrance to the alley where Madame Lefevre's wig-shop sign hung, topped with a thick layer of snow. She was waiting for Corey Johnson. Corey and the other girls jostled out of Madame Lefevre's wig shop in high spirits, pulling on their gloves and marvelling at the new fall of snow. The girls scrunched it into balls and pelted Betsy with handfuls of it. Betsy had just told them she was to be wed to Willie Carpenter, the apprentice turner at the wheelwright's.

'Leave off, you fools,' she cried, ducking her head to avoid the onslaught.

'Better than rice, this!' yelled Pegeen.

'Is it to be a spring wedding, Betsy?' Corey took Betsy's arm, and slapped at her shoulders to dislodge the snow.

'It'll be as soon as Willie's papers are signed and he's his own man.'

'What you going to wear, Betsy?' said Alyson. 'Let's hope it's sunny. We've not seen the sun for months.'

'This snow and ice is getting to me. My hands are numb it's that cold.'

'I know, it's frore,' said Corey. 'Still, there's snow, so it must be getting warmer.'

'You can never count on the weather, so I'm not having a spring gown,' Betsy said. 'My mother's making me something that'll do after for church and for high days. They're busting their buttons to give me a good dower box.'

'Ooh, what colour's your gown going to be?' called Pegeen from behind.

'Don't know yet. I fancy something sprigged. Maybes a blue, or a lavender.'

The girls giggled and chatted, swinging their bundles as they tramped down the street, pausing to let the surge of people pass or to look in shopfronts as they went.

Behind them Mercy kept just out of sight, under the over-hangs where the snow was thinnest, nipping into doorways when the girls paused, or crossing the road, her head down. She was dressed in a nondescript navy blue woollen bonnet and dark blue cloak lined with rabbit fur. Her eyes were fixed on Corey. The humiliation of her shorn hair had rankled deep. She had a mind to follow Corey and see if she could find a place where she might ambush her and take her revenge. Her brother Jacob had been outraged and had vowed to shear that Corey Johnson good and proper in return if she could find them a good place to lie in wait.

Corey was oblivious to Mercy. She carried on blithely, a wool scarf wrapped tightly over her head and ears, unaware she was being followed. At the corner she said goodbye to Betsy and Alyson with a 'see you tomorrow' and headed for home. Her feet found the driest places to walk as she threaded her way through the other passers-by, all keeping under the eaves away from the snow in the middle of the road. Everywhere was the noise of shovels scraping as folk cleared the paths. Mercy followed at a distance, keeping Corey's head within her sights.

Corey was thinking. It had bothered her, the strange business with the woman in the house by the river. The woman had said she couldn't be Corey Johnson because Corey Johnson lived upstairs. At first she had thought the woman must be touched in the head, but then Corey lay awake in bed at night, worrying at it, like a dog with a bone, and the more she thought about it, the more convinced she became that the other 'Corey Johnson' must be Sadie or Ella. Simon Reed had said he'd seen a girl with a patch on her face looking out of that house. It was just too much of a coincidence. God knows why they had chosen her name. She was vaguely affronted by it, that one of them should be masquerading as her, but then again, what would she do, if the word was out for her and there was a noose waiting. She shivered. It had been preying on her mind; she had to find out if it was them.

She stopped dead. She would be late for making the supper, but she would go there now and see if she could get in and knock at the room upstairs. The snow had stopped, it was only a step away. She swivelled round and began walking hurriedly back the way she had come. She did not see Mercy, pressed flat against the side wall of a ginnel as she hastened by.

Corey made her way back to the house by Old Swan Stairs, and by the time she got there it was full dark. Snow glistened in the alley as if the world was glazed with white sugar. There was no light at the upstairs window. Corey went to the front and tried the door. It was open. She shook her ankles to rid her shoes of snow and went in, leaving the door ajar so that she might have a little light. She looked up the stairs. It was so quiet she could hear herself breathing. She began to climb the creaking stairs, feeling her way up, for it was pitch dark, and she had no candle.

Mercy watched Corey go inside before following her. She pushed on the front door gently with her index finger; it swung open a little further. She put her head round the edge of the door and listened. She heard Corey's footsteps on the stairs, and then her voice calling, 'Sadie? Ella? Are you there?'

There was no answer. Mercy heard the creak of a door, then Corey's footsteps in a room above. The footsteps returned to the top of the stairs and Mercy prepared to run. A loud knock, and Corey's voice again, on the landing. 'Sadie? Are you in there? Ella?' Then a rattling noise of metal on metal. A pause and then descending footsteps.

Mercy did not wait for Corey to get to the bottom of the stairs. She was already running, down the alley towards the centre of the city to tell Jacob. She'd need someone to go with her to the Blue Ball on Aldergate.

Fewer people were abroad because of the snowfall, but Sadie cursed the way the white carpet threw up the light and made every step a trudge. She looked from side to side, in case a footpad or mugger should set upon her, or in case someone should recognize her. Corey's words came back to her, to keep only to well-lit streets and never to venture alone into the narrow back alleys of the city after dark. She kept her head down, ignoring the drunks spilling out surprised from the tavern, and the shivering beggars rattling their skews.

She wasn't exactly sure of the way to the Gilded Lily but she remembered snippets of information Ella had given her about how it backed onto the river, and that it was off Broken Wharf, in Friargate where the old monastery used to be. In one way she dreaded finding Ella there because that would mean she had abandoned her on purpose. But she dreaded even more that she had been taken by Ibbetson or the constable.

Several times she thought she was lost, but dare not ask anybody the way. She kept close to the Thames. This part of the river was silent and still now except for the birds tiptoeing across its glassy surface, but further down she heard sounds of revelling, and the glow of lights from the Frost Fair appeared briefly before disappearing behind the buildings. She watched the street signs more closely, hoping to see one with a monk or a friar. When she came to a dark crossroads with several winding passageways leading off, deep in snow, she almost wept with frustration. Now where? she thought.

She followed her instinct and turned down past a short row of run-down wooden dwellings and pens of sows and chickens, until she emerged at the end of a broader street. She looked to her right – there it was, the sign of the monk in the alley. Friargate. This was it. She braced herself and headed down the road. The snow had stopped now, and her feet made whumping noises as she walked. To her right she spied the weathercock with its three brass coins, above a wide entrance, barred by a pair of heavy pad-locked gates. Next to it was a smaller door in the fence.

My, it's a lot grander than Ella told me, Sadie thought. She stared at the high stone walls with their elaborate gateposts flank-ing the carriage entrance. The road was clear of snow here as if many carriages came and went, but each gatepost was topped by a massive stone ball iced with white. Further down the road, the wall changed into stout planked fencing, taller than a man and cut into points.

She was astonished at the scale of it. Though she knew it was a monastery once, then a milkman's yard, she wasn't expecting anything nearly so large. How on earth would she know where Ella was? She recalled Ella's words, that the Gilded Lily was what used to be the dairy behind the big warehouse. She peered across the yard. There was smoke coming from three chimneys, grey plumes in the night sky. One of the buildings seemed to have a candle burning in the upper room, the others were dark. She'd try the lit one first, see if she could get a glimpse of Ella. She saw straight away that the main gates to the yard were shut, and the best bet was in through the side door. It could be locked at night though, she thought.

She pushed at it, but it was solid wood bolted from the back and would not give. As she had predicted, it was locked from the inside. Sadie crept down the street to peer through the fence. As she leaned on the fence, her hand felt one of the planks give a little. She tugged at it; it was broken where it was nailed onto the supports. It made a splintering sound as she wrenched it away, leaving a narrow gap – a space barely big enough for a fox.

Sadie wriggled her way through, catching her skirt on a nail as she did so. She heard the fabric rip.

'Damn,' she said.

From nowhere a dog appeared in front of her – an explosion of barking and snarling. In the dark its eyes and jowls glistened. The dog was squat but powerful, all jaws and no tail. When it barked, saliva dripped from its mouth. Sadie clung to her skirts and backed away towards the fence.

The dog bounded forward, feet leaving black tracks in the snow. It was still barking, staccato grunts interspersed with growls from deep in its throat. From somewhere on their left, another huge dog tore round the corner of the warehouse in a frenzy of barking. She froze with fear. The dogs seemed to sense they had the better of her and the smaller one leapt towards her. Sadie reached blindly behind her and pulled out the plank, still stuck with nails. With a swipe she felled the dog with a blow to the head. It yelped and struggled to its feet, but retreated a little, more wary now.

The other, bigger dog was approaching from the side, growling all the while. With a lurch, it snapped at her hand. She felt the teeth cut through her skin, but she swung the plank back hard, the edge of it cutting a blow across the dog's cheek. It was not deterred and launched into another attack.

Sadie held the plank out in front of her to keep the dog's jaws at bay. She felt the tug as the teeth clamped onto the wood, and she tussled with it knowing that the dog's instincts would make it cling on.

The other dog kept up its frenzied barking. The yard burst into activity. The darkness bobbed with lanterns and running figures. At an upstairs window another candle appeared.

Sadie heard boots running and a gruff voice yell, 'Down, Jovis!' The dog on the other end of the plank cocked its ears but carried on growling. 'Down, boy,' said the voice again.

The dog let go of the plank to turn and look, and in that moment Sadie hurled herself back through the gap in the fence.

She ran pell-mell up the alley. Behind her the smaller dog had followed her through the fence and was barking, unsure whether or not to leave its territory. She ran faster, struggling through the snow, for she could hear men shouting, the barking of the dogs and the clank of the gates being unlocked, and the cursing and scraping as they tried to open them. She threw herself into the dark back streets, back to the shanty houses with their chicken sheds and pigsties, where the roofs were so close they had shielded the ground from the snow and underfoot was a brown mess of mud.

She panted as she ran, looking for somewhere to hide, then she dodged silently into a shabby yard and the nearest chicken house. The birds were roosting and made barely a cluck as she squashed inside and closed the door. The inside of the hut was warm and dusty, smelling of cornmeal and feathers. The barking was getting nearer. She gripped tight to the door, her fingernails in the wood. She tried to quiet her breath, motionless, listening to the sounds outside.

The growling and barking got louder until the chickens squawked and clucked and shifted uneasily on the roost. 'Up here,' someone shouted. The noise of the dogs baying was terrifying now and the birds panicked at the sound. They fluttered and screeched inside the hen hut, so that it became hard to hear what was going on outside. A woman's voice cut through the noise.

'What do you think you're about? Letting your dogs worry my hens at this time of night. Be off with you.'

'We're from Whitgift's. We're after an intruder. You seen anything?'

The dogs were still growling and letting out the occasional bark. Sadie could hear them snuffling round the door of the hen house.

'No,' said the woman. 'I was abed, like all good folk. Get your mangy dogs away. I'll be putting in a complaint to Walt Whitgift if them dogs worry my hens again.'

'Stupid dogs,' said a man's voice. 'They smelt a chicken supper, that's all. The intruder's long gone. Come on. Get the rope on 'em and let's get back to the yard.'

Sadie heard the thwack of a stick and then whining and growling as the dogs were tied up and dragged away. Inside the hut the hens settled back onto the roost, preening their ruffled feathers. When it fell silent, Sadie waited a good while, until the moon was set, before gingerly feeling her way towards the door, speaking softly to the chickens under her breath as she did so. They squawked and flapped their wings. She was about to open the door when it swung open to reveal a woman with a nightcap jammed over her dishevelled hair and a lantern in her hand. The woman's mouth fell open and her eyes widened.

Sadie did not wait for her to speak, but pushed past her, her head down. 'Now just you hold your—' The woman lunged to try to catch hold as she passed, but she twitched her shawl out of the woman's grasp and stumbled up the road. The woman seemed too surprised to follow.

A little further up the street she paused for breath. It was clear she could not get into Whitgift's at night, not with those dogs. What on earth was she to do now? She couldn't get in back home, she'd no key. She leaned back against a wall, her legs felt unsteady. There were drips of blood in the snow.

She held up her wrist and saw a gash that was steadily dripping. She held her sleeve to it with the other hand and pressed down. She couldn't stay out here all night. She had suddenly started to feel very cold. Her teeth were chattering. She would not last the night out here, she'd have to find a place indoors.

She hoped Corey was in, and would let her bed down there for the night. It was a risk – her mother might want to claim the reward – but it was all she could think of.

Chapter 34

'Let's look.' Corey took her hand. 'It's bad, that. Here, let's tie it up with this.' She tied a kerchief round Sadie's torn wrist and knotted it tight. 'You daft 'a'porth. What were you doing, going in Whitgift's at night?'

'I know. It were them dogs. One of 'em nipped me before I could get out of the way.'

'Everyone knows not to go near it nights.'

'It's a bit of a tale. I was looking for Ella. She lives in at Whitgift's now. She's changed her name.' Sadie paused.

'It's my name, isn't it?'

'Sorry, Corey. Nobody there knows who she is.'

'Cheek of it,' Corey said.

A moment's silence.

'I wondered if . . . I mean, I can't go back home . . .'

'I know. I went to find you at your lodgings after work, but there was a big lock on the door, and a hole like someone was trying to break in.'

'That was me trying to get out. I got locked in. And now I'm locked out.'

'It's all right. You can bunk in with me. But won't Ella be worried?'

'It's safer when we're separate, she says. But, Corey, something must have happened. I haven't seen her for days. She wouldn't just abandon me. She said we'd always stick together.' She could barely get the words out. 'She did. She promised me.'

'She'll be safe somewhere, you'll see. I can't make sense of all this. Tell me it proper, from the beginning.'

So Sadie told her everything. Corey frowned and listened, interspersed with, 'Well, I never did,' and 'You don't say.'

When she got to the end of her tale, Sadie said, 'So I've got to go back, to see what's happened to Ella.'

'No,' said Corey. 'You can't go in at night. Not with them dogs. Promise me you won't go back there.'

Sadie pressed her lips together in stubborn silence.

'Go back in the morning when the yard's open.'

'I've got to find out where she is. And I can't go when it's light. I'm too easy to get a fix on.'

'I know. But Whitgift's is the first place to look. No point in doing anything until we know she's not there. Tell you what, how's about I go in soon as it's open, ask after her, like.'

'Sorry, Corey, I didn't mean to get you involved in it all.'

'What else are friends for? I'll go first thing in the morning, soon as they're open and they've tied up the dogs.'

'What will your mother make of it? Me staying here?'

'Naught. She's working nights. Don't get back till four then she sleeps in. So long as the littlies are fed she won't know. They're asleep now in her bed.'

Sadie patted Corey's arm. 'Thanks, Corey.'

'Bloody Ella. She wants slapping. And I can't believe you jumped out of that window. It's a massive drop to the river. And fancy you fighting them dogs.'

'It wasn't anything. I was scared witless.'

'I used to think you were a bit quiet, you know. Always in Ella's shadow. Thought you'd not say boo to a goose. But breaking into Whitgift's – everyone knows it's set like a man-trap at night with them dogs. That's bold, that is. Just shows – appearances can be deceiving.'

'We never did those things, you know.'

Corey squeezed her arm. 'What things?'

Sadie dropped her gaze.

'I know,' Corey said.

Corey had fed her hot soup and bread and whey, and now Sadie was tucked in the bed in the garret next to Corey, top to tail. Nevertheless she hardly slept. She worried in case Corey's brothers woke and made a fuss. And her thoughts ran back to Ella, imagining her locked in some dark cell, or that she'd had an accident and there was nobody to help her. She turned over again, wincing as the spoon put pressure on her torn wrist. Corey had replaced the kerchief with another piece of torn muslin and twisted a wooden spoon in it as a tourniquet, but all night the blood continued to seep through. Dreams came, but they were confused and vague. By the morning the muslin was bright red, there was a wet patch of blood on her skirt and Sadie felt alternately nauseous and faint. When the light came, she sat up shakily and touched Corey's shoulder.

'I'm worried about Ella,' she whispered. 'Sun's up.'

'What time is it?'

'Don't know. But it's light and I heard the cocks going. Whitgift's will be opening soon.'

Corey sat up and rubbed her eyes and forehead. 'Oh, Sadie, there's blood on your skirt.'

Sadie felt the dull red patch with her fingers.

'That needs stitching,' Corey said, seeing her grey face. 'We'll have to go down to the barber-surgeon's.'

'No. He might have seen the notices.'

'You'll have to. I'll not go to Whitgift's for you this morning unless you go to the surgeon's first.'

'But you promised—'

'Only kidding. Course I'm going. Get up, let's get you to the surgeon's.'

'I haven't any money,' Sadie said. She tried to stand, but almost keeled over. Corey hauled her to upright.

'Come on, I'll loan you. Shouldn't be much, just a few stitches. It'll be done quick. You can pay me back later, when you're sorted out.' Both of them knew that was unlikely, but Corey wanted to be kind, and Sadie appreciated her tact.

'If you find her, tell her I'm here, won't you, and bring her home with you –' She paused. 'No, on second thoughts, what if the surgeon's seen the notices, or heard about me? He might hand me in, then it wouldn't be safe to bring her.'

'Well, you'll be dead soon enough anyways if you don't get that stitched. It's bad. We'll have to hope he's not heard. And it's only round the corner, you'll be back here in no time. They won't know you're here if you can get back upstairs before Ma wakes.'

'Come straight away if you've any news, won't you?'

'Soon as I can, but it might have to be in my snap break.'

Corey lent Sadie a clean bodice and skirt. They were a little roomy, and far too short, but it felt good to be clean. She put her own apron on over the skirt to keep it from getting messed up. Corey twisted her arm in Sadie's to keep her steady as they set off.

'I'll leave you at the barber's,' Corey said, 'then I'll have to go back and feed the littlies.'

'Won't they ask me what I'm doing there?'

'No, I'll send them out – up to the bridge, to the Frost Fair.'

The river's set like a road. Hurry up now. I'll have to run like the clappers to Whitgift's or I'll be mortal late for work, and you know what old Feverface is like.'

The house looked like every other house in the street – a two-roomed dwelling, half-timbered in the old-fashioned way, with an oak-panelled door sprayed with mud and gobbets of sleet from passing horses and carriages. When they knocked, he took his time opening up, and when he did they saw he was still eating, his mouth greasy with egg. He had a piece of bread in one hand. He looked at them morosely over his glasses, took in Sadie's blood-soaked wrist with the wooden spoon protruding and beckoned them in, still chewing. Sadie shook her head so her hair fell over her face.

The house was similar to Corey's, but with the open fire burning and a table containing the remains of the breakfast. He sat down, ignoring them, and slurped at the remains of his pot of ale and wiped the bread round the earthenware plate with relish. Sadie could not help looking at the other things on the table, a collection of tools such as a carpenter might have – fearsomely sharp knives, a fretsaw, a handled drill. There were several razors glinting in the light from the fire, and some strops for sharpening them. The sight of them set up a buzzing sensation in her head; she heard her breath grow shallow and fast.

She steadied herself and looked around like a nervous horse orientating itself in a new stable. A grinding whetstone operated by a treadle stood in the corner. Hanging by grubby strings on a row of pegs on the wall were a series of brushes – hogshair and black bristle – and long-handled combs. She saw a basket of blood-stained cloths in one corner, and a basket of clean ones in another. There was a strong smell of vinegar and something else, like urine.

Corey pressed a coin into Sadie's hand. 'Go straight home after. Tiptoe up, though, when you go in. Ma'll be sleeping, like as not, and snoring like a mule, but it would be better if I did the explaining.'

The barber-surgeon looked from one to the other. 'In trouble with your ma, are you? Been stopping out too late?'

Corey laughed as if sharing the joke.

Sadie pulled on Corey's sleeve. 'Come and tell me, remember, when you have news.'

'Don't fret.' She squeezed her good hand and was gone.

'Suppose you want it stitching. Open it up then.'

Sadie fumbled to untie the bandage with her other hand, but Corey had tied it tight and it was too awkward. The barber-surgeon cleared his plate with a glum air, and wiped his hands on his behind.

'Suppose I'll have to do it then,' he said. He indicated a chair behind the table with a swipe of his head, and she sat down, placing her arm in front of him. The chair had webbing straps nailed to it. Sadie had heard of people having to be tied down when they had their teeth pulled. Some of the webbing bore the dark stains of dried blood. The knives made her feel even more queasy now she saw them at close range.

He unwrapped her wrist in a business-like way, paying no attention to her, his eyes focused on the wound and his work ahead. When the spoon came free and she saw her own blood dribble again from her wrist, it made her head swim.

'Hmm. Hold it tight whilst I get my needle.' He pressed her hand down hard on the wound, which smarted and throbbed.

'You'll need this,' he said, handing her a wad of cotton.

'What for?'

'To bite on. It'll only need about five stitches. Dog, was it?'

'Yes. How did you know?'

'Seen 'em before. Now hold still. Bite down.'

She saw him thread a curved needle with what looked like button thread and tie a knot in it. His fingers moved surprisingly quickly. He measured a tot of a dark liquid into a metal tumbler and tipped a little into his mouth before dripping it over the wound. Sadie bit down on the pad as the liquid burnt and stung. The smell of alcohol hit the back of her nose. Suddenly she was back in Westmorland in their tiny cottage where the smell of liquor and pain had always gone together.

'Now then, maid, get ready.' She looked the other way.

A searing so intense that Sadie shot up in her chair, her mouth open in an involuntary scream. She looked at her arm. It was smoking; the surgeon held what looked like a small poker in his hand. The smell of burning flesh was acrid in her nostrils.

''Tis done now. It had to be cauterized first, to seal it. Now the middle can be stitched. The worst is over. Try to hold still now and bite down.'

She felt the stab and pull of the needle, but gritted her teeth. Her eyes watered freely, but it did not seem to be tears. Her arm throbbed and it jerked once or twice with the piercing of the needle. The surgeon held her arm tight as it twitched like a landed fish. She could not distinguish one pain from the other. When it was over, he patted the top of her head.

''Tis well done. There won't be much of a scar.'

Sadie looked. He wiped her wrist with a wet cloth dipped in urine. She winced, but when he had finished she turned her arm back and forth to test its movement. It moved fine, just a little stiff. She looked at the tidy row of stitches – brown thread, just like her sampler.

'Have you a sharp knife at home, maid?'

Sadie was unsure how to answer. She had no home now, no place to go, only Corey's. She swallowed, and blinked back more water.

He looked at her for the first time, as though she were a half-wit. 'The stitches will need to be cut, in about three weeks, when the wound has knitted. You just snip here,' he pointed, 'and here, then pull the ends of the thread through. Can you manage that?'

'Yes, sir,' she said, holding out the half-shilling, trying to act brave.

'Wait on, while I get change.' He opened a lidded jar and counted out some coins. He put them on the table in front of her.

Sadie stood up shakily and scooped up the coins with her good hand, thrusting them into the pocket of her apron. She would have to pull out the threads. The thought of it made her feel strange. The room whirled around her. She clung to the back of the chair, willing it to stop.

'Are you all right to walk home? You've gone white as whey.' He was staring at her face. She wondered if he had heard about the notices and the reward. She tossed her hair forward, heat rushed to her cheeks.

'Yes, thanking you,' she stammered. 'I'm much obliged to you for stitching it.'

''Tis good to help. It's what makes it worthwhile, all this. Does it feel better?'

His face was kindly, fatherly, concerned. He did not know she was a thief on the run. She began to sob. It was like a big dam breaking. He put his hand out to comfort her but she stumbled to the door in a great hurry and rushed out. She couldn't bear it, that a stranger should be so kind. She hared away. Eventually she stopped running. The cold air was bracing and she leaned against a wall gulping it in, until the stitch in her side had subsided.

She looked down at her arm. It wouldn't leave much of a scar, he had said. Another scar. Something else to mark her out. But she had survived it. The pain, the fear. It felt like an initiation. She was part of life again.

Chapter 35

'I cannot see their faces,' Titus Ibbetson complained.

'Line up,' shouted the turnkey, 'so the gent can get a look at you. Sooner he does, sooner it will be over.'

The maids shuffled into a rough line, the chains grating on the ground. They were docile as cattle. Titus's stomach turned at the sight of them, every one with some malformation or mark on their face. He cleared his throat, though he had no intention to speak, and cast his eyes down despite his desire to look them over. When he looked up again, his eye was caught by the smallest maid, who looked to be six or seven years old, with a livid red weal down the side of her face.

Her terrified eyes stared at him through the gloom. He scanned the rest of the women, looking for the girl he had caught a glimpse of at Bread Street. The sight of all those disfigured faces lined up before him made him feel peculiar. It was icy down below in the vault and the warmth drained from his body. He began to shiver despite himself.

'She's not there.'

'You sure?' the turnkey said. 'Have a closer look. Go on, you can go clean up to the bars. Best make sure.'

Titus was reluctant but leaned a fraction closer. The smallest girl began to cry silently, the big tears chasing down her cheeks.

He stepped away hurriedly. 'It's foolishness to keep that one here,' he said. 'Anyone can see it couldn't be her.'

'Them notices said maids with a red stain on their face, and she fits, right enough. You said to keep them as fits the description.'

'But that's a scorch mark, not a stain. I did not mean children like this.'

'You should have been more particular with your bill, then, sir.'

One of the women spoke up then. 'Let her go, sir, in pity's name, she's but six year old. A hot kettle fell off the fire shelf and hit her, her ma'll be frantic with worry. And Nan there's lived on Honey Lane all her fifty years, don't know nothing about the North Country. None of us do. We ain't done nothing wrong.'

There was a chorus then, all the women protesting their innocence, and as they moved the chains clanked and their eyes all burnt into him, accusing, as if he were the guilty party.

Titus backed off and turned to snap at the turnkey. 'I have already said, she's not here.'

'Sure and certain? It's been a mighty trouble to keep them if we don't get a hanging.'

'Do you think I doubt my own eyes? Let them go.'

At this the women set to wailing more and rattling to be set free, so that he could bear it no longer and covered his ears and turned and went up the way he came, leaving the turnkey to deal with the commotion.

He pulled his muffler up close around his ears. He felt badly in need of some pure air after the foulness of the Whit, but London was freezing and he regretted that he had chosen to walk back from the gaol instead of hiring a sedan or a horse. The ground was hard as flint with compacted snow and his leather-soled boots skidded over the flags and cobbles as he made his way back to the Blue Ball. On the way he passed crowds of people, shapeless hulks bundled in cloaks with their heads down, shoulders hunched against the cold. He wondered idly how many in gaol would pass away in this weather.

It was the third time he had been down to Newgate to identify the girl that had murdered Thomas. Each time he'd felt unprepared for the horror of conditions in that desperate place. Furthermore, when he got back home this day he was confronted by Isobel with her cloak and muffler on and her new jessimy gloves, and her trunk packed.

'I will not stay a moment more. My chest is so tight with the smoke of London I can barely breathe. You know I have always had a weak chest. If I have to stay a moment longer you will be calling the physician to bleed me, sure as I speak.'

Titus sat down heavily on the kist at the foot of the bed. 'You will not be able to find a carriage at this hour, especially in this freeze.'

'Not so. I have booked three places on the seven o'clock stage. Come, Titus, let us go home.'

The thought of his comfortable home in Shrewsbury with its roomy fireplaces and well-upholstered bed was almost too much for him to bear. 'No,' he said stubbornly, 'you know my mind. I will not give up, I owe it to Thomas. You presume too much, to book passages without my say-so.'

Isobel opened her mouth to speak but he held up his hand for silence. He sighed, then said, 'But I am tired of you griping about going home. It is wearing me thin, and your company befits me ill. You and Willetts may go if you wish, to keep my house in order.'

She sank down onto the bed and dabbed her eyes with the corner of her muslin whisk. 'Thank you,' she said.

They sat in silence a while, until he said, 'The whole business is taking longer than I thought.'

'I know, dear,' she said soothingly. 'But if anyone can find them, you can.'

So that evening he put Isobel and Willetts the maid on a carriage bound for Oxford and as he did so the snowflakes were swirling in the sky.

'God speed.' He said the customary words as he handed her in, but as the carriage rattled away he waved long after its lights had turned to a blur in the swirling snow. He hoped the weather did not worsen, happen she would find the way blocked if it did. He always carried a sword, and now he felt for it, feeling vulnerable. London was full of dark alleys and cramped courtyards where the unwary could be ambushed after dark. With no woman to protect, his own fear suddenly rose up.

He had no one now, he realized. Thomas his twin was gone. His father was long since deceased and since a fall in the autumn, his mother had succumbed to such forgetfulness of mind that she barely recognized him. He had no children. Isobel was unable to produce offspring; he knew not why. It made him angry with her. He deserved a son. And now she had left him here alone, so when he brought those girls to justice she would not be there to see him do it. No one would be there to see him do it. And it would make no earthly difference to Thomas – he was cold in his grave.

By the time he entered his chilly chamber at the Blue Ball he was in a mighty depression. He asked the landlord for a double measure of brandy and took it up to his room, telling himself it might stave off the cold. When he had downed it he crawled into bed still fully dressed and pulled the blankets up over his head. He was almost relieved to feel the room start to swim and soon he fell into a deep slumber.

The next day he ignored the noises from the street outside

and dozed in a stupor until he was roused from his bed by a sharp knock at the door. He tried to get up, but his legs were tangled in the sheets and he toppled out with a thud.

'What is it?' he bellowed, rubbing his knee.

It was the landlord. 'There's a young man and his lady friend asking after you.'

'What do they want?' he shouted at the door.

'They say it's urgent and it won't wait. The woman wanted to come straight up, but I said not,' came the landlord's voice.

Titus recovered himself. 'Quite right too. My wife could have been here alone. Just a moment. I'll be there directly.'

He splashed freezing water over his head and neck, brushed down his crumpled coat, and hurried downstairs. The landlord indicated a pleasant but agitated-looking young woman in a dark cloak and close navy blue bonnet, waiting at a table by the door. He recognized her straight away as one of the perruquier's girls. Sitting beside her was a tall surly-looking lad in a black hat and cloak, who stood up when he saw Titus coming.

'Jacob Fletcher,' he said, holding out his hand.

Titus greeted them both and sat down opposite the woman.

'Tell him, Mercy,' said Jacob.

Mercy smiled, showing a row of pearly teeth. She leaned in and began to whisper in an urgent undertone.

Five minutes later he was back in his chamber putting on his outdoor apparel and whistling.

After leaving the barber-surgeon's Sadie crept back into Corey's house, cradling her sore arm in a sling made from her shawl. With relief she heard the snores from Corey's mother asleep in the back room. Sadie could not settle, but sat at the window waiting for Corey to come with news of Ella. Just after the noon bells Corey's square bustling figure appeared in the alley and beckoned her outside. Sadie untied the shawl and wrapped it over her head and face to hurry to join her.

'Have you seen her?' asked Sadie as soon as they were out of earshot of the house.

'How's your arm?'

'It's all right. Stitched. Was she there?'

'No. They wouldn't let me in. Some great battleaxe of a woman in the office sneered at me – told me I needed an appointment. I tried but I didn't get past the door. There's a man sat outside, he'd break your jaw soon as look at you. It's not for the likes of us, Sadie, they'll only let quality in.' Corey said 'quality' as if it was something that smelt bad.

'But did you see her? Tell me.'

'I'm coming to it. I looked through the window and I caught sight of a woman stood there, but she had yellow hair, and looked that thin—'

Sadie laid her hand on Corey's. 'It was her, I know. She looks right different now.'

'Anyways, I got shooed off, the man outside told me it were shut for the Frost Fair. But I hung round, asked a lad. He said it was Corey Johnson in there. So then I knew it was your Ella. Bloody cheek.' Corey sniffed and grimaced. 'But I couldn't get near to speak to her. The lad told me a few things though – made me angry fit to burst, it did.' Corey blew on her hands. 'Come on, let's walk a little. My blood's freezing solid stood here. Pull your shawl over your face a bit more, we'll only go to the end of the road.'

They set off slowly, arm in arm, trying to keep a footing on the slippery cobbles.

'This lad, was he tallish, nice-looking, with sandy-coloured hair, brown eyes?' Sadie asked.

'No. He was—'

'Oh, never mind. Just tell me what he said.'

'Wait till you hear this.' Corey stopped and turned to face Sadie, her round face full of disgust. 'Your Ella's fine. Gadding about with Jay Whitgift. The lad says the other night he got the horses ready and Jay Whitgift helped her into his coach. By all accounts they were off to Whitehall, to Lord Sedley's house. He remembered she was dressed in a scarlet gown with a squirrel fur scarf against the cold, and that they didn't bring the horses back till nigh on four in the morning.'

'That can't be right. I don't believe it. To a lord's house?'

'Heartless pig. She leaves you to rot whilst she gallivants all over London in her fancy coach. I hope they do bloody catch her. Hanging's more than she deserves.'

'Don't. I can't believe she'd just leave me. Happen it's my fault, we had a terrible row, you see. She wouldn't . . . there must be some mistake . . .' She tailed off.

Corey took hold of her by the shoulders. 'Now look here. How could it be your fault? You've just got to face it, Sadie, she's a proper bitch.'

Sadie squirmed away, scuffed the snow with her boot. 'Maybe she forgot she'd locked the door.'

'And hens will lay golden eggs. Forget her, that's my advice.'

There was silence then.

'What'll you do?'

'Go back home to Westmorland, I suppose. I can't stay here. I can't even walk the streets with them notices out. I'll need money, though, and my things. Don't know how I'll get back into my lodgings.'

'That's easy. There'll be a file in my brother's workshop, he's a smith. We'll go get that door open tonight, fetch your things out. And I'm telling you – I can't wait to see the face on Lady

Uppity when she stoops to go back there and finds you gone, and the place empty as a barn. Serve her bloody well right.'

It was dark when Corey got back from work.

'No trouble with my mam?' Corey asked.

'No. I hid out the back behind the dairy when I heard her stir,' Sadie said.

Corey nodded. 'Good. Look, here's the file. Get your hood up and let's go.'

Sadie and Corey took turns to hold the lantern for the long task of grinding through the hasp. Corey was amazed when she got a better look at the hole in the door.

'Blimey, did you do that? It must have taken an age.'

The file slipped out of its groove if they tried to go too quick. There was no sign of Dennis or his mother, and Sadie was sad. She would have liked to say a proper goodbye, not just disappear into the night without settling the rent. He would think the worst of her and it pained her.

'Keep going, Corey, don't give up,' said Sadie, as they sawed the file back and forth over the hasp. Finally the lock fell off with a great clunk, and they pushed open the door.

'Is this it? Where you live?' Corey stared round her in disapproval. Sadie tried to hide her shame. It was nothing like Corey's cosy house with all the pots and pans lined up in a shining row and a fire blazing in the hearth. It smelt of mildew and rot already.

'It's better with a fire lit,' she said. Corey sniffed.

The yellow gown was where Sadie had left it on the table, with the pot of ceruse still with its lid tied on. Just looking at it made her feel embarrassed somehow. She picked up the chapbook of Barbary Bess and tucked it into her bib front.

'Come on, let's get your things downstairs,' Corey said. 'Eh, you've not much, have you? Looks like we can manage it, just the two of us. Have you got anything to put it in?'

'No,' said Sadie, 'only my apron. I could make up a bundle with that.'

'That won't do. Not to travel all the way to Westmorland. No, you start getting everything down into the hall and I'll go up the road to the fodder merchant's, see if he's got a sack for a farthing. Don't forget to keep your head down.'

After Sadie had carried the first load down, Corey arrived with a folded barley sack under her arm and they put everything in it.

'You'll need water in that flagon,' Corey said, pointing. 'Leave the sack here a minute, and we'll just nip round the corner and fill it.'

The well was in a small square, walled off from the street, with channels to drain the excess water when people took their domestic animals there to drink. There was a large trough below for washing clothes and watering cattle, and a bucket above for clean water. There was no lantern, and their breath made more white patches of fog. Sadie tried to wind up the bucket. It was heavier than usual. Corey had to help her turn the handle to wind the rope in. The bucket clinked, and when it reached the top there was a good hand's depth of ice to pull out.

'By, will you look at that,' Sadie said. 'Haven't seen ice like that even in Westmorland.'

'Thames is frozen over further up, so you'll have to walk. Are you sure you want to go? There's no boats, you know.'

'Thanks for helping, Corey. But I've decided. I'm going to go to Ella tomorrow morning and talk to her – I'll get in to Whitgift's somehow. I can't just leave London and not tell her.'

'I don't see why. She never cared aught for you.'

Sadie did not answer. Corey's words stung.

Corey stood up and stretched her short spine, her hands either side of her back. She glanced idly at the alleyway, but then her attention was taken by something and she stared hard. She laid one hand on Sadie's shoulder to stay her. Her eyes narrowed. Suddenly she grabbed Sadie by the arm and said, 'Quick, get down.'

'What is it?'

'I swear I can see Mercy Fletcher coming.'

'Are you sure?'

'I know it's near on dark, but it looks like her. Same mincing little walk. She mustn't see us.'

'What's she doing?'

'I don't know. There's some men with her carrying lanterns.'

They dropped down behind the wall, Corey craning her head over the top to see better.

'Why are you hiding from her? I thought you were friends?'

'No. She's a bully. We had a spat, and I cut off her hair.'

'You never?'

'I did. Let's hope she's not coming to fetch water. But they've no pails, or anything . . . God's truth! It's that old gent.'

'Who?' asked Sadie trying to see.

'Stay low, he mustn't see you,' whispered Corey. 'He came to the wig shop, asking after you. He's the one after catching you.'

'You mean, Ibbetson? Is he—?'

'Shh. Keep your voice down, they're getting nearer. He's marching along in a great hurry, and there's three other men with them. It's her brother, Jacob –' a sharp intake of breath, '– and the constable's men, I recognize the livery.'

'Are they coming this way?'

'They've gone past the end of the alley. Saints alive, I think they might be going to your lodgings.'

Sadie tried to stand up to look over the wall, but Corey restrained her. 'Get down,' Corey said, 'cover your face, and stay out of sight. Go further down the alley, and wait there. I'm going to see if I'm right, and they are going to your house.'

'No,' said Sadie, in a determined voice. 'I want to see if it's him.'

'Keep out of sight, then.' Corey beckoned to Sadie and the two girls scuttled across the road and dodged behind a waiting draycart. The silhouettes of four broad backs were striding down the passage towards the Gowpers' house, following Mercy's lead. By the house, Mercy stopped and held up her lantern, then pointed up at the window.

Sadie and Corey exchanged glances. Sadie rubbed her arms, they were all gooseflesh. One of the men stepped forward and banged on the door.

'That's him – Mr Ibbetson,' said Corey.

He turned round to speak to the other men and Sadie got a glimpse of lowering eyebrows and a grim set to the mouth.

'It's him all right. I recognize him.' A cold frisson of fear crept round her neck.

Minutes later the party had disappeared inside the house.

Corey tugged at Sadie's arm. 'Come on, we've got to get out of here.'

Sadie dug in her heels and tried to shake Corey off. 'No, Corey, I need to get the rest of my things. There's my sewing things and my cooking pots, and a good warm blanket . . . I'll go back and get them when they've gone.'

'Have you lost your wits? They'll be out any moment and we need a good start on them –' Corey paused. There was the glimmer of lights moving in the upstairs window of Sadie's room. 'Look,' she said.

Neither girl moved. They watched, compelled to do so, as the light went past the window inside Sadie's room. It perturbed Sadie to think they were inside, poking about in her things. Corey plucked urgently at her arm. 'Come on, Sadie, let's go. Before they come out.'

She hared across the road, grabbed the sack and swung it over her shoulder. A moment later she was pulling at Sadie's hand.

'Too late. Here they come.'

She pushed Sadie back behind the cart.

Two of the men emerged, with Mercy Fletcher just behind. Mercy's face was shadowed under her dark bonnet and hood, but the set of the head and the bouncing walk could only be hers. The men looked up and down the street, holding their swinging lamps aloft. Moments later the solid silhouette of Titus Ibbetson appeared on the threshold. He hurried to join his friends on the neighbour's doorstep. They knocked hard on the door with a cudgel, and the echo of it was loud in the night air. Ibbetson stood a little away from the others, under the house lantern, looking intently at a switch of material in his hand.

'What's that he's got?' Corey whispered.

'It's the sampler I started,' Sadie said, 'on an old kerchief. I stitched my name on it.'

'Gawd. There's no mistaking you lived there then. Wait a minute,' Corey said, 'where's the other man? There were two of the constable's men went in.'

'Are you sure?'

'Yes, Mercy and Jacob, Ibbetson and two others.' She ticked them off on her fingers. 'That means one's waiting inside. For when you come back.' Corey took hold of Sadie's hands. 'Sorry, but you know you can't go back for your things now.'

Sadie gripped tightly onto Corey's fingers. 'I don't give a spit for my things. I've got foss-all worth having anyway. Don't you see, what if Ella goes back there? She won't know there's someone waiting for her.'

'Come on, I'll take you back to mine.'

'No, it can't wait till morning. I'll have to go to Whitgift's tonight. She might turn up here.' Sadie pointed at the Gowpers' house.

'Bloody Ella,' Corey said.

They watched as Titus Ibbetson knocked on the next door, and a large woman in a buff-coloured apron opened it.

'Quick, whilst they're busy,' hissed Corey, pulling at her.

Sadie wriggled her sore arm from Corey's grasp, kept her head down and hurried after. Once well out of sight of the house, they stopped to catch their breath.

'Come back with me a little while. You can get a proper wash, and I'll make you a hot mash,' Corey said.

'No, I've told you. I'm going straight to Whitgift's, to warn Ella. I can't bear to think of them lying in wait for her. You know what they'll do to her if she's caught.'

Corey pursed her lips. 'Don't be so hasty. You're not thinking straight, you've got to be careful. Ella hasn't been here for days, you said so yourself. And you said she works evenings, so she'll be busy till the end of the evening shift, anyhows.'

'I can't stay with you. 'Twould be a risk to your ma and the littlies. No, I'll be off to Westmorland soon as I've seen Ella.'

Corey set her mouth in a stubborn line. 'You're going no-where till we've a proper plan. If you get arrested it'll do neither of you no good. Come on now. Let's work out how to get you into Whitgift's. A few hours won't make no difference. I'm not after losing you for the sake of that flibbertigibbet.'

'Oh, Corey.' Sadie put her arms round her friend and hugged her tight.

Chapter 36

When evening came, Ella could not sleep, but sat upright shivering in her bed fully dressed, listening to the sounds in the yard outside. Jay's man was still on guard. It was as if she had been living on the edge of a precipice for ever, any slight noise made her jump, and whenever the dogs barked it made her breathless with fear. The noise reminded her of the Netherbarrow Hunt. Those were the sounds the dogs made going in for the kill. Death was coming closer, she could feel it, almost as if the Reaper was standing right behind her, his cold breath on her neck. She shuddered and lit a candle, sat holding it for comfort and warmth until the light of dawn cast its pale glow in the sky.

In the morning she heard the noise of a wagon, then the Lily's door open. She hurried to the landing terrified it might be Jay Whitgift or the constable come for her. But it was Polly and Meg. They scuttled in wrapped up in mufflers and hoods; just like any other day they had come for the crates of potions they needed for the Frost Fair. Neither of them spoke, just passed with their heads down, as if she did not exist. When Polly was on her way out, Ella beckoned furiously to Meg. Meg hesitated, a box of violet comfits balanced precariously on top of another box.

'Meg,' she whispered shakily, 'go ask if Dennis is back today. And if he is, tell him to come, it's urgent.'

'You'm not allowed, Sir said.'

'Please, Meg?'

'I'll tell Sir. He's just outside. He said to tell if you went anywhere.'

'Well, I'm not going anywhere, am I? I just want a word with Dennis.' Ella looked at Meg's pouting face. 'Look, I know I haven't been right kind to you, but please – go and see if he's there.'

Meg pressed her lips mutinously together, shook her head and set off towards the door, just as Polly came back in for another load.

After Polly had gone, Meg's face came round the door again.

'He's not turned in, so there,' she hissed, plainly enjoying it. 'And there won't half be trouble when he do. He'll get the push. There's a mighty queue and Mr Whitgift's hopping mad.'

The door shut and she heard the key turn, shortly followed by the noise of hoofbeats and wheels turning. Dennis had been her only hope of getting word to Sadie. She was running out of time. No opportunity had come for her to get away, it was hopeless. Her breath steamed before her, for no one had lit a fire today. She was all gooseflesh, and her shoulders tightened as she folded her hands under her arms to keep warm. But she was glad to suffer it. It brought her closer to Sadie.

About midday she heard a noise from the back of the shop, as if something was falling. It made her startle for she had been alone with her own thoughts for so long. She leapt up, but could not see that anything had moved – the displays were exactly the same. She prowled round the shop looking for the cause of the noise and was just about to sit down when she heard it again. She felt a slight draught, and turned to see one of the shutters at the tiny trap window was open.

She hurried to the back of the shop. Two stones lay on the flagged floor. As she watched another came through and rattled towards her feet. She tiptoed cautiously over, and gently pushed the other shutter open. There was just room for her to look through if she stood on tiptoe. On the other side she could see Dennis, looking anxiously from side to side, his cap in his hand, his face wet with perspiration.

'What's going on?' he hissed. 'Why's Lutch sat outside the door? Do they know?'

She nodded and began to speak, but he was already talking.

'I guessed as much. Is she there then?' His eyes searched hers.

She hardly heard him. 'Dennis, Sadie's locked in her room.' She spoke quickly, not knowing how much time she might have, thrusting the key to their lodgings through the tiny window. 'Please, take some food and water and tell her she's to get out of London. Jay Whitgift knows who I am and he's going to hand me over to Ibbetson.'

'That's just it,' said Dennis in a low voice, 'I can't. I don't know where she is.'

'What do you mean?'

He looked from side to side again, before replying, 'When I got back home last night from my auntie's, there was a constable waiting upstairs, and no sign of Sadie. She must have known they were coming and scarpered.'

Ella could not take it in. 'She can't have done,' she whispered, 'the door was locked.'

'I don't know about that – all I know is, when I got back from Auntie's to fetch Ma's things, the whole bloody house was open. There was a man waiting for me, and he kept me all this morning asking questions.'

'What did you tell him?'

Dennis raised his eyes to the sky. 'Naught of course. Said there was a girl living there but I didn't know where she worked. They asked if she had anything that marked her out and I kept lying and telling them no, and it's God's truth anyway, I don't hardly notice it . . .' He looked sheepish, and twisted his cap in his hands. 'Sorry,' he said again, 'Lord knows, I held out for you as much as I could.'

'But where is she? You sure she's not been taken?'

'No. They were still looking. Kept asking me where she might go. Whether she had family and that. There's a big bruiser of a man posted in her room in case she goes back. But I felt sure she would've come here, somehow.'

'Oh my Lord, I've not seen hide nor hair of her.' She gripped Dennis's hand where it lay on the sill. 'She won't last two minutes with everyone out looking for her. And she mustn't come here –' Ella's voice cracked. Dennis wriggled his arm free. 'Please, Dennis, say you'll look for her.'

She saw conflicting emotions pass over his face like waves on a beach. 'I can't . . . I've got to go back to Ma, she's right badly—' He stopped mid-sentence. 'Oh my word, someone's coming. Sorry, but I can't. Sorry, Ella.'

She heard Foxall's voice saying, 'All right?' and Dennis replying casually, 'Jay told me to check the Lily's secure,' and the trap window banged shut.

Ella went stiffly to the counter. Her eyes were dry, the layer of paint seemed to be holding her together. Where was Sadie? The great wooden-headed dolt. How had she opened the door? And where could she have gone? She pictured her running, her hair streaming behind her, spindly ankles above her heavy clogs, the way she used to run across the barley fields at home. But that was in Netherbarrow. She couldn't run like that here, not in London, where every step was over a slick of icy cobbles.

Pray God she had the sense to get out of the city. She was dog's fodder here. They'd soon pick her up and she'd be done for. She wouldn't have gone back to Pa, would she? He'd get the strap to her, hand her in if he thought it would buy him more ale. A great shiver rippled up her back, a mingling of love and fear. She felt the blood connection, an instinct that knew more than she could put into words. 'Dear Lord,' she prayed, 'let her be safe.'

Chapter 37

Tindall saw Jay's boxwagon appear three more times in the dead of night before he decided to enquire of the nightwatchman what he knew. The watch told him Jay's men drank in the King's Head, so that night, instead of settling down in front of Walt's warm fire, Tindall braved the sleet to position himself in an alley opposite the tavern.

The King's was on a street in the East End with four other taverns, and so was notorious for its night-time parade of doxies looking for business. It was early yet, so there were few people about. No moll would want to stand out in this weather waiting for her customers to get drunk enough to want a flutter. At the tavern door the snow had been scraped to the side of the entrance where it had set into rigid combs of ice either side.

Tindall pulled his hat down over his ears to keep them from freezing and wrapped his long coat further over his chest. He watched several men go into the tavern from the saddlery next door before the familiar boxwagon drew up through the slush. Foxy Foxall leapt off the front, landing awkwardly as his boots slipped, and led the horse and wagon around the back, and five minutes later he and Lutch went in.

Tindall kept his hat pulled well down and his muffler up to his nose and slunk inside towards a dark corner behind a wooden spur where upturned barrels were set around a rough table. He was glad to be indoors, the sleet stung his cheeks. Foxy was already rolling up his sleeves for a game of skittles on the other side of the bar, and his opponent, one of the saddlers, was standing up the pins.

'Jug of your finest,' Tindall said to the wench in a low voice when she came over with the tray. When the ale arrived he poured it, but left it sitting in the tankard. He was not much of a drinker; too much strong ale made him queasy. He preferred plain water when he could get it clean enough, which wasn't often.

He watched Foxy's sharp aim and the rolling skittles make the saddler more and more disgruntled until eventually he was forced to concede defeat and hand over his coinage, slamming the door in such a temper that it rattled on its hinges. Tindall noticed that, like himself, Lutch did not drink much, but sat in a corner with a tray of dominoes, idly building the bones into a tower and then flipping it with his finger to topple them down.

Time passed. Foxy and Lutch seemed to be just enjoying a night's relaxation. The landlord knew them both and bantered with them over their orders, and several of the saddlers engaged them in conversation. Tindall began to feel a little foolish, and besides, he stuck out like a signpost sitting on his own. But just after the bells tolled ten, Lutch nodded, and Foxy strolled out of the door. After about fifteen minutes Lutch drew his arm across the table, pushing the bones to the side, and left. Tindall waited a couple of minutes before following.

He poked his head out of the door and at first could not see Foxy or Lutch. The street had filled up with itinerant hawkers selling pecks of oysters, roasted chestnuts, herbal elixirs and the latest broadsheets. In amongst the hawkers were the women lounging against the doorways, most with the obligatory red ribbon around their ankle or their wrist.

'Looking for a ride, mister?' The woman laughed, showing a mouth full of blackened teeth.

Tindall shook his head and quickly moved off, searching for the top of Lutch's head in the crowd. Further down the road he saw him. He was leaning against a shop shutter, watching something. Tindall stayed where he was, but followed Lutch's eyes. Foxy was cajoling and persuading one of the young women. He had his hand on her arm, and he could see her reluctance in the way she tried to move away. But Foxy leaned over and whispered something in her ear, and she laughed and allowed herself to be brought over to where Lutch was waiting. A smallish fiery-haired maid in a grey gown.

He heard her shrill voice. 'You're not kidding me? He's not jesting, is he? And a full five shillings?'

'I tell you, he often sends us down here. "Only the prettiest," he says, and the minute I set my peepers on you, I knew you were the one. Lutch here'll drive us, and bring you back again afterwards.'

'What's in it for you? What's he like?'

'A proper gent. He pays us to select for him, so's he don't have to get his feet wet. Stands to reason that – why come out in this weather if you can pay someone reliable to do it for you?'

'Well, I –'

'If you don't want the work, then there are plenty of others who need the five shillings.'

'You'll bring me back here after?'

'Course.'

And she linked her arm into Foxy's and the three of them went into the back yard.

Moments later the boxwagon bowled past with the three of

them sitting up front. The girl had her hand to her eyes to shield them from the sleet. Tindall cursed himself for not thinking ahead as he ran over to the stableyard and thrust thrupence at the lad for the hire of a horse. Once mounted he kicked the skittish horse on and rattled out of the yard gates just in time to see the wagon turn the corner at the end of the street.

From there he rode at a safe distance all the way past St Paul's, until the wagon stopped outside a large house and Foxy and the girl went inside. Tindall tethered the horse round the corner and kept a watch on the house from behind the building opposite. The area was well-to-do, he could see that from the width of the streets and the fact that all the horses were stabled out back somewhere.

He shivered in his thin coat as he waited nearly an hour before the manservant waved at Lutch from the doorstep. From there it was all action. The door burst open and the girl was thrust out onto the street. Lutch lifted her as though she were a feather and threw her in the back of the wagon, and clamped the bar down on the gates. He wielded the whip and the horses jolted the wagon forward as Foxall leapt onto the front.

Tindall leapt for his horse, cursing that he was no longer a young man and the whole escapade was making him breathless. The wagon careered down the road, wheels skidding and skewing on the icy surface. Suddenly it turned down Thames Street and was gone. He rode up and down but could not see it anywhere. At length he decided to turn down towards the river, and to his surprise he could see the back of the boxwagon parked down the alley, next to the tannery. From his mounted position he could see it was empty and there was no sign of the girl. Surely she could not have wanted to be let out here? There were no houses, only the long dark wall of the tannery and the loading pulleys jutting like gallows above.

A figure loomed out of the mist – Lutch, slapping a cane against his thigh, and he was alone. Tindall reined back his horse and retreated onto the main thoroughfare. He heard the doors of the wagon slam and the wooden clunk as the lever was ratcheted home. The wagon trundled past him with Foxy and Lutch both sat up front. From the shadows Tindall watched its retreating shape disappear round the corner before he pushed his horse into a trot down the alley towards the river. He looked from side to side but there was not a soul in sight. His horse snorted and shied at a rag blowing against the wall, but he pressed it forward to the towpath, where he slid off and looped its reins on a hitching post.

He stared out at the river. It was sliding by more slowly than usual, barely moving under a surface slick with ice. This part of the river was quiet, there were no ferries or boatmen plying their trade, just the coil of the hidden water. Near the bank it was a solid sheet, grey as polished pewter. Tindall stared. The ice here was broken as if someone had thrown something in. A shiver trickled up his spine. He could see something pale floating in the river just a little further down. He could not reach it – it was floating too far away, submerged under the skin of ice. He looked a long time but it did not move. He could not decide what to do. In the end, when he turned to go, his feet were numb. He had to hobble to his horse.

He returned to the King's Head to hand back his mount and was surprised to see that the wagon was in the yard again. When he went for a good look around it though, he could see nothing amiss. Perhaps he should look inside – but what would happen should Whitgift's men return? He had a bad feeling about it. The pale shape in the water could have been anything, he told himself, but he could not quash his misgivings.

He had had enough of this following in the dark; he needed to rest his aching joints. He rubbed his hands together to try to bring the blood back to them. Sombrely he headed back to Whitgift's, half a mind to call the constable. But what could he tell him? He had seen nothing – nothing except a phantom in the water. He walked slowly, pondering and gazing up at the sky to catch a glimpse of the stars, looking for an omen or a sign. But the sky was charcoal grey, no stars were visible. By the time he had walked back to Whitgift's yard, his teeth were chattering and he could not feel his hands.

'Get thyself inside, man, you look fair nithered,' called the watchman and he gave Tindall a wink as he hunched past the gate, head bowed against the sleet.

Tindall lifted a hand just out of his coat in acknowledgement and headed for the warmth of the offices. Just as he was about to go in, he heard the sound of a horse and looked round to see the boxwagon again parked on the road outside. Dodging into Walt's office, he pushed open the window a crack to listen. He heard the sound of another door opening and Jay Whitgift's voice. 'Aye aye, lads.'

'Wolfenden was satisfied, and there's no loose ends.'

'Good. He's going to be a regular.'

Again, Tindall saw Jay hand over a purse. He swallowed, ducked down behind the window, filled with a sudden terror they might catch sight of him. Jay Whitgift was at the heart of their racket, whatever it was. His mind went back to the river. He wished he could talk it over with Walt, but Walt would never hear a bad word against his son, and if Walt told Jay, he might have to watch his own back. He chided himself. What was he thinking of, poking his nose into risky business that was no concern of his? He was getting too old for dealing with ruffians such as Jay Whitgift's henchmen. Happen he should draw up another horoscope, find out how the land lay before doing anything hasty.

Chapter 38

At the Pelican on the ice, Jay Whitgift was crammed into the tented stall alongside Wycliffe, with Buckhurst and Sedley on the opposite bench.

'Coming over to the cockfight, gents?'

'Ah, good to see you, Wolfenden. You look a lot better,' Sedley said.

Jay glanced round and saw a tall man in a heavy grizzled wig. His face was pitted and rotted by the pox, a tarnished silver cone was tied with a leather thong where once his nose had been. Jay nodded briefly at Allsop, who hovered behind him and looked uncomfortable. And no wonder, his loans were still owing and Jay had been forced to send Lutch over to take his antique sword collection as part-payment.

'Don't mind if I do,' Wycliffe said. 'Coming, Jay?'

The makeshift pit was a pallisade of planks. They forced their way inside, past the unruly crowd of prentices with their eyes glued to the gaps. Wycliffe insisted they place a bet and Jay indulged him by pulling out his purse. The birds were mangy brutes but fought well enough. Wolfenden shouted and cursed alongside the common brewers and butchers, and when his bird showed signs of flagging shouted, 'Prick his bloody heels!'

Already the ice was daubed with blood and torn feathers, and though both its eyes were out, their cock fought savagely, ousting its three opponents. When one tried to escape the ring, Wolfenden grabbed hold and twisted its neck, casting it down before them. He smiled apologetically to Wycliffe, who hung on Jay's arm. Jay was surprised to see his companion looked mighty green. He pressed Wycliffe's hand proprietorially.

'Best way,' Wolfenden said. 'No use for breeding unless they can fight their corner. No game without game cocks, eh?'

Allsop laughed. 'They should set up pits for women. That'd be a sight to see, women fighting to the death.'

'It's probably like that in the Whit, if we could only get in there to place our bets,' Wycliffe said, and the rest laughed.

'Tell you what, as it's your birthday, we'll set it up for you, shall we, Allsop? Find you some fighting bitches for tonight?' Wolfenden said.

'Have you seen those notices for the Savage Maids?' Sedley said. 'They're the sort we need.'

Jay was suddenly alert.

'I'd pay for a roistering with one of them,' Wolfenden said. 'They'd give us a run for our money all right.'

'I'm in,' said Allsop. 'Not so old yet I can't sow my oats.'

'You can keep them. Probably riddled with the pox, anyway,' Sedley said.

'What do I care? Too late for me!' Wolfenden held up his hands in a shrug. Another burst of laughter.

'How much?' Jay said, breaking into their laughter.

They all turned to look at him.

'You're not serious,' said Wycliffe.

'If I can bring you the Savage Sisters, what would you pay?'

'Oh what sport! I don't know. What are they worth?' Wolfenden picked up the dead bird by its neck and tossed it back into the ring, where one of the fighting cocks attacked it in a frenzy of squawking and tattered wings.

'There's a fifty-pound price on their heads, so better that,' Jay said.

'Leave off, Jay.' Wycliffe tugged at his arm.

''Tis too much for two whores,' Wolfenden said. 'Do I get to keep them afterwards?'

'You can do what the hell you like with them once you've paid for them.'

'No. Not even a savage maid's worth that. Come on, Allsop, let's collect my winnings.' Wolfenden and Allsop elbowed their way into the crowd.

'What are you thinking, playing a prank like that? You could never get him those girls,' Wycliffe said. 'You'll make me look a fool.'

'I never jest, you should know that,' Jay said.

Wycliffe turned away looking sulky and walked off across the ice, back towards the Pelican. He glanced over his shoulder. He wants me to follow him, thought Jay, but he stayed where he was. It did not suit him to bend to anyone's whim; he preferred to be in control.

A few moments later Wolfenden emerged from the fray and took hold of Jay by the arm, hissing, 'It's a deal. If by some miracle you can find the Savage Sisters and bring them to Allsop's tonight, I'll give you the fifty pounds. It will be worth it just to see his face.'

'Sixty. Or I might just as meet hand them over to the law.'

'Watch out, here he comes.' Allsop's burly figure approached.

'Shake?' Jay said.

Wolfenden held out his gloved hand, and Jay shook it. But he withdrew his hastily. A thin smear of chicken blood ran across it.

Chapter 39

'We can still turn round and go home, you know,' Corey said.

Sadie and Corey hovered outside the gate to Whitgift's in the dusk, cold to the bone despite the shawls hooded over their faces.

Sadie shook her head. 'No, if I'm not ready now I'll never be ready. I'm not running away from my own sister. I've got to face her, tell her I don't give a bent ha'penny for her no more.' She moved to embrace Corey, but Corey stepped back.

'Don't go smudging your face now.'

'Thanks for helping me get ready, Corey. Sorry I kept you up all night.'

'That yellow gown was worth all the stitching. It fits you perfect, now.'

'What time is it? I'm sick of waiting. I just want to get it over. I'll see Ella, then I'm going home, home to Westmorland. I don't care if she don't come with me, or if they catch me, or if I drop down dead on the way. It's London strangles me, anyways.'

St Martin's bells pealed the quarter.

'It's time,' Corey said. 'They'll be opening any minute. Sorry I can't come in with you, got to get back for the littlies, and my mam's home tonight, it's her night off. Don't forget, your bag's round the back in the dairy. You can get it from there without my mam seeing. Are you frit?'

Sadie nodded.

'Don't worry. Carriages have to stop at the gate and announce their names, then if they're on the list they let them through, otherwise they have to go and ask in the office. But the night-watchmen change and they open the gate to let the early watch out. That's your best chance for getting in,' Corey said, 'to just walk in right behind a carriage, then act like you own the place. I'll wait here awhile, and whistle to you if I see anyone from Whitgift's coming.'

'Do you think I'll get away with it?'

'You look as fine as any lady I've ever seen.'

Corey pointed to the sign of the Gilded Lily. 'See that sign? Window above's where she lodges. Shop's beneath, under the lily and fan. I asked the lad. Just keep to the right, away from the—'

As if to finish Corey's warning, the dogs began to bark. The barking set off all the others in the vicinity. Someone was shouting, but it was impossible to hear them over the yapping and snarling. In the yard there was a commotion, the gates swung briefly open and a heavy dark figure in a long cape rode past her and into the alleyway beyond.

'It's the day man leaving,' hissed Corey. 'Go on.'

'Oh Corey, thank you.' She threw her arms round Corey's neck.

'Get away with you. And have a care, we know what those dogs are like.'

'Don't fret, they're tethered.'

A few moments later a boxwagon arrived and Sadie walked tall through the gate after it. She stopped to raise a hand briefly to Corey.

'God speed.' She heard the call to her retreating back.

The dogs barked and bounced on the ends of their tethers but the choke of their collars soon reduced the sound to snaps and growls.

She strolled past a carriage, parked outside the warehouse, her eyes fixed on the sign ahead. It was strange – there were no other women in the yard, and Corey had said it was always thronging.

A lad ran to catch up with her, 'Sorry, miss, but the Lily here is closed tonight. It's open at the Frost Fair though, right on Freezeland Street. Is that your carriage?' He pointed to a carriage parked in the street outside.

Her throat was tight with fear, but he was smiling and he did not seem to think there was anything amiss.

'Oh, yes. Yes, it is. Thanking you.' She hesitated, nervous that her north country voice might betray her.

'Pardon me, miss, but I think you'd best go back to it then. 'Tain't safe to be out on the streets alone.'

He lifted his cap and went off whistling. She turned to go. So Ella wasn't here after all. Or was she? She caught sight of a hulk of a man sitting on the mount block nearby. He wore a leather coat and cotton sleeves like a butcher might wear. He was staring at the dogs who were whining through the bars of a pen near the gate. Sadie knew a guard when she saw one. Just as Corey had said, he looked like a man put there to deter the likes of her.

Checking the boy had gone, she nipped to the side, behind the boxwagon and tethered horse. It whickered and turned its head, but then continued to pull hay from the rack on the wall. As she crouched there, the door to the Gilded Lily opened and a little dark-haired girl came out carrying a tray laden with bottles. The big man turned and she saw his eyes follow her as she tottered past towards the building opposite. The girl paused by the door trying to press the latch with her elbow until one of the bottles fell off and smattered on the cobbles. The big man lumbered over to her and plucked open the latch whereupon she staggered through. The man stooped to pick up the bits of broken glass, but Sadie did not wait to see any more. She hared across the yard and in through the open door.

At first Sadie could not see anyone for there was only a stub of a candle lit, but then she heard footsteps on the stairs. She caught her breath.

Ella was thin as a rail, chalk white, her mouth a red slash. She was dressed in the green gown laced until her waist was a mere handspan wide. Ella stopped, her hands to her face.

'Who—? How did you get in here?' Ella asked before she had got to the bottom of the stairs.

'I've come to—'

Ella leapt down and took hold of Sadie's arm, agitated. 'Is there still a man outside?'

'Yes, but he went to help the girl—'

'Oh Lord. Just look at you! I'm so glad to see you, I was near mad with worry. But you mustn't stay. You must get away from here. Go now, Sadie, before anyone sees you.'

Sadie opened her mouth to speak but Ella was propelling her towards the door. 'Go for God's sake – Jay Whitgift read the notices, he's after claiming the reward, and if he finds you he'll take you too. Please, Sadie. You've got to get out of here, and don't come back.'

'But, Ella –' Sadie stepped back, but did not turn to go. Ella gave her a push. 'I'm serious. I've told you. Get out. Anywhere. Anywhere but here! Afore it's too late.'

'I only came—'

'You stupid girl, what's the matter with you?' Ella's face was stark white and gaunt, her eyes red-rimmed. There was desperation in her voice. 'Just go, can't you.'

Sadie backed away. 'What about you?'

'Can't you hear? Are you stupid?' Ella was shouting and half crying now and waving her arms at her.

'I'm going home. Come with me, Ella, we could—' Sadie paused. Ella was looking behind her, frozen in mid-gesture like a statue.

'Hide!' she said. 'Quick, get in the back.'

Something in the urgency of Ella's tone prompted Sadie to run. She dragged open the storeroom door and plunged inside. It smelt of camphor and flowers. She peered through the crack in the door and heard the bell tinkle; the single light flickered in the draught.

Footsteps on the flagged floor, the moving shadow of a lantern. 'You say she came in here?' someone said.

'Aye,' said a deep voice. Sadie's heart sank.

'Lutch says someone came in.' Jay's voice.

'No,' Ella said.

'Foxall, search the back and upstairs.'

Sadie put herself behind the door, but knew it was hopeless. It was less than a minute before she felt a grip on her arm and she was pulled blinking into the light.

'Your sister, if I'm not mistaken,' Jay said.

'Leave her alone,' Ella said. 'She's done naught.'

Sadie wrestled to free herself, and Jay said, 'Keep ahold of her. Lutch, give him a hand. Wolfenden's paying me sixty pound for them. Fancies seeing them fight, he said.'

The big man brought her other arm behind her back and pinioned it with one of his. Jay leaned on the counter, his fancy pistol dangling from its finger-guard, watching her struggle.

'No.' Ella ran and grasped Jay by the sleeve. 'Let Sadie go free. She's done nothing. It was me robbed Ibbetson. She's innocent, I swear.'

Jay snatched his hand back and pointed the gun at her. 'Innocent is she? Is she a virgin?'

'No,' said Ella, backing away.

Sadie was about to protest but then she closed her mouth tight.

Jay turned his eyes on Sadie. 'Someone tupped you?' He was amused, his voice clearly said he did not believe it.

Sadie looked away.

'You're lying. She's never lain with anyone, has she?'

Nobody said a word.

'Even better, she'll fetch a higher price.' Jay turned to Ella. 'I hope you're right. If there's no blood, old Wolfie might demand his money back. Lutch, take this one to the storeroom. We'll lock them both up there until the carriage is ready. Don't worry, lads, you'll get your cut, same as usual.'

Lutch took hold of Ella and pinioned her arms behind her. Sadie saw something like panic in her eyes. Ella appealed to Jay, 'I beg you, let Sadie go. I'll go to Wolfenden—'

'You?' Jay laughed. 'Wolfenden likes a maid. And that, I'll warrant, you most certainly are not. Allsop's *your* man.' He looked to Foxy. 'Lock them in.' They struggled to take Ella into the back room.

'When you've finished here, send out to Wolfenden. Tell him to get his purse ready, the deal's on.'

Lutch nodded.

'You armed?'

'Yup,' said Foxy.

'Good, because I don't want any accidents getting them in the wagon.'

Sadie looked at Ella and saw her crumple. The sight of her bowed head brought about a nameless dread. Ella had always been the strong one, had always had an answer for everything.

*

407

They heard the scrape as the bolts were slid home. When the men had gone, they were alone in the chill dark. Their eyes were not accustomed to it so they could not see each other's faces.

'Have they gone?' whispered Sadie.

'I think so.'

'What will they do to us?'

'Jay Whitgift will take us to his friends and then he'll hand us over.'

'To Ibbetson?'

There was a silence then. Sadie knew what this meant. After a few moments she said, 'Give us your hand.' She felt Ella's cold fingers squeeze hers tight.

'Ella?'

'Yes?'

'Are you afraid?'

'Not of dying. Not of that.'

'What then?'

'I'm afraid of Jay Whitgift's friends. Allsop. Wolfenden.'

'Sorry, Ell.'

Ella dropped her hand. 'What are you sorry for? You haven't done anything.'

'That I wouldn't wear the dress afore now. I was afraid to.'

'That. No, you soft thing. You were right. I don't like to see you done up like that. It gives folk the wrong impression. And sooner or later someone would have found you out. It was a stupid idea.'

Sadie sat down, feeling for the wall with her back.

'What time will they come for us?'

'I don't know. But you know this is the end, don't you?'

Sadie did not answer.

'We can still beat them though.' Ella's voice cut through the dark.

'How? We're locked in.'

'This is the apothecary's cupboard. There might be poisons on the shelf if we can find a light.'

'How will we get them to take them?'

'Not them, you goose. Us. We can take them. Then when they come back we'll be dead.'

'No!' Sadie shouted, and scrambled back up to take hold of Ella by the shoulders. 'Don't dare say such a thing. It's a mortal sin. We're not doing that.'

Sadie felt how thin Ella's collarbones were. She felt limp, and she let Sadie shake her as if she was made of rags. In the dark her voice echoed strangely. 'They'll not let us go. What's the difference? Tonight, tomorrow? They'll finish us anyway.'

'We're not giving up. We'll pray, and maybe God will hear us and send us some help.'

'God?' Ella laughed, a brittle sound with no bubble of mirth. 'God won't hear me. I sent a woman to the gallows. I'm a sinner, Sadie. Evil through and through. It's the Devil wants me.'

Sadie pulled Ella close to her, hugging her to her chest. 'You're not. Don't say that. It's not true. You're my own dear Ella.'

Ella pushed her away. Her voice was barely audible. 'I'm not fit to be your sister. Do you want to know who I really am? It's not a pretty tale. It was me sent poor Alice Ibbetson to the gallows. Me, Sadie. I wanted to bed her husband, Thomas, get even somehow.' She paused and sighed. 'I don't know, I thought if I could have what she had . . . the poor wretch, I stole her husband from her. I hid it well enough, but I hated her – all her type.'

There was a silence. Sadie waited for her to speak more and when she did not, reached out to touch her, but again Ella brushed her away.

'I worry I might not see Ma, if I go to the other place. She's in heaven, I know.' Sadie listened, straining to hear Ella's voice, which was barely audible. "'Tis strange, but I still miss her, you know. You know they said I'd forget about it in time, how she died. But 'tis not a thing you forget. And I had only seven years of her. I wanted to remember it all, every last thing, even that.' A whisper. 'Ma's mistress never came, see. Left me waiting on the sands. The sands had caught her, Sadie, and I didn't know what to do, and Ma said to keep away, and the sea kept on coming –'

There was silence then in the room, except for Ella's sobs.

'What, Ella?'

'I let her drown.'

Sadie could barely take it in. All those years, and Ella had never told anyone, bore the burden of it all by herself. Sadie reached for her hand and pressed it.

'I should've done something.' Ella's voice was angry.

When Sadie finally spoke, she said, 'But you were hardly seven year old, what could you do?'

'Something. Anything.' Ella's voice broke up. 'She was our lovely ma and I just stood there.'

'Don't. Whatever happened, it won't bring her back, no use blaming nobody. You kept me going, with your talk of a fine life. When my back was black and blue, when the lads taunted me, then it were your tales I remembered – how we'd sleep on satin and eat oysters and cream pie. I knew it was all just gab, but I couldn't have borne it if I didn't think something better was coming.'

'And look where I've led you. But I couldn't leave you behind, could I? Not with Da strapping you every night.'

Sadie took hold of Ella round the waist. 'You wanted to help me. You see, you're not wicked, you're kind. See, Ella.' Ella did not speak, but Sadie could feel her ribs start to shake with weeping.

'I'm proud you came for me,' Sadie said, 'I couldn't have

stood it if you'd upped and gone without me, left me there with him. You were my hope. You did right, we could have got away. You weren't to know this would happen, it was a risk worth taking. And now, whatever happens, we've got each other.'

'Tell her I'm sorry, won't you, when you see her?'

'If I can. Though sometimes I think 'tis all just a myth, made up to keep us all in line. And anyway, if there's a heaven, then we'll walk through them gates together.'

'Oh, Sadie, I treated you so bad. I got blinded by Whitgift's. I was so selfish, I didn't mean to . . .'

'Hush, hush. Never mind, it's all over now.' Sadie patted Ella's heaving back as if she were a child. 'It's done with, all that. We've got to live for today. It might be the only day we've got left. Put your arms round me, come on now, hold me tight.'

Ella's arms fastened around her neck and her head came onto Sadie's shoulder. 'I love you, Sadie, you're the only one who really sees me.' Sadie didn't know what she meant but her tears came too, they were tears of relief. Ella had told her the truth, and it was the most beautiful sound she had ever heard, the truth from Ella's lips. They wept together, clinging to each other.

Chapter 40

Titus Ibbetson tossed and turned, unable to get back to sleep. The visions of the girls in the gaol would not leave him; stained and reddened faces with accusing eyes haunted him. He had not known so many women with this kind of face existed. He had thought to look over one or two before finding the girl he sought. Now the figure had run into dozens.

He dragged the bed covers further up over his chin. He was cold despite asking the landlady for more woollen blankets, and then piling on his cloak and the sheepskin from beside the fire onto his bed. He was surprised how much difference it made not having Isobel beside him for warmth. He climbed out of bed and went over to the dresser where the small sampler he had found in the girls' room lay next to his gloves and hat.

He picked it up and ran his thumbs over the stitches. *Sadie Apleby*. It was odd to hold it in his hands. The refinement of it took his breath away, the stitches so neat and orderly, the little flowers at the corners so finely executed. Like something a lady might make. It must have taken a deal of patience to make such a thing. Somehow he had never imagined that the girls who robbed his brother could partake in such gentle pursuits. It was not finished yet – perhaps the girl had been making it when he arrived. The thought of her sewing made him drop it back on the table, he did not want to be so near her hands.

He sighed and looked out of the window. The snow was softening in the street, stained yellow now from the frozen piss of horses and dogs. He thought of the girls' lodgings. Although he knew that people lived that way, it still surprised him to see such a grim place, bare as a board, with scarcely a stick of furniture and no glass at the window.

He was fascinated, though, to find a number of small items in the room, including several salves and pots and a bag printed by a proper press with *The Gilded Lily – Ladies' Emporium.* Mercy Fletcher had told him the stall was situated inside Whitgift's second-hand shop. He had been to Whitgift's when he first came to London, but there had been no sign of a ladies' apothecary then.

So today he was going to go back to Whitgift's yard. He might be able to trace the girls that way. It had become a matter of pride. He had been so long away, and what would he tell them back home if he failed? He had never failed at anything in his life.

It was too cold to be in bed so he began to dress. His shirt was stiff, the leather of his boots still damp from walking in yesterday's snow. He went to the window and looked out. No frost today on the windows, so the thaw must be continuing, and indeed there seemed to be water dripping from the eaves of the house opposite. London itself was embroiled in a veil of fog. He sighed again. It was hard enough to find anything, without this. Ten minutes later a carriage waited for him outside the hotel door.

'Whitgift's, Broken Wharf,' he called to the driver.

There was the usual whirr of the pocket watches as Walt Whitgift and Nat Tindall puffed on their pipes in Walt's office.

'Have you heard? There's been a riot, they've had to send in the king's life guards,' said Tindall, tapping his pipe with his thumb to settle the glowing tamp.

'What's it about then, this riot?'

'Dissenters against the king – led by someone called Venner. Wild man he is, so they say, but there's more than twenty dead on both sides. Imagine that. His head's going up on the bridge. Didn't I tell you there'd be blood?'

'You did. That strange dream you had – about the Thames turning red, and a mighty lightning bolt from heaven. Odds fish, you were right.'

'These are curious times. It's common knowledge in my business, that when the year can be reversed, then fortunes can turn on a horseshoe.'

'Is that right?'

'1661. The same writ backwards as forwards.'

'Aah.'

'Chance for Lucifer to push his nose in and turn things about. Shouldn't be surprised if we don't see more fighting before the month's out.'

'No, Nat, we'll not go back to that. Funny, I was just thinking, my Jay's had it easy. When I was his age I was fighting for the common man alongside most other young men my age. And trying to set up shop here. Do you remember?'

'Those were good times. The best times. Your Bessie was still alive then.'

'Aye. She was a good lass.' They sucked on their clay pipes, savouring their memories.

Walt withdrew one of several baize bags from the drawer and tipped out some signet rings, seals and cameos onto the desk. He bent to the task of pricing them up, pushing back the russet woollen cap that kept his balding head warm.

Nat talked and talked. Often Nat's words were about matters so arcane Walt could have no hope of understanding them, and they would drift past him so that later he would not be able to remember a thing Nat had said. But he liked the noise of him in the background, and Nat always seemed to be glad to be in the warm office. Walt passed the price tickets to Nat to write. His penmanship was far superior to his own, and it made the whole business companionable. Their quiet activity was broken by a loud clang from the St Stephen's bell outside. The two men looked at each other.

'I'll go. You carry on,' Nat said.

A few moments later he was back with a dark-suited gentleman in tow.

'Please sit down,' Walt said.

'I won't, thank you.' The man stood away from the chair as if it might contaminate him. He cleared his throat.

'Who is in charge of the Gilded Lily Ladies' Emporium?'

'That'll be my son. But it's closed in the day while the Frost Fair's on. They've got a stall there you see—'

'You mean it's shut now? There's nobody there?'

'All the serving girls are on the stall.'

'Ever heard of two girls called Ella and Sadie Appleby?'

Walt and Nat looked at each other, raised their eyebrows and shook their heads. 'No,' Walt said. 'Can't say I have.'

The man blew out a long sigh. 'I have an inventory here, of goods that were stolen from my late brother. They tell me at the inn that stolen goods are often sold forward here.' He emphasized 'stolen goods' as if it pained him to say the words. 'My name's Ibbetson. I want you to look at your records and see if any of them have come in.'

Walt sucked on his teeth and frowned. 'We don't deal in stolen goods here. Only honest transactions.'

'They say you're a pawnbroker.'

'We are not averse to making a charitable loan if the person's need is pressing.'

'But you do have records of all your sales?'

'Of course. It will take time. There's a fee for this sort of thing. It's my son who normally deals with those enquiries.'

'I'll make it worth your while if it can be done today.'

'It depends. I'll need dates and descriptions. I've no time today, maybe tomorrow.'

Ibbetson looked disgruntled. 'But I have the list here, already prepared.' He drew out a folded paper with two long columns of spiky writing and placed it facing Walt. He flattened it out as if he would glue it to the desk.

Walt coughed, embarrassed. 'Nat, I haven't got my eyeglasses. Would you?'

Tindall picked up the list. 'It is quite a comprehensive list.'

'Do you want me to check each item?' Walt asked.

'That's why I gave you the list,' said Ibbetson, ignoring Tindall and prodding the paper with a well-manicured fingernail. 'My brother was murdered, and his house turned over. I don't know what the world's coming to – I can't get justice from the law, they are taking for ever. These days you just can't rely on them. And servants are the same – if they're not out to rob you, they're witless, most of them.'

'Shame,' Nat said. 'We'll do what we can to help.'

'When did it happen?' Walt said.

'October last year. Anything that's come in since then.'

'That's a lot of work, we've dealt with scores of items since then. Nat, I think it would be best to fetch the right ledgers. We need Dennis here for this really, but I suppose his ma's still bad, poor lad. Ask the prentice, would you?'

Tindall duly went and fetched the apprentice, who lowered

the pile of inventory books heavily onto the desk. They were grubby and stained and the edges of the papers were furred with use.

Tindall began to read the first entry on Ibbetson's list. 'Item. One silver charger . . .'

'There's hundreds of silver chargers,' Walt said. 'It'll take weeks to go through all of them. Can't we start with something else?'

'It's very particular, inscribed with a—'

'Look,' Walt said, dreading his quiet office being taken over, 'you'll have to find another place to do this. Take the ledger to the plate room, and do it there.'

Ibbetson started to demur, but the apprentice dragged the pile of books back off the table and tucked it under his arm. As he did so he dislodged the baize bag from the table and it scattered its contents onto the floor, where they spun and rattled across the flagstones.

'Begging pardon, sir,' he said, stooping to retrieve them. Ibbetson and Tindall bent to help him.

'What's that you've got there?' Ibbetson said.

Tindall looked down into his palm. 'What, this?' He held it up. 'Just a seal. Quite a nice one too, well-chased, with a bevelled ruby stone.'

'Let me see.'

Tindall dropped it into his outstretched hand.

'I'd know this anywhere. See, it's got his initials on it. T.W.I. Thomas William Ibbetson. I've got one just the same.' Ibbetson pulled out his own from his pocket and dangled it before them. Nat and Walt exchanged looks.

'Second of February.' Ibbetson was reading the label on the seal. He held it out before them.

'Well, what are you waiting for, boy? Find it in the ledger.

I need the name and address of who brought it in. We've found one of the girl's lodgings, but she's not there. Maybe she's gone to her sister's. We need that address.'

The apprentice let the book thump back on the table. Nat licked his forefinger and riffled through the pages. 'Here we are. Second of February.' His finger scrolled down the page. 'It's not here.'

'It must be,' Walt said.

Ibbetson and Walt both pored over the page. 'He's right. It's not there.'

'It'll be one of Jay's then,' the apprentice said.

'What do you mean, "one of Jay's"?' Walt said.

The apprentice looked suddenly scared. 'The stuff he's ticketed himself. When it sells, if it's not in the big book we keep the money aside, give it him at the end of the week.'

'What?' Walt said. 'Let me get this straight. Not everything goes in my book?'

'No.' He dropped his gaze. 'When goods come in from Jay's folk, they're kept to one side.'

'I see,' said Walt. He turned to Ibbetson. 'Beg pardon, sir. We will find record of it soon enough.'

He turned to the lad. 'Go ask Jay to bring me his ledgers.'

There was a chilly silence until the boy returned. 'Out, sir. Door's locked.'

'Then I will keep this, as it is my property.' Ibbetson dropped the seal into his pocket.

'You can't do that,' Walt said. 'Someone might have sold us that seal in good faith, not knowing where it came from. Nat here will go through the list this afternoon, and when my son returns we will get to the bottom of this transaction. Best leave the seal here, until we can unravel its history.'

'I'll wager the rest of my brother's goods have been sold already through Whitgift's. Either that, or they are still here somewhere.' He tapped the ledger. 'You must have something on your records. The maids have given us the slip twice. We need to find out who brought this in – trace them that way.' He weighed the seal in his palm again. 'Maybe this will persuade the constable to take action at last. I am going straight to his house now to ask him to return with me. He will make a thorough check of your premises to see if we can recover any more of my brother's goods. I expect you to check my list and have all the relevant records to hand when we return.'

'Damned inconvenient,' grumbled Walt. 'We've got better things to do than chase after your silver.'

Ibbetson leaned over the desk glowering. 'Now listen to me. If those inventories are not on the desk when I come back I'll get the place closed down whilst I turn over every last corner myself.'

'Don't worry, sir,' Nat said in a placatory manner, seeing that Walt was glaring at the visitor with open hostility. 'We'll have everything ready for you.'

They watched him stride across the yard in his shiny boots and call for his carriage. When he had gone, Walt told the apprentice to keep an eye out for Jay and to bring him straight to the office when he returned. 'Where is he?' grumbled Walt.

'Out and about in the coffee houses or at the Frost Fair I expect,' Tindall said.

'He's supposed to be with the clerk, doing the month's accounts for the chambers, not jaunting about town.'

'That man'll bring the law though, so you'd better dust off your records. I'll wager he's a Taurus. Bull-headed, I could tell. He won't give up until he's found every last button.'

'Do you think so?'

'And your Jay's got a bit of explaining to do too. It doesn't sound right to me – him making deals behind your back. You should know what goes on in your own yard, Walt.'

'It's just a bit of a misunderstanding. We'll sort it out.'

'Let's hope so. I worry about his friends, Walt.'

'What do you mean?' Walt didn't mean to snap, but found himself always on the defensive where Jay was concerned.

'He's mixing with some real penny stinkards, not the sort of company I'd want to turn my back on. Maybe he should be settling down, finding a nice maid, someone who'll be useful in the business. And I don't like to say it, but he should be more of a help to you, if you ask me.'

'He's just young. Time enough for him to settle down.'

Tindall sighed. 'Give me that list then and we'll make a start. Perhaps if we can find it all, Ibbetson and the law will get off your back.'

They combed the place for the items on the list. It was difficult on two counts – first because Ibbetson's handwriting was sprawling and hard to read, and secondly because there was just so much stuff cluttering the yard. And though it was all supposed to be sorted into categories, somehow it never was, and although the top layer looked ordered, beneath was such a muddle that Walt became quite tetchy, demanding to know who was responsible.

By noon they had found several items matching the list, but could not actually be sure that these were the ones Ibbetson was after. There was still no sign of Jay.

He called the apprentice over. 'Do you know where he is?' Walt said.

'Lord Allsop's carriage came for him, with Wycliffe and Sedley. Frost Fair, sir, meeting some other gentlemen at the Pelican on the Ice.'

Tindall raised his eyes to the ceiling.

'All right, Nat. I'll have words with him, when I see him,' Walt said, and went out, slamming the door. They watched his bent shape go in through the door of the warehouse.

'That son'll be the death of him,' Tindall said. 'Is that today's broadsheet?'

'Yep.' The lad passed it over. 'I'm a-taking that home. Man at the end of our alley can read. Ragman says there's been another body found. A woman. Same as the last, throttled she was and dumped in the Thames.'

Tindall took hold of the paper and scanned the words. He sat down at the desk and read it again.

The prentice carried on talking. 'That's seven all told. Whores mostly, but there were two that were just young girls, fourteen year old. They say one was a milliner's prentice and one a pelterer's girl. Hey, tell us what it says about them, mister?'

But Tindall was not listening, he was reading the description. Red hair, it said. And the girl he had seen getting into Whitgift's wagon had red hair.

Chapter 41

Sadie and Ella sat together on the same side of the wagon, holding hands. The boxwagon Jay had sent had no windows, just two bench seats either side. It was empty but for a few sacks and blankets. At the front was a small barred window through which Sadie could see the back of the man who drove the horses.

Sadie glanced at Ella. Her eyes were dark pools in her white face; there were smears around her eyes where the paint had run from crying; she looked frightened and it wrung Sadie's heart. But Ella turned to her then and gave her a thin smile. It was a sudden light, like the way that landscape changes under the play of sunshine. It can change the world in an instant.

Sadie smiled back.

'Sing for me, Sadie.'

'What, now?'

'I thought it would be nice to hear something beautiful.'

'What shall I sing?'

'Anything. Nothing sad though.'

Sadie thought. Most songs she knew were sad. There was a beauty in sadness, when you put it to song. A yearning of the heart.

'Go on,' said Ella.

'All right.' Sadie began to hum a tune very softly. It wavered slightly with the jolting of the carriage, but the rhythm of the horses' hooves barely disturbed her own internal rhythm. She did not sing the words though they both knew them.

> *The oak and the ash and the bonny rowan tree,*
> *They all grow sweeter in the North Country.*

Sadie hummed as she always did, with her head cocked slightly and her eyes closed, the better to hear the tune. When she had finished she opened her eyes to see Ella wipe her face with her cuff.

Foxy's head appeared at the grille. He was scowling. 'Oy!' he said.

'Let her be,' she heard Lutch say, 'there's no harm in it.'

But the tune was finished and it was for Ella; she did not want to sing for these men. She clasped Ella round the waist and hugged her hard.

The wagon jolted to a halt. Her own fear was reflected in Ella's eyes.

'When we get inside, act meek,' said Ella. 'Whatever you do, don't fight. He might not want us if we're quiet.'

'What do you mean?' Sadie asked.

'He wants us to fight. Promise me you won't fight.'

Sadie nodded.

'Is Jay to meet us at Allsop's?' she heard Lutch say.

'Went on ahead on his horse,' the other man said. 'He must be here – that's his big roan tied up over there. He said to bring them both in here. Wolfenden's set it up. Jay reckons he can do a deal for the pair of them.'

'Is it a cane job?'

'Dunno. Perhaps. There's a price on their heads. Reckon he'll double-cross Wolfenden and hand them in to the law tomorrow. Make himself look like a model citizen. We've to be ready with the wagon when he calls us.'

'How much are they worth?'

'No. Don't even think about it. Not worth the risk. He'd have us behind bars if we scuppered him, an' he can't half hold a grudge.' She heard footsteps move to the back of the wagon.

'I don't like Allsop.'

'Who cares. Jay never asked you to marry the bugger. Go tell Allsop we're here.' The noise of someone unbolting the doors.

Sadie twisted the lace of her bodice round and round her fingers. Ella took her by the shoulders. 'If there's a chance, then for God's sake take it. If you can run, then go, don't wait for me, but just run, like the wind, like you've never run before.'

'No, Ella. Not without you.'

Ella's eyes burnt into hers. 'Do it for me. And for Ma. If you get a chance, remember.'

The wagon doors shuddered then and they were thrown open to the night. Sadie looked out. There was a row of grand stone houses with lanterns hung outside. Where they had drawn up the big back door stood open, and in its light she saw the silhouettes of some men waiting. She clung tight to Ella's hand, feeling her shivering, whether from fear or cold she could not say. Outside the door Foxy's face was pale, and she caught the flash of a knife as he silently beckoned them out.

The men approached the carriage. One of them pushed the other from behind, but he was so drunk that he fell into the slush, guffawing with laughter.

'Get up, Sedley, you fool,' said the other man, kicking him in the ribs with his shiny boot.

Ella made use of the diversion. 'Now!' she screamed, knocking the knife from Foxy's hand and setting off at a run. Hitching up her skirts Sadie ran clumsily down the garden embankment.

'Catch them, Wycliffe!' she heard one of them shout. 'Quick, fan out.'

Sadie heard them and put on a further spurt of speed, looking left and right. The ground was uneven, the snow and mud frozen into ruts and furrows. A moon was reflected in the patchy cloud and she searched for somewhere to hide by its greying light, but the buildings loomed dark and forbidding and she realized with growing panic that she was in a huge courtyard. She heard the thud of footsteps behind her. She looked over her shoulder. One of them must have got up and now he was gaining on her. The flash of his white shirt caught the moonlight. He swung his arm towards her, but she twisted out of the way and headed for an iron gate glinting beneath an archway. To her right, she could see the other sprinting to cut her off before she could get to it. She thought her chest might collapse with the effort to push her legs to move faster.

'Oh, what a lark!' she heard a breathless voice behind her. She turned to see that her pursuer had stopped running and was bent double, holding onto his knees with both hands, panting with the effort of running.

Realizing Sedley was nearly at the gate, she doubled back on herself, searching for another way out, but her pursuer saw her intent and sprang towards her. 'Oh no, you don't, you minx!' he shouted and his body landed heavily on hers, knocking the wind out of her. She rolled over coughing and tried to scramble to her feet, but the others were upon them now too, blowing like horses.

'Oh, shall we let her go and play that again! I haven't played chase since I was a child!' said Wycliffe, holding her by the ankle with both hands.

Sadie struggled to free herself, but Sedley ran to help and

clung onto her. Tears of frustration seeped from the corners of her eyes.

'Go on then, I'll let her go and we'll have another chase,' said Sedley.

They stood away, leaving her sitting on the grass. She saw then that Lutch and Foxy had taken Ella and were holding her fast. Ella caught her eye and shook her head. She looked beaten. Jay Whitgift lounged in the doorway watching, an expression of amusement on his face; he was playing with a stick rapier, idly tossing it up and catching it.

'Oh, Whitgift, she's spoiling our sport, she won't run,' said Sedley. 'You didn't tell us she would give up so easily. You said she was wild.'

'How can he help it if she's too dim-witted to run?' Wycliffe said. 'Come on, let's take her inside.'

In the brighter light of the chamber a tall man with a horribly disfigured face helped himself to a glass of port from a decanter. Sadie could not help but stare at the metal cover over his nose, though she tried not to. She had been on the receiving side of such stares. The man looked irritable and his hooded eyes flicked round the room.

'Are these they?'

'This one's wild as a cat,' said Wycliffe, hanging onto Sadie's arm. 'We had a job to hold her. She's quieter now, though.'

'Let's take a look at them. Then I'll decide if they're worth my silver.'

She caught Ella's eye. Ella shook her head, and Sadie stayed motionless as Wolfenden circled them. 'I told Allsop to expect a surprise – he's waiting in the drawing room.' He thrust his hand into Ella's bodice and pinched her on the breast. Her eyes widened slightly but she did not react. 'This one's the one that recites,

The Gilded Lily

isn't she? She's a bit thin, not much meat on those bones. A man likes something he can sink into, isn't that right, boys?'

'Speak for yourself,' said Wycliffe. Sedley brayed like a donkey.

Wolfenden walked round Sadie, lifted her chin with a rough hand. She looked impassively into his face, seeing how his skin was festering around the nose, how his hair seemed to be worn away into wisps under his heavy wig. When he spoke his lips were cracked over yellowing teeth.

He slopped back into his chair, a disappointed scowl on his face. 'She won't do, Whitgift. She's not what I imagined. She's like a mouse.'

Sadie held her breath, keeping silent. Perhaps they would let them go.

'I know she looks quiet now,' Wycliffe said, 'but you should have seen her before – she was that wild we had to hold her down.'

Wolfenden's face registered a little more interest.

'Yes, you can still see the mud and wet on this one's gown, where we had to wrestle her onto the ground,' Sedley said.

'Where?'

Jay walked over and turned her round by the shoulders. She felt a hand brush down her back, but she stayed rigid. Sadie's skin crawled. Jay turned her back to face Wolfenden, whose eyes were glinting now with something like greed. He leaned forward in his chair.

'She ran like the blazes. Hitched up her skirts to show her bare knees and everything,' said Sedley.

'Bare knees?'

Jay lifted her skirt with the tip of his stick rapier. Wolfenden leaned over. His voice turned husky.

'Lift your skirts, girl.'

Sadie did not move. She was sinking inside. She cast her eyes to Ella while Jay bent over and twitched up her skirts. She heard Wolfenden exhale, and saw the beads of sweat break out on his brow.

'All besmirched with mud,' he said. His voice was breathy.

Sadie looked down. Her bare ankles were white against the vibrant red and blues of the rug, her legs wet and dark with dirt.

'She'll do.' He drew a pouch from his coat and held it out to Jay. 'We'll get some sport out of them somehow.'

Jay let go of her skirts and they covered her feet again. He pocketed the purse with a small bow.

Wolfenden stood up unsteadily and said, 'Allsop's waiting in the drawing room. If he don't want them, then I'll tup this one myself.'

'No!' Ella protested, struggling wildly, but Foxy put his hand over her mouth. She sank her teeth into his palm.

'You bitch,' he said, letting go in surprise and shaking his hand. 'She bit me.'

Wolfenden laughed. 'That's what I like – a bit of spirit. This way.'

Chapter 42

Walt was restless. He took out all the watches one by one and wound them. Tindall was still searching through the back warehouse with Ibbetson's inventory, but they had turned up nothing that could conclusively belong to him. Walt was worried about Jay. He hadn't seen him all day, and he needed Jay to tell him where that seal had come from. He didn't want a constable asking questions. He knew he wasn't supposed to make loans on goods, but there was such a demand, it would have seemed churlish not to fulfil it, like turning away a plate of food. And he remembered when times had been hard well enough, when the crops were burnt in the days of shaking.

And he did not like it when Nat disapproved of his son. It was as if he was disapproving of Walt himself, it gave him a pang inside. He hoped Jay might have come home by now, but although he had heard carriage wheels several times, he had seen nothing of Jay. He was probably at the Frost Fair. Walt himself had been along there earlier in the week and had been amazed by the scale of it. In his day they hadn't been such grand affairs with troops mustering, and crowds thick as at the coronation parade.

When the bell rang for his office he hurried to the door,

expecting to see Jay standing impatiently as he always did with his hat in his hand ready to duck under the lintel. But when he opened the door it was to see a stout constable in the king's livery, and behind him Ibbetson, in a long dark cape and a tartan muffler against the cold.

'Good evening, sir,' said the constable. 'May we come in?'

'Of course,' said Walt, his heart sinking. Now he wished he had not set Nat on searching the warehouses. He felt old all of a sudden, and tired. He would have liked his friend with him. He sighed as he shut the door.

'Have you found out where this seal came from?' Ibbetson said.

'One of my men is on it now,' Walt said faintly.

'Your son is not here then, to explain how he came by it?'

'No. He's out.'

'And it is he, who is in charge of the Gilded Lily, isn't it?'

'Yes,' Walt said, 'but it's shut right now. They've taken the business to the Frost Fair. Everyone's up there nights now.'

'Ask him again about the girls,' Ibbetson said.

The constable frowned, 'I was getting to that. Do you know if he employs two sisters there – Sadie and Ella Appleby?'

Ibbetson sat down on the leather chair Nat usually sat in.

'Well, he does have two girls, but they are Miss Johnson and Miss Bennett,' Walt said.

'Does one of them have a stain on her face?'

'A stain?'

'Like a big red mark from here to here.' Ibbetson drew his hand over his face.

'No.' Walt did not understand. 'They're very pretty girls. What would Jay need a girl like that for?'

'It's just that we found some jars from the Gilded Lily in her room.'

'Well, I'm not surprised, sounds like she needs it. Every girl buys their salves and pomades from my son's emporium. The Lily's the talk of town.'

Ibbetson stood up again and said, 'I'm still not satisfied. There's the business with the seal. Tell him about the warrant to search his chambers.'

'Now hold your fire,' Walt said. 'I've said Jay'll be back soon, then I'll have a talk to him. Come back tomorrow.'

'It won't wait,' the constable said. 'Someone's given us information that links this place to the murder of a young girl. If you won't open up, then we'll force entry.'

'What? I don't understand. What's all this talk of young girls and murder?'

'Where is your son, Mr Whitgift?' the constable said.

'I've said. He'll see you tomorrow.'

'He's just wasting time,' Ibbetson said.

The constable sighed in irritation. His voice had the resigned tone of someone who had had a very long day. 'Come on, old fellow, we'll break the lock anyway if you don't let us in.'

'All right, all right. I have a key. I have keys to all the buildings. I'll just have to find it.'

Walt opened his desk drawer to find the key to Jay's office. Jay did not know he had this key, and Walt felt a little guilty about it. Jay would have been very annoyed to think that his father had a key to his private chambers, but Walt had not been up there in months. He used to go up regularly because he liked to see what his son was doing, handle his fine things. It made him proud. But now he hated those stairs, they hurt his knees and he was frightened of taking a tumble. These days Jay never offered to give him his arm and take him up.

Walt unloaded various grubby items from the drawers onto the table whilst Ibbetson frowned and tutted. Eventually he found the key with its faded green tassel.

'I think this is it.'

'Right then. Lead the way. We need to find the ledger and see if we can find an address, or something to trace that seal,' Ibbetson said.

Walt sighed and made a great show of putting on his cloak and scarf and a beaver fur hat which he pulled down over his ears. He plucked a lantern from the table and set off without so much as a glance behind. But he heard their footsteps behind him as he limped across the yard.

When the door was open he led the way up the stairs, feeling his knees creak mutinously with every step. 'Careful,' he said, 'there seem to be a few boxes on the stairs.' He must have a word with Jay about those crates, they could cause someone to trip.

He pushed open the door, but it would not open very wide, something was jamming it. Walt held out his lantern for a better view. He stopped dead, astounded, unable to go a step further. The room was piled high. There was scarce room to breathe for boxes and baskets, crates and chests. Some of the piles were teetering at an alarming height. Not a square inch of wall could be seen.

'Wait there,' he croaked, finally able to speak.

'We'll come up if you don't mind,' the constable said.

'No, no. I'll look for the ledger. You go back down.' Walt wiped his brow. He could not understand it. What was all this? Supplies for the Lily? He squeezed his way carefully through a narrow passage towards the desk, marooned like a valley between mountains. He was afraid that he might knock into something and send a stack tumbling about him. When he got to the desk, he could see there were more small cabinets and chests and cases piled beneath it, and small jewellery cases and tea caddies crowding round the edges. In front of him was a cabinet with rows of small drawers. He had no time to take this in, though, because he heard the constable call from the doorway, 'Are you in there, Mr Whitgift?'

'Yes, yes,' said Walt faintly.

'What's in the boxes?'

'I don't know. Requisitions most likely. Pots and jars for the Gilded Lily. You know, the ladies' chambers.'

'Let's have a look then.' The constable bent to pick up one of the nearest boxes. The stack behind him swayed slightly as his back nudged into it. Walt put his hand out to steady the stack as the constable lifted his hand out of the straw to reveal a tortoise-shell and gold card case. He handed it to Walt. Walt stared. It was an expensive item, that he could tell. The constable dug deeper down and found several more, all gold, all polished to a high sheen. He lined them up in a row on the only remaining space on the desk. Walt could not believe what he was seeing. Where had they come from? What was all this gold doing in his son's chamber? He was stunned, could not take it in.

'Where are the ledgers?' Ibbetson's voice broke in.

'I don't know.' Walt was stumbling over his words now. 'I can't see them, I mean, I don't know where he keeps them, you see I don't come up here much, but I'm sure he'll be back soon enough to tell us where they are . . .'

The constable meanwhile was pulling a silver-backed looking glass from a drawer. 'There's a few dozen more of these in here,' said the constable, accusingly.

'Just stock,' Walt mumbled.

But the constable had an intent expression on his face. Shining the lantern close to the cabinet he was examining another drawer. Walt caught a glimpse of something flash and twinkle in the light as he drew it out, before the drawer was shut and another opened. The constable pulled a whole drawer out and pushed aside the other small cases and boxes, leaning over it so that his shadow was projected eerily on the towers of crates as he picked out one object after another.

Ibbetson said, 'The ledgers won't be in there. The drawers are too small.'

The constable was too engrossed to answer. Walt leaned on the table; he felt as though his legs might give way.

At last the constable turned, and fixed Walt with a grim look. 'For the last time, where is your son?'

'Out. On business,' Walt said.

'If I'm not mistaken, one of those bracelets in the drawer belongs to Mrs Cecily Rowlands. But I'll need a second opinion. I believe these goods to be stolen property. The bracelet has an inscription on the inside from her husband that is most particular, and I must enquire exactly how your son came by it. And just look at all this stuff.' He gestured round the room.

'Just a few bits for the shop,' Walt said.

Ibbetson said, 'My God. I'll bet my brother's belongings are in here somewhere. Let me see.' He reached up to take down a crate precariously balanced on top of several others.

'Careful,' Walt said.

'No, sir, don't touch anything,' the constable said. His voice had taken on a new authority. Ibbetson put down the crate. 'There's a small fortune in here. I want it thoroughly checked. Is there a boy available?'

'No,' Walt said, hoping to stave off the inevitable. 'The lads are down at the Frost Fair.'

'I need a runner to fetch the guard. You are not to leave the premises, and when your son comes home, he must wait for us here. Do you understand me?'

'Yes. But I'm sure he can explain it all,' Walt said. The constable was treating him like an old man. It upset him. His thoughts ran round his head like rats in a trap, asking what all this stuff was, but a small voice inside him was whispering that it already knew.

'Look at this,' said Ibbetson. 'Looks like a notebook of some sort – best take this. Maybe it will have the information we seek.'

'I thought I said not to touch anything, sir.' But he held out his hand for the calfskin book, flicked it open for a look, raised his eyebrows. He went very still, sucked in his breath, then tucked the book deliberately into the pouch at his belt.

The constable's eyes had turned hard. 'Let us descend,' he said. 'I cannot do more without help. Mr Ibbetson, go find a boy, get someone to send for the king's guard. I'll wait in the office, keep my eye on Mr Whitgift.'

Ibbetson looked disgruntled but manoeuvred his way back to the door, and Walt heard his boot heels clatter down the stairs and the noise of crunching snow as he strode across the yard. Walt followed the constable's broad back. 'Better lock it,' said the constable tersely.

'Oh. Oh yes,' Walt said. It felt strange to lock the door again now he knew what was behind it. And he dreaded to think what might happen when Jay came back. He walked to the office in silence and slumped into his chair. The fire had sunk to cinders in the office and the room seemed grey and dull.

A few moments later the office door burst open and Ibbetson came in, followed by Nat Tindall, who appeared anxiously at his shoulder.

'Ah, good day again, Mr Tindall,' the constable said. Nat looked guiltily at his feet and slid out of view into the yard.

'The son's at Allsop's,' Ibbetson said, breathless. 'Trinity Lane. Mr Tindall asked the nightwatch, and he saw him go out. Jay Whitgift told him to send his men straight there in the box-wagon. And wait till you hear this – the watch said he saw them open up the Gilded Lily and hand two girls into the wagon. He said it was too dark to see their faces, but he says the wagon's gone on to Lord Allsop's.'

'In that case we'll apprehend Whitgift there,' said the constable. 'I'll ride and fetch some back-up. Like as not we'll have need of it. And better have men to wait down here in case he returns.'

It was all happening too fast for Walt. He couldn't make sense of it.

'Tindall.' The constable put his head out of the door and shouted for him. He shuffled in, looking sheepish. 'Wait with the old gent until my men arrive. Make sure he stays where he is.'

'Old gent' was it now? Walt caught his friend's eyes and felt ashamed. He dropped his chin to his chest.

'I'll ride on ahead, sir, meet you at Allsop's,' Ibbetson said, top-buttoning his riding cloak.

'Don't go in, though. Safer to await some protection,' said the constable.

'Of course not.' Ibbetson and the constable hurried out of the door together. From the yard came the sounds of the horses side-stepping as they mounted them, and then the squelch of hooves receding into the distance.

When the sounds had died away, Walt turned to his friend. 'Don't say anything, Nat. I know, I've been stupid. Did you know? About all the stuff, I mean?'

'No, Walt. You weren't to know.'

'Happen there'll be an explanation.'

Nat merely shook his head.

'Will they bring him home?'

'I don't know. They'll need to go through the evidence.'

'They said something about a murder. A young girl.'

Nat dropped his gaze and looked at the floor.

'His mother would have broken her heart. I've never seen anything like it. Constable thinks it's all stolen.'

'What do you think?' Tindall said.

Walt looked up and met his friend's eyes. 'He'll hang,' he said simply.

Tindall walked slowly home to his lodgings. He had ignored the constable's orders and refused to play the role of guard. Not with Walt. Walt had looked broken enough when he left, hollowed into himself, his usual bright eyes dull behind his eyeglasses. Tindall no longer felt able to poach a bed in front of his fire, for he carried his own guilty secret. After Ibbetson had left that afternoon, and whilst he was supposed to be hunting the goods on his inventory, Tindall had walked over to the constable's house and told him everything. About what he had seen the night he had followed Foxall and Lutch, about his suspicions about Miss Johnson in the Gilded Lily, and how the perruquier was looking for a girl that looked like her. About the shady transactions that took place in the night, and about the red-haired girl who disappeared from the wagon and the floating shape in the Thames.

Tindall dragged his feet through the slush, ignored the drips from the eaves landing on his broad-brimmed hat and trickling down his neck, for he was deep in thought. His friend would never forgive him when he found out it was Nat who had betrayed his son, and it was no use fooling himself, Walt would guess soon enough who had given them the information.

'Hackney carriage, sir?' A cab pulled alongside him, spraying him with sludge from the gutter.

'No, I bloody don't. Sling your hook,' he yelled with venom. Damn fool driver, he said to himself. Then he sighed. He would miss Walt. Nigh on thirty years they'd known each other, and nary a bad word between them. 'Curse the bloody boy,' he said.

Walt had sat in his chair a long while, but now he paced up and down the office. It was cold, but the peat stayed in the basket by the fire, the candles stayed unlit. The yard was empty and quiet, except for the drip, drip of iced water from the gutters. There were no customers because the stall was still at the Frost Fair, even though Tindall had said it was thawing. Jay had not returned, and Walt did not know whether they had found him at Allsop's. He imagined his son's face, when the king's guard came, the closed look he always took on when he was accused of anything. The same look he had at six years old when he denied taking the sixpence from his mother's purse.

Walt looked across the yard. The dogs were sleeping, curled nose to tail by the railings. The weathercock creaked slowly round in the wind. Every now and then he would hear a soft whump as a wedge of snow slid off the roof to land on the cobbles outside.

He had tried to persuade Nat to stay, but he had gone home early. He recalled the slight yeasty smell that accompanied Nat everywhere, and how it lingered in his office in the mornings, and how at first he had thought how odd it was, that even if he forgot to bank the fire, it was always only just sinking to ash when he arrived. He probably thinks I don't know he sleeps here every night, he thought. Nat had looked embarrassed just now when he left. Bless his old bones, he'd been insistent he was not going to keep watch over Walt as if he was some highway felon.

Walt eyed the key to Jay's office where it lay on the blotter. He picked it up and weighed it in his hand. He had known all along there was something odd about his son. Something he did not understand. His mind worked in a way he just could not fathom, for example he never seemed interested in the usual things – he had never brought a girl home, not a single one. And he spent far too much time in the coffee houses with the fast set.

Walt suggested he take up with Sally, the smith's daughter, a handsome broad-boned girl, but Jay would always have an excuse ready. Walt had thought it was because Sally was not good enough for him, and had suggested Miriam Edgware, but he had even turned his nose up at her. All the time he could have been a-courting Jay'd been filling those boxes up above the Lily. What for? What on earth for? What hurt the most was the fact that he had not known. That his son had a secret life that went on without him, that he had been shut out, made to look a fool.

Walt swung the key from his palm by its tassel, his nose wrinkling as he bit back tears. There was enough stolen plunder there to string Jay up. And there was not a hope of shifting it, even if he had the men, there was just too much. There was no way he could get rid of it, unless –

Dennis was at his mother's house when he saw the smoke. It was strange to think she would never come back here, that her bed would always be empty. And there was nobody upstairs still, not even the constable's man. The table where Sadie used to sit was already dusty, his fingers left dark smudges where he leaned on it. He supposed he would never see Sadie again. He pictured the way her hair parted, showing the fine line of her white skin and the nape of her neck, when she bent over his books. There was a great stone weighing on his heart and he didn't know if it was for his ma or for her. When Ella had told him she had not seen her either, he ran back home again on the chance she'd go back there, but there was not a sign of her, and he didn't know where else to start looking. Then the messenger boy came to tell him his ma had not lasted the night. Already the room felt empty without Ma's cough.

Of course he'd been expecting it, but it was different when it happened. He didn't know what to do so he changed into his best dark suit. He supposed he should go back to Epping, but there was no hurry now. Absentmindedly, he picked up the corner of Ma's crocheted blanket, but let it drop as he followed the thick grey plume in the sky.

He walked to the window and watched the smoke unfold into the foggy air, one roll upon the next in an ever thickening cloud. He barely noticed it, until Widow Leadbetter from across the way hammered on his door.

'Thought you might like to know,' she said breathlessly, 'it's Whitgift's. It's afire.'

'What?'

'You'd better go. Looters are out already. Come on, lad, shift yourself.' She held out his coat.

Dennis stared at the smoke. It couldn't be true. Not Whitgift's.

'Word's out the gates are open. Folk have gone to get their goods – and a bit more besides if they can carry it.'

As he looked, a huge flower of flame shot up into the smoke.

'Oh my word, Ella!' Wordlessly he grabbed the coat from her hand and, without thinking, plunged out of the front door. By the time he got there the Gilded Lily was fully alight. The yard teemed with shadowy figures scurrying into the building and running out with armfuls of goods. The warehouse doors were open, and there was no sign of the nightwatchman, or Jay. Jay's chambers were well alight, smoke pouring from all the windows and the roof.

'Stop!' yelled Dennis to one man. 'Where's Walt Whitgift?'

But the man did not falter, he put his head down and scurried away. Just then a king's guard arrived with a fire machine. Dennis waited for him to dismount. As he did, several other lads he recognized from the yard joined him.

The warehouse was now a burning wall of flame behind them, the flames licking up the side of the wooden stalls and creeping along the stacks and bundles of clothes. The heat intensified, red floating particles drifted into the air, the fire began to blow, a sound like wind rushing through trees.

Dennis ran back into the yard shouting, 'Ring the bells, we'll need all the help we can get, it's dry as a tinderbox in here.'

'It started in Jay Whitgift's office,' said the stable lad breathlessly, 'but I can't find the gaffer, or Jay. There's nobody in charge.'

'Where's Miss Johnson?'

'She's out, gone with Jay.'

'Tell them to ring the bells backwards, maybes it'll bring them home.'

'And like as not the other half of London on the make,' said the lad ruefully before running off.

'It's no use,' said the king's man, 'we can't get water whilst the river's iced over. We'll have to use the fire hook.'

'Is there anybody in the buildings?'

'Lad says they're all out at the Frost Fair.'

As he spoke the wind blew a flurry of sparks into the sky. The smoke belched thicker from the Gilded Lily's windows. As the bells of St Martin began to peal a crowd gathered, jostling to get near the warehouses. Dennis saw a woman run by, her arms piled high with pewter.

'Wait!' he cried, but it was hopeless, people poured like ants from inside the doors. More came in from outside and seeing the looting quickly joined the pillagers.

Dennis felt a tug on his arm. 'I saw the smoke.' Tindall was breathless, coughing. 'You can see it from Blackfriars. Where's Walt?'

'Don't know. No one's seen him.'

'Oh my lord, where can he be? Dennis, you've missed a right to-do.'

'What's up?'

'The law's on to Jay Whitgift for burglary and murder. They're sending more men. The constable's gone haring over to Allsop's on Trinity Lane with Mr Ibbetson, chasing after Jay and those poor girls. And now this.'

'Which girls?'

'Miss Johnson and another girl. The nightwatch saw them go. Be more than an hour ago now.'

'Two girls you say?'

'Yes. That yellow-haired Miss Johnson and another dark girl.'

'Did you see her face?'

'No. I didn't see her at all, 'twas only the nightwatchman saw, 'twas he who told me. Said they were hanging onto each other like they were drunk.'

It could be Sadie. Dennis felt an unfamiliar sensation in his chest.

'Trinity Lane, was it?'

Tindall nodded.

'Sorry, Nat, I've got to go.'

'But—'

It was not a thought that made him run, more like an instinct, something his heart knew although his legs did not.

Chapter 43

Sadie held tight to Ella's hand as they were pushed into Allsop's small drawing room. She stayed quiet now, as Ella had asked, with her head bowed, her hair covering her face. Ella had stilled her face too into a neutral mask, but Sadie could feel her tremble.

At first she did not see the other man, for he was sitting in the chair with his back to them. He was not wearing a wig and his bald head was stubbled and wrinkled at the nape with rolls of flesh. When he heard them come in, he stood up and turned, his eyes bleary in their pouchy sockets. Ella gripped Sadie's hand more tightly and, keeping hold, moved in front of Sadie to put herself in between them.

'What's all this?'

'Said you wanted the Savage Sisters, did you not?' Wolfenden smiled and winked at Jay. 'Spared no expense, as it's your birthday.' The other men laughed at his discomposure.

He stood up. 'You bloody coxcomb. You never did.' He looked genuinely taken aback. 'No, these are not they. You can't fool me – where did you get them?'

''Tis true,' Whitgift said.

'I wasn't serious! Bloody fool, Wolfenden. What the hell am I supposed to do with them?'

'Oh come on now, Allsop. Never known you short of starch when it comes to a skirt. The fellows have a few ideas even if your ale-addled brain has not.'

Sedley grabbed Wycliffe by the arm and mimed pumping his fist up and down.

'I thought one of them was supposed to have the Devil's patch on her face?' Allsop said.

'Take a look then,' Jay said. He drew his rapier and with the tip of it nudged Sadie forward into the empty space between Allsop and Ella. Sadie stepped forward, head held high, and as Ella had told her, she said nothing.

'Show me her face.'

Wycliffe took hold of her hair as if he did not want to touch it and pulled it back so that her head was forced backwards. She stiffened but remained silent.

Allsop walked towards her and leaned over her. He threw the liquid from his glass into her face. She gasped but stifled it. Allsop handed his kerchief to Wycliffe, who rubbed at her face at arm's length. Sadie winced as the liquid stung her eyes.

'Well, I never,' Sedley said. 'Take a look at that. It *is* the bloody Savage Sisters.' He laughed uproariously.

Jay looked towards the door where Foxy and Lutch were leaning either side, watching impassively. 'You two can wait outside now,' Jay said. 'Remember your orders.'

Foxy and Lutch nodded and went out, banging the door behind them.

'So this is the famous patch-faced girl,' Allsop said. 'Well, she's a curiosity, all right. Ugly, isn't she? She doesn't look much of a fighter. Wolfenden can take her. I'll take the other.' He walked to Ella, who flinched as he placed a hand on her shoulder.

'She can watch while Wolfenden has her sister. Maybe that will make her wild.'

'No. Please no. I'll do anything.' Sadie saw Ella sink to her knees before him. 'Please – I'll do anything you please, but let my sister go free.'

'Get up.' Allsop kicked Ella with the tip of his buckled shoe.

She stumbled to her feet. 'I beg you—'

Allsop punched her hard in the side of the face and she staggered and fell, clutching her cheek.

'I'll take the young one first.' Wolfenden pulled Sadie's arms behind her and pulled her towards the ground.

'No, please,' Ella wept.

Sadie wanted to scream and shout, to struggle. But Ella had told her not to fight back, hadn't she, and so she was silent.

She closed her eyes as she felt Wolfenden's weight come down on her. Allsop's voice: 'Come on, fellows, want to see some sport?'

'Leave her alone, you bastard.' It was Ella. Sadie heard sounds of a scuffle and tried to turn to see what was happening, but Wolfenden had her in a tight grip, one hand on her chest thrusting her back to the floor, the other pudgy hand fastening around her throat. She closed her eyes as if asleep. Wolfenden kept a hand at her throat whilst he lifted her skirt. She felt him fumble at his breeches. She turned and fixed her eyes on Ella. Ella's eyes sought hers and in that moment Sadie felt Ella's love blaze like anger.

A staccato knocking made Wolfenden start, and slam Sadie's head hard against the floor. Her eyes opened wide and she cried out. The pounding of the iron knocker at the door was insistent. Wolfenden rolled off, fastening the flap of his breeches.

Allsop paused, his hand wrapped over Ella's mouth. He listened as they heard the manservant open up. 'You can't come in,' she heard him say, 'his lordship is indisposed.'

'Help us!' Ella had managed to free herself from Allsop's grip. There were more men's voices, and a commotion in the hall.

'Hold her,' Allsop yelled at Sedley, but he was already opening the window.

Wolfenden and Sedley made a dive for the opening and scrambled out. Jay Whitgift made to follow them, but Wycliffe took hold of his sleeve.

'Hey, fellows, don't go without me,' he said.

Jay was still trying to shake him off when the door burst open.

'Stay where you are.' A roughneck constable levelled a pistol at Allsop's chest.

He flung his hands up. 'What's going on? What are you doing in my house?'

'Which is Josiah Whitgift?'

'I am,' said Jay, his rapier already drawn. 'What of it?'

'Into the hall. Now. You too.' He waved his pistol at Sadie and Ella.

'Do as they ask,' Sadie shouted, dragging Ella away, and they stumbled through the door. There were two armed men in the hall and Foxy and Lutch were face to the wall with pistols pressed to their necks.

Sadie turned to see Jay Whitgift, with a face like thunder, followed by Allsop who was looking from side to side in a panic.

'What's this about?' blustered Allsop. 'You will hear from my lawyers.'

'Much good it will do you,' the constable said. 'You are all under seizure. We are investigating the murders of several young women –'

Allsop threw Jay a desperate look, before making a clumsy run for the front door. He shoved the terrified manservant to the side and put his hand on the handle. A king's guard drew his sword but Allsop ducked out if its way and punched him in the jaw. The

sound of it was like the crunch of broken glass and the guard toppled. The constable spun on his heel and fired. Sadie heard Ella
scream as the noise of the shot reverberated in the room, before
the blast turned her momentarily deaf. Allsop slumped to the
ground – a red hole like a flower split open in the back of his coat.
The noise seemed to galvanize everybody into action.

The guard who was still holding Foxy and Lutch ran over to
Allsop, his pistol ready, and rolled him over. Allsop's eyes stared
up in an expression of disbelief. A wet patch of red crept out from
under him.

'Dead,' the guard pronounced.

Wycliffe crouched on the ground, his hands over his ears and
head.

Foxy and Lutch exchanged a brief glance before they made a
sudden lurch down the corridor.

'Quick! The back stairs!'

The guard who had been punched staggered to his feet and the
rest plummeted after them, leaving the constable alone in the room.

Sadie was still staring at Allsop's body when Ella shouted her
name. But the warning came too late. An arm snaked around her
throat and pulled her backwards. She recognized the dark velvet
of Jay Whitgift's coat. He had hold of her from behind, the crook
of his elbow was like a vice on her neck as she staggered, half
falling, towards the door. The constable's gun pointed directly at
her chest. Jay was using her as a shield. She kicked out now and
struggled, but he held her firm. The constable began to reload his
gun with powder and cocked it back.

'No!' Ella shouted and grabbed him by the arm. The shot
went off but hit the plaster in the ceiling, so that a shower of
white powder added to the smoke. Ella coughed and staggered
before running after them into the hallway.

The door was suddenly open and Sadie was stumbling

backwards, being dragged down the stone steps. She choked, Jay's arm was cutting off her breath. From the side of her eyes she saw the black boxwagon draw up at the side of the house.

'Get in!' yelled the red-haired man from the front seat.

The constable had reloaded his gun and fired a third time, but Jay kept Sadie in front of him as he threw himself backwards into the wagon and the shot went clean through the wagon door.

She heard the whip crack and a voice shout 'Gerrup!' The horses sprang into action, the back doors of the wagon flapped, clanging against the sides, and she was jolted into motion, Jay's arms still around her throat. Over the noise of the wheels she only heard one sound:

'Sadie!' screamed Ella.

The two guards rounded the corner and pelted down the road, firing after the departing carriage. Ella leapt down onto the pavement, ran alongside as fast as she could run, shouting after the wagon, but she turned to look behind and her voice petered away. Two guards had their weapons levelled at her. She slumped to her knees in the wet. They had taken Sadie. She beat at the ground with her fists. It was only then that she saw the man in the long cape standing staring as the boxwagon turned the corner out of sight.

He had found her then. She would recognize him anywhere.

Ibbetson raised a pistol and pointed it at her chest. Behind him more of the king's guard waited, swords drawn.

Ella slowly put up her hands.

Sadie hunched as far from Jay Whitgift as she could. She rubbed her elbow, which had cracked on the wooden bench-seat as she landed. The wagon was jarring and jerking, listing as it turned the corners, the back doors flapping as it went.

She watched Jay warily. He clung to the railings at the window to the driver's seat and shouted from the back telling them to turn left down a small alley. When the wagon keeled to the side he threw a glance out of the back to see if they were being followed. The doors crashed against the body of the cart as they went. After a short distance Jay yelled, 'Pull up.' The wagon slowed a little.

'We've lost them. There's nobody following us,' he yelled. 'The river. We need to get rid of the girl.'

Lutch replied, because she saw his profile turn, but she could not hear what he said. Jay's voice went on. 'Safer to make sure. The usual place. Then we can make a clean break. We'll head for Oxford, Wycliffe has a country house there.'

The hairs on the back of Sadie's neck stood on end. They're going to kill me, she thought. There is nobody who can help me now. Ella had surely been taken by the constable and there would be no one coming to rescue her like in Dennis's chapbooks. Dennis. She wondered if she'd imagined he liked her. It wouldn't matter now, anyway.

The horses trotted on down the side street. Through the square aperture of the back doors Sadie saw the houses replaced by the walls of a tannery. The smell of rotting fish, bonemeal and the damp fog blew in. The road was darker and wetter from many wagon wheels coming and going. The packed snow was gone, the road looked like a black sea unrolling behind them. Sadie prayed with all her might. She hung on to Ella's words – that if she should find a chance, to run like the wind – and she was ready.

The wagon skewed abruptly to a halt. Sadie made a desperate dive for the doors, but Jay was too quick. He grabbed her arm in his wiry grip and there was a brief scuffle before the wagon lurched to a standstill and he pinioned her to the floor, his hand clamped on her mouth.

'Why have you stopped? What do you think you're playing at? Help me, you bloody imbeciles,' he yelled.

'Here. We'll have to do it here. The river's frozen,' said Foxy, his thin freckled face looming over her as he hauled on her arms to drag her out of the wagon. She kicked out at them as hard as she could, but they half lifted her so she was forced to totter between them as they dragged her a few more feet into the dark shadow of a dripping tannery. Next to it was a raised wooden pit full of the nameless stinking parts of dead cattle and sheep. Two dogs growled at them as they tussled over a piece of gristle. She looked desperately about her for someone who could help, who she could call to, but there was not a soul abroad. Oh God, she was really going to die. She heard Lutch's heavy tread behind her. She glanced behind. Lutch flexed a long cane between his palms.

'Just get on with it,' said Jay. 'With any luck we'll be long gone afore anyone sees her. I'll wait at the wagon.'

Lutch moved round to stand next to Jay. There was a moment's silence. Sadie saw Lutch and Foxy exchange a look.

Sadie felt Jay let go, but with a deft movement Lutch grabbed hold of Jay, twisted his arms up behind him and propelled him forward to the dark slimy wall. Sadie was rooted to the spot.

'Hold him,' Lutch said.

Foxy latched onto Jay's arms from the front, and in one deft movement Lutch swung the cane round Jay's neck. He pulled sharply on both ends. Jay staggered back until he leaned on Lutch's chest and began to speak but it was silenced instantly.

A small soft moan was all she heard.

Jay's knees sagged and a stream of liquid trickled from between them. Sadie stared in fascinated horror. Lutch let go and Jay hit the ground with a soft thud. Between them, Foxy and Lutch heaved him into the offal pit. He landed face up, his spreadeagled limbs splayed. One of the dogs leapt in on top of him and began to pull at his coat. The other let out a stream of frenzied barking. It was all over in a few moments. She could not believe what she had just witnessed.

She felt a great wave of nausea rise inside her. She reeled away and hung over, spitting into the slush at the edge of the road. When she looked up Lutch and Foxy were walking back towards her. Dread engulfed her, she backed away towards the wall.

'You din't see that,' Lutch said.

Sadie nodded dumbly.

'Then what are you waiting for, maid? Get outta here.'

Sadie turned tail and ran.

Lutch threaded his cane into his belt. He banged the doors of the wagon shut and unhitched the reins. The horse was standing quietly, waiting. Lutch rubbed its neck before throwing the reins over its head.

'God, Lutch, what've we done?' Foxy still stood staring at the offal pit. 'Are you sure he's dead?'

'Heard his neck crack.'

Foxy began to laugh, a hysterical laugh until he had to put his hand over his mouth.

'Quiet. Don't want nobody coming.'

Foxy's laughter stopped abruptly. 'Why did you let the girl go? Thought you said it didn't bother you?'

'It don't. It's just – well, she reminded me of Titan. The blaze and all. And her being so quiet.'

'You let her go for the sake of a bleeding horse? I'd never have thought you sentimental. We'll have to lay low a bit. Do you think she'll blab?'

'No. Not her. Too scared.'

'You're a strange one.' He climbed up alongside Lutch. Lutch clicked his tongue and the wheels began to turn. 'Can't see the girl now,' Foxy said. 'She's got clean away.'

Lutch merely nodded.

'Hey, Lutch.'

'What?'

'Don't half feel different now Whitgift's gone, don't it? He would have scuppered us to save his own skin, like as not.'

'The law was on to him. Safest to cut and run. Better without him.'

'By, I feel like a new man – my own man,' Foxy said. 'Freedom, eh, Lutch? Now ain't that a pearl worth having.'

Dennis ran as fast as his legs would take him, dodging the other folk swarming through the gates into the yard. He had tied his coat around his waist and ran in his shirtsleeves to give more freedom of movement. His heart felt heavy as if it jolted in his chest. He found himself chanting in his head *hold on, hold on my little nightingale* to the rhythm of his footfalls as he pelted up Broken Wharf towards the centre of town. He was glad of his boots for they gave a good grip, but he was terrified Jay might already have handed Sadie over to Ibbetson for the reward, that they might have already taken her. He did not know what he was intending to do when he got to Allsop's. Just knew he had to get there, that was all.

He skidded to a halt on the corner of Friargate to get his bearings. The grand houses rose up in the distance, over the bridge, with their lanterns hung out making small haloes in the dark. Shouts and music drifted up from somewhere downriver. Unused to this chasing about, he panted, doubled over, his hands on his knees. As he stood up a woman turned the corner and ran down the road towards him. Another looter, no doubt on her way to the yard like the rest. He paid her no mind, but stumbled forward, able to run now he had caught his breath. He set his sights on the bridge and lengthened his stride.

'Dennis!' The sound of his name brought him skidding to a halt. He looked round behind him, confused. But there was nobody there. Across the street the woman was flying towards him now, yellow skirts flapping, hair loose from its cap. Her face was streaked with white.

It couldn't be Sadie.

His legs began to move of their own accord. She carried on running, eyes fixed on his.

'Sadie,' he shouted. He scooped her into his arms. A small mewling sound escaped from her lips.

'There,' he said, holding her tight to his chest, 'there, there.'

'Thank God,' she wept. She clung on, her fingers dug into his back, he could feel her heart thudding against his chest. She was sobbing so hard it rocked him. He clasped her tighter, enjoying the sensation of holding her, it made him feel strong, keeping her safe. 'I didn't know where else to go.'

'Safe now,' he said, rubbing her back until she quietened a little. 'Where's Ella?'

'At Allsop's.' She pulled away, and looked up at him. Her eyes looked different, older. Her face was smeared with patches of white and wet with tears. 'At least she was – but now I don't know. The constable came.'

'Oh no, you don't think . . . and what about Jay Whitgift? Tindall told me they had sent somebody to arrest him.'

'No.' She swallowed, and pulled away. 'He's –' She did not finish. 'Dennis, will you come with me to find out what's happened to Ella? I'm too scared to go by myself. Will you ask after her for me?' She tugged at his arm. He saw that her wrist was bandaged and that dried blood had seeped through.

'Your arm, what have you done to it?'

'It's nothing, a dog. But it's been stitched. Now hurry.'

'Should we fetch help?'

She was pulling him into a run. 'There's no one we can trust, and they might have taken her already. I just want to know where she is.' He clung tight to her hand as they weaved their way through the alleys and yards. She seemed to know exactly where she was going. He concentrated on the feeling of her small palm in his. Finally she slowed.

'He's down there. Jay Whitgift.' She pointed. But it did not look like the sort of ginnel that Jay Whitgift might frequent, or that a fine gentleman like Allsop might live in. He paused and started to move towards it.

'No, don't go down.'

'What's the matter?'

She shook her head, her eyes glinted with new tears. Some sixth sense alerted him and he released her hand and walked the few yards up the street. He cast his eyes hurriedly down the narrow lane into the darkness. The place stank. Probably it was used as a piss-hole by the tanners passing from the tavern. He was about to go back, when a movement in the shadows caught his eye. The growl of a dog.

Sadie appeared at his side. 'He's dead, Dennis.' She was tugging on his arm all the while, but from a few feet away he had seen enough.

'Who did this?'

She shook her head, her lips pressed together. He guessed the answer anyway. But the sight had shaken him. He folded her in his arms again. It felt good. He could have stood there all night, but Sadie turned her face up to his and he knew what she was going to say before she even opened her mouth.

'Leave him. We've got to go back to the big house. For Ella.'

Chapter 44

Ella held her hands above her head. Titus Ibbetson walked towards her, a pistol levelled at her. To his right were the constable's men. They were armed with swords and muskets. Her legs felt like lead, her mouth dry as cornmeal, she did not think she had any more fight left in her. Her heart hammered behind the whalebone of her bodice.

He walked towards her and she looked back at him defiantly.

'Arrest her,' he said.

Out of the corner of her eye she glimpsed the constable's men make their move. She groaned. There was only one path open to her and she took it. She made a sudden dive to the left, and it must have taken them by surprise for she heard no shot. A new strength filled her. This was it, her last chance. She threw herself around the corner from the house. The ground was slippery with melted snow but she did not look back, just picked up her skirts and ran.

A shot exploded just to the right of her and threw up a spatter of icy slush, and she panicked, veered left into an alley. She did not dare stop, footsteps splashed behind her. She could barely breathe, her stays were choking her, but she forced herself to run on. If she could get down to the Frost Fair, she could lose herself in the crowds. Fortunately, there was a young couple walking arm in arm up the alley and she pushed past them, knowing that she had a moment's respite from the gun.

At last she saw the stairs. Two men shouldering sacks were about to come up but she grabbed at the wooden rail and hurled herself down to the wharf. The two men leapt aside and cursed and shouted 'Whoa!' at her back. She turned. The men laboured up the steps and she glanced back to see Ibbetson craning his neck and panting impatiently at the top. She stumbled on. Ahead of her the great stone arches of London Bridge rose out of the flat grey ice. In the distance the torches and fires of the fair twinkled as the silhouettes moved in and out of the light. There was the dark hulk of the ship embedded in the ice, and the white flapping canvas of the stalls, luminous in the moonlight. Strange, the ship's mast looked to be upright now. She skewed her head to look back again. Ibbetson had descended and was behind her, his cloak flapping as he sprinted after her. And behind him, the constable's men. Even as she looked, he was gaining ground. Oh Christ in heaven, she thought, let me make it.

Holding her skirts above her knees she leapt onto the ice. Her feet skidded away and she slithered to the ground. She scrabbled to her feet, frantic, her breath rasping as she tried to suck in more air. She forced her legs to move though her body was resisting, her eyes fixed on the lights in the distance.

Away to her left, a waterman waved his arms at her but she did not stop. She jumped over an oar that was embedded in the ice, one end jutting up out of the flat surface. Ibbetson was closing on her fast and she could only concentrate on her breath. The ice was wet, as if it had recently rained, and splashed round her feet. She looked over towards the centre of the river and saw with horror that the surface was greyer, the ice patchy, white floes surrounded by water, grainy like porridge. The surface was moving, sliding.

She stopped dead. There would be no way across. The ice was melting. Dark figures over by the tents had stopped what they were doing and gesticulated at her, waving her over to the edge. She could see now that the stalls were packing up.

She paused and as she did so the ice tilted slightly under her feet and she heard a creaking noise like a ship's timbers. She turned to look at her pursuer just in time to see him jump over the oar. As he landed he seemed to crumple and the ice gave way beneath his feet, his legs and body disappearing under the surface. A black pool rose round his chest. His arm flailed wildly and grabbed for the oar. He floundered until he had the oar wedged under his arms. He was gasping with shock, thrashing in the water. The cold had punched the air from his lungs.

'Help me,' he choked.

The world fell silent, the ground creaked again beneath her feet. She watched him in the middle of the expanse of shifting ice, his fingers fumbling on the oar. His knuckles stood out red against the ice as he took hold. He was clinging on. Gingerly, her eyes still fixed on him, she walked deliberately backwards, away from him to the left towards the bank.

The water slopped under the frozen crust, and above the sound Ibbetson's voice, less ragged now, calling, 'Please. Help me.'

Ella paused. She could not take her eyes from his face. His hair was plastered to his head. His mouth hung open, grey with cold. He looked like Thomas. If she walked away he would die. But that was what she wanted, wasn't it? To be free of him. But what would Thomas think of her if she left him there? Thomas is dead, she reminded herself. She took another step away. She couldn't just leave him, could she? She looked around; there was nobody else nearby.

'Please,' came the voice from the ice. She stopped. Something in its tone touched her. Some humility. In an instant she was seven years old again. Her feet moved of their own accord. Falteringly she crept towards him, a quivering in her stomach, the fear that the ice would give way any moment. The surface was cracking. Ibbetson's face was bloodless and pale. The sound of the ice held her in its thrall.

'Can't hold on,' he murmured.

Ella crouched and slid herself flat on the ice stretching out a hand towards him. Straight away he grabbed for it, but his hand was cold and wet and slipped over hers, and his head disappeared momentarily into the blackness. Panic-stricken she pulled her hand away lest he should pull her in too. He clutched for the oar again.

'I can't pull you out,' she said, staggering to her feet. 'I'll fetch help.'

'No,' he said weakly, 'don't go. It's too late. Don't leave me alone.'

She stayed where she was, her eyes on his face.

'I can't get out,' he struggled to form the words.

'Don't speak, save it till help comes.'

'I might not last,' he said.

'Hush.'

She cast her eyes back to the shore and saw that there were people running down the stairs.

'Ella!' Sadie's voice drifted over the ice.

Ella's head shot up. 'No,' she screamed. 'Don't come near! Go back! It's breaking up. It'll give way.'

She saw her hesitate, and the constable's men in a ragged group on the bank. Another figure stepped out onto the ice. Against the white she saw Dennis, dressed only in his shirtsleeves, taking a round-about route, tiptoeing gingerly across. At the same time she became aware of shouts behind her and she glanced over her shoulder. A group of watermen were approaching from the direction of the fair.

Ibbetson was grey as the ice now, his eyelids were closed, his knuckles white on the oar. The black water rose and fell round his chest.

Dennis appeared at her side and eased himself with tentative slowness onto his knees. 'Don't move,' he said.

'He can't last much longer.' She whispered it, lest he hear.

'Take hold of my ankles.' The ice rocked as he lay down. She gasped.

He took hold of Ibbetson by the wrists. Ibbetson's hands were welded to the oar. Ella pushed herself back on the ice inch by inch and grasped Dennis's ankles. Her own hands were numb with cold, she did not know if she could hang on.

Dennis turned his head round to Ella and voiced her own thoughts, 'If he lets go I might not be able to hold him. Help's on its way.'

Behind them there were the shouts of a group of watermen approaching from the bank upriver. She glanced briefly in their direction, to see them dragging a ladder and a plank between them. Ella concentrated on holding the stiff wool round Dennis's ankles. The ice was burning her chest, her teeth chattered uncontrollably.

A brief discussion in low voices between the men, followed by: 'Careful now, it might not bear more weight.' A voice from behind them.

'Pass us the ladder, Jake.'

The noise of wood scraping the ice and a ladder slid out next to them.

'It's all right, milady, you can let go, we have him.' Two pairs of hands grasped Dennis firmly by the calves.

Ella sat up and rubbed at her hands, but there was no feeling in them, they were like dead things. Dennis was rigid, holding tight to Ibbetson's wrists. Ibbetson did not move, his eyes were closed, his lace jabot floated round his neck. His hands still clasped the oar but Ella feared he was already dead. The other boatmen were standing on the shore on the firmer ice, shouting instructions. The top rung of the ladder was right next to Ibbetson now, but he made no move to take it.

'Sir, take hold of the ladder,' Dennis said.

Ibbetson half opened his eyes. Dennis tried to pull his hands free so he could grab the ladder but Ibbetson would not let go of the oar.

'You've got to let go, take hold of the ladder,' Dennis said. He turned to Ella. 'He won't let go.'

'Mr Ibbetson,' Ella said, almost weeping with cold, 'please take hold. We can't pull you free else.'

Ibbetson's face did not move.

'You've got to help yourself. Take hold, in God's name,' she said. 'Do it for Thomas.'

He opened his eyes then, screwed up his face and lurched through the water making a grab for the ladder. His hands latched on.

'Now kick!' shouted Ella, 'kick for all you're worth! You need to swim out.'

Ibbetson began to feebly move his legs.

'More. Kick harder.' His legs gradually came up to the surface. She could see the dark of his breeches beneath the grey sludge.

'Pull!' shouted Dennis, and the watermen heaved the ladder back over the ice, dragging Ibbetson with it. As he came free of the water Ella looked to the bank; she could see Sadie was still there, the yellow of her dress shone out. She was surrounded by the constable's men.

Ibbetson lay like a beached seal on the grey surface, unable to speak, but moaning. A waterman helped lug him on a sled and they towed him over to the bank. The sled scraped on the ice. Pockets of black water oozed up under it. Dennis followed, leading Ella the long way round, past the cracked and shifting surface to the edge. When the sled reached the bank, the constable leaned over Ibbetson; she saw him speak, but could not hear his words. By the time she arrived the watermen's wives were clustered around him, with earthen flasks of hot ale. Someone had stripped off his wet clothes and given him a dry shirt. He looked vulnerable without his coat, like a baby, a sheepskin pulled up to his chin. A man laid a blanket over her shoulders and escorted her to solid ground, but as she neared the shore she shook him off and ran towards the waiting figure of Sadie on the bank. Sadie's eyes searched hers.

'You're safe, God be praised,' Sadie said, and she threw her arms about Ella's neck. They stood for a while just holding each other, before Ella pulled away. 'Sorry,' she said.

'Nothing to be sorry for,' Sadie said. 'Is he all right?' She nodded her head towards the gaggle of people surrounding the sled.

'I think so.' She hooked Sadie's arm through hers and pulled her over to the crowd. They stood a little apart until Dennis beckoned them through.

Ibbetson held out his hand from under the rug, and Ella took it. His hand pressed hers. She looked into his eyes. Neither of them smiled.

He turned his head to the waiting men. 'These are not the girls,' he said with great effort.

Dennis beckoned the constable, who stepped up.

'Tell him again,' Dennis said.

'Not these girls. Never seen them before in my life.'

DEBORAH SWIFT

The constable narrowed his eyes and looked from one to the other. He stared at Sadie clinging to Ella's arm, and then back to Ibbetson. 'Right enough, sir, if that's what you say.'

Ella smiled then, and nodded, and found her eyes were glassy. She squeezed Mr Ibbetson's hand tightly.

'Has someone sent for a carriage?' asked Dennis. 'He lodges at the Blue Ball on Aldergate. Send ahead for a fire to be lit in his chamber.'

'My Agnes has sent for a carriage,' said the waterman, 'and a physician's on his way. The gentleman'll need a draught to get rid of the excess cold and damp. Or he'll take sickness, sure as I stand.'

A carriage arrived with the physician and they watched as Mr Ibbetson was carried up and bundled into the back. Someone offered Ella a hot draught, and she watched the running footmen close the door, and the carriage move away.

After they had taken warm ale with the watermen, they said their farewells. Dennis untied his black coat from round his waist and put it on.

'You look different. I've never seen you look so smart, were you going . . . ?' Sadie's voice petered out. 'Oh, Dennis, not Ma?'

Dennis looked down. 'Yesterday. At my auntie's. I guess she couldn't hold on no more, she was that weak.' He paused a moment, intent on some memory of his own. ''Tis a mercy, when I think on, but I'll miss her that sore.'

'I'm sad to hear it,' Ella said. 'You were a good son to her.'

'I was just thinking earlier, Father's been gone these six year, and now Ma. It feels awful strange, like I'm floating. I've got nobody now.'

'You've got me,' Sadie said shyly.

Dennis drew her into a big bear hug. 'Dear Sadie, oh my little one.' She smiled up at him, surprised, her face open as the sunrise. Ella looked away, embarrassed. A few moments later he tapped Ella on the shoulder. 'Come on, the pair of you, let's get you home,' he said.

There was a stench of burning in the air, and now they neared the bank they could see that the snow and ice there was flecked with floating particles of charred debris. Over to their right an orange glow lit the sky. But Dennis did not stop. The three of them hurried onwards through the dark, arm in arm, back to the little house in Blackraven Alley.

Chapter 45

⁂

Sadie went down to Whitgift's the next morning with Dennis and Ella. The thaw had set in and the air was damp, water dripped from all the eaves. On the Thames, streams of brownish meltwater trickled through the ice. Slabs had broken loose and were floating, making a clunking sound as they jostled downstream. Watermen, anxious to get their familiar trade back, hit at the ice slabs from the bank with oars and sticks to try to break them up and send them on their way. The three stopped a while to watch and marvel at the thickness of it, before moving on. Even before they turned into Friargate the sour smell of smoke caught the back of the throat.

Sadie looked through the gates at the ruins of Whitgift's yard. What had been the Gilded Lily was now a gaping blackened wound. Wisps of smoke yet curled from the debris on the floor. Wooden buckets lay cast about, along with charred remains of chairs and broken bottles. The lead from the roof had melted and turned into a solid pool of grey lava, and embedded in it were blackened tea chests and a man's scorched steeple hat along with other less identifiable objects. To the left, one of the warehouses had been pulled away to save what was left of the old stone monastery.

Dennis pointed to a jut of broken and charred timbers like a crow skeleton against the grey sky. 'Not much left of Jay Whitgift's office.'

'I didn't think it would be so bad,' Ella said.

The three of them stepped through the gates, they were wide open now.

'I can't take it in,' said Ella. 'Seems only a few hours ago this place was full of fine ladies and gentlemen in sedans.'

Sadie hooked her arm through Ella's and squeezed her hand. Now there was just a hushed gaggle of folk staring, shaking their heads and pointing. Ella pulled her nearer to the Lily, at least what remained of it – the two walls still standing and the scarred earth. She went so close that she could see the charred wall-covering, the gold bamboo pattern blackened with the heat, the scaled varnish of the wainscot peeling away like bark.

'That's where the counter was,' Ella said in a whisper.

'Don't go too close, Sadie, those timbers don't look safe,' Dennis said.

'Aye, 'tis a sorry sight,' Tindall's voice cut over Dennis's warning. 'We could have done with more men. Too much ice in the river, we couldn't get the pumps working.'

'Sorry, Nat,' Dennis said, 'I had to go. Sadie needed me.' He pulled her forward, and she smiled at Tindall. He doffed his hat, stared at her face. She returned his look with an open smile.

'Any sign of Jay Whitgift?' Tindall said. 'Walt's out of his mind thinking they've arrested him.'

'He's—'

'No,' Sadie said firmly, 'no sign.'

Dennis shut his mouth.

Tindall looked at Sadie's defiant face. 'I can see there's a tale hangs there, but one you are not for sharing. What shall I tell Walt?'

Dennis turned to him then and said, 'I don't know, Nat. But I'll own you this – he'll need a good friend right enough. One to stand by him, no matter what comes.'

'There's a deal of clearing to be done, and no way to pay wages whilst the business is closed,' Tindall said. 'It's a disaster. I told him it was coming – in the stars you see. But thank the Lord at least some of the stock was out at the Frost Fair. Walt's worried to death over his son, and he says there are all manner of debts, and people hammering on his door demanding payback for their loans, and then there's the whole question of stolen goods. So you can see, there'll be no work for you,' he said to Ella. 'Merciful heavens, just look at it.'

'I know, sir,' she said, 'but I want none. I'm glad it's gone. I don't want to look on it again.'

'Sadie!' Corey hurtled out of the crowd. 'And Ella too. Blimey, what a shiner!' Ella brought her fingers to her eye where Allsop had hit her.

Corey cocked her head from one to the other, her hands on her hips, as if to gauge how the land lay. She turned to Sadie. 'You found her then. Oh my word, am I glad to see you. I feared the worst when I heard the place was afire. I asked everywhere after you, but nobody knew nothing.'

Sadie embraced her and then said, 'Corey, I don't think you know Mr Gowper.' Dennis's face flared red with pleasure. Ella bowed her head, she seemed embarrassed to see Corey again, but Corey paid no mind, she was looking Dennis up and down with a broad grin.

'Pleased to meet you,' Corey said, with a little bob. 'Terrible, ain't it. Such a shame. My mam's told me to ask after her Sunday shoes. She hocked them last week. But I don't hold much hope.'

'I will take you to the office,' Tindall said. 'Dennis, maybe you would come with us. I'll wager Walt will be glad to see another friendly face in amongst all this.'

Dennis set off with Tindall and Corey. Halfway across the yard he turned and waved at Sadie, as if to check she was still there. She lifted her hand in reply.

'He's smitten with you,' Ella said.

'I know,' Sadie said, shy again, patting the lavender ribbon that tied back her hair.

'You could do worse. It's a good match.'

'Oh, Ella.' She put her arm around Ella's waist and held her tight. 'What will you do now, with no work?'

'Don't know. Maybes I'll learn a trade.'

'What, like weaving or baking?'

'Perhaps.' And then casually, 'I was thinking I'll maybes sign with a milliner, find out how to make fancy hats.' Sadie opened her mouth and shut it again. She knew Ella had no patience with crafts. Ella must have sensed her wariness, for she said, 'I want to master it. It's a proper skill you know, one you need instruction in to do well. I'll make you such a bonnet then, no one will have seen the like!'

Sadie laughed. 'I'll bet you can say that again.' She squeezed Ella's hand. Millinery would be a hard task for Ella, but she recognized that it might be the place for Ella to shine. Her sister could go her own way, make the life she chose for herself, just as she could make her own.

Just then Tindall came hurrying across the yard with a lad at his side. 'A messenger boy, for Miss Ella Appleby. I am sorry to presume, but I take it you are she?'

Ella stepped forward.

The boy recited the words in a gabble as if he had repeated them over and over to remember them. 'Mr Ibbetson is very much better. He asks that you call on him at his inn, before sundown.' He beamed, pleased with himself. 'Oh yes, I've to give you this with the address. Blue Ball he said.' The boy held out a piece of paper. Ella reached out her hand and took it.

'Thank the gentleman for me,' she said.

'Is there any message?'

'No. No message.'

Tindall pressed a coin into the lad's hand, inclined his head and shepherded the boy back to the gate where he sped away without a backward glance. Ella did not even look at the paper. She tore it into small pieces and let them flutter from her fingers like snowflakes. She put her arm around Sadie's shoulders and watched as the particles blew in amongst the ashes.

'Why did you do that?' Sadie said.

'I can't read.'

'Maybes he wanted to thank you.'

'He's thanked me already. I don't need him. We can manage fine by ourselves, isn't that right?'

Sadie smiled at her.

'You hungry?' Ella said.

'I thought you'd never ask,' Sadie said.

Just then Dennis came trotting back across the yard, his black hat in his hand, his eyes fixed on Sadie.

'Hey, Dennis, we're going to treat ourselves, go get a hot pie,' Ella said.

'Sounds good to me. I've got a few hours before it's time to catch the coach over to my auntie's. Tell you what, I'm paying. You can tell me everything then, how you got that shiner, the whole bit and tackle.'

'You'll be needing something more than a bloody pie to sustain you then,' Ella said, 'and anyhows,' she added, looking at Sadie, 'I don't know as we're ready to tell it yet.'

'I'm a good listener,' he said, taking Sadie by the arm.

'Aye,' Sadie said, reaching out to link Ella's arm in her own, 'he is that.' She smiled up at him. 'And a tale's naught without a good listener.'

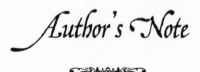

Author's Note

Those readers familiar with the Restoration period in England will already know that the Thames did not freeze in the winter of 1661. The worst winters of the decade were in the years of 1662 and 1666. I have taken the liberty of transposing the freeze of 1662 to 1661 in order for the novel's timescale to fit as a companion volume to *The Lady's Slipper*.

Mohun, Sedley and Buckhurst were real historical personages; all other characters who appear in the book are fictional.

The observant reader will notice that several characters in *The Gilded Lily* believe different things about the fate of Alice Ibbetson. The truth of her story can be discovered in *The Lady's Slipper*.

For those readers interested in exploring the history of this period or themes from *The Gilded Lily*, I suggest starting with the following books:

Restoration London: Everyday Life in the 1660s by Lisa Picard

Frost Fairs on the Frozen Thames by Nicholas Reed

The Illustrated Pepys edited by Robert Latham

Constant Delights: Rakes, Rogues and Scandal in Restoration England by Graham Hopkins

The Elizabethan Underworld by Gamini Salgado

Seventeenth and Eighteenth Century Fashion in Detail by Avril Hart and Susan North

The Artifice of Beauty: A History and Practical Guide to Perfumes and Cosmetics by Sally Pointer

And finally, I highly recommend the meditations of Helen Humphreys in her volume of vignettes, *The Frozen Thames*.

To discover more about my writing and research, please visit www.deborahswift.co.uk or contact me on Twitter @swiftstory.

Acknowledgements

I am grateful to all the people who helped bring this book to the bookshelves: my editor, Will Atkins; my agent, Annette Green, and the team at Pan Macmillan – they all worked enthusiastically on the book's behalf behind the scenes. I would also like to thank fellow writers James Tippett, Jenny Yates and Peter Fisher, who were the first readers of *The Gilded Lily* and whose responses when I took my drafts to our monthly meetings helped guide my progress. And my thanks as always to my husband John for his unstinting support, and for Dennis's story of the standard-bearer.

1. How are Sadie and Ella different from each other? Does their relationship to each other alter, and did your sympathies for them change through the book?

2. Titus Ibbetson says his mother referred to him as "the roguish one who would get himself into trouble," whereas his brother was spoken of as "the good one." Amongst you and your siblings, have you ever felt you have been cast into a particular role by your parents? How does this theme play out in the book?

3. The book starts with a quotation from a fairy tale. Ella and Sadie often refer to stories they have been told as children. To what extent do fairy tales affect their perception of the world? How strong is the influence of childhood stories in your life?

4. As a reaction to the end of Puritan rule, the world of Restoration London is dominated by fashion and beauty. How does Sadie, whose appearance is at odds with the prevailing standard, change and adapt to life in London? How important is the character of Dennis to this process? Have ideas of beauty changed over time?

5. There are several burglaries in the novel. Did you have sympathy for the victims in every case? If not, why not? How much is greed a theme of the book?

6. Discuss what the character of Jay Whitgift brings to the novel. Does he evoke your sympathy at all?

7. The extreme weather of the Little Ice Age in Europe forms the background for much of the book. Have you experienced severe winters, and what was their effect on you and your community? To what extent is the weather symbolic, and how is it integral to the plot?

*A
Reading
Group
Guide*

St. Martin's
Griffin

8. Ella often tells Sadie lies—she says that "with Ella, the truth moved about, like tussocks on shifting sand." Is there a difference between a story and a lie? Have you ever told a deliberate lie for a particular purpose? Does the truth "move about" depending on the point of view?

9. Dennis tells Sadie a story handed down to him by his father that explains why he did not fight in the English Civil War. Dennis says that you cannot hate someone when you know their story. Is this true in Ella's case? Do you have more sympathy with her behavior because you know a little about her past?

10. Could this story have taken place in any other place or period? If so, when? What common features does the period of the English seventeenth century share with your home? Can you picture Ella and Sadie in a big city today, and would they fare differently?

For more reading group suggestions, visit
www.readinggroupgold.com.